SWEET SOLDIER

KALI SWEET URBAN FANTASY SERIES, BOOK 3

MISTY EVANS

Beach
Path
Publishing
LLC

Sweet Soldier, Kali Sweet Urban Fantasy, Book 3

Misty Evans

©2010 - 2024

ISBN: 978-1-964028-06-4

Cover Art by Fanderclai Design

Formatting by Beach Path Publishing, LLC

To Mark—my Damon, Rad, Cole, and Dru all rolled into one.

ACKNOWLEDGMENTS

Every story I write is a collaboration between me, my readers, editors, cover artist, friends, and family.

To those who supported me during the writing of this book when my precious dog, Max, passed away, I send you love and light.

Finding creativity in the midst of such great sadness is difficult, if not impossible, for me, but knowing I had your support and being able to channel some of my grief into this story saved the day. Max and I thank you from the bottom of our hearts. I miss him every day, and know that he's with me in spirit.

"The more we seek the light, the denser the Shadow becomes."
~ *Introduction, The Dark Side of the Light Chasers by Debbie Ford*

1

L ife is one battle after another. Having lived three hundred years as a vengeance demon, I've won a lot of battles.

I've lost a few, too. Those are the ones I remember the most because each one involved a human I couldn't save.

That's me, Kali Sweet, a demon with a soft spot for humans.

A hundred or so of the humans I loved so much jumped and gyrated to electronic music in an abandoned warehouse on the South Side of Chicago. Their auras were all over the map and I tuned them out, instead tuning in to my overachieving sense of smell to track my prey. He wasn't human although most of the time he appeared as such. The demon in question was bald with a meth-user, bug-eyed stare. He was also a good two hundred years older than the kids at the rave.

His aura was black.

Not in the sense of color, in the sense of magic.

I was still getting used to the aura thing. Reading auras was a new talent oi f mine. I don't see colors in the way humans read auras, but rather, feel emotions and the different kinds of magic various creatures—human and supernatural—project without realizing it.

Like my hypersensitive nose, my sixth sense had grown extraordinarily perceptive in the past few weeks thanks to a dose of Master vamp blood. Reading everyone's feelings and thoughts like a billboard advertisement was new territory for me. It took getting used to.

As far as raves went, this was a small one. The warehouse was undersized for this deserted part of town. In the 1920s and '30s, the building had been a dry cleaning business. One used by the most notorious gangsters of long ago Chicago. When you're in the business of disposing of bodies, things get a little messy, so a cleaner comes in handy. Rumor had it the back of the building had been used for the disposal part and since it sat near a dock, the rumor was probably true. Who knows how many people had been fish food at the bottom of Lake Michigan? You could torture and shoot your enemy in the back of the warehouse, weigh their feet and dump them into the lake, remove your soiled clothing, and have it cleaned and pressed in under an hour. Hi ho, hi ho, back to work you go.

This was the third rave I'd attended in the past week looking for Lamir, the Bosnian demon who only came out of his hole every fifty years to feed on human young. The raves were a cornucopia of underage high-schoolers as well as college-age kids wanting to make the most of the night without realizing the night was filled with monsters wanting to make the most out of them. As in a seven-course meal.

Lamir was like a bear emerging from hibernation—hungry and cranky. He was a supernatural bully with three times the strength of a human and not an ounce of empathy. He liked to mark his victims with an X on their foreheads before he ripped out their throats and ate their hearts.

I hate bullies. Demon bullies even more. Using my city to

hunt, and my neighborhood in particular, would be Lamir's undoing.

Two DJs pumped the crowd with loud beats, flashing strobe lights and words of encouragement between tracks. A layer of smoke hung near the ceiling from cigarettes and joints. The sharp tang of meth permeated the skin of several humans I passed. Nearly every hand held alcohol of one kind or another.

Demons have no trouble seducing humans so Lamir's obsession with nabbing impaired humans from illegal raves made me wonder if he was getting lazy in his old age. Or maybe he preferred them with drugs and alcohol in their systems. Drugs don't affect demons like they do humans but they do give human flesh and blood a different taste. Whatever his reasoning, Lamir had scored multiple human dinners at raves like this one in the past week, and I was determined to stop him. Not only because it's my job as the Bridge Institute's enforcer, but also because, as I said before, I like humans.

My two sidekicks worked their way through the crowd on either side of me. Maddy, my teenage vamp friend, and Arman, my shapeshifter blood slave, looked like ravers themselves. As I made eye contact with each of them, they shook their heads, telling me they hadn't spotted Lamir.

That made three of us.

I've been hunting demons a long time. Nearly three hundred years, in fact. My instincts are never wrong. Instead of parting more dancers and scanning the crowd with my eyes, I stood still, fine tuning my senses and letting them take inventory instead.

There were, indeed, supernaturals in the human mashup. My blood buzzed under the surface of my skin with a low voltage warning me there were two Chicago House vampires besides Maddy in residence. I tucked that bit of information away for later.

A female shifter was making out with a frat boy in a dark

corner. She was in full mating mode; he was in heaven. While I don't judge, the situation rang warning bells. Things could quickly get out of hand if she developed feelings for the kid and tried to turn him. I'd have to talk to Ranulf, the local pack leader, about having her spayed.

Two low level demons were selling cocaine and ecstasy out back, but neither one's aura indicated they were indulging in human snacks on the side. Still, I added them to my mental watch list and would include their information in a written report to Damon, my boss, when I got back to the Institute.

Chicago had taken action several years ago to battle illegal raves, giving its citizens the illusion they were dealing with the drugs, underage drinking, violence, and date rape that often happens at large gatherings of young people. And like some cities, Chicago now had events *called* raves that were legal and endorsed by parents and kids alike. Hardcore ravers laughed at these 'virgin' raves and their PLUR—Peace, Love, Unity, Respect—credo, continuing to do what they'd always done... taking their movement to the underground.

A guy with curly hair and a cheeky grin bumped me from the right, bouncing off my protection spell and catapulting into a couple who were slow dancing even though the music was anything but. The male in the couple shoved the guy back toward me and I sidestepped his outstretched hands. He fell at my feet, looked up at me, and the grin widened. "Who are you?"

In the light of day, he would have been drop-dead gorgeous and old enough to play with. Under the strobe lights, he looked wicked and still of playing age. But he was all human and I wasn't interested. "No one you want to know."

"Xena, Warrior Princess or Red Riding Hood?"

The leather mini dress and thigh-high boots I wore conjured images of Xena, and the red cape hanging around my neck—technically a capelet, Maddy had informed me –with its

4

interior pockets filled with weapons, often tagged me as a role-playing Red Riding Hood. In reality, I was more like the wolf in that Grimm storyline.

My demon blood made me attractive to males of all species. That whole predator-prey thing. Add in the vampire cocktail and I was irresistible, especially to human males. They flocked to me in droves, and I was like a bitch in heat, thanks to the demon and vampire DNA running amok under my skin. Every look, every gesture, turned me on. A sexy voice, the right shape to a jawline, a broad back, a tight ass...you name it, I was enthralled with the male species. Thing was...there was only one male I wanted. The only male I'd *ever* wanted.

Radisson Beaumont.

The rock god, half-Chaos demon, and *il pistolino* who stood me up at the altar three hundred years ago.

A group of females bopping up and down and yelling at the top of their lungs at something one of the DJs said nearly trampled him. A new song started—the Chaos Demons' latest number one song—and the women squealed. Grabbing the back of cutie-pie human's jacket, I hauled him to his feet. "Go find someone your own age to play with."

He wobbled and tried to grab hold of my arms, but his hands slid off my shields. He cocked his head and stared intently into my eyes. The dopey grin left his face and the faked drunkenness disappeared. "You a cop?"

The scent of metal and gun oil filtered through his aftershave and the beer he'd spilled on his shirt. His youthful appearance gave him a *21 Jump Street* advantage with the current crowd, and I wondered who he was there for. The drug dealers? The underage kids? A particular criminal?

I gave him my best wolfish smile. "Takes one to know one, Officer...?" I let the question hang between us.

Convinced I was also undercover law enforcement, he gave me a careful once over. "Moreno. And it's detective."

Merde. I so did not need to come to the attention of a Chicago PD detective. "Detective Moreno." We shook hands, and I kept my smile in place. "Homeland Security. Sorry I can't give you details about myself or my assignment tonight, but I assure you I'm on your side."

Homeland Security was a blanket Get-Out-of-Jail-Free card that worked on most law enforcement officials. Especially the younger, less experienced human variety.

Moreno may have looked young, but he hadn't made detective by being easily brainwashed. "Credentials?"

Out of the corner of my eye, I saw Maddy headed my way. She gave me the signal—a two finger point to her right. Sure enough, the strobe lights flashed over the bald head of Lamir less than a yard off to her side.

"Again, Detective Moreno, I apologize that I can't share more with you, but my suspect is about to exit the building and I'm charged with bringing him in tonight. Please excuse me."

I stepped around him, heading in Maddy's direction. Arman's werecat scent tickled my nose, indicating he wasn't far behind.

Before I took three steps, Moreno slid into step with me, jostling human blockades out of his way. "Who is the suspect? What do you want him for?"

Seriously? This was how it was going to go? "I must insist you don't interfere."

We parted to get around some dancers. "And I insist you produce your credentials and a valid reason for being here."

Sometimes the good guys were a pain in my ass. With a nod from me, Maddy came to the rescue. She grabbed Moreno, said, "Hello, arm candy," and swung him away, dragging him into the crowd with her lovely face and superior vamp strength.

Toward the back of the warehouse, I spotted my target half carrying, half dragging a drunken girl toward the rear of the building. The strobe lights didn't reach that far, but I could feel the various human and supernatural energies of couples making out in the dark as I fought through the crowd. Arman raised his hand and pointed at a side door. I gave him the go ahead and watched him slip outside. Lamir was headed for a rear garage door we'd scoped out earlier. I'd follow him out that way and Arman would come at him from the west side. My blood tingled, telling me Maddy had already lost Moreno and was covering my six.

Sensing my approach, Lamir glanced up, his gaze meeting mine across the dark expanse. He froze.

My nerves shifted into overdrive. Volante, my whip, vibrated against my hips. I'd used her as a belt around my skirt since in such tight quarters she was useless as a weapon.

Beelining for Lamir, I hustled several kids out of the way, pushing for the rear of the building. In those few seconds, understanding dawned, and Lamir's fight-or-flight instinct kicked in.

Lucky me, he decided to try both.

2

As I cleared the crowd and dived into the darkness at the back of the building, Lamir held the girl like a shield in front of him. Her long, blonde hair swung over her shoulders as she laughed, high and loose, seeming to think he was playing a game. Grinding her hips against his groin, she kept her head down and ran her hands over his body.

His unblinking bug-eyes stayed locked on me. I'd made it within twenty feet when he picked up the girl, raised her over his head, and threw her like a Frisbee.

Her high-pitched laughter turned into a scream. Reflexively, I dropped my protection shields so she wouldn't ricochet off them and hit the concrete walls or floor. I raised my hands to catch her, not missing the fact Lamir used that moment to run outside.

The girl's dead weight hit me hard, but I stayed standing. I righted her, ignoring her continuing screams, and took off after Lamir.

Behind me, I heard a familiar voice yelling at Red Riding Hood to stop. I kept running.

Bursting through the garage door and into the night, the January air chilled my overheated skin. I drank in several deep breaths to clear my lungs and nose as I scanned the area. My sensitive ears locked onto Lamir's retreating footsteps, and after a few steps in that direction, my nose picked up his demon scent—a combination of mold and sulfur. Arman came around the building, his nostrils flaring as he, too, fastened onto Lamir's scent.

Maddy dropped down from the roof. I didn't need to say anything to my team. I motioned for one to go right, the other left. I would take the middle. Between the three of us, we'd sandwich the sucker.

Five minutes later, the demon bully groveled at my feet, held down by Maddy. Damon and the other Bridge Council members had already determined that past demands for Lamir to stop feeding on humans had been disregarded. Three times. The old three-strike rule was in play. Hence, my job as enforcer was to send him back where he belonged—hell. Placing my ring fingers and thumbs together, I raised my magic. Cool blue light encircled me and a powerful energy charged my blood. Goose flesh rippled over my skin.

From a hidden pocket, I withdrew a silver blade. Maddy forced Lamir's head up so I could look him in the eye.

"Please, don't kill me," he pleaded. "I'll start over. Live human-free."

Right. Like I hadn't heard that before. "Vengeance is mine," I said and plunged the knife deep into his heart.

When it comes to revenge, I dole it out like candy. Demons like Lamir are the worst of the worst. If I ran the Bridge Council, they wouldn't even get one warning, much less three.

As his physical form shriveled and turned to watery mold, Maddy made vomiting noises in the back of her throat. "So gross. I need a drink."

With nothing much left of the demon, Arman sidled up

next to her. The poor kid had it bad, his werecat eyes jumping to her face and away, back to her face. Needy. "We could go back to the party. You know, if you want to hang out."

Maddy, oblivious to his crush, turned to me. "Can we go back to your place?"

My place was akin to O'Hare Airport these days with five new roommates, each of them a combination of one of the deadly sins and its opposite virtue. Like me, each *vitium* was a hybrid of good and evil. I found their virtues as annoying as their vices. "Might as well. You can't go back to the rave."

"Why not?"

"That undercover cop questioned me, and he'll be looking for answers to Lamir's dramatic exit."

"I mind-melded him." Maddy made some kind of Vulcan whirling motion with her fingers around her temples. "The guy won't remember a thing."

"Fancy." That was a skill I wish I had. No such luck even with the vampire blood running in my system. "Still, I better ditch my cape for a while. He'll remember that."

Arman raised the hood of his sweatshirt and shivered. "Who's up for some hot chocolate and a bad action flick?"

My phone rang the beginning notes of *Whisper in the Dark*, a haunting ballad a certain half-Chaos demon posing as a rock star had written for me. Earlier that evening, I'd left him in my bed playing his favorite guitar and prepping for his upcoming Super Bowl half-time performance he and the guys were doing. The short winter days and long nights provided substantial working time, but were hell on my love life.

Me with a love life? The thought made me chuckle. Here I was, an uptight vengeance demon who'd been stood up at the altar and sworn off the very notion of love, knee-deep in it.

I held up my phone. "Gotta take this. You guys need a ride?"

Maddy shook her head no. At the same time, Arman nodded yes. Poor kid. Being a vamp, Maddy preferred leaping from rooftop to rooftop and running at high speeds, even in the dead of winter, over riding in a warm car. She grabbed his hand and took off running.

I walked east through the deserted neighborhood toward the vehicle I'd left a block away. If the South Side vandals hadn't stolen the tires, I'd be back at the Institute shy of fifteen minutes. "What's up?" I said into the phone.

Radison Beaumont's voice was dark, sexy, and all-male. "Me. How soon can you get here?"

Potent heat surged in my body. "My night doesn't end until sun up. I'll bring breakfast and see you in a couple of hours."

"Make it twenty minutes."

Il pistolino was too demanding for his own good. I bristled at being ordered around, but the female side of me couldn't help teasing him. "Or what?"

He chuckled low and soft. Dangerous. "Or I'll show up at the Institute wearing nothing but my Fender, and I'll give your boss something to remember when I take you on his desk."

Rad in his birthday suit was drool-worthy, and I enjoyed the image. There was no love lost between him and Damon, and I was the reason for their ongoing pissing match, but I wasn't impressed with the threat that he was going to mark his territory.

"Yeah, yeah, promises, promises. The ugly truth is, Radison, I'm not a rock star. I don't get to make my own hours, and I have two more items on my enforcer list and a dozen Sweet Investigations cases waiting at my office. So keep your clothes on, write a new song, and I'll see you in a couple of hours. For breakfast," I emphasized.

Before I made an idiot of myself and gave in to his demands, I hung up. Thinking about Rad made my blood boil—in a good way—and it always, *always*, got me into trouble.

I jogged the last half block to my car. Things were eerily quiet just past midnight. It was only nine degrees out. The human population in this part of town was rough, tough, and mean, but not stupid. Even the independent and mentally unstable homeless folks found shelter when it was this cold.

I raised my protective shields anyway. A few minutes later, I was glad I did.

3

My car still had tires, windows, and headlights. Bonus. I blessed the locals for leaving it alone and punched the key fob. The driver's side door unlocked, but before I got in, I stopped and scanned the shadows of a nearby abandoned house. Someone's aura tickled over my exposed skin.

The yard was covered in snow. A leafless tree stood wearily in the corner of the lot, its limbs sinking toward the ground. A chain-link fence, now ripped open in spots and rusting, lined the property.

Scanning...scanning...

There. Along the north side of the building. A presence.

Human or supernatural? I sniffed the air, reached out with my other senses.

Human. Female.

"Hello," I called. "Do you need help?"

No answer. No movement. Her aura was clear, no distress. Maybe a touch of excitement, but nothing negative. No drugs or alcohol impairing her body.

Okay, then. She didn't need help. Maybe she was on her

way to the rave or meeting someone in secret. None of my business. "Do you need a ride somewhere? Do you want me to call you a cab?"

Again no answer, but I would have sworn I heard a breathless chuckle, saw a small white plume of breath freezing in the bitter cold air where she stood.

My hackles went up. The hard scent of metal drifted past my nose, followed by the ominous stench of the Catholic Church.

Noctifector.

Merde.

Shifting slowly, I withdrew Volante from my waist and palmed her handle. She coiled around my arm, vibrating at the adrenaline and dark intent flowing through me. She loved the taste of blood and was hoping for a snack.

The problem with Noctifectors—a demon-slaying group of highly-trained humans—is that they travel in packs. It's the only way they can overcome their supernatural targets, and they consider all supes an abomination to God. Doesn't matter that I protect humans, I'm still number one on their 'Most Wanted' demon list.

I scanned the area more intently, searching for more humans. Except for the ravers behind me, there were none in a three-block spread. What was a Noctifector doing in this section of Chicago in the middle of the night without backup?

As if reading my mind, she stepped away from the house. There was no moon, only dirty snow and shadows playing tag. Her boots made soft crunching noises; the hood on her coat hid her face. "He can't leave the Order, you know."

That voice. Cultured, soft around the consonants. A whiff of peppermint on the night air.

"Parker?" My blood ran hot and vengeful. Human or not, I wanted her dead. "Rad can do whatever he wants. He owes you nothing. You forced him into servitude. Forced him to hunt down his own kind. If that's not sinful, I don't know what is."

"I didn't come to argue semantics, Kali Sweet. I came to warn you. The Church is pressing for an all-out manhunt—or should I say, *demon* hunt—to bring him back to Rome. You know what will happen to him if my group succeeds, right?"

She let the threat hang on the cold night air. "He'll be tortured and burned at the stake. His heart will be cut out and he'll be damned to Hell for all eternity."

I blanched, gripping Volante's handle tighter. Of her own volition, she slid off my arm and cracked her tip against the street. "I won't let you get anywhere near him."

Her voice was purposely light. Her aura growing more excited. "Can you protect him twenty-four, seven?"

Rad could protect himself. If Parker thought her silly mind games would work on me, it was time to give her a dose of her own medicine. "You love him, Parker. Why would you allow the Church to hurt him?"

"He deserves to be hurt."

"You're sick."

She cocked her head under the hood. "I'm a vessel of the Divine, and Radison Beaumont is the antichrist. It's my job to hunt him down and make him pay for his sins against humanity."

"The antichrist?" I laughed loud and hard. "You really need to see someone about these delusions."

She stepped closer, adjusted her hood so I could see her face. A weird sort of pleasure shone on it. There was a manic gleam in her eyes. "You don't know, do you?"

More games. "Know what?"

Giggling, she paced in a small circle. "How is that possible? Or perhaps you *do* know, but you're protecting him..." She stopped, met my eyes again. "Is that it? You think you can protect the White Horseman from us?"

"I have no idea what you're talking about."

"Sure you do. You broke the first seal of the apocalypse, you and the other deadly sins, and now you're harboring the antichrist."

I reached for the car door handle. "Go get your meds checked, Parker. You're losing your grip on reality."

"Wait." She advanced, standing on the other side of the car, looking at me across the roof. "You want to protect Rad? Let's make a deal."

I hate deals. Negotiating is one of my strong points. "I'm listening."

The manic light was still present in her eyes as she smiled. "Let me arrest you and turn you over to the pope. In return, I'll derail the Church's mission to crucify Rad."

This would be why I hate deals. "You could do that? Get the Church off Rad's back?"

"Could I do it? Of course, but *would* I do it? That's the real question. I'm offering you a once-in-a-lifetime deal here. Think about it." Her voice exuded confidence, but she walked backward until she reached the house's shadow, keeping an eye on me. "I'll be in touch."

Snow crunched under her boots as she drifted away. I stood, waiting. Thinking.

Planning.

"Before the moon is full," I murmured to her presence still lingering on the edges of my supernatural radar, "I will grind your bones to dust and sprinkle them in my morning coffee."

4

To the casual human observer, The Bridge Institute looks like an oversized warehouse surrounded by a couple of similar but smaller buildings and multiple parking lots along Lake Michigan. Glamours hide the true façade of an elegant modern building encased in enough magical protection spells to scare the devil himself away.

Although it was after midnight, the interior was lit like the middle of the day. We work at night when supernaturals are most powerful and most active. Damon and his counterparts, Kirill and Yasmin, live at the Institute and work pretty much nonstop. At least Damon does.

So when I climbed the stairs to the second-floor offices and found his empty, I was surprised. He refused to have an assistant or secretary to track his whereabouts and keep him organized. Mostly, I suspect, because his previous six secretaries had all fallen hard for him, creating more drama and turmoil than he cared to deal with. Besides, no one in the Institute was more organized than Damon.

My bloodhound nose tracked his smoky wood scent to the basement training center, where I stopped and stared in shock.

He was wearing nothing but black drawstring pants and sparring with Cole, our resident War demon. Cole regularly trained me and the other supernatural soldiers working for the Council with regimented glee.

But I'd never seen Damon, or any of the Council members, in the training center working out with him.

I'd also never seen Damon in anything but three-thousand-dollar Italian silk suits. I kept blinking, thinking my eyes were playing tricks on me.

Holy cow, my boss is...hot.

The shock on my face drew Damon's attention. As he noticed my gaping jaw and wide eyes, he smiled and then proceeded to land a solid blow to Cole's right kidney.

Showoff.

"Impressive," I called over the smacking and thudding of their gloved fists as they continued to spar. "Do I get to go next?"

"I'm next," a diminutive voice said from the bleachers.

In my shock, I hadn't noticed there was an audience. Three of my fellow *vitiums* watched the show from the sidelines.

"Kali, luv, join us," Shayne, also known as Leviathan and owner of gluttony, patted the bench next to him. He was the size of a Viking and had an accent I associated with the Australian outback, although I was sure he'd never been there.

Seraphina, our female Amazon warrior and owner of envy, watched the show with stern attention, her turquoise eyes like neon lights against her dark skin. Her complete opposite, Akimo, the owner of the tiny voice, even tinier frame, and a boatload of greed, nodded her head at me. She was going to take on Damon? *That* I had to see.

Parker's proposal couldn't be ignored, however. "I hate to interrupt the show, but I need to speak to you," I said to my boss. "It's important."

Shayne stood and spread his hands. "Speak freely. What is important to you is important to all of us."

"It's..." Admitting the truth seemed weak, but there it was. "Personal."

Damon and Cole continued their sparring, but hearing the tone of my voice, Damon stepped back from the fight and slit his eyes at me. "Did you not dispatch Lamir?"

His voice was chastising, stabbing at my pride. His assumption, however, was warranted, given that I'd hunted Lamir over multiple nights, and every time, the bugger had gotten away.

Didn't stop the reprimand from stinging.

"I *dispatched*"—what the hell kind of word was that for killing a demon?—"Lamir just fine, thank you very much, and my report will be on your desk before sunrise. This matter has to do with a certain...Noctifector."

Cole was breathing hard, but Damon didn't seem to need any extra oxygen after the vigorous workout. I had the uncanny feeling he'd been holding back. All of us could probably have jumped him all at once and still ended up dog meat in short order. Archdemon magic was nothing to mess with, even for a superfreak like me.

A warm rush of energy tickled inside my temporal lobe. I heard Damon's mental question, *Radison?*

Damon's ability to communicate with me in this fashion drove me crazy, but it was handy at times. *Parker Burkett. She's a complete psycho, but she offered me a legitimate proposition.*

My boss bowed to Cole in standard martial arts fashion, then said out loud to me, "Meet me in my office in ten minutes."

Cole faced me and lifted one of his dark brows as Damon disappeared into the locker room. "You in need of a bodyguard?"

"If so..." Shayne jumped up from his seat. "I'd be most happy to assist."

A controlled sigh escaped Cole's lips, but he didn't so much as glance at the Outback Viking. "I'm sure you would."

"I don't need a bodyguard." At least I hoped I didn't. Poor Cole had been tagged enough with me already in the past couple of months. "What I need is some good advice."

Shayne bounded over the bleacher, taking his cell phone out of his pocket. "I'll call the priest."

"No." I held up a hand and turned to Cole. He knew me better than most and cut me slack where Rad was concerned, even though my boyfriend had been a Noctifector until recently. "I've got to get that report on Damon's desk. I'll catch up with you later."

Cole understood my code. He nodded and I took off.

Ten minutes later, on the dot, Damon strode into his office, his lips thinning when he saw me sitting behind his desk typing on his computer.

"Just finishing my report on Lamir's execution." I saved the report with a click of the mouse and relinquished the cushiony leather chair reluctantly.

We traded places, him taking his seat and me pacing the floor in front of his desk. Inactivity makes me want to crawl out of my skin these days.

His gaze skimmed the report on his computer, and I covertly breathed in his reassuring fresh-from-the-shower smell. The archdemon was ancient, uptight, and a stickler for rules. He often made my job harder, and he was comfortable blackmailing me when necessary to get what he needed for the Institute's highest good.

But when push came to shove, I trusted him to keep me in line, tell me the bald truth, and stay emotionally detached. All qualities I respected and lived by myself. Damon could yell at me, curse me, and threaten me, and I still felt safe.

He frowned as he read the computer screen. "Your report is five sentences."

"Time, date, and place." I ticked the necessary information off on my fingers. My brief reports never failed to aggravate him, although I always figured he of all the Council members should appreciate my concise accounts. "Subject and manner of disposal. What else is there?"

If possible, his lips thinned even more. He closed the report, sat back in his chair, and steepled his fingers over his stomach. "I assume Miss Burkett's proposition was not sexual."

Eww. "Devil take me, no."

"And it was not about Radison?"

"It was about both of us. She claims if I turn myself over to her, she'll make sure Rad goes free from persecution by the Church."

Damon rocked his chair in quiet consideration. "Do you believe her?"

"Hell, no, I don't believe her. Well, maybe. But she was talking nonsense." I decided to hold off telling Damon about the antichrist malarkey. Damon didn't have much use for Rad as it was.

While Parker may have been off her rocker, Rad had been a Noctifector up until a few weeks ago, and therefore, Damon would give weight to any and all accusations against him, no matter the source.

He stared at me, eyes searching my face. The communication center in my brain warmed. "You want to deceive her. Use yourself as bait to...?"

I slammed my shields into place. "I want her gone. If she won't leave us alone—if she's purposely coming after either of us and endangering someone I care about—then I have every right to end her."

"She's human."

"Give her a cookie."

"You don't kill humans."

"Noctifectors don't count."

He fell silent, but he didn't try to read my mind this time. "And your plan?"

Since I'd only had a flash of inspiration and the details were still fuzzy, I hedged. "If Parker captured me, would she attempt to kill me here in Chicago or take me to Rome?"

Damon loved logic and big-picture thinking. He loved the hunt for answers. This question, however, seemed to stump him. "The laws of the Church require her to return a demon such as yourself to Rome, where the pope will make you an example to others of our kind."

As if I'd allow *that* to happen. "Would she follow the rules? Her vendetta is personal. What if she attempted to kill me here for her own purposes, not wanting to risk my escape during transport? She could say I broke free and threatened the members of her Order."

"That *is* a possibility, but Miss Burkett's nature is one of obedience and the desire for acknowledgment. She seems unlikely to trade her current status as leader of the Noctifector Chicago Order or the approval of her superiors, which she obviously craves, in exchange for any personal satisfaction she might gain exterminating you on her own."

From my experience, Parker was not the subservient Noctifector Damon painted her as, but his profiling capabilities were legendary. If he believed she would follow the rules, I believed it too. "That could work in my favor."

His brows dipped. "If you're considering the idea of using yourself as a Trojan horse to get inside the pope's private quarters and murder him, I will be forced to stop you."

How did he do that? I had barely thought that much through—with my mental shields firmly in place—and here he was, a step ahead of me. "It's the perfect plan to put a kink in the Church's biggest weapon against us. We tried getting them to work with the International Bridge Organization and they refused. In the art of war, take out the leader and the soldiers scatter."

"Have you forgotten we are preparing for the apocalypse? When the time comes, the Church may be all that stands between us and the demon hordes loosed from hell."

Chicago was already overrun with demons from the looks of stacks of cases on my desk at Sweet Investigations and the missions Damon handed out like candy. "Have *you* forgotten that I sent Maria's ghost to the afterlife? Without the seventh sin walking the earth, there is no apocalypse."

His face told me he wasn't convinced Maria was gone. That made two of us, but thanks to me, the queen from my past had gone somewhere filled with light. If she came back in any form, I'd take her down again.

Damon pointed at a stack of papers on his desk. "In the past twenty-four hours, Bridge employees around the globe have reported an increase in supernatural activity. Here in Chicago alone, we've seen a dramatic rise in human death and suffering." He flipped through the sheets. "Water is running red from Oak Park to downtown Chicago. Two high-rises along the lake have reported infestations of rodents. Every emergency room in Cook County is swarming with patients with flu-like symptoms."

He released the papers and met my gaze. "Kirill believes this is an outbreak of malaria, dengue fever, and several other infectious diseases. So you tell me, should we not be preparing for the apocalypse?"

"That's why you were going one-on-one with Cole, isn't it? You're worried. You think you might actually have to fight to survive."

"I'd be a fool not to worry about this, Kali, and I've lived too long to be considered a fool."

His sharp tone told me he wasn't kidding. The reports on his desk seemed to mock my confidence that I had stopped

Maria...and that I could stop her again. "What do you need me to do?"

"Your father was a skilled historian and scholar for his time. He kept extensive journals on notable demons, including Maria. I'm told he also detailed elaborate hypotheses about the Beast and the potential for a biblical Armageddon. He figured out how to stop them. His journals were confiscated by the Church many times over the years, the final ones taken on the night he, your mother, and your sister were murdered."

The mention of my family hit me like a fist to my solar plexus. It took me a minute to get the red-hot anger suddenly pulsing through my veins under control. Another minute to resume breathing. "You never told me this before. Why?"

"The journals are stored in the Vatican's underground libraries where clandestine records and protest literature against God and the Holy Catholic Church are kept under lock and key. The answer to the coming Armageddon may be found in your father's writings...and our only hope of retrieving those writings may be a Trojan horse."

Conflicting emotions raged inside me, but the conspiratory gleam in my boss's eyes gave me hope. "So you'll consider my plan to infiltrate the Vatican if I agree to find those papers?"

The phone on Damon's desk rang, interrupting whatever he was about to say. He answered with a curt "yes" into the receiver, and his eyes narrowed at me. "You're sure? What time did the attack occur?"

A pause. "Anything else you can tell me?"

Another pause, this one longer. Damon's eyes narrowed farther, creating lines in the corners. "I see. Yes, she's one of mine. I'll send her to have a look at the crime scene once you've vacated it. Thank you."

He returned the handset to its cradle with slow, deliberate movements. Damon wasn't one to sigh, so when he blew out a deep, troubled breath, no longer looking at me, a chill went down my spine.

"What is it? What happened?"

"There was another attack on a young female human twenty minutes ago in Millennium Park. Her throat was ripped out along with her heart. She had an X carved into her forehead."

Lamir's MO.

The clock on Damon's wall read one a.m. "It couldn't have been Lamir. I offed him over an hour ago. Is your source reliable?"

"He's a CPD officer. One you met at the rave tonight."

"Moreno? *He's* your source inside the police department?"

Damon nodded. "One of them. A good male."

"But I didn't sense an ounce of magic in him."

"He's all human. And unimpressed with your Homeland Security cover."

Few humans knew about us and that was how we liked it. Knowledge was power, as evidenced by the Noctifectors and their ability to find our weak spots. But why would Moreno snitch for the Bridge Council if he was human?

Damon took out a notepad and pen from his top desk drawer. "He lost his wife, a woman with latent demon blood, two years ago to the Noctifectors."

So the detective had a vendetta. My estimation of his character rose. "He was tracking Lamir at the rave?"

"A legitimate assignment since he's in violent crimes." He scribbled words on the notepad. "His superiors believed the recent murders to be the work of a serial killer. This fourth incident will solidify that assumption. The FBI was already reviewing the cases. Now they'll take over, especially since the CPD is overworked with the uptick of crimes in the past twenty-four hours."

"So if it wasn't Lamir, who or what killed that girl?"

Damon tore off the sheet of paper, handed it to me. "That is your new assignment."

So old-fashioned. The paper held the name of the victim and the precise place of her attack. It also had Moreno's private number on it. "What about Parker?"

"The Institute can offer Radison sanctuary so we can better protect him, but I can't offer round-the-clock security off-site because of the current crisis. We barely have enough soldiers, even with Alexandru's vampire unit, to cover all of these trouble spots." He tapped the stack of papers. "And since Parker is also after you, I must insist you move back into your apartment suite here as well."

The idea made me want to stick out my tongue in true Maddy fashion. "Rad's living at my place and there are five other *vitiums* there most of the time. As long as he doesn't go anywhere without backup, he's safe." I decided not to mention there was no way I was moving back in. "I'll take Cole with me as security detail on my jobs."

"I can't spare Cole. He's the best trainer and strategist we have, and we *are* at war, Kali. But I will request Alexandru loan us Brianna Mullins to escort you on jobs. Cole recently passed her with the highest of clearances for security operations. He claims she's almost as good as he is."

Oh, joy. Nothing like having the Master vamp's undead snack source hang out with me. Brianna and I had a love/hate relationship and there was no way either of us would be on the love side of her playing my bodyguard.

Damon rose, came around the desk, and placed a hand on my arm. "If I could, I would insist you stay here around the clock until we could deal with the Noctifector situation, but I'm afraid you're the best field soldier I have. The Bridge needs you out there, stopping as many of these supernatural monsters as possible."

A hundred and one questions swirled through my brain. Parker, Rad, Maria...

"Take care, Kali." Damon squeezed my arm. "We'll discuss Parker and her proposition when you get back."

"But..."

Go, he interrupted, breaking through my shields. *Make sure this attack isn't Maria.*

Maria. I would always be looking over my shoulder because of her. "Yes, boss."

I heaved my own sigh and headed for my car.

5

Moreno warned me over the phone that the crime scene was too hot for me to be poking around. He would call me when the cops were done. I wanted to see the body, but calling attention to myself was out of the question. He promised to email me a picture of the vic's body as soon as possible and give me a heads-up when the scene was clear.

I had time to kill, but wasn't in the mood to work on any Sweet Investigation's cases. Instead, I headed home.

The place was hopping, as is normal these days with all the supernaturals living there. Shayne, Akimo, and Seraphina were still at the Institute, but Salmad, the priest, and Bronwen, the sixth *vitium*, representing sloth, were in the sanctuary.

I live in an old church that resembles an ancient castle. A few years after the Civil War, it was abandoned and condemned. I used my magical talents and a lot of elbow grease to turn it into a home. Never did I guess that the east wing I'd closed off would eventually become Hotel Kali for five of the seven deadly sins.

My Sweet Investigations computer guru, JR, was also in

attendance. He was on his laptop, Bron was hanging maps and sheets of paper on the walls, and Sal had a handful of markers and was making colored X's on various spots on the maps.

"Why aren't you at SI?" I asked JR.

He glanced up but didn't meet my gaze. "I'm using social media and other online resources to detect disease outbreaks, violent crime upswings, sudden crop failures, and mass deaths."

Nice.

Salmad turned, pointed a marker at me and then the map in front of him. "JR has found over a dozen reports claiming the water in the Mississippi River has a reddish cast."

"And that means...?"

"Pestilence. The first of the Four Horsemen of the Apocalypse. The red tide, parasites, boils, plague. Chicago appears to be ground zero for six different deadly viruses, and two fatal disease epidemics and the waterways are carrying most of it. Even Lake Michigan is darker than usual. One of the last seven plagues will be inland waterways turning black."

Bronwen yawned. "Can we take a break now?"

I cocked my chin at the map. "What are the X's for?"

Sal's sad eyes met mine. "JR has his way of tracking. I have mine. Green for Pestilence, Red for War, Black for Famine, Yellow for Death."

There were green X's on multiple points on the Chicago map. All at once, the weight of what we were facing made my knees weak. "The Horsemen signal the Apocalypse?"

He nodded.

Because of Maria. "How can Maria be back? And where is she? How do I hunt a ghost I can't find?"

Bron leaned against the wall and closed his eyes. "You could kill one of us instead."

The thought had occurred to me on the drive over. I looked at Sal. "Would that do it?"

"Once the Horsemen appear, it means the first seal is broken. There's no going back."

A part of me felt relieved. I didn't want to kill any of my fellow *vitiums*.

Okay, except when they ate all my food and wrecked my house, but that was different. They may have strained my patience, but I'd grown fond of them. "So hunting down Maria won't do any good either, right?"

Salmad tapped the marker against his chin. "I don't believe Maria is back, only that her ghostly arrival last month tripped the apocalypse switch before you could send her from this world. According to prophecy, each *vitium* is supposed to have a certain time on earth. We rotate, in other words, every three to four hundred years. A couple of us may overlap, but we are never here all at once. And yet, for some reason, we *did* end up here at the same time, only Maria was here as a *revenant*, a ghost. Apparently, that was enough to complete the circle and open the door to the Four Horsemen."

Somehow, that seemed worse. If Maria walked the earth and I could hunt her down, at least I would have a target—a mission to focus on instead of drowning in a sea of 'how do I stop plagues, war, and certain death for most of the world's inhabitants?'

I needed time to think. To take in the fact that humanity was about to be destroyed. "I'll be back in a minute."

I found Rad upstairs pretty much how I'd left him the previous evening...pants, no shirt, a guitar in hand. His music was raucous and upbeat—a scintillating song about a hook-up. Not his usual angst-y rock song, and yet, this almost pop-sounding version worked for him.

Humans...their ability to create something from nothing always enthralled me. Rad was only half-human, but that half was one hundred percent creative, ingenious rock god. He lived for his music the way I lived to wreak vengeance. I'd have traded all my supernatural abilities for one ounce of that creative human gene.

Because he was my blood slave, I felt what he felt, especially when we were within a few feet of each other. Right then, he was high on life. High on the chords coming from his guitar and the words coming from his mouth. His back was to me as I stood in the doorway, the muscles in his shoulders and his biceps working as he strummed. His dark hair had grown a few inches in the past month and was curling slightly around his ears and down his neck. For a split second, I forgot about Maria and the apocalypse and my job. All there was was Rad and his perfect back. I wanted to kiss my way down the vertebrae and run my hands through his hair. I wanted to hear him sing to me as he stroked his fingers over my body the way he did his guitar.

The last note of the song drifted away. I'd been so lost in my fantasy I hadn't noticed he'd quit singing. "What do you think?" he asked without even turning around.

I cleared my throat. "It's got a good beat. Easy to dance to."

The old American Bandstand cliché wasn't lost on him. He'd lived as long as I had. "Dick Clark. I met him once, a long time ago. He was a good guy."

He rose, unhooked the guitar from the amp and made his way over to me. A wicked grin lit his face. "You're home early."

I walked into his arms without saying anything, burying my face in his neck. He could read my emotions, limited as they were, and didn't ask what was wrong. His strong arms encircled me, and he stroked my hair, my back. His lips pressed a kiss against the top of my head. "Rough night?"

I was used to rough, and whining about the obstacles facing me wouldn't solve any of them. With a Herculean effort, I stepped out of his embrace. "Parker paid me a visit."

He dropped his arms, a crease forming on his forehead under his bangs. "Did she attack you?"

A little voice inside my head told me not to share the fact

that she'd offered a trade. If Rad knew I was considering her proposal, he'd find a way to lock me up. Not that I'd allow that to happen, but I had enough fires to put out at the moment without expending energy fighting him. "I think it's time you moved into the Institute."

"What?" He took a step back. "Wait...you think I'm scared of Parker?"

I planted my feet, preparing for the fight to come. "Of course you're not scared of Parker, but she was pretty explicit about what The Church plans to do if they catch you. From the way she talked, you've surpassed me on their wanted list."

His eyes burned with indignation. He crossed his arms over his well-sculpted chest. "And you want me to hide and let you fight my battles."

Here we go. "I want you to stay alive. You'll be safest at the Institute until this blows over." *Or until the apocalypse kills us all.* "Security by obscurity. Stay out of sight, under the radar. You know the drill. Once things quiet down and Parker finds a new boy toy, you can go on with your life."

His face turned impassive. I held his gaze and kept my whirling emotions under control. He uncrossed his arms, stepped close once more. The scent of salty ocean air invaded my nose. "You're not telling me the whole story."

Damn. He knew me too well, even if I was shielding my emotions. Time for an evasion tactic. "Have you been downstairs tonight?"

A slight narrowing of his eyes told me he knew I was changing the subject. "I know Salmad and JR are predicting the end of the world."

"You're not worried?"

He chuckled, low and deep. The sound made me long to touch his naked chest. "Why would I be worried when I know you're here?"

My heart pinched. I started to speak, had to swallow a sudden tightness in my throat. "I can't stop Armageddon, Rad."

Unless I somehow stole my father's journal from Vatican City, and it did, indeed, contain the antidote.

Rad gave a nonchalant shrug. "Then we'll go out together."

So cavalier. No wonder I was in love with him. "Boy, that makes me feel *so* much better."

He rubbed my upper arms and gave me a smile. "We're a team, K. I'm not hiding out at the Institute, nor am I letting you face pestilence or any other damn plague alone. I'll handle Parker. You have bigger things to worry about."

"Parker threatened to harm you. That is not insignificant to me. Since the day I lost my family to Maria and the Noctifectors, nothing pisses me off more than when someone threatens me or mine. You're the one she wants, and it's now my goal in life to make sure she never, ever lays a hand on you."

My voice got quieter as I said the words, my scarce supply of emotions effectively shutting down as the vengeance demon in me came to the forefront. She was controlled and calculating. A cold-hearted bitch who felt nothing and lived only to do her job serving justice and disposing of anyone who got in her way.

Emotionless powerhouse. That's me.

Rad's beautiful golden eyes widened as my demon peeked out. Usually, only my enemies got that little show, but at that moment, slipping into vengeance mode was necessary. I needed a clear head to make the hard decisions ahead of me. "I have to get back to work. Regardless of Parker, you should pack your things and some of mine too. If the end of the world is coming, we'll be safer at the Institute. I'll let the *vitiums* know they need to be prepared to move at a moment's notice."

My logic seemed to pacify him. "What about Aphrodite and Neve? Want me to round them up?"

I felt that odd pinch in my chest again. Radison Beaumont...

breaking through my walls by being a nice guy. Again. "Yes. Thank you."

"Done." Paying no attention to my standoffish attitude, he drew me into an embrace and kissed me. His lips were firm and hot, teasing mine open with a practiced, reassuring touch.

A shiver went down my spine. I couldn't help but give in. Like I said, he could break through any barrier I put up. With a kiss, an embrace—hell, with a simple look of those golden eyes. I don't know how he does it, but I turn into a mushy, worthless demon every time.

He stroked a piece of hair from my face, rested his forehead against mine. "Parker is good—top of the Chicago Order of demon slayers—but she's no problem for me. I can handle her."

Rad probably knew her better than anyone. "I know you can."

A breeze suddenly blew strands of hair around my face. The salty ocean scent intensified. Rad drew back his face a few inches, his gaze locking on mine as his Chaos demon showed up front and center. "If she as much as sneezes on you, I'll end her."

"She sneezes on me, and I'll detach her sinuses and feed them to Satan's hell hounds."

He smiled and winked. "That's the Kali spirit."

My phone buzzed inside my cape. Caller ID said it was Moreno. Pecking Rad on the lips in goodbye, I left him and his beautiful body and went back to work.

6

Millennium Park—Chicago's wave at Y2K—stretched north as I lounged on a bench in the Lurie garden. Four a.m. and the bandshell was quiet, the sounds of traffic along the lakefront a soft, intermittent drone in the distance.

The sticky-sweet scent of Fae hung in the winter air, cloying and thick in my nose. Other smells, mostly human, were nearly drowned out by the odor. Minty gum wrappers, wet dog fur, newspaper print, car exhaust, molding leaves...the normal smells of the city.

Roiling dark clouds overhead were fat with rain instead of snow. Towering buildings on the west and north sides looked down on me with dozens of tiny lighted windows. Humans resisting the call of sleep. What were they doing in their high-rise condos and offices?

As I sat scanning the night, I thought about the humans in those buildings. To be so passionate, so emotional, so screwed up, and so mortal fascinated me. The fact they were oblivious to the supernatural world and the contingent of demons, vampires, shifters, and an assortment of other evils who all wanted to use them for one reason or another, scared me.

I couldn't save them all. Couldn't protect everyone.

Stalks of brown prairie grass and Allium globes held their stems high in the garden, their plumes and flowers long dead. The stalks reminded me of humans as well; their birth, life, and death all happened in such a short time, leaving their hollowed-out remains behind. How fragile their lives were, and yet, how tough they tried to be. I admired that about them—their ability to ignore their mortality.

To my left, Cloud Gate—otherwise known as the Bean, due to its shape—had been roped off. My acute hearing picked up the faint slapping noise of the yellow crime scene tape as it blew in the wind. The female human had been killed under the sculpture, her neck ripped to shreds. The third female since Christmas to die that way in this part of town, and Chicago's finest had squat for leads. I doubted the FBI had anything solid, either. I'd taken care of Lamir, but this killer mimicking his MO was still running loose...*running* being the key term. From the looks of the wounds on the photo Moreno had sent to my phone, it was most likely a shifter. A large dog shifter.

I never took things at face value. Hence, my lying in wait for the killer to return to the scene of the crime or for my nose to pick up evidence. The sweet stench gave me pause and also confirmed my suspicions. There were many types of Fae demons. This one was a succubus.

Succubi live to drain emotions from others. Their favorite meal is human, and they can feed off the same one for months, sometimes years, before eventually killing them.

But ripping out a human's neck? Not the typical succubus MO. Vampire? Check. Werewolf? Double check. Demon? Possibly, but atypical for succubi.

In my three hundred years on Earth, I only knew one

succubus who enjoyed physically hurting humans in such a brutal manner. I also knew she was dead.

At least, I hoped she was still dead.

Shifting on the bench, I scanned the area. The crime scene told me little, and besides what my highly sensitive nose was telling me, all I had to go off was Moreno's photo and a sketchy autopsy report. Was it too much to hope that the perpetrator would return to the scene and make my job easier?

Even better, if it was Maria, could she appear and give me a reason to blow off the tight anger simmering under my skin?

A new scent drifted over the dead landscape. Strawberry daiquiri lip balm and the smooth floral notes of Chloe perfume. Underneath those lay a whiff of fresh blood and old leather.

Vampire.

This particular vamp had given me a tube of watermelon lip balm for Christmas and stole my favorite perfume. Not to mention she regularly raided my closets for clothes and was currently on a vintage leather kick.

Beneath my cape, a tingling started in my blood. Now, all vampires set off warning bells in my system, but I was intimately linked to the Chicago pool.

"Hail, oh queen of mine." Maddy's teenage snark cut through the night and echoed over the open space. Her boots clomped on the sidewalk as she walked arm-in-arm with a young man in a hoodie. The smell of werecat tickled my nose. "Thought you might be here."

Her companion lifted his eyes from under his hood. His teeth flashed white in the shadows as he smiled. "I came to help."

Arman. If the perpetrator *was* a shifter, no supernatural being was better equipped to help me hunt him or her down.

"Glad you're both here. Any word on the shifter grapevine, Arman, about our mystery killer?"

He shook his head. Maddy shook hers as well. "Nothing on the vamp grapevine, either. You sure it's a supe?"

I crossed my legs at the ankles, settled farther down on the bench. The lack of chatter by either shifters or vamps confirmed my theory. "The MO is Lamir's, but we took care of him, so this is a copycat killing. But our perp wants to throw off both the human investigators and the Bridge Council by making it appear that Lamir did the job."

Arman lifted his nose and sniffed the air. "I smell succubus."

"Exactly."

"And..." Arman blinked and his eyes widened. His gaze swung around and locked with mine.

"What is it?"

His hands were stuffed deep in the pockets of his hoodie. Breaking eye contact, he balled them into fists and stretched the garment out, let it fall. Stretched again. "Nothing. It's just..."

The nose went back up and he stepped out of Maddy's embrace, walking toward the Bean. Maddy followed. "Just what?"

He didn't say anything else, ignoring the footpaths and crossing through the dead plants and grasses as he headed for the crime scene. Keeping a wary eye out, I trailed several yards behind.

At the scene of the crime, Arman ducked under the tape, kneeled, and swiped his fingers across the ground. Raising the ends to his nose, he swore under his breath and swung around to find me.

Earlier, a group of kids hanging around the Bean had dared each other to tear down the tape and reenact the crime. Gruesome, but humans had a natural curiosity and morbid fascination with violent death. Demons and most supernaturals reveled in it. My own teenage years in Maria's court had been filled with it.

Now the area was as dead as the victim. Ironically, Arman, who'd killed his fair share of humans during the time he couldn't control his werecat side, was far more serious than his human counterparts, and seemingly more shocked at what had transpired there. "I don't believe it."

Maddy shot me a questioning look. I shrugged. "Believe what, Arman? What do you smell?"

His voice was barely a whisper. "Wolf."

Granted, the wet dog scent here was stronger, but plenty of people walked their dogs around the area. I was disappointed my nose hadn't picked up the difference.

So had the succubus come along after the killing? Maybe watched it happen?

In my mind's eye, I could imagine Maria watching, even egging on the werewolf. Feeding her hunger and flooding the area with her strong dark magic.

But why did it look like Lamir's work?

A tight sigh left my lips. Maria could make it look like anything she wanted.

Arman's face tightened further. It was a wolf, but not just any werewolf.

A thought dawned...one I didn't like any more than the fear on my young blood slave's face. "*Merde.* Please tell me it's not who I think it is."

Maddy frowned. Arman stood and started stepping backward, placing each foot with care, as if retreating from a landmine. "It can't be. Ranulf would never kill an innocent female."

Chicago's pack leader wouldn't have been my first pick for this, either. "I have to look into the possibility, Arman. You know that."

His eyes blazed with defensiveness. "He preaches peace with the humans. He's the Bridge Council's biggest and most outspoken supporter. Ranulf wouldn't jeopardize our community here in Chicago. He would never kill a human."

Never is a long time. And a supernatural's propensity for killing humans is high.

Now that I'd become queen of the Undead, the vampire nation was the Bridge Council's most important ally. Could it be that Ranulf was pissed about this new arrangement? Maria would do anything to get back at me. Had he and Maria struck a deal to do just that?

Motioning for Arman and Maddy to follow, I tucked my hands inside my cape pockets and checked for my snub-nose gun and the silver bullets it used. Check and check. "Come on. Let's go talk to your werewolf king."

7

Arman grabbed my arm and spun me around. He was more of a threat to himself than to me, but that didn't stop my hackles from rising. The mix of vamp and demon blood inside my veins roared to life.

Maddy felt it, too, and her blood answered mine. Arman was my blood slave and wouldn't hurt me, which Maddy knew, but I was her queen. The blood bond we shared would force her to protect me at all costs. She stepped between us. "Back off, bro."

"Sorry." Arman released me, held up both hands, but his eyes pleaded with mine. "If you walk into Ranulf's den and accuse him of murder, it could start a new war between the shifters and the Bridge Council. Let me talk to him first. Find out why his scent is here. There may be a good reason."

There was no good reason I could think of. "If he's guilty, he'll run the minute you tell him we found his scent here."

"He won't run. He's innocent."

A new odor wafted past my nose. Maddy's head whipped around as she caught a whiff of it as well.

Arman followed our gazes to the east, his nose twitching. "Noctifector."

Maddy and I automatically fell into a back-to-back warrior pose, protecting each other's six while circling so we could both scan the area. Sensing danger, Volante hummed to life where she was wrapped around my right forearm. I let her handle slide into my palm. "Not just a Noct. Parker Burkett."

Arman looked confused. "Rad's fiancée?"

"*Ex*-fiancée," Maddy corrected. "And he never loved her or anything. He's *totally* into Kali."

Totally. Right. The male screwing up my emotions on a daily basis was *totally* into his music. Since Parker's father happened to be Rad's producer...well, things had gotten messy around Christmas and Rad was still dealing with the fallout of firing him and breaking up with Parker. Parker had been suspiciously absent, but I'd been too busy with a houseful of unexpected visitors to care.

Until now.

"Two visits in one night," I called to her. "In case I wasn't clear before, we're not BFFs."

She floated out of the shadows, dressed in Noctifector black and wearing more leather than Maddy. Her hooded monk-type robe billowed out behind her as she strutted down the walkway toward us. "I was tired of waiting for your call."

While Parker walked alone, I sensed the presence of other Nocts spread out in the other three directions. Nothing like a little good versus evil in the heart of Chicago.

I stopped circling, undid the clasp of my cape and let it fall to the ground. If Parker wanted a fight, I was up to the task.

But I was also highly paranoid—you don't live for three hundred years if you're not über careful. Maria, Ranulf, Parker and a dead body. Something stunk and it wasn't the garbage scattered around the area. No one knew better how tricky and conniving Maria was. I'd learned at nine years old to never, ever underestimate her.

I had the same inclination about Parker. She was no demon, but she was crazy. Religious crazy, demon crazy, ex-boyfriend crazy. A deadly mixture ready to explode.

She stopped, smiled at my fighting stance and removed her robe, letting it fall to the ground in an imitation of me and my cape.

I hate imitators. "You really want to do this here?" I waved my free hand at the expanse of Millennium Park. "In public?"

Her answer was to draw a set of slender and oh-so-sharp daggers from matching thigh holsters and dance around with them in a choreographed display.

A challenge. And a ridiculous-looking one at that.

Maddy stepped up behind me, her jacket brushing my shoulder. "Kali, you know I've got your back, but this is a bad idea."

Battles were never a good idea. Some you had to fight anyway. Even in public. "I'll distract Parker and her minions. You grab Arman and get out of here."

Arman's breath touched the back of my neck as he stepped in behind my other shoulder. His body heat engulfed me. "We're not leaving."

I flicked my wrist and Volante cracked against the concrete. Challenge accepted. "This is my fight, not yours. It's personal. She's mine."

Maddy sighed dramatically. "You don't take anything personally, remember? The vengeance demon code of honor, or code of bullshit, or whatever it is."

That *was* part of my code. *Don't take things personally. Don't get emotional.* I couldn't take vengeance for myself, only others. Parker is Rad's ex-fiancée. She's also a Noctifector who kills supernaturals for no other reason than they were abominations in the eyes of The Church.

Touching my thumbs and ring fingers together, I raised my shield of protection. A cool, blue light enveloped me. Once secured, it became invisible. "Vengeance is mine."

"She's human." Maddy drew out the word so it sounded like *huuu*man.

"She's a Slayer, and I'm the number one demon on her kill list. All I'm going to do is defend myself when she attacks."

The *click, click, click* of Maddy's fingernails on her cell phone emphasized her next words. "I'm texting Cole."

Around us, Parker and her Noct buddies inched closer. Parker's sly smile said she thought this battle was already in the bag.

"*Porca miseria.*" Parker was highly trained, but her cockiness would be her undoing. I didn't need the War demon to help me out of this situation. "Forget Cole. This will be over before he can get here."

I stepped forward, ready to get the show on the road. Parker sped up her forward motion as well, accepting my counterchallenge. As she moved to meet me in the center of the plaza, she swung her daggers in a series of movements meant to intimidate me.

Yeah, whatever. I kept walking, boring and un-Hollywood as it was. Volante trembled in my hand.

Behind me, the Nocts moved in on Arman and Maddy. I heard Maddy hiss, her vampire nature taking over. Arman shifted into his cheetah persona, letting go of a cat cry that raised the tiny hairs on the back of my neck.

The two of them could hold their own against a couple of Noctifectors, but there were close to a dozen closing ranks on them. Time for a distraction.

Magic rippled down my arm. Volante rose in response. I cracked the whip at Parker and she jumped out of the way. Working her around to the left, I kept cracking the whip, driving her in an arc so I could keep an eye on Arman and

Maddy. The Nocts bearing down on them were avoiding Arman's claws and Maddy's fangs, but that wouldn't last long. And there was no way I'd let my friends get hurt.

The Bean is a sculpture consisting of one hundred and ten tons of highly polished steel plates that create a mirrored surface. Maddy and Arman secured themselves under the high arch, forcing the Nocts to come at them in pairs from either side, rather than standing in the open and facing all twelve enemies at once. Clever.

I'd always wanted to stand on the top of the sculpture and look down. Seemed like now was my chance.

Climbing the structure, with its slippery mirrors, was a challenge. Good thing I had both demon and vampire blood in my system, and my lucky studded boots had three-inch military-style soles that could climb anything.

Parker advanced on me, swinging her daggers in tight semi-arcs up, around, down, and out. She was slightly taller than me, but reed-thin, and a sword would've been clumsy and too heavy for her. Also harder to hide. Daggers could be secured anywhere on her body. They were lightweight and could slice or stab her victim. Most Nocts, male and female, preferred daggers for all of these reasons, but I knew from experience, they also preferred them because daggers were a more intimate weapon. In order to do damage, you had to get up close and personal with your target.

Less skilled Nocts preferred swords and guns. Highly-trained ones liked daggers and knives.

While waiting for Parker's show to be over, I noticed a tiny line creasing her forehead. Worry or concentration?

Standing completely still, I let her get close enough that I could see the hate in her blue eyes. They looked nearly black under the street lamps. She swung a dagger at my throat. Missed, thanks to my speed when I ducked.

Being the well-trained little Noct she was, she adjusted

faster than I expected. Instead of swinging the second dagger at my body, she threw it.

The sharp tip sliced through my protective bubble, slit open my leather bustier, and bit into two of my ribs below my heart. A stinging sensation set up camp.

What the hell?

Sure it was a silver blade, but it shouldn't have penetrated my protection shields. But this was a Noctifector, so this blade had to be pure silver and blessed by The Church.

Still…it might have cut into my shields, but it shouldn't have blasted all the way through and done damage to my body so effortlessly.

Parker smiled. "Nothing personal."

Yeah, right. Everything with Parker was personal.

Using my gloved hand to remove the dagger from my ribcage, I examined the blade. Blood sizzled against the silver, evaporating into the chilly air. With the odd steam, an unusual scent flooded my nostrils. A chemical smell, part gasoline and part something I couldn't identify.

My demon didn't care what it was, only that it stung.

A lot.

She peeked out from my eyes and smiled back. Black magic surged in my veins. Pain in my demon's world was a good thing, and now she was ready to rip Parker's head off.

Letting Parker see my demon had the desired effect. She sucked in a breath and hesitated.

That heartbeat of hesitation was all I needed. Snapping my wrist, I sent Volante at her ankles. At the same time, I threw the dagger back at her. Her gaze naturally followed the knife, while the whip sliced through the air hitting its mark with a solid *snick* as it wrapped around her ankles.

She screamed and I jerked back on the whip. All the Nocts looked in our direction as Parker was swept off her feet. She hit the ground with a sickening thud, rolled several times, and sent me a hateful look when she finally came to a stop.

Another flick of my wrist and Volante released her ankles. "Nothing personal," I murmured as I sprinted past her and headed for my friends.

Musical notes rang out from my cape where it lay on the ground. *Whisper in the Dark*, that damn haunting rock anthem of Rad's, filled the wintery air. The gazes that had been on Parker swung to my cape, then up to me as I jumped on the slippery surface of the Bean.

Thirty-three-foot sculpture? No biggie. I hit square on, but the soles of my boots slid out from under me. So much for all that military tread.

I righted myself with a single pinwheel of my arms, slashing Volante through the air and taking out two Nocts on the ground at the same time.

"Shazam!" Maddy yelled, laughing at the Nocts.

Raj Nudra's blood injection hadn't given me supervamp powers, but a later dose of Alexandru's had. The Chicago House Master, and direct descendent of Vlad the Impaler, had cut a deal with Damon to give me his blood when I had experienced such extreme withdrawal symptoms that I nearly died.

Mixing the oldest and most powerful vampire blood with my ancient demon blood turned me into a freak. A Super Woman of Evil. I could leap farther, run faster, and astral project if I concentrated hard enough.

The flip side? I was also part virtue. One of the seven deadly sins Jesus had cast out of Mary Magdalene back in the day. I was cursed—or blessed, depending on how you viewed the glass—with a side helping of virtue.

Vice, virtue, demon, vampire...my blood, bones and very cells were a complete Frankenstein-ish mess. And everyone wanted a piece of me. The Nocts wanted my head, other supernaturals wanted my blood. According to Maddy, who kept one ear on the supernatural underground, it was the new ultimate drug, even though no one but my blood slaves had ever tasted it. Neither of them showed enhanced abilities, although Rad's performances in the bedroom had certainly kicked up a notch. The bedroom, the kitchen, my office...

The ringtone of *Whisper* played again. I mentally smacked a palm against my forehead. Talk about getting distracted. *Il pistolino* always did that to me. One of the reasons I kept trying to keep some space between us. One of these days, he was going to be the death of me.

Parker yelled at her minions and they resumed attack positions. I skipped across the steel plates to the other side, doing a mocking imitation of her and her daggers. Volante buzzed with joy, reaching for the Nocts she could reach below. They darted out of the way, but she followed, nicking their hoods, faces and necks.

On Parker's command, throwing stars, more daggers and even a sword came flying my way. I danced out of reach with each assault and the weapons fell harmlessly on the mirrored surface of the Bean.

The stinging sensation in my ribs burned hotter with every movement.

Parker pursed her lips and whistled. Not at me or her soldiers. Someone else. Some*thing* else. My blood tingled.

A pack of vampires materialized from the gardens and headed our way, fangs bared and claws extended.

"Kali?" Maddy's voice, coming from below, held a note of anxiety. "You seeing this?"

My blood registered the new vampires, but it didn't sizzle like it did when a Chicago vamp got close. This group belonged to another city. Another country even.

Or maybe...from the looks of their ragged clothes and lack of personal hygiene, they could be renegades.

Sweat broke out along my hairline and the burning sensation spread throughout my chest. I'd never felt this type of pain and a tiny seed of fear made my legs go weak. The silver dagger hadn't just been blessed by The Church or dipped in holy water. It had been forged with something stronger. Much, much stronger.

But what?

I'd heard stories about blades forged in angel fire. The ultimate demon killer.

Was it possible? If so, how had Parker gotten her paws on one? It wasn't like angel fire blades were commonplace.

The Noct in question crossed her arms, staring me down as the vamps closed ranks around the Bean. The lead vamp jumped to the top of the sculpture with the grace of a gazelle and faced me. He smelled like all the Undead...a mixture of old and new blood and lusty magic. But he was young. Younger than Maddy if I guessed right and he was full of conceit and a deep craving. His eyes burned an intense red so he'd either been turned very recently or he was starving.

Definitely a renegade vampire. I glanced at Parker. "You're stooping low these days, Parker. Turning human kids into vamps to do your dirty work. You disgust me."

Through the years, Noctifectors had recruited other supernaturals—Rad being one of them—to help them wage war on the rest of us. 'Recruiting' being a politically correct term. Rad had been tortured and blackmailed into becoming a Noct. No telling what Parker had done to turn these young kids into her vamp bitches.

"War is hell," she replied. "Sacrifices have to be made."

The vamp took a swing at me, all arm and no hip. I only had to shift my head to avoid the obvious punch. This was going to be a snap.

Literally.

It saddened me that I hadn't saved this kid. Unfortunately human-on-human violence wasn't under my jurisdiction. One of these days, though, I'd find the vampire responsible and dole out some revenge.

My entire chest ached now. Ignoring it, I casually wiped the sweat from my hairline while the vamp bounced on his toes. Before he could throw another punch, I used my hyperspeed to lunge forward and hook an arm around his neck.

I jerked up once and snapped his head to the side, breaking his neck. His body convulsed once and then he fell at my feet.

He wasn't dead, and without a stake, I couldn't kill him unless I decapitated him. But there wasn't time for that. I kicked him off the sculpture and curled my fingers at the next vampire waiting on the ground. *Bring it.*

All at once, the other nine vamps launched themselves at me.

8

They hit me from all sides, taking me down in a pile of arms, legs, and gnashing teeth. Through the tangle of bodies, I heard Maddy scream my name. Arman, still in Cheetah form, bellowed. One vamp's teeth sank into the back of my neck; another clamped down on my calf.

Superman had kryptonite, while I had holy water and angel fire. Thanks to Parker's dagger, my protection magic was definitely on the fritz, and the infection was spreading like poison, an acid coursing through my body via my bloodstream and engulfing my heart.

The blade had to have been forged in angel fire. The thought made my head swim.

The edges of my vision darkened, or maybe that was the vampire blanket covering me. My pulse raced, my skin crawled. The demon inside clawed at the secure prison I held her in, desperate to get away.

It would have been easy to free the evil living inside me. Too easy. And once free, my demon would destroy everything in sight until someone reined her back in. Prior to my transformation into Frankenstein's monster, I believed Damon could do that if necessary. Now, I wasn't so sure. I wasn't just a demon anymore.

Bracing myself, I called on my superfreak mojo and felt it bunch my muscles and pump hard in my heart. I compressed my bones, cells, blood, and tendons and then exploded out of the pile, throwing vamps in every direction.

They hit the shiny surface, limbs flailing, blood running from their mouths. Half of them slid off the sides. The other half lay dazed.

The exertion took its toll on me. My legs shook. I couldn't raise my arms. Warm, sticky blood oozed down my neck, side, and calf. The sculpture's surface ran slick with it.

Darkness encroached on my vision once more and the plaza's lights made the rest a blur. My tongue stuck to the roof of my mouth, and I dropped to my knees. The angel fire had created the purest silver dagger around. Add in a dip in holy water and the pope's blessing, and it was a triple whammy my system couldn't seem to shut down.

Along with everything else, my shields were broken. To my right, a vamp rose, eyeing me. If he'd waited another minute, he probably could have had me as a snack. As it was, when he leaped at my head, I forced my weak arm to shoot up and grab his neck. His Adam's apple exploded in my palm.

Oops. Not as weak as I'd thought.

I tossed his body over the edge and wiped off the worst of his blood, but my fun wasn't over yet. The young leader, whose neck I'd broken earlier, had come back online. Teeth bared, he vaulted onto the sculpture and reached for me. His long fingers closed around my neck and he brought my face to his. He cursed me in Spanish.

Interesting. A Spanish renegade vampire group created by the Nocts? Damon and Dru would have a field day with that information.

I would have returned the cursing in his native tongue, but my mouth was too dry for speech and he was cutting off my air.

Balling my bloody hand into a fist, I punched him square in the stomach. He caved but held onto my neck. We both fell off the Bean, thirty-three feet straight down to the plaza's concrete.

I landed half-on, half-off of him, his weight nearly breaking my arm and causing my head to bounce into the ground. Shouts erupted around me. I was burning with fever and my body felt like every bone was broken. The vamp attempted to shove me away, but my arm was pinned under his torso. I made another fist with my free hand and brought it down on his throat, collapsing his windpipe. He jerked and went still.

My demon fell quiet. I rolled onto my back and closed my eyes. I needed to finish off the vamps and get Maddy and Arman out of there, but my limbs refused to move. The air in my lungs seemed trapped, and the side of my head throbbed where it had hit the concrete. I struggled to open my eyes, but they wouldn't respond. I called on my demon and vamp blood to get a move on with the healing process but got no response.

Out of the pain and emptiness came the salty smell of ocean water. A soft caress of warm air caressed my face. A deluge of half-human, half-chaos demon emotions washed over me.

I licked my lips and fought to open my eyes. They refused to cooperate. "Rad?"

Callused fingers touched my neck, checked my pulse, and then rose to cup my face. The softness of his touch belied the anger and fear rolling off him in huge, undulating waves. "I'm here."

Embarrassed by my weakness, I swallowed hard and finally managed to open my eyes. My breath hitched. Blackness met my vision.

I blinked.

Still zero dark everything.

Satan's balls, I was blind.

"Angel fire," I whispered. "Parker's dagger is primo stuff. I'm infected and it's not going well."

Rad's voice floated above me, the clang of swords and the hiss of vampires a distant sound. "I'll get you out of here."

"Arman and Maddy first."

His hand moved to the spot where Parker had cut me. He murmured something in French and probed the cut with his fingers. A fresh wave of pain set off an explosion of fireworks underneath my eyelids. I moaned.

A second later, I felt the tip of a knife against my skin. Lines forming over my ribcage. A jolt of magic ripped through me. A renewed sense of strength came with it.

Powerful magic, that. I sat up, blinked. Whatever he'd drawn on me revived me in record time, but my sight was still AWOL. "What the hell was that?"

"Healing rune." He patted my shoulder. "Stay here, stay down, and I'll be back in a minute to get you out of here."

Healing rune? Those didn't work on me because of my demoness. Or at least that's what I'd believed until now. Maybe the virtue side had some influence in that department. If so, I was all for it.

Before I could ask Rad about the possibility, the ocean smell moved away in a clash of metal on metal. That tiny seed of fear returned and rooted in my stomach. I couldn't see what was going on, only hear and sense it.

Unnerving to say the least.

A vamp approached on my right. I heard his quiet footsteps, smelled his desire and hunger for my blood. I also felt his essence—his aura—hovering just out of my reach like a ghost. Slowly, step by careful step, he hunted me.

Keeping my head up and my heightened senses on alert, I patted the ground for Volante.

She wasn't there.

Touching my fingers together, I tried to raise my protective shield. A cool blast of air stroked my skin, the bubble snapping into place.

Ahhh…

And then it popped.

No cloak of weapons, no whip, no protection magic. Just me. Blind, injured and exposed to my enemy.

Cries rent the air. The vampire stalked closer, not as impulsive as his counterparts had been, but just as eager to try his hand at taking me down.

"Kali!" Cole's voice came from my left. He must have arrived with Rad. "Volante. Incoming."

I jumped to my feet, holding out my hand. A slicing sound whistled through the air as the whip flew toward me, thanks to Cole's accurate aim and her ability to hone in on me. A second later, she lay secure in my palm, her tail lashing out at the vampire hunting me.

I gripped her tight and let her fly.

There was a sharp smack, a horrible screech, and a juicy sounding *thunkthunkthunk* when the vamp's head hit the ground and bounced.

Breathing deeply, I forced myself to hold still and pick up the next threat. Sure enough, I heard the barely there footsteps of someone else sneaking up behind me. Female. Human. Smelled like a traitor.

Parker.

The scents of silver and human sweat invaded my nose. Volante trembled in my hand, anticipating the command to attack.

"What are you waiting for?" I couldn't resist provoking her. I might be blind and in pain, but I was just getting started in the make-her-pay department. "Finish the job, Parker."

"You were never the job," she said, *sotto voce*. She was close enough that her breath brushed my neck where the vampire bite was already healing.

Confused, I searched for her angle. She'd attacked me and my friends. Sent a renegade group of vamps after me. "Then why are you here?"

She leaned in so her mouth was next to my ear. "For him," she whispered.

And then she was gone.

Anger made my hands tremble. A trap. Parker had attacked me in order to get to Rad.

I had to give her credit. She was a bitch, but she was a *smart* bitch.

"Rad!" I yelled over the noise of the battle. What was she planning? Payback for him ditching her? Payback for him firing her father? Payback for him rejecting the Noctifector way and going dark side again? Check, check, and check, but it didn't matter. Payback was payback, and that was a subject I knew everything about. Her earlier offer had been a test. A test I'd failed. Now she'd pulled out the big guns...using me to get what she wanted.

I'd walked right into her trap.

Her angel-fire forged weapon could kill Rad as easily as me. I had to warn him.

I yelled again but got no reply. Being blind on the battlefield was worse than being paralyzed.

Slowing my breathing, I also stopped my racing thoughts. Rad could handle one scrawny Noctifector. He was one of them —*had* been one of them. He knew their MOs. Especially Parker's.

The smell of lip balm hit me right before I felt Maddy's hands on my arms. "Kali, are you all right?"

"Where's Rad?"

"Why are you looking at my stomach?"

"I'm not looking at anything. I'm blind." Spots now danced

in my field of vision and the heavy darkness seemed lighter, more translucent. I hoped that was a good sign. *"Where is Rad?"*

"Blind?" Her hands ran up and down my arms. Vamp magic poured off her as her tension spiked. I sensed her scanning my face and trying to get my eyes to track her fingers. "How did that happen? When you fell? Do you need blood?"

The rune cocktail Rad had infused me with was wearing off. My arms felt like hundred-pound weights, and my wounds throbbed in time with my heartbeat. The only positive thing was that my vision was definitely clearing, the temporary blindness wearing off as fast as it had come on. I could suddenly see Maddy's outline.

"Listen. This is a trap. Parker's after Rad. She attacked us to get him here. Can you see him?"

"Yeah, he's right..."

"Here."

Rad was suddenly in front of me. His features were a blur, but I could make out his broad shoulders and his bedhead hair sticking up in all directions. I smelled his scent, felt his emotions.

He leaned close, scanning my face. "Can you see me?"

An unexpected bubble of relief burst inside my chest. I *could* see him. Not in high-def or anything, but well enough to see the worry crease dance across his forehead and the tight set of his generous lips.

"Yes," I murmured. My eyesight might be returning, but my strength was fading faster than ever. "I can see you now."

The last ounce of strength I had disappeared. I fell into his arms, the world once again going black.

9

I regained consciousness at the Bridge Institute's infirmary. Like human hospitals, it was cold, sterile, and rocking the white-on-white effect.

Kirill, the closest thing we had to a doctor, was holding a mean-looking needle in one hand and feeling around for a vein in the crook of my arm with the other. An archdemon and one of the three top dogs on the Bridge Council, he looked annoyed to be relegated to what appeared to be a common blood draw.

An IV pole, with some funky yellow liquid in a bag, stood sentry next to the bed, pumping the yellow goo into my forearm. Kirill poked me with the syringe, narrowed his eyes, and started probing the tip around under my skin.

"Ow." I tried to jerk my arm back.

He held firm, his black-eyed gaze shifting to my face. "You're awake."

Everything, including his pudgy face, seemed to have a fuzzy gray shadow around it. I blinked a couple of times but the shadow outlines didn't disappear. How had I ended up here, and what was going on with my vision? My memory was unclear, so I mentally poked and prodded my brain, but it only produced disjointed blips. Like a book with a cartoon picture drawn on each page. You flip them in running succession to produce a motion picture. Only my individual memories didn't flow into a bigger picture. They simply produced confusion.

I flexed muscles in various places on my body and was happy to note everything seemed normal. My magic felt fine, as well. Once my memory came online, I'd be good as new.

Except for the fact that Kirill was torturing me with that damn needle. The tip sank deeper as if he were purposefully trying to hurt me.

"You're not exactly Florence Nightingale, are you?"

"Don't be such a baby." Finally, he hit a vein and dark red blood with a viscous black and green tinge began filling the tube. "Nightingale. That old bitty put a crimp in my infection rate during the Crimean War."

Kirill was better at spreading disease than curing it. But his knowledge of diseases, infections, and poisons made him invaluable as our resident demon doctor. There wasn't a sickness on the planet he hadn't dabbled in and knew the cure or antidote for.

Another memory surfaced. "Pestilence. You're friends with the Red Horseman, aren't you?"

"Friends?" He snorted. "He's my boss."

"But you work for the Bridge Institute now. Damon's your boss."

"Damon is not my boss. We're equals."

Uh-huh.

Kirill watched the blood fill his syringe. "Pestilence is not a demon, and once you belong to him, he's your boss forever. He currently doesn't know where to find me. I prefer to keep it that way."

The map of Chicago Sal had decorated with red X's flashed

in front of me. "Oh, I think he does. He's in town. Do you know how I can track him down?"

"He can't find me." Kirill's gaze rose from the vial to meet mine. "And you can't kill him, Kali, if that's what you're thinking. The Horsemen are invincible. God created them to bring about Armageddon."

"So they're like angels?"

"Not angels. A separate species. They're not human, angel or demon. They're simply the Horsemen. Haven't you ever read the Book of Revelation in the Bible?"

"I live the war between good and evil on a daily basis. Why would I want to read about it?"

He cocked his head, withdrew the needle. "Point taken. However, you probably should brush up on the basics about the Beast, the Horsemen, the False Prophet, etc."

I'd get right on that. "Why does my blood have that greenish tint to it?"

Kirill frowned. "I'm not sure. Could be holy water poisoning. It's killing off your demon cells. Rotting them, like a blood gangrene."

Yuck. Bits and pieces of the fight at the park came back to me. Renegade vampires, Parker, and her plan to capture Rad. The cut from her dagger. "Is it possible the dagger Parker used on me was forged with angel fire?"

He looked like I'd struck him. "Possible, I suppose, but highly improbable." He fixated on the blood vial, his forehead creasing deeply. "I've never seen that type of wound or its effects on demon blood."

He held the vial away from him, his chubby cheeks hanging even lower from his frown. "I'll take this to the lab and see what I can find out."

"Is everyone else okay?"

"A few cuts and bruises, but otherwise fine. Radison and Cole are transferring your personal belongings to the upstairs apartment. Maddy and Arman are downstairs in the cafeteria. Radison stated your friends Neve and Aphrodite will be here in the morning."

Relief loosened the tightness in my chest.

"How's the vision? Maddy stated you experienced blindness during your encounter with the Noctifectors."

I blinked again, took another scan of the room just because I could. It was good to have my sight back, even if everything did have a shadow. "Sucks to be blind, but the baby browns seem to be working okay now."

He taped the injection site. "Could have been caused from your head wound or from Parker's blade. Either way, it's good it was only temporary."

I touched my temple. There was no lump, tenderness, or pain. That rune packed a punch.

I pointed at the IV bag. "Do I really need that?"

Kirill made work of labeling the vial of my blood and collecting his plastic carryall loaded with lab supplies. "Yes."

"What's in it?"

"You don't want to know. For now, it's your sugar daddy. Whatever you do, don't pull that IV out, or your ass will be dirt."

"Ass will be *grass.*" I really needed to hook him up with an urban dictionary. He and Damon both needed a jolt of modern-day American lingo. "If I've been poisoned, why don't I feel sick? Is it because of the healing rune Rad carved into my side?"

He held up the tube. "I'll know more about your condition once I analyze this."

He left, taking my blood and his white cart of supplies with him. I studied my surroundings and twiddled my thumbs. No TV, no magazines, not even my MP3 player. This was *so* not going to work.

Throwing off the covers, I slid out of bed and gave the

bleached hospital gown a frown. I was naked underneath. Had Kirill undressed me, or Damon's right-hand groupie and fellow council member, Yasmin? She was nowhere to be seen, nor could I smell her burnt sugar scent. Probably hanging out by Damon's side. Better him than me.

A square bandage covered part of my ribs. When I probed it, the area wasn't sore to the touch, and a faint scar lingered silvery-white where Rad's healing rune was imbedded. I had never used runes. Up until now, I hadn't believed they'd work on me, and the act of carving into someone's skin brought back too many bad memories of my days in Maria's court.

I grabbed the IV pole and dragged it with me to the attached bathroom. There I found my clothes. My sweater wouldn't go around the tubing attached to my arm, and there was no way to work a bra around them either. I considered rejecting Kirill's order not to pull the damn thing out, but in the end, the thought of the greenish blood stopped me.

At least I could cover my ass. I left the room a few minutes later in my leather pants and the stupid hospital gown tied securely around my torso.

In the hall, I ran into Lainie, the Institute's house mother. She didn't ask me what had happened, just looked me over and made motherly clucking sounds. She ordered me to stay put, disappeared for five minutes, and returned with a red and black flowered kimono. I didn't see how that would help until she revealed that the sleeves and sides had no seams and were held together by ties. She covered me in the beautiful satin material and I took the elevator to the second floor, pushing my IV pole ahead of me into Damon's office.

He sat at his desk, his aura dark and disturbed. Across from him sat Alexandru, House Master of the Chicago vampires and my partner in the world of freakdom.

Upon seeing me, both males rose. Old fashioned but kind

of charming. Blood pounded in my ears as Dru's blood called to mine. Embarrassing heat pooled between my legs.

Damon looked annoyed, Dru looked happy. Nothing new there. Damon was generally annoyed at me and Dru was constantly trying to get me to sleep with him.

Damon searched my face. "How are you feeling?"

Dru motioned me to the chair he'd vacated, taking my hand and rubbing a thumb over my wrist. He leaned his head close to mine as I sat, murmuring in my ear. "You look stunning as always."

I rolled my eyes and withdrew my hand. Outside the office window, the night sky was still dark. Gusting winds whipped the lake's waves into a white-tipped frenzy. The antique wall clock showed it was a few minutes after six a.m., but the sun was nowhere to be seen.

I caught Dru's eye. "Did you come to see me or to talk business with Damon?"

His brown eyes danced, sending me an unspoken message. Vampires didn't seem to have an aura, but they rarely cloaked their emotions. A combination of lust and powerful magic rolled off him and reached for me. He was in the beginning stages of laying claim to Vlad's position as head of the entire vampire nation and he wanted the Institute's backing.

He wanted my backing too. Regardless of whether the Bridge Council stood by him in his quest, he wanted me as his right-hand demon queen. He'd purposely kept his plans nonspecific, but the fact we shared each other's blood gave me insight into his mind and emotions. When the time came, he was going to offer me a world of supreme power and unlimited possibilities.

A warm rushing sensation, followed by Damon's voice, entered my head. *He came to check on you. But he's always hoping to talk business.*

"You were my first concern," Dru admitted. "I'm glad to see you're up and about. Kirill said you'd been poisoned. I brought a pint of my blood in case you need an extra boost."

Dru had saved my life with his blood and I'd returned the favor shortly afterwards when his heart had been nicked by a stake during a fight. By sharing my blood with a pure-blooded Master vampire, I'd broken every cardinal rule the Bridge Council had—demons, especially those who worked for the Bridge Council, never shared their blood with another supernatural.

But here I was, their top enforcer, with not one, but three blood slaves. Dru and I were friends—a rare thing in my world —and he'd earned my loyalty. That loyalty had nothing to do with him saving my life.

Well, maybe a little, although being tied to a vampire was my worst nightmare on many, many levels. In essence, I was now his blood slave and he was mine. We were both Frankenstein monsters in the supernatural world. That was saying something, considering supes are freaks of nature to begin with.

I knew without a doubt, Dru would be my friend and confidante long after the Council terminated my employment. And that could be any day. I was hardly a model employee.

The biggest thing I brought to the table was skill. Demons who would protect humans were few and far between.

Damon resumed his seat. Dark shadows edged his eyes. Or maybe that was my off-kilter vision. "I debriefed Madison and Arman earlier about tonight's affair and shared the information with Alexandru. We have grave concerns about the renegade vampires you encountered and about the idea that Chicago's shifter leader may be involved with the recent attacks on human women. If you're up to it, we'd like to hear your version of tonight's events."

We had bigger things to worry about, but I had the feeling

Damon wasn't up for sharing the end-of-world stuff with Dru just yet. *You could have just said, 'What happened, Kali?'.*

A nerve under Damon's eye twitched. "What happened, Kali?"

I pinched my lips to keep from grinning, took a deep breath, and started at the beginning. As I told my story, the crease in Damon's brow deepened. Dru, who'd pulled up another chair, sat forward, frowning as well. Neither interrupted, even though I could see dozens of questions in their eyes.

When I finished, Damon picked up a pencil and started flipping it end over end. "Let's start with Ranulf. The evidence is circumstantial at best, and in all the time he's lived in America, he's never been involved with any human killings."

Dru sat back, kicked his long, Armani-clad legs out in front of him and crossed his ankles. "That you know of."

Damon raised an eyebrow in question. Dru shrugged. "He ran the woods between Germany and Russia for two hundred years before moving here. You really believe he gave up hunting humans simply by changing locations?"

Vampires and shifters hated each other. Did Dru know something we didn't, or was he simply pointing fingers because he had no use for Ranulf and his large, Chicagoland pack?

Damon was thinking the same thing, but he was an expert at keeping his cards close to his chest. "I'll call him and set up a meeting. See if he has an alibi for the night of the killing or can explain why his scent was at the scene."

"Calling him is a bad idea," I said. "If he is guilty, he's not coming in for a meeting. He's running."

Both males considered that while I continued. "Better to let me show up on his doorstep and ask the hard questions."

Damon looked at me inquisitively, and Dru just looked amused. The IV may have had something to do with it. It's hard to travel with that thing on my arm.

"What about Maria?" Damon asked. "Any sign that she had a hand in this?"

"The scent of succubus was hanging around. Arman and I both picked up on it. As for a direct tie to Maria? No. I found nothing."

"I'll send Chigaru to talk to Ranulf." Damon picked up his phone and dialed. "He has canine in his ancestry. The pack leader will be more likely to talk to him."

Chigaru was a new recruit from Africa who'd been sent to the Institute for me to train. Fat chance I had time to take another demon under my wing and teach him anything about being an enforcer. I'd met Chi once, found him to be quiet and likable, but I wasn't a teacher. I'd set him up to train with Cole, gave him some handbooks JR had developed for me and left him to his own devices.

The canine ancestry Demon referred to included a touch of hell hound. I doubted Ranulf would find that reassuring enough to trust Chi with the truth, but it was still a good call. Ranulf would immediately bristle at my presence since I tended to bring the wrath of the Bridge Council with me. Chi could pretend to be on a fact-finding mission as a rookie Bridge employee. If he played it right—acting like this was his first big assignment, which it was—he could probably garner a lot of help from Ranulf.

Still, it rankled to have Damon hand off this job to a newbie. If I didn't have the Parker situation and the Red Horseman breathing down my neck, I might have objected.

While Damon called Chi to give him the details, Dru and I struck out down the hall. "I should grab Arman and make it clear to him not to warn Ranulf before Chi has a chance to question him."

Dru took my arm and supported me, even though I didn't need it. He was always touching me, most of the time in a lascivious manner, but this time, it was a friendly gesture, nothing more. "I saw him and Madison when I arrived. Madison didn't want to leave you, so they were going to watch a movie in the media center."

The media center was on the second floor and was Maddy's favorite hangout at the Institute when she wasn't in the training room ogling Cole. Like most teenage girls, she loved movies and music. The center contained a theater, a library, and a hub for listening to and recording music.

I was touched she'd stayed to make sure I was okay, but not surprised. Maddy had attached herself to me several months ago, becoming my shadow after her parents rejected her new vampire way of life. In some ways, she reminded me of Pippa, my little sister. Or maybe it was simply my longing to have a younger sister in my life again, but I enjoyed Maddy, even when she was a teenage pain in the ass.

We headed away from the elevator and toward the media center, my IV pole bumping along on one side of me and the vamp Master hovering on the other.

"Have you seen the news?" Dru asked.

"JR, Damon, and Salmad have kept me up to date. They believe it's the start of Armageddon."

"Funny how Damon didn't mention that during my conversation with him."

Dru's voice said he didn't think it funny at all. We stopped in front of the entrance to the media center. I turned to look at him and the hallway swam before my eyes. Tightening my grip on the pole, I swayed, closing my eyes.

"Kali? Are you all right?"

"Yep, just shifted my head too fast." I blinked, swallowed, and opened my eyes. Dru had three heads instead of one.

They blurred and floated in front of me. A weird tingling zipped down my legs, my ankles and knees going wobbly. "I think I need to sit down."

The words had barely left my mouth when my legs gave

out. Dru caught me, easing me down to the floor. "Look at me. Let me see your eyes."

I did as he said, and he gave a curt nod when he saw them. "Your pupils are red. You need to feed."

Red pupils? That was a vampire's calling card, not a demon's. "Are you sure? They've never been red before."

He placed his wrist to his mouth and bit, drawing blood. "My blood is at war with the poison in your system. The vampire in you is fighting for control."

I swallowed hard at the sight of his blood, the scent of it like a fine wine to my nose. His face blurred again and I blinked to try and right it. "I'm not a vampire. I'm a demon. And it'll take more than a Noctifector's blade to bring me down."

He smiled, once again amused at my bravado. "Drink, demon."

I wanted to resist. *I hate vampires*, I reminded myself. *I will not drink directly from Dru's wrist. Ever. In a million years. Not even if he's the last male on earth who can satisfy this awful...*

As if I had no power over my body, I reached up, latched onto his wrist, and sucked on his open vein.

My brain screamed denials. My body ignored them. At first taste, the blood was tart, but by the second swallow, it was intoxicating. I only ever drank his blood from a glass bottle. This experience—the warm blood pumping across my tongue in time with his pulse—was carnal, primitive. A low groan escaped my lips.

Freak.

I drank long and deep, and afterward, a warm glow suffused my body. My brain continued to berate me, and I tried to tell Dru I hated him, but when I opened my eyes, there was only one of him, and there were no odd shadows around his body or the objects I saw. Without thought, I closed my eyes again in complete and utter satisfaction. I was satiated, quenched...

Content in his arms when he lifted me from the floor and carried me to the infirmary, my IV pole tagging along.

Sinking into sleep, I barely noticed when he crawled into the bed beside me and wrapped me in his arms. My brain yelled obscenities at him, but my body was too gone to do anything about it. I snuggled down into the covers and drifted off.

10

I woke to shouts outside the infirmary door. An argument between males that loaded the air with so much testosterone and crackling electricity, the hair on my arms rose.

I sat up in bed, my chest tight. A mix of ancient magics swirled through the crack under the door as the shouting grew louder and more intense.

Fight.

Icy snow crystals beat against the outside windows. Either it was still night or the storm made it seem so. How long had I slept?

Another burst of furious words and tangled magic hit me. The glass in the windows rattled. Bending forward, I sucked oxygen into my lungs and noticed it stung like I'd gulped in salt water.

Rad.

My brain clicked into gear, but the argument I was overhearing didn't make sense...and then it did when I realized the males outside my door were arguing in French.

My name was said, along with a string of curses directed at Rad.

Dru.

Threats were exchanged. The vamp blood in me responded with a sharp spike of adrenaline. My Master was being threatened.

It annoyed me that Dru's blood exacted that response, but I couldn't deny nature. I threw back the covers, climbed out of bed, my body ready for a fight. Except for the vise around my lungs, I felt good. Healthy. Ready to take the males arguing over me down a notch, shred Parker into a million little pieces, and stop the Red Horseman and his buddies from decimating the world. All at the same time.

Flexing my hands, I forced my lungs to relax. Forced Dru's blood demanding my protection to settle down. Although I didn't doubt Rad would love to kill the Master vampire, no one was going to get hurt. Amidst the shouting was Damon's steady, commanding voice, trying to appease both males.

Good luck with that, I mentally told him through the walls.

He started at the mental intrusion, then regained his calm, controlled persona. *Perhaps you'd lend a hand? You are the cause of this row.*

I needed a shower, some food, and a toothbrush. All that would have to wait.

Dragging the damned IV pole behind me, I threw open the door. "*Non più!*"

Rad was restrained by Cole. Dru by Damon. Brianna was halfway between them, ready to defend her Master. Maddy, Arman, and my best friend Di stood to the side watching. Neve, also a good friend of mine, and totally human, sat in her wheelchair rubbing her Celtic knot necklace.

Stretched down both ends of the hall behind the combatants was just about everyone else I knew. The *vitiums*, the other Bridge Council members, even a set of vamp soldiers Cole was training. All eyes bounced from the males to me and back to Rad and Dru.

Rad's gaze locked with mine, his magic rippling through the air. The lights up and down the hallway exploded, making everyone jump and dousing us in darkness. My IV bag exploded at the same time, and yellow goo landed on me and splashed onto the floor at my bare feet.

With the exception of Neve, all of us were supernaturals of one persuasion or another, so we had no trouble seeing in the dark. Shaking goo off my hands, I yanked the needle from my arm and tossed it to the ground. Then I walked between the two males, shoved Bri out of the way, and grabbed each by his shirt, bringing their faces close to mine. Since I was shorter than both without my heeled boots, they loomed over me.

First, I looked at Rad. His emotions were a chaotic ball of anger and pain, and I could easily put two and two together about the reason for this fight with Dru. He'd discovered us together or Dru had told him about my drinking directly from his wrist. It was an intimate act. One that usually led to sex and a deeper bond between the two participants.

Rad and I shared that bond. I didn't blame him for jumping to conclusions. I hated that I'd succumbed to drinking directly from Dru. If the situation were reversed and I'd found Rad in bed with someone like Brianna, say, it wouldn't matter the reason. I'd be madder than hell, too.

But I wasn't about to discuss what had happened or air my dirty laundry in front of Satan and all. "Calm down. Nothing happened between us."

He knew the *us* meant me and Dru. I didn't need to spell it out.

A snarl curled his lip.

Ignoring it, I switched to the vamp. "And you. Stop with the theatrics. I'm not your slave any more than I'm your Master. We share a blood bond, yes, but that's for our mutual benefit to stay alive and kicking. I won't let you twist our friendship into something ugly."

Dru's Master vamp magic rolled over me, pushing back on Rad's demonic energy. A white-hot tingle burned in my veins. "We are more than friends, *mon petit chaton*. You are my queen."

Oh for hell's sake. I shot a glance at Damon. The corner of his mouth quirked. He found humor in the strangest things. "Well, your queen is going to stake you if you don't stop being an ass."

Now Dru's mouth quirked. *Bastard.* To him, this was a game. To me—and to Rad—it wasn't. We'd spent nearly three hundred years apart. Nothing as insignificant as a vampire was going to come between us.

I conveyed that in my eyes to both males, released them and stepped back.

"Save the fighting for the Horsemen. We have work to do. Everyone to the conference room." I pointed at Neve and Di. "You two as well. We have a lot to discuss and not a lot of time."

Supes started filing past us, giving me questioning looks. Maddy gave me a *brush your hair* command in hand signals. My fingers automatically went to my mane and tried to smooth it down. Great. Nothing like being badass with bedhead.

Damon did that quirky eyebrow thing at me and I returned it, not quite managing the height of the arch he achieved, but getting my point across nonetheless. "I'm going to put on some decent clothes and then I'll join you. We have a battle plan to discuss."

Cole rubbed his hands in anticipation, giving me a wink as he joined the crowd heading downstairs. Didn't matter what we were fighting...a fight was a fight. Good times in his book.

Kirill stepped forward, snapping his fingers at Lainie. "Bring snacks to the conference room."

"Please," I added.

The archdemon was forever worried about food. He turned his attention to me. "We need to get you back on that IV."

"I feel great. Dru's blood healed me."

Dru smiled. Rad harrumphed. Kirill looked doubtful. "I

need to perform another blood draw to ascertain if that's true or not."

I didn't have time for blood draws. The itch under my skin to get out of the Institute and back on the streets made me jittery. Ideas on how to handle Pestilence and knock Parker out of the ballpark formed and solidified in my brain faster than I could catalog them.

But Kirill wouldn't be mollified until he had my blood. Which meant Damon wouldn't either. "Give me fifteen minutes to talk to the troops. Then I'll give you some blood."

Damon started to argue, Rad and Dru both taking his side.

I interrupted before any of them—now an unexpected team working *with* each other and against me—could get on a roll. "Kirill can be standing by with a fresh IV in case I go belly up. It's all hands on deck right now, and I won't stand in front of my friends and fellow soldiers and issue orders while looking like an invalid who's going back to bed while they risk their lives."

Rad sighed. He stepped to my side and laid a hand on my shoulder. He gave it a squeeze and stood next to me in solidarity. About damn time.

Kirill looked at Damon. Damon stared at me, scanning me from head to toes. We butted heads as much as two old married people, and maybe because of that, he knew from the gleam in my eye, this was one battle he should concede. "Fifteen minutes. Not a second more."

"Thank you." As Kirill headed for his medical supplies, I faced Dru. "Put your vampire soldiers on alert. All that training they've been doing? Time to put it in action. And call Juliana and Rafael. We're going to need their troops as well."

Juliana and Rafael were Master vampires in the South and East regions. Their troops had helped us before and I knew the score sheet was unbalanced, but this was the ultimate favor to ask. Dru knew this too. "And what will you have my vampires fighting?"

My vampires. Interesting. Was Dru trying to put me in my place after I refused the idea we were more than friends? Good luck with that. "All vampires, despite their regional allegiance, will be fighting alongside the rest of us to stop the coming apocalypse. Those who don't fight will die anyway, so if they want any chance of surviving, they better grab their swords and start swinging."

Dru cut his eyes to Rad, back to me. Gave me a slight, but professional, nod. "As you wish, my queen."

The title was said in a mocking tone. Vampires, what a pain in the ass.

He sauntered down the hall, pulling out his cell phone and placing a call. Brianna fell into step behind him.

Rad, Damon and I were left standing there. Damon snapped his fingers and the lights in the hall repaired themselves. He stepped forward and glared at Rad. "Fighting is allowed in the training center and *only* in the training center. In the future, if you threaten anyone with physical violence inside the Bridge Institute, it will be the last thing you ever do. *Tu me comprends?*"

Rad nodded, aggravated at the French, even though he and Dru had just been going at it in his native language. I understood. Damon could turn anything into a beat down.

"I understand." Rad stepped forward, so he and Damon were nose to nose. "And if you ever allow someone *inside the Bridge Institute* to manipulate Kali again, I'll level the place before you can snap your fingers, archdemon."

Wonderful. Another pissing match.

Grabbing Rad by the arm, I dug my nails into his skin and marched him away from the confrontation. "Help me get dressed," I said, leading him to the stairs. My temporary living space was on the top floor across from Damon's permanent one.

Before we turned the corner, the familiar rush of Damon's voice filled my head. *Be careful of your alliances, Kali.*

11

My alliances were also about to be challenged by a certain Chaos demon.

Inside my apartment suite at the Institute, Rad leaned against my chest of drawers, his face a storm cloud. "So you're drinking from the bastard directly now?"

How many times were we going to have this conversation? His tone rubbed like sandpaper and I didn't want to fight. Fight we would, though. Being a blood slave to a Master vamp was my worst nightmare, even if Dru and I were friends, but it was also the least of my worries at the moment.

"Direct from the source is the most satisfying. You know that." I stalked over to him, flipped him around so his hands were on the wall and withdrew the silver dagger he kept hidden at the small of his back. Scoring my wrist, I tossed the dagger aside and slipped between him and the wall, lifting my bleeding wrist to his mouth. "Drink, slave."

His aura flashed with need, a hot, pulsing sensation that engulfed me and started a throb between my legs. Pressing me against the wall, he kissed my lips thoroughly, parting them and teasing me with his tongue. I returned the ardent kiss and encircled one of his legs with mine.

He sucked on my wrist next, gently tormenting the edges of the wound with his tongue and lapping at the blood. His talented fingers had no trouble de-robing me. One hand toyed with my breasts, the other slid up and down my inner thigh, building a terrible, wonderful craving between my legs.

I arched into him, slamming my hips against his and feeling the bite of his belt buckle into my bare skin. His mouth left my wrist and he lifted me, carrying me to the bed. I'd just unzipped his pants when a sharp knock sounded on the apartment door.

"Kali? What's taking so long? Everyone's waiting."

Yasmin. I searched the floor for the dagger I'd tossed away. "It hasn't even been five minutes," I added *bitch* under my breath. "I'm getting cleaned up."

"It's been twenty minutes. Get your ass in gear." *Slut*, she said under her breath, just loud enough for me to hear.

Touché.

Time had slipped away from me. Always did when I was with Rad.

He chuckled softly as I gave Yasmin the middle finger and the front of his very full jeans a disappointed look. "I am going to kill her one of these days."

"We could leave. Get out of town for a while. Fly out to Hollywood early for the awards ceremony."

"What ceremony?"

He frowned. "The People's Choice Awards. Remember? I told you the Chaos Demons have been nominated for a couple of awards."

Oops. "Sorry, I forgot. Awards ceremonies are not at the top of my list right now. You know I can't leave town."

He was pissed, but he helped me off the bed, slapped one of my ass cheeks as I headed for the bathroom. "At least Yasmin's honest about hating you."

Change of subject. Definitely pissed.

I stopped in the doorway and grabbed my chest, doing my best Maddy gesture while trying to lighten the mood. "Yasmin hates me?"

"I know your job comes first, I just wish you could take a vacation." He motioned at my hair. "Probably need to brush that."

"I need a shower and three days of uninterrupted sleep, but neither is going to happen. I'd kill for a vacation. That's not happening either." Avoiding the mirror over the bathroom sink, I washed off my wrist, which was already healing and snagged my hairbrush, attacking the tangled mess the same way I attacked everything else in life.

The simple act of straightening and smoothing the hair into a ponytail calmed me. I snapped a band around the base and got dressed. Rad watched me with his golden eyes. His aura was contained, the emotions forced down behind a wall. He was still thinking about Dru and stewing about it.

I sat on the bed next to him, tugging on a pair of thigh-high boots with a bevy of weapons hidden in their silver hardware. "Jealous much, demon?"

My tone was light and teasing, but his response was all heat and desire. His gaze dropped to my feet, then traveled up my legs, lingering on the juncture between my thighs before continuing its slow perusal upward. One of his fingers traced the top of my cleavage, now held up by a leather bustier. My nipples tingled, the pulsing sensation returning to my lower body. His fingers trailed up behind my ponytail, latching onto my neck, and his lips stopped just short of mine.

They grazed my cheek, trailed down to my neck. His low words vibrated against my skin. "The vampire's blood may give you sustenance, but I'm the only male who will ever satisfy you, demon."

My head spun, my nipples puckered. I licked my lips,

thinking about all the ways Rad could satisfy me. A shudder ran through my body and his magic gripped me like a vise.

Rad lifted his face to look me in the eye. Sex magic snapped between us, but there was more. Much more. "*Tu me comprends, mon couer?*"

Did I understand? That I was his heart? His only love? The one and only thing that could damn him to hell?

"*Mais oui,*" I answered in French the way I had two hundred and eighty-plus years ago. "I understand."

12

How do you fight a titanic enemy like the Four Horsemen of the Apocalypse?

That was the question circling my brain as we entered the conference room. A jostling of voices and magics met us at the door. Inside, I tried twice to get everyone's attention, and when that didn't work, Rad placed his finger and thumb between the lips that had kissed me only minutes before and blew hard.

The piercing whistle echoed around the large room. The two dozen people in attendance fell silent, all eyes on the two of us.

I nodded a thank you at Rad. He smiled and found a seat next to JR.

"Just so everyone's up to speed, Damon, will you tell us the latest?"

Damon was excellent at being the boss. He rose from his chair at the end of the table and succinctly covered the list of problems erupting in our city. After he finished, I asked Salmad to fill the group in on the Four Horsemen.

As the priest finished laying out the specifics of what we

were up against, I paced and looked over the powerful group in the room. Elite warriors, six of the seven deadly sins, archdemons, and a goddess. A pure-blooded Master vampire with demonic proficiencies, a Chaos demon who had a legion of fans all around the world, and me, a vengeance demon who embodied dark magic, Jesus-given virtues, and all the enhanced magical abilities of a natural-born vampire.

It wasn't enough.

A sense of foreboding stole up my spine. "When fighting an immense enemy, you amass your forces. Even if we add the vampire and Bridge foot soldiers to this group, our forces,"—I motioned a hand at the group—"are too thin to face the coming apocalypse. We'd only make a nice, tidy target for the Horsemen."

Wary eyes stayed on me. I shook off the foreboding and continued to pace. "If we can't conquer our enemies with one concentrated assault, we borrow a page from the industrious Viet Cong. We embrace guerrilla warfare."

Cole, leaning on the wall next to the door, brightened. "Small, nimble attack forces. We've got those. Unpredictable and unconventional strikes—no problem. They advance, we retreat. They rest, we attack."

"Exactly." I pointed at Kirill. He was reaching for a plate of pastries Lainie had set on the table. "Kirill, what does the Red Horseman look like?"

His hand stopped in midair, and he gave a confused shake of his head. "Why does that matter?"

I walked over to JR. "Do you have that sketch artist software on this laptop?"

"Face ID 4.5." My tech guru's fingers raced across his keyboard. A new program opened. "Has over four thousand facial features in its database."

"Put it up on the screen." As JR connected to the Institute's internal Wi-Fi media server, the projection screen on the far wall came to life. I turned back to Kirill. "What does Pestilence look like?"

Everyone stared at the pudgy disease expert. Forgetting the pastry, he adjusted his lab coat and leaned back in his chair. "Usually poses as a doctor, but he can shift into a rat, a fly, even a flea to spread disease."

He rattled off height, weight, bone structure, eye and hair color. On the screen, a man's face evolved. As things like eyebrows and lips were added, Kirill gave JR instructions. "The eyebrows are thicker and not so arched. Yeah, that's more like it. The nose should be narrower."

Over the next couple of minutes, they tweaked the sketch until Kirill was satisfied. "That's him." He swiveled his chair to look at me. "At least the last time I saw him in Europe."

"He's been on Earth before?" This from Di. "I thought the Horsemen's only purpose was to kick off Armageddon."

Kirill gave her a smug glance, his aura indicating he reveled in the attention. "He's been responsible for a dozen or more plagues and pandemics going all the way back to 430 B.C. Before then, actually, but record keeping was poor in ancient times so few humans know about those outbreaks. I know because I helped with all of them."

Kirill had been around longer than I thought, but this was good. *Know your enemy, know yourself.* The first rule of battle.

He saw we were still waiting for him to explain how it was possible Pestilence had visited Earth before. Leaning his elbows on the table, Kirill shifted his gaze around the room, making eye contact here and there. "The Horsemen have tried kick-starting Armageddon at least a dozen times. Never worked. They send in the False Prophet, then Pestilence and War initiate the first waves of disaster and wait for Death to show up. The four of them working together have started cataclysmic world events, but they never close the deal. Up until now, anyway."

"Why is that?" I asked.

"Because they need the help of the archangels to bring an end to humans. The angels can't lift a finger to help until all seven seals are broken. The False Prophet, the Whore of Babylon, the Horsemen...they're all seals. All we've seen so far is Pest."

"So the others haven't been broken yet?"

Kirill shrugged.

I looked at Damon, and he straightened in his chair slowly as if deep in thought. Or maybe he was already exhausted thinking about the problem. I knew the feeling. "The breaking of the seals happens in stages. The stages can take weeks or hours, days or months. All we know at this point is that Pestilence is here. We can assume the other Horsemen are on their way. And after that?" He tossed his hands in the air. "Even if this *isn't* the final apocalypse, things are going to be bad for supernaturals as well as humans."

I thought of Parker's words: The White Horseman...the Antichrist. Was it really possible Rad was one of the Four Horsemen?

"Humans don't know about us," Salmad interrupted my wayward thoughts, pointing a finger at me and then at our fellow *vitiums*. "But our combined presence on Earth is what tripped the switch, and from my research, this is the real deal. The Horsemen will succeed this round, but to wipe out the planet filled with billions of humans, they'll need the help of the archangels."

"So if we stop the Horsemen, we stop Armageddon," I said.

Sal shrugged. "According to Revelation, The Horsemen represent the first four seals, but according to other ancient texts that predict the end of mankind, there are far more."

Lovely. "Do we know how to stop any of them?"

Damon waved off the question. "Moot point. If we don't

stop the Four Horsemen, humanity will not survive whatever comes behind them."

I couldn't help it. I shot a look at Rad, who was slouched in his chair watching me. Cutting Pestilence off at the knees to stop the apocalypse was one thing. Taking out Rad?

My chest heaved at the thought. Fucking Parker. This was just a stupid mind game. Her wanting me to doubt Rad. To believe he was my enemy again.

The drone of Neve's electric wheelchair broke the silence as she maneuvered it next to Sal. Unease creased the corners of her eyes. "Aren't the angels supposed to be on our side? Um... you know, the side of humans?"

A collective snicker went around the room from the supernaturals. Sal gave Neve a sad smile. "I'm afraid the only angels who were ever on your side were cast from Heaven in the days before Adam and Eve."

Neve rubbed the cross pendant at her neck and swallowed. I stepped up behind her and rubbed her shoulders. *Don't worry, friend. I'll protect you.*

Cole's calculating War demon gaze zeroed in on the face looming before us on the projection screen. "If Pestilence is in physical form, we can make him bleed, right?"

Kirill gave a reluctant shrug. "His blood? What good would that do us?"

"If he bleeds, I can kill him."

My kind of guy, that War demon. "I agree. We have to be proactive in this war. We find Pestilence and engage him on *our* turf. We get in, strike fast and hard, get out. And then we do the same with the next Horseman."

As long as it's not... I stopped the thought as I caught Damon watching me again.

Shields!

The mental click of them snapping into place reassured me, and I drew a deep breath.

Murmurs rippled through the room, many of them full of surprise and doubt. Di turned frightened eyes on me. "Kali, even for you, that's...well, that's plain crazy. You can't fight the Four Horsemen. They'll slaughter you."

I paced the floor, my feet unable to stay still. "If we bring the battle to them—a battle they won't be expecting—we'll control the fight. That's the way you win. Advance, retreat, and when they think you've given up? You advance again and attack. It's a proven battle strategy for small, dedicated groups of natives, and that's what we are. This territory is *ours*. We care about it far more than they do, and they cannot win if we stay out of their reach and strike quickly, quietly, and effectively, over and over until they give up. Our first mission-critical...take out the Red Horseman. The rest will be a cinch."

More murmurs, fading to silence. A very uncomfortable silence.

Most of the auras in the room suggested my friends and comrades still thought I was crazy. I took hope in the fact no one got up and left.

Damon sat forward. "In a metropolis the size of Chicago, how do we locate the Red Horseman?"

"*We* don't." I ambled over to Kirill, tapped his shoulder. "Our disease specialist does."

The archdemon reared back and glanced between me and Damon. "But I...I have no idea where Pest is, nor would he do anything but strike me dead if he saw me. I work for the enemy now, in case you hadn't noticed."

Pest. A fitting nickname. I pointed a finger at my tech guru. "JR, where did the initial outbreaks occur?"

The sketch of Pestilence morphed into a Chicago map, showing a bright red dot. "Rush University."

"And where do you predict he'll go next?"

"The second largest hospital in Chicago proper."

"Northwestern." I paced to the screen and back. "Kirill, you head over to Northwestern and put out feelers. Tell your friends and enemies alike that you're looking to rejoin Pestilence's ranks. You have skills he can use and insight into how the Bridge Council will try and stop him."

Kirill gave a derisive snort. "He's not stupid. He'll know it's a trap."

"Then give it to him. Tell him what I'm planning. Make him believe I'm going to be his worst nightmare and that he needs to take me out before I ruin the best chance he and his brethren have to fulfill the biblical prophecy. Once he's on board, lead him to my place, the church. Give us a heads-up before you get him there. Cole and I'll do the rest."

Dru, positioned in the far corner with his arms crossed over his chest, rocked on his heels. "And what exactly *is* the rest?"

Rad gave me a look that said he wondered the same thing.

He and Dru weren't the only ones. I had no idea what I'd do once Pest was within reach. I'd figure it out later. "Let me worry about that." I pointed at the third archdemon in the room, who, as usual, paid little attention to me or anyone else when Damon was in her presence. Yasmin, you and JR work on upping security around the Bridge Institute. Once we hit Pestilence, all hell's going to break loose."

She seemed startled that I'd spoken to her, but recovered quickly when Damon glanced at her. "Of course. The Institute will be safe."

At least Damon would be. Yasmin would give her dying breath to save him. "Good. Dru, you and Seraphina set up vamp patrols at all the major Chicago hotspots. Sporting events, concerts, anywhere massive groups of humans are gathering. I want eyes on the ground so we can ferret out Pestilence in case he's being social outside the hospitals. Also, keep an eye out for the other Horsemen. War will start riots and cause supply transportation breakdowns. Death will cause food to spoil, water mains to break, and mass carnage. Anything that seems out of the ordinary, no matter how small, report it to Damon. He, Sal, and JR will track everything so we can see the big picture."

Seraphina gave me a solemn nod. Dru glanced at her, and I saw him sizing her up. For him, everyone fit into one of three categories: food, sex, or sword. If he considered you food, your neck would meet his teeth. Sex, the same. And if he considered you the enemy, your neck would meet his sword. It would be interesting to see how the Amazonian warrior would handle him. Unfortunately, I didn't have time to keep an eye on the two of them.

"Our second most pressing issue is stopping the Red Tide and the rodent population from spreading Pestilence's diseases."

Arman raised a hand. "My friends and I can handle the mice and rats if you tell us where they are."

Werecat shifters were definitely a plus in this situation. JR performed his techie magic, and the Chicago map spun and zeroed in on the docks and large-scale condo units by the lake. "Here, here, and here," he said as three yellow Xs appeared on the areas in question. These are where the worst infestations have been."

Arman stood. "We're on it."

I liked a supernatural who didn't wait for instructions to go to work. "Check in," I said as he headed for the door. "And let me know how bad it is and what we can expect going forward."

He gave me a smile and a salute, seeming glad to be leaving our discussion. Maddy, however, sighed as the door shut. No doubt Arman was more fun to hang out with than me.

"Now the Red Tide." I turned to Rad. "Your strongest element is water. What do you think? Can you kill the bacteria in Lake Michigan?"

Sal raised a hand. "You need to boil it."

Rad's face didn't change, but his aura conveyed suppressed shock. "You want me to boil Lake Michigan?"

"Can you do it?"

He drew a deep breath, rubbed the stubble along his jawline. "I've never worked magic on such a large body of water, but...what the hell." He shrugged. "I'll give it a shot."

"Take Sal and Shayne with you."

"Me, too," Akimo volunteered from behind Dru. "I'll be the bodyguard in case the Nocts get wind of what we're doing."

The Noctifectors. Parker. Too bad she was so focused on me and Rad. Her team would have done more good helping us slay the Horsemen.

Except, Parker believed Rad *was* a Horseman.

What a load of crap. "Kill anyone who tries to stop you," I told Akimo. "Especially the Noctifectors. If they show up, kill them all."

13

Blood, blood, blood. No matter how I tried, I couldn't get away from it.

Kirill poked and prodded at my vein as I tried to sit still on the examination table. I bit the inside of my lip and mentally cursed him in Italian and English.

"You need more practice," I ground out, refusing to flinch as the needle missed the vein again and dug into something else in my arm.

"I'm not a doctor."

"Or a nurse, apparently, because the nurses I've known over the years are experts at blood draws. You suck at them."

"I'd be better at this if I wasn't contemplating my own demise."

The inside of my elbow throbbed. "What are you talking about? I'm not going to kill you for missing the vein." Although the thought had merit...

He struck gold, and we both relaxed as the red liquid, minus the greenish tint, slowly flowed into the tube. "I have to find a way to get myself recruited back into Pestilence's ranks. He's more likely to torture and kill me than accept me back."

Wah, wah, wah. "Scared, Kirill?"

No archdemon liked to be challenged. "Scared? Damn right, I'm scared. The Four Horsemen are nothing to mess with. But then, what do you know about tangling with the devil?"

I chuckled. "I went toe-to-toe with Lucifer a few months ago. Lucifer, as in *fallen angel. Prince of hell.* The Four Horsemen don't scare me."

Kirill removed the tourniquet with a snap. "Then you're a fool."

Been accused of worse. "What about the other three Horsemen? You know any of them?"

The vial was full. He withdrew the needle from my arm. "Never met them."

"Ever seen 'em?"

"Nope."

Damn. "Do you know anything about the White Horseman in particular?"

He swabbed the insertion site and stuck a bandage on it. "Just that she's not what everyone expects."

"She?"

Capping off the vial, he marked it with a large K and took off his gloves. "Personally, I think it's Oprah."

I laughed, thinking he was making a joke. He wasn't.

"Who has millions of followers all over the world and the power to sway everything from what they think to what they read?"

"Any number of famous people." *Including Rad.* "But wouldn't the antichrist be more like Jesus? Humble, lowly, possibly a carpenter?"

"In the twenty-first century?" He snorted. "Jesus would have to be more popular than Taylor Swift or the Kardashians to get noticed these days."

As far as I knew, Swift was one hundred percent human. The Kardashians...I wasn't so sure. A hunch told me they had siren blood in their veins—maybe vamp blood—but that wasn't the point.

"Oprah. Wow." I swung my legs, unconvinced. "So you honestly have no idea what the White Horseman looks like?"

Kirill narrowed his eyes. "What is it with you and the White Horseman?"

Nothing, I hope. "I just want to keep an eye out for him. Or her, as the case may be."

"Oprah came to power right here in Chicago." Kirill pointed at the floor as if we stood on sacred ground. "Now Pest is here, too. Take my word for it: this is ground zero, and we're all going to die."

He stomped off, the vial of my blood in hand. Cheery guy.

"Nice talking to you," I called as he went through the door. Yeesh. I didn't even get to ask him whether I needed to be hooked up to an IV again. My blood had looked normal. I felt good as new. Must be time to vacate the premises before he remembered the yellow goo. He or Damon would call me with the news about my blood and I had work to do.

I took the stairs two at a time to my temporary apartment upstairs. I wanted to talk to Rad before he headed to the lake.

My hand was on the doorknob when Damon opened his apartment door behind me. "Radison has already left. He said to tell you he'd call after he scopes out the lake. Also, he has some TV show appearance at eight a.m. I don't believe he's taking our predicament seriously."

"Oh." Funny how my chest twinged a bit that he'd left without saying goodbye. These days, we didn't know when all hell would break loose and we'd never see each other again. And I had to agree with Damon. Putting his rock-star life above our *predicament* seemed wrong.

What could I do about it, though? "Um, well, I guess I'll get to work then."

"Kali." Damon's dark eyes bored into me. He opened the door to his apartment wider. "We need to talk."

Talk? In his private quarters? A strange sensation took hold in my chest, and this time, it had nothing to do with Rad. I'd never been inside Damon's apartment suite. As far as I could tell, no one ever had. "Sure. I'll meet you in your office, *boss*."

Reminding him of our working relationship did not have the desired effect. He stepped back and motioned me inside. "Please come in."

Said the spider to the fly. Or in this case, the archdemon to the freak. A prickling awareness of magic skittered over my skin.

The room was straight out of the masculine edition of House Beautiful. A sprig of bay leaves was tucked over the top of the door frame. Other than that, there was little in the classy interior that denoted Damon's Basque heritage. The three-room apartment dominated the top floor of the Institute and resembled an upscale hotel. Black hardwood floors, white leather chairs, modern artwork.

And a damn lot of old, powerful magic.

Seductive magic.

I covertly sniffed the air. A wood fire burned in a built-in, glass-fronted fireplace, but there was something else. Not burning wood...more like melting beeswax. "Is Salmad here?"

I stepped across the threshold, following the priest's scent. Damon closed the door behind me. "We'd like to discuss a contingency plan with you."

"Contingency plan?"

Like in, I don't survive?

Damon ushered me into his private study. Sal stood near a bookcase, arms crossed over his robe-clad chest. He gave me a serious nod and said to Damon. "You haven't told her?"

"Told me what?"

"Sit." Damon held the back of a chair. "This goes no farther than this room, Kali."

Cloak and dagger wasn't Damon's style. Mine either. I stayed standing. "I'm not going to like this, am I?"

Might have been my imagination, but I could've sworn Damon's shoulders sagged a little. "No, enforcer, I'm afraid you're not."

14

few minutes later, I stared at Damon in shock. "You want Sal and I to walk into Vatican City in plain sight and raid the Secret Vatican Archives for my father's journals?"

"Yes." Damon stood relaxed in front of the fireplace, one arm resting on the mantle. The fireplace was two-sided. I could see through the glass into the living area. No sounds met my ears except for the crackling of wood and the ticking of the clock on the wall. "Your Trojan Horse plan using Parker is fairly sound, but as usual, you've left out an important element to ensure its success...no team to extricate you once you have retrieved the documents we need."

I hadn't given further thought to my father's journals. Well, I had, but other things had been more pressing. Now, I realized, nothing was more important than finding those journals and figuring out the key to stop all this madness.

The only light in the room came from a Tiffany desk lamp and the fire in the fireplace. I wondered if the suite was sound-proof since I had yet to hear anything from outside or below us. "I'll be walking into the lion's den. Things are going to get rough. No way am I jeopardizing anyone's backside but my own."

Sal remained seated near the desk. "I was a prefect of The Secret Archives until last year when I came to Chicago in search of you. I'm well acquainted with the Church's libraries and documents held inside them—those available to the public *and* those hidden deep in the bowels of Vatican City that the Church denies exist."

"You've seen my father's journals?"

He shook his head, light reflecting off his short blond hair and visible skin beneath. "I have not, but I do believe they exist, and I have a fair idea where they may be located."

The idea of passing the job off didn't appeal to me, logical or not. "Why don't you retrieve the documents on your own then?"

Damon regarded me with the faintest of smiles on his lips. He did like logic. "The secret archives are restricted, even to friends of The Church. Salmad cannot simply walk in and take the documents. He needs a distraction. A lengthy one that will give him time to enter the underground vault where the documents are hermetically stored."

Salmad had the chronic look of exhaustion about him, as if the world rode on his shoulders. "The Church appears to have embraced the idea of transparency in the past couple of years, allowing the public to view a hundred documents and other curiosities from the Archives, holding press conferences about leaks, and being very visible and interactive in mainstream media. Its hand was forced to do this since it's been dealing with one public-relations disaster after another. This transparency is staged. With the advent of the Internet and the popularity of tell-all books, it seems the only way the pope can maintain control of the Church's image. An attempt for them to appear they have nothing to hide in this new age of social media. Behind the scenes, it's politics as usual."

The only nation that could compare with the politics of the Catholic Church was the Undead Nation. Even the relatively small group of vampires in Chicago did nothing but fight for power and prestige.

Sal sat forward, resting his elbows on his knees and staring at the luxurious carpet beneath our feet. "The information in your father's journals is considered heresy by the Church. It was not destroyed when discovered because, like Galileo and Da Vinci, your father wove enough verifiable facts about demons and angels through his predictions that the Church considered the journals a valuable tool in the fight against evil at the end of days. Therefore these documents would have been buried deep in the archives, where I'm sure they still exist. But because of the secrecy and the extensive security system in place, it'll take me time to locate the journals and smuggle them out." He lifted his sad blue eyes to me. "That's where you come in."

"Playing side-kick isn't my usual role."

"I understand your personality does not lend itself well to being part of a team. You've made that quite clear with all of us *vitiums*."

Heat rose in my cheeks, and a spark of irritation flared in my gut. He spoke the truth, but I didn't much care for it. "I opened my home to you and have done my best to keep you apprised of everything that's going on so that we—as a team— can fight Maria, the coming apocalypse, the Noctifectors, you name it. I even shared my tech manager with you."

He nodded, solemn and patient. "Your experience, innate skills, and magical enhancements will serve you well on this mission. But only if you have a partner to assist."

No '*Thank you, Kali*' or '*We know you're trying not to be an island.*' Not that I expected a pat on the back, but I couldn't deny the urge to justify myself. "I've been a solo act for most of my three hundred years, Sal. I don't play well with others, and I don't like them taking risks for me."

The phone on Damon's desk rang. He answered it, nodded at the incoming information, and hung up. "Your blood is clear. Kirill says there is no lasting damage from the poison, although he's still unsure as to what exactly the poison was." Damon still had the faintest trace of a smile on his lips. "Back to the matter at hand, Salmad can hold his own. The two of you together will make an impressive team."

"Oh yeah. The Dream Team, that's us." I blew out a breath, lifting my bangs as I set my hands on my hips. "What kind of distraction do you need?"

"We'll discuss that en route."

Damon left us, disappearing into the back room, where I guessed his bed and bath were located.

I tiptoed to the doorway and peered around the corner. Yep, a master bedroom fit for a king. Or an archdemon. Big bed. Silk linens. Huge framed nude oil painting hanging over the headboard.

Damon emerged from a walk-in closet, a coat in one hand and a leather overnight bag in the other.

My gaze returned to the oil painting. If it was a reproduction, it was a damn good one. "A painting of Nyx? Is this the one done in 1883 by French painter William-Adolphe Bouguereau?"

He nodded.

"That's what you hang over your bed? The goddess of night and secrets?" I snickered at the archdemon's version of pornography.

He stopped and stared at the painting. His aura—always so hard and demanding—softened. "Lovely, isn't she?"

"Wait." I followed his gaze, then gawked to his face. "Is this the original?"

"Yes, indeed."

I bumped his shoulder with mine. "You dog. You stole this from a gallery?"

He looked momentarily confused. "The one in Paris is a reproduction. The original has always been mine. I commissioned it."

Mamma mia. My boss was one hard-to-figure-out male. "The woman posing as Nyx, she was your lover?"

"The woman posing as Nyx is Nyx. And yes, she was my lover."

"Get. Out."

Damon faced me and smiled. "I had a life before this, you know. Before you and I met in Spain. There is much I would share with you if the occasion presented itself."

His eyes were rock steady on mine. Magic danced in the air, sending a warm flush down my arms and legs. I was in my boss's bedroom. Talking about his former lover. Watching his archdemon aura go all warm and sexy.

I needed air. And a change of subject. "How freakin' old are you?"

His aura stopped oozing magic and sexual invitation. The slightest of chuckles escaped his lips. "Our plane is waiting. We should be off."

"You're going with us?"

"The Dream Team needs a coach, yes?"

Satan's balls. I hated it when Damon tried to orchestrate my jobs. But since I was unclear exactly what my job was in this instance, and invading the Holy Roman Church might be my biggest one yet, wisdom dictated I make nice. *Team player, that's me.* "Of course."

Turning on my heel, I headed for the suite's front door. "Let me make a few calls to let Rad and the others know where I'm go—"

Damon's hand on my arm stopped me. "This mission is top secret. No one can know what we're about to do."

"But..." I glanced at him, then at Sal. Intuition blared loudly in my head. That's why we met here—so no one could overhear us in your office. Do we have a leak in the Institute?"

He released my arm. "Caution is our best weapon. Salmad will pose as he is, a priest who has captured the Noctifector's most wanted demon and is returning to the fold. No need to chance that the Noctifectors might learn of our subterfuge and warn the pope."

"In other words, you don't trust Rad. You think he's still working for them."

"There are many entities staying at the Institute these days, all with their private agendas. Logic dictates that the fewer entities aware of our mission, the safer you and Salmad will be."

As safe as a demon could be walking into Vatican City. "Won't they be suspicious when no one can find the three of us?"

Damon patted my shoulder. "I've taken care of everything, Kali. Trust me."

Trust was a hard commodity to come by in my world and he knew it. Which made it easier for me to understand his position, even if I didn't like it. "You've made a deal with the pope to hand me over in exchange for absolution, haven't you?"

That got a laugh out of him. A real laugh. The deep, resonant sound rippled over my skin, making me smile in response. As the generous sound faded away, he tipped his face down and put it close to mine. "Not even absolution would be worth giving up my favorite demon."

A trickle of sweat ran down my spine. His aura was all warm again, only this time it had a new layer to it. A layer of protectiveness and...

No. Not from Damon. Sure, he loved me in that friend-to-friend way, but that's all it was.

My throat tightened. My voice came out soft and breathy, even though my words had steel in them. "If things go bad, that's exactly what I want you to do. Cut a deal with the pope or the devil or God, if necessary, and leave me behind. The important thing is for you and Sal to get out safely. Stop the Horsemen and keep Armageddon from happening. Are we clear?"

His aura hardened. His eyes did, too. "I will take care of Salmad. You have my promise."

Tucked between those words was another message.

I'll take care of you, too.

15

Two steps inside the private jet, I pulled up short. A certain War demon sat in a beige leather chair, his gun spread out in pieces on the table in front of him. "Cole?"

He dry-fired the weapon, picked up a cloth, and started cleaning the barrel. "Yep."

I rounded on Damon. "You said this mission was top secret. That I couldn't tell anyone."

Damon pressed by me, choosing a seat across the aisle from Cole and taking off his coat. "Cole knows nothing about what we're doing or where we're going. I asked him to meet us here, and he is one of the few Bridge employees who performs his job without questioning my authority."

Cole kept his head down and continued cleaning his gun, but I saw his lips tighten in a suppressed smile.

The plane engines kicked in, making me raise my voice. Sal stood patiently behind me, my bag and his in his hands. "Blind loyalty is a virtue."

"Watch it," Cole muttered just loud enough for me to hear. He hated being labeled virtuous.

Damon sat in the chair, pulled out a laptop, and went to work, speaking to me simultaneously. "You and Cole are my two most valuable employees, although you demonstrate your loyalty to the Bridge Council in different ways."

Cole and I exchanged a look. Neither of us had ever heard Damon so complimentary. "Cole's supposed to be lying in wait for Pestilence."

Damon continued to focus on his laptop. The pilot announced our destination, the weather conditions we'd be flying in and asked us to buckle up. When he finished, Sal brushed me aside and hustled into the seat across from Damon. The priest's forehead glistened with sweat. Not a flyer, apparently.

Damon buckled in. "Kirill will need a day or two to lure the Red Horseman into your trap. Cole's services are more effective in our service for the next twenty-four hours."

"You said you couldn't spare him from the training center when I wanted to put him on Rad's protection detail."

With what might have been a sigh, Damon turned his dark eyes on me. "Radison Beaumont is not my concern at this time. You are. Sit down and buckle up."

The plane lurched forward, challenging my balance. Huffing, I did as instructed, throwing myself into the seat. I didn't buckle up, though. Score one for rebellion.

The plane's engines grew loud as we taxied down the runway. Cole finished assembling his gun, laid it on the cloth-covered table, kicked back, and gave me a hooded look. Questions lit his eyes, but I wasn't in the mood to talk. Probably wasn't allowed to tell him the plan anyway. I had a dozen questions of my own, most of them surrounding Damon's suspicions about Rad. What did my boss know that I didn't? And why was he keeping it from me? My own suspicions were easy to stomp on. Damon's, not so much.

But there was no way Rad was working for the Noctifectors. That I was sure of.

A hundred years had passed since I'd left my European home to journey to America. Nearly three hundred since the last time I set foot in Rome. A brick of dread sat heavy in my stomach, and because of my boss, I couldn't talk to the one person who would understand.

Rad.

Facing the window, I sunk down into the leather seat and watched as the ground and Chicago grew farther and farther away.

THREE HOURS LATER, everyone in the cabin was asleep. I tip-toed to the restroom, cradling my phone.

Locking myself in, I sat on the toilet seat and scrolled through the names in my contact list. My phone didn't ring once—not even a text from Maddy, who sent me all types of unnecessary messages every hour on the hour. What had Damon done to keep everyone from contacting me? Every time I thought about it, a warning bell rang in my head. Something wasn't right about this trip; I just couldn't put my finger on it.

The restroom was spacious compared to commercial planes. And clean. There were even decorative soaps in a dish on the vanity. But the motor noise here was worse than the cabin. No way could I carry on a discreet phone call.

I pulled up JR's number and texted him. *What do you know about the Vatican Secret Archives?*

The text took several seconds longer than usual to go through, but the supped up cell phone Damon made me carry got the job done. A minute later, JR responded. *Everything.*

That's why I kept him around. Well, that and his gift for technology. When dealing with supernaturals and religious cults on a daily basis, you can't go wrong hiring a guy with the golden touch for bits and bytes and a master's degree in religious studies.

I need details about the underground vault where the extra-secret stuff is kept, including blueprints, diagrams, diagnostics, etc.

Again, there was a pause as my message flung itself across the Atlantic and back to Chicago. JR responded. *Fifteen minutes. Check your inbox.*

Speedy as well as knowledgeable. But was he as omniscient as he appeared? *Do you know where I am?*

Even though I was safely tucked into the privacy of the restroom, I scanned the walls top to bottom, looking for hidden cameras (found none), sent out a thread of magic to check that my companions were still sleeping (they were), and tapped my foot, waiting for JR's reply. When it came, I had to look at it twice to decipher.

43.068888°

-26.71875°

Longitude and latitude. My tech guru had my coordinates as I winged my way over the Atlantic toward Italy.

I breathed a sigh of relief. Whatever Damon had done to take me off the grid, I still had the ability to contact the people back home, and JR could find me. Seemed silly to be comforted by those two simple facts, but I was. Maybe I was making a big deal out of nothing. Letting my paranoia get to me.

I texted Rad, then Maddy, with nonchalant messages. *How's it going? Any new developments?*

In rapid succession, I received two *undeliverable* messages from the phone carrier. Paranoia set in again. Why could I communicate with JR and not the others?

I tried Di and Neve next. Undeliverable.

Was it magic or something else? Why did I suddenly feel like I'd entered the Bermuda Triangle?

JR got a new message. *Testing. Reply if you receive this.*

Tapping my foot, I counted the seconds, then the minutes until he replied. *Success. Trouble with phone? I can run diagnostic.*

Nope, just trouble with my boss. Why had Damon allowed the link to JR to still work? Had he simply forgotten to cut him off from me like he'd done the others?

Damon was nothing if not meticulous with his planning. He didn't forget things.

Send me a test message every hour, would you?

Sure thing.

JR didn't question why I was over the Atlantic Ocean or why I was acting cryptic. The sign of a good follower. Eyeing the decorative soaps, I almost wished he'd been a bit more proactive and asked what I was doing, where I was going, and why.

Ironic I'd hated having so many people living at my house and interfering with my life over the past two months and now that I was finally free of them, I wanted nothing more than to make contact.

Six minutes had passed, but I was too antsy to wait any longer. I hacked into Damon's Wi-Fi hub and checked my email —JR was rubbing off on me. His code name appeared in my inbox with six different emails. Nothing from anyone else. Again, I wondered what the hell my boss was up to that even my emails were culled so I only received JR's.

I shoved that problem aside. Understanding Damon's thought process was too time consuming and probably fruitless. A plethora of information regarding the Vatican Secret Archives awaited me. Settling in as best I could on the toilet seat, I opened JR's emails and went to work.

16

Stato della Città del Vaticano, otherwise known as Vatican City, is its own country. The Italian government labeled it a 'sovereign city-state', and behind the walled enclave built inside Rome lies the pope's personal island.

Vatican City has its own government, issues its own passports, and the only absolute monarch in Europe. Looking to enlighten yourself with history and culture? Check. Some of the most famous paintings in the world can be found in the Vatican's museums and churches. Searching for the meaning of life? Check. You can find philosophers, spiritual leaders, and an abundance of theories on life, the afterlife, and good versus evil. Need to launder money or blackmail the church? Check and check. Ways to do both abound behind those walls.

Of course, I've never seen the art or the architecture or talked to any priest about my sins and the afterlife. Never once ventured into Vatican City, assuming all the time that I was one-hundred-percent demon. Demons and consecrated ground don't mix. Throw in a bunch of self-righteous do-gooders who want my head, and you've got a recipe for the apocalypse right there.

Since discovering I'm one of the seven deadly sins Jesus cast out of Mary Magdalene, I've also discovered Jesus' mojo gave me a hefty dose of virtue. That virtue drives me to save and protect humans from supernaturals who would harm them. It's also a free pass on consecrated ground.

Hello, Vatican City.

Except we didn't land at da Vinci-Fiumicino or Ciampino airports in Rome. VC doesn't have an airport, but Rome has two nearby. Nine hours after leaving Chicago, we landed on a long, pot-hole-filled runway fifty miles north of the city, coming to a stop in front of a rundown building with floor-to-ceiling glass windows that reflected the plane's running lights back at us. In the distance, a huge military-type castle outlined a cliff overlooking a large lake.

"What the hell is this?" was all I could say.

Rain tapped against the windows. Damon donned his coat. "*Castello di Guerriero Feroce*. The Italian Bridge Institute. They moved from Milan a few years ago."

Cole and I exchanged a look. I drew on my cape, fingered my weapons. "Why are we here?"

"I have business with Marco Agresta, a friend of mine. We'll spend a few hours here, preparing for your entrance into Vatican City, and allowing me and Marco to catch up and share news."

Damon had friends? Friends he needed to catch up with? "That's what email is for—catching up. Besides, you're on the phone to the Bridge people over here all the time."

Heat filled my head. *Please refrain from questioning my actions in front of others.*

I stifled my middle finger's reaction. If Damon felt the need to visit Marco and the Italian Bridge Council, it was for a good reason. What I didn't like was the fact it was a false reason. Combined with him lying to me about Cole and the communication isolation from everyone but JR, the subterfuge made my skin itch.

I also felt uncomfortable because I didn't like meeting new people. I didn't like being in Italy, where so many memories from my past haunted me.

Fog was creeping in, cradling the castle and inching its way toward the hangar and runway. Two males emerged from the building riding a truck with some kind of seal on the side and a large liquid tanker on the back. They stopped near the plane and went into maintenance mode, docking the wheels and running a hose to the plane's fuel tank.

A woman appeared at the entrance to the building, and suddenly, Damon's stop at Castle Fierce Warrior made more sense. She was classic Italian—long black hair, a pointed chin, and full lips. Her dark eyes seemed to look right through the plane's walls and search for Damon's presence.

She was dressed in a black, conservative suit, underneath which was a lacy tank top with an overtly generous V to it. Her breasts pushed up to full attention, showing as much olive skin from the top as was covered by fabric. The moment her gaze fixed on Damon, I felt him freeze.

Salmad grabbed our bags and rubbed the top of his head in a gesture I'd come to recognize as nervous relief. Cole sidled up next to me and whispered in my ear, "Marco, huh? Are you buying that?"

I shook my head no, swinging my attention from Damon to the woman. Both of them were way too still for my liking. I moseyed over to the archdemon and rubbed my shoulder against his. "Hey, boss. Everything okay?"

His lips formed a thin, tight line. His aura exuded a weird mix of lust and hate.

Mixed feelings I had a time or two myself. Had that recipe down to a science. I patted him on the back. *If you need me to play your girlfriend, just say the word. I hear I'm pretty good at making others jealous.*

It was ridiculously forward of me to invade his brain—although he did it on a regular basis to me—and suggest we act like lovers. The mental push, or perhaps the psychological one, broke the spell she seemed to have on him.

He gave me a grateful nod. *That won't be necessary, but I appreciate your concern.*

Who is she?

An old friend.

And I was the pope.

Damon picked up his laptop case and made for the stairs, which had lowered while we talked. I gave Cole a shrug and followed.

The magical energy between Damon and the woman nearly lifted me off the ground. The moment Damon exited the plane, her features tensed. She stood stock-still, but her aura bounced and gyrated like a small child jumping for joy.

Friend, my ass.

There was an awkward moment as they faced each other and then Damon smiled. A generous, if not overly friendly, making her tension ease. The full lips brushed kisses on his cheeks and she gripped his arm to lead him inside.

Once we were all out of the rain, Damon introduced us. "Valentina, these are my employees, Kali and Cole. The priest is Salmad." He took his eyes off her face long enough to address us. "Everyone, this is Valentina Bellucci. She's head of the Bridge Council here."

What about Marco? I almost said it out loud, but Cole must have sensed my rudeness because he stepped on the side of my booted foot as he stepped forward and offered Valentina his hand. "A pleasure to meet you."

The woman's breasts jiggled as she shook his hand. "The War demon. Damon speaks highly of you."

Cole smiled, suddenly smitten with her. I almost kicked him to snap him out of it.

Sal set down our overnight bags and took his turn exchanging greetings with her.

Then she turned to me. Instead of a handshake, she grabbed my arms and pulled me into an embrace, air kissing my cheeks.

I'm not a touchy-feely demon. Recently, everyone from Maddy to Dru had had their hands on me, hugging me, carrying me, feeding me their blood. I was less sensitive to being touched now than previously, but I still wasn't prepared for Valentina's assault.

I did not return the air kisses, nor did I find being pillowed by her gigantic breasts comforting or titillating.

"You!" she said, stepping back and regarding me with a smile that didn't quite reach her eyes. "Damon's enforcer. What an honor it is to finally meet the famous Kalina Dolce."

She was lying, and I didn't like the way she massacred my name, making it sound like *Kee-a-leena*.

My mother, a Greek demon whose family name was Kalinikos, had wanted to use a K rather Ch to begin my name in memory of her home. Italians had difficulty pronouncing Kalina and Chalina, and my parents had settled on Calina. A few Italians, like Val, threw an *i* after the *ch* and turned it into *Chi*alena. A pretty version, but not my name.

I didn't go by Calina anymore; only Kali, and Damon had introduced me as such. Val's misstep—on purpose or not—raised my hackles.

Her fingernails dug into my skin, right through my cape and shirt sleeves. Her magical fingers probed at me as well as she assessed my powers. Her eyes scanned my body and conveyed she found me lacking in all areas.

My assessment of her was less emotional and more objective. She was a Kopek—a female nightmare demon—with a little greater demon thrown in for good measure. She haunted humans' nightmares and got them to make crossroads deals in their sleep. Underhanded and devious...but if she worked for the Bridge Institute, she had to keep her hauntings to supernaturals only.

My boss appeared to be a living example. His aura continued to be a wild mix of desire and hate. Those emotions clawed at my chest where my demon resided. I had no doubt Val had haunted him, but before or after his wife died? His fling with Nyx had to have been centuries before his beloved Spanish wife happened onto the scene, but he seemed too edgy for a fling with Val to have been so long ago.

I almost let my demon peek out at her just for fun. Instinct told me to keep my cards close to my chest. I didn't know her or any of the other demons here...tipping my hand or appearing in any way to be ruffled by her rudeness only gave her more power.

And the male between us was the best weapon to fight her with. "Funny, Damon never mentioned you."

Shazam, as Maddy would say. The she-demon tightened her hold on me while inside, she roared with anger. But she was no giddy young girl who couldn't control her emotions. As fast as her anger surged, it shut off, like a lid being dropped on a grease fire, smothering it. Her lips formed a cat-like smile. "He said you were cheeky."

Cheeky? That was rather mild for Damon and not a word I'd ever heard him use. "Cocky, imprudent, annoying as hell... those are more like it."

"And honest. I like that."

Liar.

Damon's voice filled my head. *Kali.*

Just my name, but stated with enough reprimand—even mentally—to make me return Val's smile. "It's nice to meet you. Quite a place you have here."

Her smile turned more genuine. She released my arms. "Come. Marco is waiting."

A set of Maserati SUVs waited on the other side of the hangar to drive us to the castle. The luxury cars seemed extravagant for the hundred-yard drive. I considered suggesting Val and her demon council members think about scaling down the autos and fixing the runway instead. A swift glance from Damon squelched that impulse.

On the side of the stone gates hung a sign as old as the castle itself, greeting us as we pulled into the courtyard:

Castello di Guerriero Feroce

Semper Paratus

Always ready. Ready for what, I wondered as the gates to the castle closed slowly behind us.

17

The castle was home to nearly two hundred supernaturals from all over the globe. Apparently, while Damon and I were doing our thing in America, the European Bridge Council had established a new directive, recruiting demons and other supes from all walks to train for war.

Boot camp, weapons management, and Battle Psychology 101 were all on the list of graduation requirements. Castle Fierce Warrior was the magical equivalent of the United States Department of Defense.

Where they found so many supernaturals willing to help humans was beyond me. Times were obviously changing. As one of the female cat shifters who was showing me to my room said with a lift of her shoulders, "It's a brand new world for us."

Her name was Isi, and her shifter was close to the surface. Her white hair flowed thick and full around her baby face, contradicting her human genes. She shook my hand with feline grace, and nearly purred when we were introduced. "Kali Sweet. I can't believe you're here. I'm a huge fan."

Beside me, Damon smiled. Cole looked as confused as I felt.

"Fan of what exactly?" I said, my hand still caught between both of hers.

She giggled and her eyes snapped with playfulness. Something about her eyes looked familiar. "Your work, silly."

Hanging onto me, she took my bag from Salmad and tugged me toward an enormous set of stairs. "Can I get your autograph? My sister will scream with jealousy when I tell her I got to bunk with you!"

I cast a *save me* glance at Damon and Cole and found them both snickering as Isi marched me away. Behind Damon, Valentina shot me a cold, hard look.

The castle sprawled in all four directions. Moisture dampened the stone walls and the place had the distinct smell of an institution. The room Isi took me to, however, was cozy and had a small fire burning in the stone fireplace. There were two beds, a sitting area near the fireplace, and an attached bathroom. I had no intention of staying longer than necessary, but my new roommate seemed to think I was moving in. Curious, I let her assume what she wanted and encouraged her to talk. The more she said, the more I worried. Damon's plan was becoming clearer.

Demons come from the earth. So does our magic. As she chatted, I laid my hand on the stones of the room and let my demon get a read on the place. I expected strong vibrations from the stone, but the intensity of the magic surprised me. The stone acted like a magical light socket of energies and very dark, very strong magic lived inside these walls. High levels of all the deadly sins and their offspring. For a group of Bridge employees, that struck me as odd. Where was the benevolent energy? The desire to help rather than hurt?

Ignoring the burning sensations in my hand, I probed deeper. What I found were the magics of young vampires, recently changed, and upper-level demons, like Valentina, who were older than the rocks used to create the castle. There was a concentration of mischief and friendship on the west side of the castle, but beyond that, nothing but evil.

My demon did a little dance. This was her kind of place.

So many different types of magic in one location created a great deal of tension in the land, air, and water. Every natural element in the area was overloaded, and the magic pulsing into my hand and up my arm radiated all the way to my head.

Instant migraine as my virtue fought back.

What was going on here?

Breaking the link, I shook my hand, then rubbed it, trying to get rid of the lingering maleficence. I also rubbed my forehead to ease the sudden pain there.

"Would you like a tour of the place?" Isi asked, jumping up from her Barbie-pink bed. She had no accent and could have been from America from the sounds of it. "Damon will be tied up with Marco and Valentina for a while, and dinner isn't until seven. This place is awesome! You'll love the training center and weapons room. I know you will!"

"Great," I said, motioning for her to lead the way. Sitting in the room wasn't going to help me figure out what was going on here and what Damon was doing about it. He had to have caught on that the European Bridge Council had something up its sleeve, and I would bet money that's what this trip was really about. "Can we pick up Cole along the way? Those War demons, you know. Nothing they love better than a fully stocked weapons room."

Isi nodded her head and giggled again. "So you date Radison Beaumont, right? My sister and I have all his trading cards and we know all his songs by heart. We're, like, obsessed with him!"

Uh-huh. "That's nice."

Lame, I know, but what was I supposed to say? He rocks *in* bed as well as out?

She grabbed my hand again like we were best friends. "So tell me..." Giggle. "What's he *really* like?"

Mamma mia. Kill me now.

18

Dinner provided me with my first glimpse of Marco. The archdemon was dark-skinned, with a wide, relaxed smile that belied his aura's convoluted structure. No one in this castle—with the exception of Isi—was easy to read. Deception, duplicity, and machination seemed to be the hidden agendas of the day.

Of course, Marco *was* a demon. One of the top dogs in demon-land, too, right up there with Damon.

But as I watched him and Damon talk and laugh at the head of the long, rectangular dinner table in the dining hall, I couldn't help but compare the two males. They may have both been archdemons working for the Bridge Institute, but they couldn't be more opposite from each other in personality.

The dining hall was Hogwarts-like, with the castle's occupants sitting on benches around three enormous wooden tables. The energy in the air was suffocating, the smells of the food and all the different magics overpowering. My eyes watered, my nose ran, my ears rang. My demon scratched and clawed at her prison, desperate to come out and play.

Thanks to all the magic, my head continued to pound. Even

if the guests in the hall hadn't been magical, it would've been too much for me. Large groups of living beings—human or otherwise—are irresistible to my demon. A living smorgasbord she can't resist. She was desperate to tempt, torture, and kill everyone in sight.

Magical security barriers were thick, constantly shifting, and held poisons and spells designed to keep us in, as well as the big bad out.

All the while Isi had been showing me around the grounds and castle, I'd been working on my plan to get to Rome and my father's journals. Damon insisted we were staying overnight and hitting Vatican City at sunrise. Security barriers and boss aside, I had a different plan.

As if someone were reading my mind, every time I made an excuse to head back to the room, a supernatural would grab my arm and ask for an autograph. Or shake my hand and ask me to tell them about the time I killed and disembodied Queen Maria or some other supe on my hit list. My reputation had spread further in the international community than I'd suspected, exaggerated stories spreading with it. I found myself clarifying and setting straight more than a dozen false accounts, disappointing my audience until I gave up and went along with whatever they thought. Arguing was pointless.

After dinner, we were invited to a fighting exhibition in the training center. Instead of watching mindless TV or playing Xbox games, the supes gathered under a dome and showed off their skills for a couple of hours.

Cole and I had just gotten settled in to watch the show when I was challenged by a male vampire whose hair dangled down past his waist. He swept the long, straight strands into a high ponytail, emphasizing his aristocratic features, and for half a second, I swore I saw Vlad the Impaler looking back at me. I begged off the fight, but the bastard wouldn't take no for an answer.

"Chicken, Miss Sweet?" the cocky vampire called out.

People in the audience made clucking noises. Volante, in her usual spot on my arm, trembled from the challenge. From a balcony overlooking the ring, I caught Damon's eyes. His thoughts overrode the internal cursing inside my head with a warm, familiar rush. *Put the vampire in his place but don't kill him. Yet.*

I snickered under my breath, my demon laughing as well. The whole arena watched to see if I'd acquiesce. "Thunderdome," I murmured to Cole, who sat on my right.

"Roman coliseum," he murmured back.

The group gathered here looked more like Mad Max than a gladiator to me, but Cole had been a the later back in the day. Had to give him credit; he knew what he was talking about.

Which meant I was about to be tiger meat.

Sal, on my left, shook his head. "I don't like this."

Join the club.

"Cut him off at the knees." Cole slapped me on the back, not appearing to be at all concerned for my safety. "His weakest link is below the waist."

I rose to accept the challenge, and the crowd went wild, calling out, chanting my name, and yelling obscenities just for the hell of it. "Every male's weakest link is below the waist," I murmured.

This was so not my cup of magic. I glanced at Damon again and found Marco studying me closely. So was Valentina. The three of them formed a stunning threesome of demonness. Suddenly I realized this wasn't just a fight to provide good-natured entertainment. This was a test.

I hate tests.

Pissed, I stomped my way across the open floor to my opponent. He didn't scare me, but the idea that I was being tested didn't sit right. I had nothing to prove, as my reputation seemed to show, and yet, there had to be a very real and urgent reason for Damon to ask me to perform in this ridiculous dog-and-pony show.

The vamp grinned, flashing his pearly white teeth and fangs that were already descended. His aura was half cocky-shit and half superior self-righteousness. He'd thought about this moment. Planned for it. Thought about handing me my ass on a silver platter.

Why?

At the moment, it didn't matter. *Alright, buddy boy. Let's see what you've got.*

I smiled back, letting my demon flash in my eyes. His grin faltered for a second, then he turned in a slow circle, waving his hands in the air to further rile up the crowd. They cheered their pleasure at the theatrics.

Magic flooded the dome. I coughed and blinked several times to clear the tears in my eyes. Was this what it felt like to be on stage for the WWE?

When in Rome, I told myself, releasing my own magical energy. I brought up my protective shields and snapped Volante to attention. She shuddered and reached for the vampire, ready to go to work. "*Semper Paratus*," I yelled over the crowd.

The crowd roared, their voices echoing under the dome to the point of deafening me. Something in my blood rose to the occasion. I shot a glance at Cole—he was on his feet, yelling with the rest of them.

Adoration is a funny thing. Once you get a taste of it, you only want more.

I swung Volante with lightning speed and cut the vampire off at the knees.

19

Two hours later, the wounded lay in piles at my feet. The cheering ceased five minutes after the aristocrat fell, and a new energy had emerged. It was suddenly me against them. All of them.

After the vamp, their best warriors came at me one at a time. Some were better than others. None had my hybrid Frankenstein blood. All fell.

Then they came at me in pairs, and finally, in groups. Took me longer to fight the groups, but in the end, they all went down and didn't get back up.

Blood and other bodily fluids dotted my clothes, hair, and face. Volante dripped red. My left shoulder was out of place, and my right kneecap shattered. Bruises and cuts covered my body.

My blood couldn't keep up with mending all the damage. I could have used one of Rad's healing runes.

I glared at Marco and Valentina who'd insisted more of their warriors come at me even after I'd damaged so many. I flicked the whip as Marco called out to another of his lieutenants. "Beldon!"

"No." I staggered to the edge of the arena as best I could with a broken kneecap and stared up at the archdemon. The knee was mending itself, but I was sick to my stomach. "Enough. Whatever you wanted to prove, we're done. I won't hurt anyone else."

Marco vaulted over the edge of the balcony, landing gracefully in front of me. That grace contradicted the brutal anger in his aura. "He said you could do it, but I didn't believe him."

No need to explain that Damon was who he was talking about and my boss had told him of my extraordinary abilities. "What do you want?" I countered. "Why would you put your followers through this?"

His arm reached out so fast I couldn't follow. His fingers went right through my shields, weak from the constant hits of both fists and magic, and wrapped around my neck.

In a heartbeat, Cole and Damon were by my side. Cole took a swing at Marco, but Damon blocked his fist.

Only because Damon wanted to do the honors. Grabbing Marco by the neck, Damon lifted him from the ground and threw him into the seats.

Those with medical training streamed onto the floor of the arena, tending to the fallen. At the sight of Marco taking a whooping from Damon, Valentina swung into action, but not before I noticed the subtle, calculating grin on her face.

She ran to Marco's side, helping him sit up. As she tended to him, she shot daggers at me and Damon.

Cole grabbed me up in a bear hug and swung me around in a circle, crushing my bruised and cracked ribs. "Amazing, Kali."

He set me on my feet and my knee gave out, but his hands held me up as he grinned down into my face. "You're a machine."

I was a machine, all right. Rubbing my neck where Marco had grabbed me, I faced Damon. "I don't know what kind of game you're playing with your dickhead Bridge friend, but I'm done."

I left him there with his cronies. Cole put an arm around me to help me to the nearest exit. Sal and Isi waited for us.

"Are you hurt?" Isi said in a small voice. Her eyes were wide, and she hung back as if scared of me. "I can get you medical attention if you want."

"Go help your friends." I brushed past her. "I don't need you."

It was rude and I berated myself for it as I dragged my tired limbs upstairs, Cole and Sal silent on either side of me. But I was wiped out and pissed off. Not even the super cocktail of mixed bloods could fend off the pain and emotions rolling through me.

When I reached the room I shared with the shifter, I motioned Cole and Sal inside. "We need to talk."

With everyone in the dome, this was my only chance to speak to them without worrying about someone overhearing us. Cole sat me on the bed, then disappeared into the attached bathroom.

Most of the cuts and bruises were already healed, thanks in part to the extra dose of Dru blood I'd had the night before. The knee, shoulder, and aching ribs would need more time. Cole emerged with a wet washcloth and handed it to me. As I dabbed at my bloody lip, he motioned for me to brace myself so he could pop my shoulder back into place. Hard to do with my busted kneecap. "Help me out here, Sal."

The priest paled but did as instructed, holding me firm as Cole yanked on my arm. The pain was sharp and I felt it down to my toes. I didn't cry out, just added it to the throbbing my entire body was doing.

Sal released me and I hung my head between my knees to keep from retching. Once I could manage it, I raised my head. "I'm heading to Vatican City at midnight. There's a tunnel I can access outside of Rome that will take me to a spot where I can access the archives. Once I have the journals, I'm out of there and headed back to America, with or without Damon. You in?"

Cole didn't even blink. He hefted my feet onto the bed, despite my protest about my knee, and wrapped it tight with some strips from one of Isi's white cotton shirts she'd left lying on the floor. "Why midnight? Why not now?"

It seemed obvious that I was in no condition to take off right at that moment, but my shoulder already felt better.

"Now?" Sal rubbed his head. "This isn't the plan. *I'm* supposed to retrieve the documents, not K—"

"Are you in or out, priest?" I flexed my shoulder, then my knee. Cole's brace would support my leg while the knee cap mended. My arm moved stiffly, but I could rotate it without blacking out from pain. "Your assistance may be useful but is not required. I can do this without you."

Flustered, he ping-ponged his gaze from me to Cole and back. His jaw tightened, relaxed. Tightened again. He blew out a disgusted breath. "In, I guess. God help us all."

I leaned back against the pillows and looked at Cole. "I have something I have to do before we take off. That's why midnight."

He searched my face for answers as to what I was planning. "Need backup?"

"It's a girl thing."

Both of them looked skeptical, and I almost laughed. I'd just taken on close to a hundred supernaturals in the arena all by myself, and they were still questioning my abilities.

Males. My life is blessed with more than my fair share.

After several minutes of Sal grilling me with questions I wouldn't answer, he took his leave, agreeing to meet us at the carport behind the castle. I wasn't up for threatening Damon's pilot to fly us to Rome. We'd borrow one of those fancy SUVs from Marco and Valentina. The least they could do for siccing their soldiers on me.

"How's the shoulder?" Cole asked, rewetting the washcloth and cleaning dried blood from my temple.

Exhaustion set in. I needed a shower, a nap, and some protein, but what I wanted were answers to my questions.

I moved my arm in an arc, showing the War demon it was healing. I even held back a grimace. Cole needed to be focused on our mission, not my minor aches and pains.

"There's no better feeling than standing victorious in the arena," he said.

"Satan, save me. You're not going all Spartacus on me, are you?" I tried to take the washcloth from him, but he smacked my hand away and continued his ministrations.

His aura was full of pride. Not for himself, but for me.

That pride made me wonder. "Were you in on it?"

His dark eyes met mine. "On the gladiator showdown? Of course not. I had no clue that was coming."

That made two of us. "Why would he do that to me?"

A lift of his shoulders. Continued cleaning of my wounds. "Proving something to his friends?"

"That was my thought, too, but why? Aren't we all on the same side?"

"Maybe not."

"There's dark magic in the walls. In the very air. I'm not sure what's going on."

His fingers lifted a section of my hair. The cuts on my scalp and face had already healed, but blood remained clotted in my hair. "A lot of demons in one spot. Could be nothing more than simple genetics."

I grimaced as he tugged at the knots. "It's more than that. I can feel it. But even if there *is* something underhanded going on behind the scenes with Marco and his employees, why wouldn't Damon simply tell me he wanted me to show them what I could do? Why did he..."

I broke off, and Cole read my mind. "Throw you to the wolves and hope for the best?"

Exactly.

Betrayal. That's what the show in the arena smacked of.

Giving up on his quest to clean my hair, he tossed the washcloth on the floor. "You're his prized weapon, Kali. He wanted to show you off."

"It was more than that." I scooted around so I sat next to Cole with my feet over the edge. I flexed my knee, sucked in a breath at the sudden pain. Close, but not healed yet. I willed a little magic into it, hoping Dru's blood would follow. "Have you noticed the weird dynamic between him and Valentina?"

He snickered and gave me a knowing look. "Who could miss it?"

"There's a personal agenda here. I'd stake my life on it."

"Seems like you already did. You may have held back and not killed the supes in the arena, but they were out for your head."

I'd thought the same. Another reason being thrown in the arena smacked of betrayal. "But were they acting on Marco's orders or Valentina's?"

He rubbed my shoulders, gave the good one a squeeze. "Doesn't matter. You *kicked ass*, Enforcer."

"I did, didn't I?" I smiled, slid off the bed and forced my knee to hold my weight. Better. Stronger. "And I'm about to go kick some more."

20

As expected, it took time for the castle's inhabitants to settle down. Those who weren't badly injured or who recovered quickly went to work in nearby towns and cities. Those who were still recovering went to their beds or stayed in the infirmary.

Isi was nowhere to be found when I snuck out of our room and to the wing on the west side that faced the lake and harbored the archdemons.

I positioned myself outside of Damon's room. I'd expected him to seek me out after he finished giving Marco a piece of his mind, but he never showed up. This complicated things since I was too stubborn to reach out to him. So I'd spent the better part of the past four hours stewing, my ego raw. I hated being treated like a pet on a leash, and no matter what logical reasons I could come up with for him asking me to fight in the arena, none of them seemed legitimate.

That didn't mean I was going to leave him unprotected from a certain Kopel demon. I'd seen it in her aura during dinner and afterward in the arena when she'd gone to Marco's side.

She planned to pay Damon a visit in his dreams. Maybe in the flesh as well.

Darkness blanketed me, allowing me to stand guard in the shadows across from Damon's door, my shields firmly in place once more. Normally, I would have worried he might sense me there, but he was distracted.

His presence was a powerful one, so powerful I could feel it bleeding through the stones. He paced, sat, paced some more. Seductive magic seeped from his pores along with something else.

Nerves.

A pinch of pity bit deep into my heart. Me, pitying Damon? Absurd. He was a big boy and could take care of himself.

Or could he?

Love and lust did funny things to us. No one, not even demons, are immune to making stupid choices based on them. I, better than anyone, knew this.

A butler arrived with a cart filled with room service...all the plates sporting gold-domed covers, complete with elaborate finial handles. The dinner looked big enough for two. I couldn't see the label on the bottle of wine that accompanied the meal, but I noticed two crystal goblets standing guard on either side. You don't put cheap wine in fine crystal—not if you're Damon.

And you don't drink fine wine alone when you have two glasses.

He was expecting her. From the looks of it, her impending arrival would be soon, and he was relishing the idea of serving her food and drink.

Serious stuff for an archdemon. At the top of our demon ranks, archdemons serve no one. They snap their fingers and lower-level demons scurry to do their bidding. It's innate in our blood. They are our gods. We are their servants. For one archdemon to cater to another expressed deep desire. One archdemon feeding another was a mating ritual.

Ew. The image of Damon getting it on with Valentina was the stuff of nightmares to me. She didn't deserve him. He didn't deserve to be haunted and tortured by her.

But apparently, that's what he wanted.

Was I wrong to defend him? Save him from himself?

Most definitely.

I stayed where I was.

When the butler knocked on the heavy wooden door, I sank farther into the shadows and reinforced my mental shields to be sure Damon didn't detect me lurking. He called to the butler to enter and the male did, hustling the cart inside before I got more than a cursory look.

No Damon in sight, but I did notice the large bed in front of a floor-to-ceiling window overlooking the lake. Flickering light to the right suggested a fire was lit. The familiar scent of wood smoke teased my nose, a mix of the burning wood in the fire-place and Damon's natural smell.

The door closed; an exchange of words happened between my boss and the butler over the food and wine. The wine was uncorked and Damon gave his approval after a sample taste. A few seconds later, the butler left with a smile on his face.

This is none of your business.

I fidgeted, torn between leaving and staying to have my say. *He's a big boy and can make his own decisions.*

But he still owed me an explanation.

Hiding in the shadows wasn't my style anyway. I stepped across the hall and raised a hand to knock...and the weight of Kopel magic hit me like an iron beam.

Valentina's voice was hot coals on the back of my neck. "What are you doing here?"

Bracing, I faced her, putting my back toward Damon's door. I started to say, "I could ask you the same," but the female in me came to life with an unexpected ferociousness I couldn't explain. Words flew out of my mouth without forethought. "He invited me for dinner."

Her brow knitted in confusion. "To talk battle strategy and gloat over your win today?"

Again the female in me rose to the challenge. I gave a giggle worthy of Isi and felt Damon's presence shift to the other side of the door. "Battle strategy? I don't think that's what he has in mind for us tonight." I cocked my head as if a thought had just dawned on me. "You don't know, do you?"

I hated it when people said that to me. My guess that Valentina would hate it as well was accurate.

"Know what?" she ground out.

Damon's magic enveloped me. His mind reached out to mine, hit the shields, and promptly broke through them. *What are you doing?*

Give me a minute. Out loud, I spoke to Valentina, "Look, I know you were hoping to renew your relationship with Damon during this visit, but if you're planning on screwing him over the way you did before, I have to warn you—Marco gets wind of what you're up to? He'll be looking for blood. And if he's the jealous type, which we both know he is, he'll be out for Damon's black blood."

Her inky-black eyes flashed green. I'd hit the nail on the head. But there was more to it than making her current lover jealous of her ex-lover. "And?" she prompted, killing me with her eyes.

This new talent for reading auras really came in handy. "And your plan to have the two of them take each other out in the process isn't going to happen."

She gave a tiny, startled gasp. "I have no idea what you're talking about."

Right. I leaned against the door in a nonchalant pose. "Well, let me clear it up for you. You or Marco, either one, come after my boss or attempt to hurt him in any way, waking or asleep, I'll cut you open and feed your own intestines to you for breakfast."

Damon's magic sucked in and released slowly, as if he were containing his aggravation only by the tips of his fingers.

He didn't like me blowing date night? Tough.

I felt him reach for the door knob. *Don't you dare interrupt us*, I ordered, grabbing the handle and holding firm. I hoped it looked as if I was done talking to Valentina and heading in for a night of debauchery with him.

At least the *done talking* part was accurate. "You know I can do it, Val. Think hard about your choices right now. I strongly recommend you walk away and head back to whatever hole you crawled out of. Take Marco with you. I owe him a beat-down for manhandling me earlier."

With that, I left her standing in the hallway with her mouth open, pushing my way into Damon's chambers with a big smile on my face. "Hello, lover boy," I said loud and clear, throwing my arms around Damon's neck and kicking the door shut with my foot.

My boss was stone under my hands, his dark eyes bearing down on me and his aura crackling with irritation. He started to speak, but I put a finger to his lips. "You can thank me later," I whispered.

I slunk back to the door, put an ear against it, and listened. Valentina's floor-length dress made soft swishing noises as she turned on her heel and headed off toward Marco's room. Her night-air magic went with her.

Mission accomplished.

My satisfaction was short-lived as I turned to Damon and saw the storm cloud on his face. "You ambuscade my dinner guest and undermine our professional relationship with a counterfeit flirtation?"

Ambuscade? Seriously? "I'm not sure exactly what you said there, but I think the answer is yes, I *ambushed*—a modern-day term you may not be familiar with—your guest. She wanted to do you harm, and I pretended to have a personal relationship with you to make her jealous and send her on her Kopel-demon way. To top it off, I threatened to rip out her intestines and feed them back to her for breakfast if she or Marco hurt you. Check, check, and check, boss. My job here is done."

His scowl deepened. "I'm capable of fending for myself."

Ah, love. Makes us stupidly brave. "Not against her. I noticed it in your aura from the moment we landed. You hate her, but you still want her."

Making a disgusted noise in the back of his throat, he curled a lip at me. "You take liberties where you have no right. This is a complicated matter, one which you'll never understand."

"Oh, I understand. She's with Marco now, but she'd love to have you and Marco act like Neanderthals and fight over her. That's what happened before, isn't it? She pitted you against your best friend, and he won. What I don't understand is why either of you are interested in a nightmare."

He paced away from me. I gave him the space. Damon saw fit to be pissed at me on a regular basis. Nothing new there. But I'd never seen him hung up on any female except his wife, Zandra, and while it might have been wrong of me to interfere in his love life, I didn't give a shit. He regularly interfered with mine.

Friends didn't let friends jump off cliffs. "You and Val hook up before Zandra?"

His chest heaved as he drew a deep breath. Absently, he glanced at his ring finger, the gold band that had once graced it long gone, at least in physical presence. Its ghost, like his dead wife, still lingered.

Damon was a Psukhe demon, one that lived and fed on the psyche. In Greek, *psukhe* meant breath, life, soul. Although Zandra had been nearly all human—a tiny amount of demon blood in her system had been repressed—she'd been Damon's psukhe, his breath, life and soul.

She'd lived a long life by human standards, but her death had nearly done him in. I'd never thought much about the fact Damon had lived far longer than Zandra or me...it made sense he'd been around the demon block with other females before and probably after Z. I just hadn't known of any. At least until the past day. Now I knew about Nyx and Val.

I'd never given Damon's love life much thought. On several occasions, he'd made it clear he considered me a potential bedmate, but we were so not going there. I respected and cared about him—and he was incredibly sexy—but my heart was Grinch-sized, and apparently, I loved only one man—a man Damon had strong misgivings about.

He didn't answer my question and that silence told me what I needed to know. "Val's your Achilles heel, isn't she? That's the real reason we came here. So you could see her."

He turned on me, righteous fury pinching his handsome face. "I never place personal reasons above our mission."

"I would." Being a demon might have given us superior abilities, but our vices also gave us significant weaknesses, and I accepted that. In matters of the heart, demons were no better at love than humans. "Just because you're head of the North American Bridge Council doesn't mean you're a saint."

The fury lessoned. He rubbed his forehead, his shoulders slouching. "The personal and professional are tied together, I'm afraid."

At first, I didn't get it. Then a couple of brain cells clicked together. I pointed at the room service, which smelled absolutely divine and made my stomach growl. Fighting off a hundred or so demons by yourself can make a demon hungry.

"Wine her and dine her and see if she spills company secrets? Don't you already know all there is to know about this place?"

His gaze met mine, and my brain warmed. *Best not to speak of this out loud.*

I sat up straight and eyed the door. *She's back? Listening to us?*

Wouldn't you be?

Touché. *I can pop her eardrums.*

Ignoring me with a frustrated shake of his head, he sauntered to the table and poured the wine, handed a glass to me, and sat in the chair across from mine. "*Salute, amore mio.*"

My treasure. Uh, huh. More like his hired gun. *Well played, boss.*

We need to play this well, Kali. He winked, egging me to go along.

Being Italian, I've drank my share of wines. I like 'em red, rich and bold. The variety Damon had picked was all three. *If she's listening, let's give her a real show.* "*Salute, caro mio.*"

One of his gorgeous eyebrows rose seductively. *What do you suggest?*

Making Val believe I was Damon's latest conquest wouldn't be that hard after my jealous performance outside his door.

I set down the glass, crawled into his lap as he was taking a sip, and kissed him on the neck. "Did you like my show tonight?" I murmured against his skin. "In the arena?"

The shock on his face was priceless. Whether it was the kiss or the seductive tone of my voice, he choked. After another sip, he recovered quickly, running a hand along the top of my thigh-high boot. "Nothing turns me on more than watching you in action."

For once he sounded like he lived in modern-day America. I almost smiled, but then my breath caught. In his eyes was a kernel of truth that matched his words and his massaging hand. My pulse quickened.

Shifting in his lap, I started to stand, but he grabbed my leg and held me in place. Under my butt, I felt the hard press of something very male. Very archdemon.

Momma mia. I stopped squirming. That would only make it worse. Mentally reaching for safer ground, I came up mute, but pissing him off would wipe that look off his face. *You used me like a trained seal to show off to your friends.*

Setting down his own wine glass, he kept a hand on me. *And now I'm going to use you to make my former lover jealous. Wasn't that* your *plan?*

His other hand went around the back of my head to keep me from escaping his lips. As he brought our faces together, his hooded gaze never left mine. His lips were firm and unyielding as he kissed me into a type of submission. If I fought, Val would hear it, so I acquiesced.

It was torture, I tell you. Pure torture that I melted under. His warm lips offered magic and something more. A promise. *This is just a game*, I reminded myself. *Only an act.*

Is it? His voice countered.

I was so startled, my magic snapped out of me with the force of a bull, attempting to shove him away. His magic was stronger than mine, and it was prepared for my knee-jerk reaction. It blocked my whipsaw retort and blanketed it, once again pulling me under his spell.

Attempting to rein in my magic, I lost control of it, and it shot off around the room. The glasses shattered into a mess of blood-like puddles of wine. The fire in the fireplace geysered, shooting sparks all over the hearth and an expensive Persian rug.

Damon released me, a sly smile on his face. I scrambled off his lap, lips and magic tingling, and nearly landed on my ass in the process.

"You didn't even set your demon loose, Kali. I was a little disappointed. You know how that turns me on."

Huh? I blinked, trying to clear my head. My legs shook. Wisps of smoke rose from various spots of burnt carpet. A dozen sconces around the room vibrated against the walls like an earthquake's aftershock. My voice came out sounding similarly. "I didn't need her."

He appeared amused. "Your injuries are healed properly?" His aura was bright with desire.

"Yes."

"Good. I want you in peak condition when I take you to bed. Otherwise, you may not survive."

He winked. I backed away, studying his face, his aura, his mind. Nothing suggested he was in any way kidding.

But he had to be. He was feeding me a dose of my own medicine.

Hardy, har, har. Relief washed through me. Relief so profound that I almost collapsed.

Instead, I called up my earlier indignation over the fight. Time to address that little situation.

Why did you do it? Send me to face Marco's army like that? What were you trying to prove?

Avoiding the question, Kali?

Damn straight, I was. Taking a stabilizing breath, I squared my shoulders. My demon got ornery. I'd started this stupid charade, and by god, I'd finish it. "My wounds are healed, and I can handle anything you dish out, *lover.*"

I stroked Volante and raised my brows in a challenging gesture. *Touch me and your stones will never be the same.*

To my dismay, he laughed. The bastard was enjoying this. *Is that how you seduce the Chaos demon? By threatening his manhood?*

Rad. My heart twinged. I missed him and I hated myself for it. Reining in those emotions, I narrowed my eyes in answer. No way was I bringing Rad into this fight. "I could use some protein before our...lovemaking." *I could also use some insight into what the hell we're doing here if you're not hooking up with Val.* "Will you feed me, archdemon?"

A mental chuckle echoed the previous verbal one. He gave me a nod, desire still present in his eyes. "It will be my pleasure."

Exactly what I was afraid of.

21

I could diagram my entire history through my three hundred years of earthly existence, all based on being a vengeance demon born in Italy in the eighteenth century. Parallel lines of time and place running alongside demons like Cole and Damon. Black holes of evil miring me in magic quicksand with Maria. Spirals of behavior and choices—such as those with Rad—that had taken me away from my goals, only to circle me back around to them.

I had been haunted by my past as Maria's weapon, encumbered by my present as a demon bent on saving humans, and filled with false hope for a future now threatened by the coming apocalypse.

The sum total of my life wasn't worth much, but it provided enough to accept my fate.

As Cole, Sal and I left Castello di Guerriero Feroce by the light of the quarter moon at three minutes past midnight, my head swam with the messages Damon had delivered, both verbally and mentally. The European Bridge Council was not our ally. No surprise there.

They were, in fact, out to destabilize the international

Bridge community and resurrect demon leadership over all supernaturals. While vexing, this only mildly surprised me.

Damon suspected they wouldn't stop there. Humans would be subjugated, turned into sex slaves, blood sacrifices, and meals-ready-to-devour. Evil—always close to the surface of every demon —had infiltrated our organization and was preparing its ultimate downfall.

Now I was well and truly pissed.

Emasculating Damon was one thing. His position, temperament, and ancient, all-powerful magic were nothing to mess with, but Marco and Valentina had been secretly plotting to overthrow him for years—probably since the early days when Val had confessed her love for him.

Emasculating me, the Bridge Council's enforcer, who was also an original vice blessed by the hand of Jesus, was another.

Add the Master vampire blood in my veins and my position as Queen of the Central United States Undead population, and I was nearly indestructible with an army of supernaturals at my disposal. Marco and Val had refused to believe the reports coming out of Chicago and needed, according to Damon, to see firsthand what I could do.

Ah ha. There was the rub.

I'd done what he needed. Knowing why didn't mean I liked it any better than before. Damon had always taught me to downplay the extent of my abilities in order to surprise my enemies. Right now, my enemies knew everything about me.

"You all right?" Cole asked. He'd hot-wired one of the SUVs and we were speeding down a narrow, gravel and grass road away from the castle. Sal was in the back seat, reviewing the maps JR had sent me and rubbing his peach fuzz.

"Of course," I lied. Checking my weapons, I allowed my fingers to linger on the silver, steel and leather. They comforted me in a way nothing else could. "According to JR's calculations, we can reach the catacombs under Vatican City via a bookstore called Libreria Madonna Belle Strada off Via della Concili-azione. It's owned by a Jesuit priest whom Damon says will help us. He lives over the bookstore and has access to a tunnel underneath the building that runs parallel to the catacombs."

Salmad's head came up. "Father Reese?"

"You know him?"

He nodded. "A human priest is helping us? Why?"

My exact response when Damon had told me about him. "His mother was raped by a Swiss Guard servicing the Vatican when she was thirteen. That guard was half demon. Reese's mother was forced to marry an older, human male to cover her unintended pregnancy and gave birth to him several months later. The trauma affected her mental health and she committed suicide when he was five. His step-father put him in a Jesuit boys' home where he grew up to embrace the life. He has no love of demons, but he also has little love for the Swiss Guard and has evidence about some pretty big Vatican cover-ups, so no love lost there either. He's been using his bookstore as an underground railroad for religious martyrs and supernat-ural prisoners to escape from Rome for the past fifty years. Damon claims he's running his own miniature Bridge Institute."

Cole whistled under his breath. "So Damon knows all about our little heist tonight?"

"We had dinner. Talked. I convinced him this was the best plan of attack. No spectacle, no show, just get in, grab the jour-nals and get out as quietly as possible. The pope won't even know we're in town."

"Why didn't he come with us?"

How to answer? *Marco and Valentina are the tip of the iceberg,* Damon had told me, *but they are the head of the beast. If I can cut the head off, the rest of the beast and their mission to take over the Bridge Institute will fail.* "He has important matters to attend to with Marco and Valentina." I played with a string trailing from the hem of my cape. "Matters that should be wrapped up by the time we're done in Rome."

Neither male was satisfied with the revelation, but Cole didn't ask anything else, and Sal went back to his paper map, pointing a bony finger at it. "The bookstore is here. The Secret Archives are...here. That's probably less than half a mile."

"The tunnels under Vatican City follow a circuitous route, and not a very good one at that. The catacombs we'll be trekking through are not ones the Church recognizes, so they're not public and, therefore, not in good condition, from what JR says. Our route will probably be closer to a mile in distance and may take longer than usual on foot."

"The catacombs are sacred ground," Cole interjected. "I can't go in."

The Italian countryside gave way to suburbia, then to urban sprawl. All around us rose modern high-rises and ancient architecture. Street lights glistened off the wet streets as the windshield wipers worked overtime. Traffic was sparse, but the cars that passed us seemed to be running from the devil, they went by so fast. St. Peter's Square beckoned ahead.

Rome. *How long has it been, dear city?*

Dark magic skittered over my skin in response. The tiny hairs on my arms sat up and took notice. Certain buildings we passed, especially the ancient churches, seemed to loom over me, their blessed energy pushing me away. "Salmad and I will be fine. You be ready when we reemerge to drive us away. Hopefully, we can get in and out without detection, but in case we come out hot, we'll need a good driver to get us out of Rome."

Cole hated to miss out on the action. A muscle in his jaw pulsed, but he knew I was right. Casting a glance out his window, he shook his head. "Things sure look different than the last time I was here."

My birth city had changed. Even the street leading us into Vatican City and the bookstore was new, thanks to Mussolini and some other industrial sorts. The path to St. Peter's Square and onto VC had been reconstructed into a straight line in the past century. Too bad I couldn't follow that straight line to the Secret Archives.

Sal was giving Cole directions when my cell rang, the familiar ringtone telling me it was Maddy. How had she gotten through? Even JR's texts had stopped right before my fight in the arena. "Maddy? Is everything all right?"

"If you call a dead enforcer and a missing werewolf all right." Her voice sounded very far away, but it was the best sound I'd heard in the past twenty-four hours. "Ranulf killed Chi and took off. We don't know why or where Ranulf went. Kirill and Yasmin are bringing charges against him, and the shifters are in an uproar. Dru wants me to hunt down Ranulf, and Arman's telling me not to, that there has to be something going on we don't understand with the pack leader. I don't know what to do. When are you coming home?"

Home. Rome called to me because of my past, but Chicago was my future.

If I could save it.

"Don't do anything yet. Have Arman put out feelers for Ranulf. Do some detective work and find out if the werewolf's been acting odd or has been sick. Arman's right, this doesn't add up, and the Council and Dru may make matters worse by going after him. By all means, *do not* engage the shifter. Wait for me. I'll be home by this time tomorrow." I hoped. "Did Rad have any luck with Lake Michigan and the Red Tide?"

The line went fuzzy and then she came back on. "...not working and Parker's getting in the way. Where are you anyway? Rad's threatening to hunt you down."

Parker. That bitch. "What is Parker doing?"

"She showed up at your house and told Rad you were as good as dead."

"My *house*?"

Cole glanced my way and Salmad looked up.

"She was also downtown at Chloe's trying to buy blood."

A cold chill tickled my spine. "What kind of blood?"

"The kind a certain vengeance demon stores there for her blood slaves. Chloe turned her away, of course. Told Parker she didn't handle your blood."

Porca miseria. "What does she want *my* blood for?"

"What else?" Even across two continents, Maddy exuded annoyance. "She wants super powers too."

"She's human."

"So is Victoria. Look what your blood cocktail—even before the addition of Dru's powers—did for her."

Victoria, a witch who'd raised Lilith from hell, was rotting at that moment in the Chicago Bridge Institute's underground prison. "I'm certain she has throwback demon blood in her heritage. That's the only reason my blood gave her power. It only increased what she already possessed."

"Maybe Parker, baby, has throwback blood too."

That thought made me slightly dizzy. Mostly because it rang true. Her skills were off the charts for a human, but if she had demon blood in her system, it was nominal. My supernatural radar would have gone off otherwise. "Have you run that theory by Rad?"

A terse chuckle. "Rad is a jackass right now because you're gone. He mumbled something about you didn't have time for a vacation with him but you could take off with Damon, yada, yada, yada. And he's caught up in all his rock star stuff. Got nominated for a new award and has all kinds of interviews and performances lined up. *He's busy.* God, if I hear that one more time..."

The vacation statement made it all clear. "He thinks I'm on vacation?"

"Since none of us know where you are or why you left, that's as good a guess as any. Kali," she lowered her voice, "Rad caused a blizzard with hundred mile-an-hour winds when he found out you left with Damon. We lost power for four hours. The only reason the storm stopped was because he had to get on a plane to Hollywood for that awards show."

Damn it to hell. So much for Damon explaining my absence.

But this was the part of my life that others didn't understand, even those closest to me. I belonged to the Council. My life was not my own. I worked weird hours, weird cases and sometimes I had to leave in the middle of the night without saying goodbye. Up until Rad came back into my life, it hadn't been a problem. I had few friends, no family, and no lover to worry about. This new relationship with him was a wrinkle in my world, as was becoming a stand-in mother for Maddy, and accepting my responsibilities as queen of Chicago's Undead. Even the other *vitiums* looked to me to lead them.

Times like this, I felt pulled in too many directions. Everyone wanted something from me.

Right now, I seemed to be letting all of them down.

"Don't worry about Rad. I'll be home and straighten things out as soon as I can. Meanwhile, steer clear of Parker. She's up to no good."

"Ya think? That bitch is as bad as Victoria."

Not quite, but close. "As long as neither of them raises the queen of hell again, we'll be okay."

There was a pause. "I'm not so sure about that, Kali. Things are bad here. Like *bad* bad. Have you seen the news? All the wackos coming out and talking about the end of the world? They're citing things like the red water in Lake Michigan and all the cooties going around. Rad's freak blizzard added to the mayhem they're stirring up."

The good news kept coming.

False reassurances weren't my style, and I was positive I could stop the Horsemen. The *libreria* sign appeared on the next block. "Hang in there. I'm on the trail of something that's going to help us out. Something my father knew about. Once I get hold of that, I'll stop the apocalypse, and you and I will take care of Parker and Ranulf. 'K?"

A heavy sigh. "Yeah, whatever. But just so you know. If Parker baby shows up at the church again, I'm going evil vampire on her ass."

"Not a good idea, Maddy. Wait for me to get back. Please."

"What? You're breaking up..." She made interference noises. "Hurry home!"

The line went dead.

Brat.

Cole parked across the street from Belle Strada, a narrow, three-story high structure connected on both sides with similar buildings made of artificially aged stone to make them look older than they were. A few soft security lights illuminated the inside, but the street and the shops were locked up tight.

I was already armed to the teeth. Cole and Sal raided the Maserati's trunk for items we'd stolen from the weapons room at the castle. Once they were satisfied with their haul, we ducked our heads from the rain, bypassing the front entrance and heading for the small courtyard at the back.

A lion's head door knocker hung centered on the red wooden door. Above the door, an inscription was written in bold italics: *Verba volant, scripta manent.* Words fly away, writings remain.

Italians. A famous quote from an ancient Roman ruler used as an apt motto for a religious bookstore. Even in the simplest of things, my people could find a way to incorporate art, politics, and religion in an ordinary four-word quote.

A minuscule camera tracked our movements. I lifted the heavy knocker and let it fall twice in quick succession. In the distance, a dog barked. Far away, I heard the sound of a siren.

Cole stood with his back to me, a gun in each hand as he watched my six. One gun was equipped with holy water bullets, the other with silver. To my right, Sal kept his hands hidden inside the bell sleeves of his robe. He'd covered his head with his hood, like I'd done, to keep the rain off and conceal his identity.

Above our heads, a light came on. A disembodied voice spoke to us from a speaker hidden inside the cursive motto over the door frame. "*Cosa vuoi?*"

I'd believed Reese was Italian, but the accent accompanying *what do you want* sounded British. And young. I'd had the impression Reese was in his fifties.

"We're looking for a book." I said in English. I gave him the code word title Damon had shared with me to make sure Reese knew not to shoot first and ask questions later. "*Angeli e Demoni di* Dan Brown."

There was a rustling noise, a soft buzz, and the click of a latch. Above those sounds, I heard the kid mutter, "*Che è inutile.*"

Worthless.

Us or the book? I opened the door and stepped in, palming Volante's handle and ready to find out.

A young man in a threadbare white T-shirt and low-slung flannel pajama pants met us in the hall. He scratched his head, making his brown hair stand on end. A beard sprouted here and there along his jawline as though he'd forgotten to shave yesterday. He looked us over with bored, sleepy eyes—a college intern perhaps studying all night for finals?

His assessment of us slowed only once—when his attention fell on Cole. A slight tension entered his aura even though his nonverbal body reaction was too muted for most to pick up on. "This way, mates."

British? Check. Young? Check. Not Reese. Double check.

Definitely not human either. At least not entirely.

My supe radar buzzed as I walked behind him. I sniffed the air and let my new heightened senses take over.

He gave off plenty of human odors but also those of metal, fresh blood, and calculated precision.

A Mercenary demon? This kid?

A visual scan of his body revealed no obvious weapons, but my nose didn't lie. I'd faced enough Merc demons in my time to know how they smelled.

I shot a look over my shoulder at Cole and arched an eyebrow. He gave me a sharp nod, his attention swinging all over the place as he watched for potential attacks. Mercenary demon, check. But not one Cole was worried about.

I relaxed a little. The kid led us up a flight of stairs, bypassing the main library and into a small kitchen. From the other side of the room, an older man wearing a pair of small, round Harry Potter spectacles entered.

Upon seeing us, he stopped in mid-step, adjusted the glasses and seemed to pull himself up a notch. After a pause, he motioned at the kid to get lost.

The Merc demon seemed happy to comply and disappeared the way we'd entered.

Reese touched the cross hanging from his neck. "Kali Sweet, *si presume.*"

I nodded, introduced Cole and Salmad. No one shook hands, but the two priests sized each other up and apparently found each other acceptable.

"You know why we're here," I said.

He switched to English as he grabbed a tea kettle and filled it with water. "You will not find what you're looking for in the Secret Archives."

Cole and I exchanged a look. We came all this way for nothing? "How do you know?"

Setting the kettle on the hot plate, he dug into a cabinet, pulled out mugs and teabags. He brought his haul to the kitchen table and held out a chair for me. "I have been in the archives many times. The documents you seek are not there."

When I refused the chair, Sal sat and folded his hands on top of the table. "You've been in the archives? What are they like?"

Reese's eyes were a washed-out hazel color that had blended in with his olive skin and plain brown hair until now. He drew a breath, held it, and smiled, staring off into the distance. "*Bellissimo*! The art, the industry, the imagination! God-inspired artifacts that man cannot begin to appreciate."

His eyes closed and he swayed as if listening to a Beethoven sonata. He even hummed several bars of something close. "It is like hearing the anthem of the angels, *mio fratello*. Nothing on earth compares to the riches inside the archives."

I had no doubt the archives could fascinate me and many others for hours—days and weeks, probably—there was so much history there. "But my father's journals don't exist?"

Reese's eyes popped open and he raised his pointer finger. "Not in the archives. Your father's texts still exist, as do your mother's oracles, but they are hidden in a very special place inside Vatican City. A place where no one other than the pope has access."

"Oracles?" Adrenaline made my pulse race. "Are you saying my mother was a prophetess?"

He seemed surprised I didn't know this. "*Sì*. Your mother was a Sibyl."

"A what?"

"A Sibyl. A Greek prophetess who uttered divine revelations in a frenzied state."

I knew what a Sibyl was, but the very thought was preposterous. My mother had been a simple, low-level demon with few skills and even less magic.

Cole cared little about my past. He was ready for action. "So where is the book her father wrote?"

"*Appartamento pontificio,*" Reese said.

I was still mentally stuck on my mother being a Seer, but like Cole, I was ready to get the show on the road. Only 'the show' appeared more and more impossible. Surprise tightened my voice. "The pope's private chambers?"

"He, like the heads of the Church before him, store certain documents and heretic texts in a special safe hidden in the papal chapel. The safe exists behind a painting of the Black Madonna of Czestochowa."

Salmad crossed himself. Three times. I have to admit, I added my own *mamma mia* to the heavy pause. Cole was the only who seemed unfazed. "And what makes you believe her dad's stuff is stored there?"

The kettle whistled. Father Reese gave a knowing smile, eyes flashing with a conspiratorial light. "Because her father, John of Patmos, wrote the Book of Revelation based on her mother's prophesies. Prophesies the Church has held a tight rein on since the time of Christ."

22

A familiar ache set up shop inside my chest as images of my parents floated in front of me. This was all too weird and almost...blasphemous.

My parents and sister died because of me. Because I wasn't there to protect them the night the Nocts came for them. Listening to the priest make wild claims about my mother and father felt as if I were dishonoring their memory.

I snorted in disbelief to cover my vulnerability. As Reese made his way to the kettle and poured tea, I asked, "What have you been smoking, *padre*? My father lived in the 1800s and was murdered along with my mother and sister by Noctifectors. The queen of the supernatural court, Queen Maria, set the whole thing up. My mother wasn't a Sibyl demon and *mio papá* definitely did not write the Book of Revelation."

The priest appeared unruffled. He brought mugs of steaming tea to the table for all of us and returned to stand at the sink with his. "How much do you know about your parents, *soldato della notte*?"

Soldier of the night. Wasn't that cute. The priest had given me a nickname.

It had only been a few months since Lucifer had told me I was one of the original sins. I doubted anything Reese said would surprise me more than that, especially since he appeared to enjoy making shit up. So even though I didn't have time for a family history lesson, I decided to give him some rope and listen to his ridiculous theories about my parents. "Go ahead, *padre*. Shock me. What do you know about them?"

The mocking tone in my voice made him smile ever so slightly. "When Jesus cast you and the other sins from Mary Magdalena, you were granted human form. Except in His infinite wisdom, He decreed that all seven of you should not walk the earth at the same time because of the immense damage you could do to humanity. You, the woman you call Maria, and you" —he pointed at Salmad—"were not allowed to live in human form. You were put in purgatory in a soul-only state—a type of stasis—for over a thousand years, only taking the earthly place of one of your brethren as Jesus deemed suitable.

"The three of you did not walk the earth until the seventeenth and eighteenth centuries. Kali, you were born to Goffredo and Rachele, who escaped persecution in Greece centuries before and settled in Rome under new identities. Your father was determined to retrieve the Sibylline Oracles from the Church. He also planned to save the other texts left out of the Biblical Cannons, such as the Life of Adam and Eve, the Psalms of Solomon, and the Assumption of Moses. These texts and others are considered Biblical Pseudepigrapha—religious literature written between 200 BC and 200 AD and falsely attributed to another author, which in most religions renders them suspect. He managed to secure a couple of the texts, but not all, and not the oracles your mother had provided."

Through this Salmad inhaled his tea. He set down the cup, rubbed a hand over his peach fuzz. "All of those texts are or have been hidden in the pope's chapel?"

Reese nodded. "Many have been allowed into mainstream academia, but only to keep those who seek the truth...how should I say it...mollified. As is always the case with the Holy Catholic Church, they allow enough access and information to the public to appear helpful, but in reality, they hide much more than they share. For instance, the Book of Revelation, like the Book of Genesis, gives us only a taste of the truth. Eve's rendition of The Fall would be heresy in today's religious world."

Questions sprinted through my brain, but I was quite simply speechless. Reese had done what I'd asked...he'd shocked me. Not about the Church withholding documents from the public, but about my parents. What else didn't I know?

Reese read the look on my face and supplied the answer. "The revelations John of Patmos transcribed in the Book of Revelation were based on your mother's visions. But there is more than one book. There are, in fact, three in sum. The first one is found in part in the King James Version of the Bible, but the second, which describes the necessary measures to stop the Whore of Babylon and the Beast, and a third, which reveals the whereabouts of a divine army who would assist those on earth to stop the apocalypse are hidden in the papal chapel."

I finally found my tongue. "How is it you know all of this?"

Again he offered me that slight smile. "Because I've seen them."

23

"You've been in the papal apartments? In the chapel?" Sal seemed more astounded by this than by my parents' history or real identities. "I worked inside the Vatican for twenty years and never entered them."

A faint charge of supernatural energy wafted into the room. The Merc demon followed, dressed in loose black clothing that hid an assortment of weapons. "Ready to rock?"

"Yeah." Cole stood, gave the kid a nod. The War demon wanted to get the show on the road and seemed to accept the Merc without any hesitation. "Will you use the catacombs to get in?"

Reese set down his tea. "There are many tunnels under Vatican City. We will use the catacombs and an evacuation tunnel of the pope's. He uses it in case of emergency to access his apartments."

"How will we do that?" Sal asked, echoing my thoughts.

"Four lay members of the *Memores Domino* serve the pope. All four women are friends of mine."

There was a slight pause on *friends*. Because of my recent

encounter with Damon's past lover, I immediately surmised the priest wasn't all that priestly, but who was I to throw stones?

"The two of us"—Cole waggled a finger between him and the Merc demon—"can only accompany you to the catacombs. Who'll watch your back after that?"

"There are many areas under Rome no longer consecrated, demon, even though they house Christian and Jewish remains. Too much unholy blood has been shed above and below these spots over centuries of persecution and secret murders. That is how I've been able to assist supernaturals fleeing the Vatican's secret prison under the city. You and my assistant, here, will be able to accompany us until we reach the papal apartments. My friends there will assist our mission and we will return to you at the entrance with the credos Kali seeks."

"I'm more worried about Kali than the books," Cole said. "Just so we're clear."

The War demon's intensity seemed to surprise Reese, much like my lack of knowledge about my parents. "*Non si preoccupi.* I will keep her safe."

Cole's look suggested that's what he was afraid of. I gave him a slight shake of my head. *Down, boy.* "We need entry and exit strategies. And how are we going to open the safe?"

Reese's face firmed. "I am your entry and exit strategy. I assumed you could open the safe with your...powers of magic."

"I missed the Safe Cracking 101 class in school but I might be able to pull something off. What kind of safe is it?"

"Borgdona recently gifted one of its Zero safes to the pope. It is said to be cracking and fire resistant."

Great. A luxury safe only millionaires could afford. But then, the Church was a billionaire.

I thought about it for a moment. I rarely channeled magic into anything other than protecting myself, but a demon's energy came from the earth. A safe was simply a set of earth's resources molded by human hands. No magical barriers, no hexes, no supernatural energy of any kind.

At least I hoped. "Resistant is the key word. Any safe I can touch, I can probably open."

Reese nodded and bade us follow him. We clomped downstairs, where he retrieved his coat and hat. "The pope takes morning Mass in the chapel in two hours. We'll wish to have the documents and make our exit before then."

Two hours. Cole set the timer on his watch. I set my internal timer.

24

Early European peoples buried their dead in underground chambers. Romans preferred cremation but eventually succumbed to burial when Christianity became popular. Christians believe in the Second Coming of Christ and want their body to be reunited with its soul when that happens.

There are nearly a hundred known underground catacombs in Rome, many used by the persecuted Christians of old to bury their dead in secret. Jews and others used the catacombs and underground tunnels as well.

And they weren't always used for burials. Memorials were performed, persecuted sects hid in the tight tunnels, and even a few pagans along the way used the ground, bones, and blood for performing ceremonies. Numerous passages and extensive galleries depicting the life of martyrs were built on top of each other. The wall graves carved into the ground served as mausoleum, church and art gallery.

Maintenance of the catacombs lies with the papacy.

As with so many other areas, the Church decided which ones to open to the public and which to keep off limits. From the basement of Reese's religious bookstore, we entered one I was sure was not only off-limits but didn't exist even on the pope's extensive map of the underground tunnels.

Flashlights in hand, the five of us moved quickly. Which was a shame once we passed under St. Peter's. The art on some of the slabbed tombs our lights flashed across was medieval but fascinating. Frescos of biblical stories, like the fish and the loaves. Martyrs. The poor, the sick, the holy and not so holy...all were saints here.

Out of the corners of my eyes, shadows hunched and skittered around. The scent of unconsecrated ground teased my nose. Bloodshed. Black magic. Sulfur.

Demons had been raised here. Demons still existed.

I'd already locked in my shields, but it didn't stop the call of the unholy from warming my blood. My demon hummed, reaching out for the magic pulsing this deep underground. The seeping walls carried more than rainwater runoff. They carried the tang of death, and my demon lapped it up.

The energy ebbed and flowed. I shuddered in its wake, usually warm from my elevated temperature, but here, my bones were ice cold. Consecrated tombs pushed me away; others pulled me to them like steel to a magnet. The Merc demon led our conga line; Cole brought up the rear. The two priests sandwiched me, but even their holy auras did little to stop the evil coming up from the ground. It clawed at me, making my stomach churn.

The floor seemed to blur under my feet. Was it the shadows playing tricks on me or the demons who lived here? I blinked and blinked again. Pressure filled my lungs.

Maybe it was due to the smell. The bodies were long past the decay stage, but the bones emitted a certain smell as well. Mixed with the dank, moldy water and wet stone, it was enough to make anyone sick to their stomach.

I covertly checked my companions. None of them showed any distress.

Taking a deep breath, I tried to concentrate on something else. Anything. I turned Damon's predicament over in my mind but found I had no real feelings about it. Odd, but true. I attempted to come up with a reason Ranulf had seemingly changed his stripes and, again, found I didn't give a damn.

Uh-oh. The old Kali—the one who had lived under Maria's firm rule all those years ago—was resurfacing. Once Maria stripped me away from my parents, I'd shut off all emotion. Shut off logical thought. I'd lived to avoid her abuse and make her happy. What remained was a demon with a hard-on for vengeance and nothing else.

The thought overwhelmed me. I stopped short and laid a hand on the nearest wall grave to keep from losing my balance. Big mistake. The evil energy trapped there clawed at my hand, grabbing onto it and charging through my skin.

The shock was so strong I yelped, my voice echoing off the tunnel's low ceiling. I had a vague awareness of Cole and the others crowding around me and asking me questions, but all I saw and felt was darkness. Consuming, heartless and entirely demon.

No, no, no.

My demon danced with the evil, drawing the magic into her like water through a straw. My shields should have kept it out, but they seemed to do the opposite, wrenching it toward me. Absorbing it and begging for more.

Fight it!

My lip curled as I steeled my blood, my body, and my magic. Light flared around my peripheral vision. The scar on my neck from Dru's original bite heated abruptly, as if he'd seared me with a brand.

"Break...the...seal," I ground out between clenched teeth. I tasted blood. Must have bitten my tongue as I spoke. "My hand...from...the wall."

Cole reached out to grab me, but Sal said, "Wait. Look."

With great effort, I ignored the demon rising inside me and turned to where he pointed.

There on the wall, a thousand pinpricks of light glowed forming a wheel pattern that started at my palm and reached outward in all directions. The lights twinkled, giving the illusion of seven rays, each one ending in a rune. Old Latin was written along the lines. Magical symbols were grouped in threes between them.

"I know that symbol." Salmad unbuttoned the upper half of his wool cloak, revealing his chest. The words and runes I'd long ago carved into his skin reflected light from the glowing stones. "It's what you branded me with."

Reese's brows shot up to his hairline. He shone his flashlight on Sal's chest, then read the stones. "The words are similar, but not the same." He moved closer to me and adjusted his light. "*I, master of vengeance, conceal here runes of virtue, power and resurrection. Cleanse this maleficence ground with goodness. Reject any insidious death. I am the way of hope. Vengeance is mine.*"

"What does it mean?" Cole asked.

Reese's flashlight shifted to illuminate my face. His eyes snapped with indignation. "You've been here before," he accused.

The evil was still coursing through my body and his human flesh made me lick my lips. I met his gaze, my demon peeking through without my consent. "Never."

He started at the sight of my demon, but his focus returned to the light show. "Then it could only be Raguel."

The Merc demon, who'd been quiet until now, eyed me with curiosity. "Is that some kind of female disease?"

"No." Sal's tone was clipped. "Raguel, also known as Rufael and Akrasiel, is one of the seven archangels found in the Book of Enoch—another of the cannons not found in any modern-day Bible. He's the angel of justice, fairness, and harmony."

"The angel of vengeance," Reese added, almost in awe as he traced the flickering lights and runes while keeping an eye on me. Dropping his hand, he met my gaze, this time with a smile. "Your heavenly counterpart."

I was going to show him heaven if he didn't step back. Although technically, hell was more like it. "Break. The. Damn. Connection."

Cole responded, grabbing my arm and wrenching. Did no good. I was stuck.

"Sorry about this." He slipped a large silver knife from inside his coat and slid it between my palm and the stones.

Burned my skin, but did the trick, searing the earth magic on one side and my demonic magic on the other. I sank into Sal's arms for a minute, willing my normal, controlled self back online. The churning in my gut continued, but I focused on the one thing I knew would clear my mind of all the other thoughts pounding in my head.

Rad.

Closing my eyes, I reached for him, knowing there was no way he could feel me, but not caring. In my mind, I heard his voice singing to me. My lips tingled with an imagined kiss. I rubbed my hands together, feeling instead the callused skin of his guitar-playing fingers.

Another shiver. This one full of emotions I wanted to feel. The haunting evil in the catacombs receded. Renewed strength flowed into my limbs. "I'm fine," I told the males around me, their auras suggesting they thought otherwise.

Reese gave me a thorough once over, reevaluating his opinion of me. "Divine order."

"What does that mean?" My shoulders ached from a tension not even thoughts of Rad could relieve.

"Raguel brings all angels, even the archangels, to account

for their misdeeds, especially with humans. You, Kali Sweet, bring supernaturals to account for the same."

I needed a drink. I looked at Cole and Sal. Both shrugged.

"Don't you see? You're part of divine order." Reese's smile grew and so did the awe in his aura. "You really will stop the apocalypse from happening."

I huffed, once again shutting the door on my demon and straightening my cape. "Not if we don't get those books, padre. Let's go."

25

Reese led us through a maze. The tunnels grew narrower and deeper. At one point, we were forced to crawl through a tight opening hidden behind a grave marker. The grave was empty and had long ago lost its original dimensions as people burrowed from one passageway to another. I had to remove my cape full of weapons to squeeze through.

That was the spot where Cole and the Merc demon—I never got his name—were forced to stay behind. We were about to pass under St. Peter's Square and into the courtyard.

"Don't take unnecessary risks," Cole warned as he passed my cape through the hole.

Any risk I took at that moment was necessary. "I can't play it safe. The world is depending on me."

His forehead creased and he sighed, bent down to eye me through the small channel. His aura spiked with annoyance. "Right."

He agreed with me, but didn't like it. Making a fist, he held it out. I mimicked the fist and bumped it with mine. His eyes told me what he wanted to say but couldn't. *Hey, it's been nice knowing ya, but you don't stand a chance in hell without me,* so I guess this is goodbye.

"Don't count me out yet, War demon."

"Are you kidding?" He grabbed my hand and squeezed. "I'm betting everything on you."

He smiled. I smiled back. A sinking sensation set up camp in my stomach. No one knew me or my skills better than Cole. If he didn't think I could pull this off, maybe I couldn't.

A lot of supernaturals had doubted me through the years, a certain goddess and my entire handful of human friends as well. I'd proven every one of them wrong at one point or another. I appreciated that they worried about me, but I couldn't stop being who I was to make them feel better.

Nor could I back out of this mission, no matter the odds.

I nodded at Cole, attempting to reassure him, and then faced the priests. "Let's rock and roll."

A new energy permeated the air; the air itself was lighter here, less tepid and cloying. No demons scurrying in the shadows. No dark magic riding the air currents or the dank smell of rotting bones. The next hidden passageway showed me why.

"The pope's private underground subway is on the other side of this door," Reese said. He pointed at what appeared to be another stone slab. "All you have to do is open it and we're in."

The slab sported a fresco of the shepherd and his flock. I lowered my shields and let my hand hover over the stone. After my last encounter with bare rock, I was hesitant to touch it. I scanned the stone with my eyes and even sniffed it. It smelled of earth and men and carried their faint energies—probably those who'd carved the slab from the ground and the one who painted the shepherd's likeness on it. Gingerly, I touched the stone with my fingertips, ready to pull back if anything tried to grab hold.

A slight buzz against my skin made me jump back. Both

priests jumped as well. Embarrassed, I shook out my hand and drew a deep breath. *Focus, Kali. You have to do this.*

Calling up my bravado, I went all in, slamming my hand against the rock and tensing in response to the shock I was sure was going to come.

Instead, the sensation of warm butter slid over my palm. In the far reaches of my mind, I heard singing. Faint, lilting, beckoning. My chest expanded and I saw dizzying lights behind my eyes. Felt the impression of lightness again.

Like a kid digging into ice cream, I placed my other hand against the stone and leaned in, opening all my senses.

Buoyancy filled my mind and body. I floated there, free of pain, free of anxiety.

What *was* this sensation? Where was it coming from? The closest thing I'd ever felt to this was...

An image of Rad's face bloomed. Rad and I making love. Him bringing me to climax over and over again. *You glow, Kali,* he'd said to me.

I felt like I was glowing now, although when I looked at my hands, they were the same as ever.

"Kali?" Salmad eased into my peripheral vision. "What is it?"

I took his hand and pressed it against the stone. He was a *vitium* like me. "Do you feel it?"

Our faces were close and I could see the confusion in his eyes. He strained toward the door, pressing his hand firmly. After a few seconds, he shook his head. "What am I supposed to feel?"

I released his hand, laid my ear against the slab. The singing rose and fell like a wave in the ocean. "Do you hear the singing?"

He mimicked my gesture, placing an ear against the stone. We were face to face, his aura one of expectation. He wanted to hear what I did, but disappointment clouded his features. "All I hear is the sound of dripping water."

I whirled on Reese. "Why can't he feel and hear what I do? We're both original vices. Both hybrids of good and evil. Shouldn't we both be tapped into the energy here?"

Reese only shrugged. "God works in mysterious ways."

After what I'd been through in my lifetime, I meant it when I said, "*Dio cano.*"

God is a dog. A common enough Italian swear, but both priests crossed themselves at my blasphemous words.

I wasn't done. "God's *mysterious ways* are bullshit. I'm not here to play games or get all mystical." I lifted my hands from the door and raised my shields, effectively cutting off the euphoria and the singing. "Let's get moving."

The security system on the door was high-tech compared to the stone itself. A few zaps of my magic and it was disabled. Not wanting to trigger any silent alarms upstairs, I didn't fry the system, only blanketed it with a bit of energy to keep it numb to the door's movements. The slab probably weighed close to seven hundred pounds, but my strength had tripled since ingesting Dru's blood. I moved it easily, then shoved open the door on the other side.

Turning to the priests, I held out a hand. "After you."

As Reese passed me, I noticed him praying under his breath. I figured he was praying that we didn't get caught, but when my sensitive ears turned into his Italian mumblings, I realized he was praying for me.

26

The pope's subway was a modern-day work of art. I caught myself staring at the arched ceilings, gilded statues, and copies of the frescos from the Sistine Chapel. Of course, I'd never seen those frescos in person, but the copies in the tunnel were so good that they could have been originals to me.

The subway rose to ground level in the basement of the Apostolic Palace. More security—all electronic—was quickly disabled. The basement was like none I'd ever seen. Rich paneled walls, thick carpet. A library behind etched glass doors. An art room filled with pagan statues and erotic paintings. I thought of Damon and his Nyx portrait and gave a small chuckle. More from nerves than humor. Everything about my life at that moment seemed surreal.

There was a mahogany-paneled elevator. "This goes all the way to the papal apartments, but Swiss Guards are stationed outside the doors on the third floor. We'll take the servant stairs. My friends will be waiting."

I checked my watch. Only fifteen minutes until the pope went into the papal chapel for Mass.

It wasn't enough time. I wished I had a comm link to Cole, but he'd nixed the idea due to fear the security team inside would pick up on the transmission. Sal and Reese were my only available backups. They would have to do.

I stood at the bottom of the stairs on the northwest side of the building, watching Reese climb to the next level. Sal stood behind me, his energy nervous but eager. I knew the feeling. No matter what happened, I was determined to see my father's writings. Read my mother's predictions.

Reese turned back, a question on his face when he realized I wasn't following him. Sal laid a supportive hand on my shoulder.

I started climbing.

27

Reese's friends from *Memores Domini* were waiting for us. Or at least they were waiting for *him*. On the third floor of the papal apartment, a woman Reese called Nicola greeted him at the secret door to the pope's study with the delighted air of a secret tryst.

Apparently these 'meetings' were somewhat normal between them.

The *Memores Domini* didn't need to know about us or our visit—Reese insisted they be found guilt-free in case our little B&E was discovered, so Sal and I stayed back in the shadows of the stairwell as per Reese's instructions. My priest didn't like the idea of a relationship between his fellow padre and the woman, but it hardly shocked him. Disappointed him, yes, and that made me wonder if Sal had ever had a fling.

I had no problem with staying out of sight. The fewer people who knew about our heist, the better our chances of success.

Nicola was one of the four laywomen who cooked, cleaned, and played secretary to the pope. I sensed sexism but held my tongue. In the overall scope of things, it didn't matter. I wasn't there to pass judgment.

Didn't mean the vengeance demon inside didn't castigate those who'd persecuted my father and mother and misled humans under their charge to believe falsehoods. But I had to stay focused. Doling out justice under the circumstances would only sabotage my mission. The women here chose their place in the order of things. I respected free will whether I agreed with the humans' decisions or not.

During the next hour, Sal and I waited in silence for Reese's return. On the other side of the walls, the pope rose for the day, took Mass, ate breakfast. I opened my senses as far as they would reach, scanning the presences inside this part of the building. Human, human, human. And then...

Not human. At least not in full. Half human and half supernatural.

I had the impression of wet hair, sharp teeth, glittering eyes. A shifter.

Female.

Cat?

She moved purposely but with an aura suggesting youth and a certain...flightiness.

Hmm. Did the pope realize he was entertaining a female shifter? She must have been one of the *Memores Domini*. The irony made me smile into the dark.

The Church had persecuted us, exorcised us and killed many of us. Sent a lot of demons back to hell and thousands of other supernaturals into the fires as well. And here they were with what they considered an abomination to God within their very walls.

Although I couldn't see him well in the dark, my keen eyesight found Sal's outline. His aura sweated...much like he was probably doing. Waiting in the bowels of the enemy's camp was nerve-wracking, no doubt, but if push came to shove and we were balls to the wall screwed, Sal would set loose his inner demon, just like I would mine. I sensed it in him. He struggled with his inner vice the same way he struggled to maintain his inner virtue.

A war neither of us will ever win, will we? The thought sobered me.

Too much thinking. I needed action.

Reese had made sure the door was unlocked, so I placed my ear against it and listened for telltale signs of anything moving on the other side. Heard nothing. Felt no aura. Where was Reese? Had he left us hanging? Was he enjoying himself with Nicola while we sweated it out?

According to the pope's schedule, he would spend the morning in the study beginning at nine a.m. Sal and I needed to get to the chapel soon. If we didn't, we might be stuck in our hiding place until the afternoon. More people would be in residence then, coming and going from the study for meetings and whatnot, reducing our odds of success to nil.

What would Jesus do? I asked myself and then almost laughed.

Jesus wouldn't be in this situation.

But *I* was.

Sal's hand touched my back. "What are you doing?" he whispered.

My answer was to open the door.

28

The study was another example of inspired art, right down to the rug on the sixteenth-century inlaid marble floor and the beautiful Renaissance desk. Tightly packed shelves of books surpassed those Reese had in his bookstore. The smell of old parchment and worn leather accosted me. Faint magical energy did as well. More than one of those books, ledgers and atlases in the pope's collection had been written by a supernatural.

The same held for the art in the room. A soft buzzing emanated from a medieval sculpture on the pope's desk and a large oil painting of avenging angels striking down the devil on the far wall.

The energy made me shiver the same way I had in the tunnels. The entire length and breadth of Vatican City held much more than piety and sacrifice in the name of God. It held remarkable history, dark magic and the answers we needed to fend off the Four Horsemen.

Looking at the paintings, sculptures, and books, a part of me was in awe of humans' creativity. The other part wondered if any of this would survive the coming apocalypse.

As I turned in a circle, taking it all in, Sal hung back in the doorway. The smell of breakfast foods, aging humans, old wood and melting wax drifted in from various places. There was a cake in the oven, robes recently delivered from the dry cleaners and the presence of dedicated, subservient males and females.

Not a bad way to live.

If you liked that kind of thing.

Instead of longing for a similar lifestyle, I wished for my own. I wanted to be back in my castle with Rad in my bedroom and a bunch of rowdy vices hanging out downstairs.

I wanted Maddy to nag me about my wardrobe and steal my perfume. I wanted to be torn over drinking vampire blood and hating the whole queen of the Undead thing. Hell, I even wanted Damon to give me his evil eye and threaten to fire me. The South Side of Chicago had never seemed so attractive.

Now *that* was my kind of living.

Motioning for Sal to follow me, I tracked the smell of melting wax, which, as expected, led me to the chapel.

Enormous cross on the wall? Check. Kneeling bench? Check. Candles, Bible, stained glass windows? Check, check and check.

Most importantly? The Black Madonna portrait.

Must be a small safe.

The painting wasn't the original Black Madonna of Często-chowa, but a reproduction. Still, the Madonna's eyes chastised me as I ran my fingers around her frame, searching for the best way to remove her from my way.

The gold frame was heavy, but not overly so. I lifted a corner and peered underneath.

A clean beige-painted wall met my eyes.

No safe.

Must be hidden. I pressed my fingers around the perimeter, scanned the wall with my senses. Nowhere did I detect a hidden anything. No metal, no steel, only plaster and lath.

I turned to find Sal but he was nowhere to be seen. I ran my eyes over the room, searching for another painting or anything else that might house the safe. When that turned up nothing, I closed my eyes and called up my magic, my heart fluttering like a bird inside my chest. My father had been dead for two hundred and eighty-three years. Could I still find a trace of his energy?

For several heartbeats, I concentrated. I called up memories of my father...tall, with a swimmer's body and a bearded face that was always smiling...

A faint magic in the other room called to me.

In my head, I heard my father's deep, kind voice. *Kali... come...*

I returned to the study, searching for Sal and following the trail of magic. My priest was hidden behind one of the floor-to-ceiling bookshelves, running his fingers along the spines. "Look at this," he whispered. "A whole section of apocalyptic literature."

I stood beside him, eyeing the spines. Most had nothing written on them, but a couple had symbols. I matched his whisper. "There's no safe in the chapel."

Sal's finger stopped and he frowned at me. "Reese was mistaken?"

Or he'd lied. Which meant this might very well be a trap. "Any of these books written in Greek?"

We both scanned the spines, and as Sal laid a finger on the ones he knew to be Greek, I also laid a hand on them, reaching for my father's aura. Dozens of them were interspersed with other texts. A few were written on bark, some carved into shallow stone tablets. When I touched a strangely colored leather-clad journal, magic tickled my fingers. "This one."

Sal gently removed it from the shelf. It was tied shut with several leather cords. The leather was worn down to threads and the pages inside were yellowed and loose as if stuck in helter-skelter.

"What is it?" I whispered, feeling the draw of the words.

"The codex. It's written on papyrus and uses Greek lettering." He pointed to the symbols on the page. "This is the date. 90 A.D."

With shaking fingers, I touched the odd symbols of faded ink. "Does it mean something to you?"

"No, but it does to you."

The bird in my chest beat her wings in a furious staccato. "My father. He wrote this?"

The frown still darkened the priest's face. "Why is it stored here, rather than the archives or safe, as Reese claimed?"

Trap, my instincts shouted.

But we'd been inside the study and chapel for nearly twenty minutes. If it was a trap, why hadn't anyone tried to apprehend us? How would they have known we were coming?

I scanned the apartments again with all my senses. As before, there were people present, but none seemed agitated or focused on anything other than their normal morning duties.

"Reese said there was more than one. See if you can read any of that and I'll keep looking for the other."

Sal nodded and began ciphering, his index finger guiding his focus across the faded and aged papyrus papers. When he turned the page, the paper made the sharp sound of rigidity.

I wanted to scan those rigid papers, touch my father's handwriting. Instead, I went back to work searching for his other codex.

The books were lined up like soldiers, waiting for me, but I couldn't tell anything from the spines alone, so I pulled each one out far enough that I could lay on a hand on the cover. If I felt nothing, I put it back and went onto the next one.

Minutes later, I'd found nothing, and curiosity flared from Sal's aura. Pausing in my ministrations, I glanced his way. Sure enough, he was reading and rereading a certain passage. "What is it?"

His piercing blue eyes left the page and met mine. "This is the third book. The one that tells how to fight the Horsemen and stop the apocalypse."

Bingo. "What does it say?"

Even whispering, his tone held reverence and amazement. "You fight Heaven and Hell with the one group who represents both."

I waited, but he didn't spell it out. "Sal, I suck at riddles. What group?"

His gaze held mine, his awe morphing into consternation and I knew I wasn't going to like his answer. "The Fallen, Kali. You fight the Horsemen with the angels who fought beside Lucifer and fell with him from Heaven."

A cold emptiness invaded my stomach. "Let me see that."

Sal held out the codex, but I couldn't read the Greek lettering. *Lucifer, Lucifer, Lucifer*, my brain chanted, making the unsettling cold in my stomach spread to my chest.

"This means *Lightbringer*." Sal pointed to a set of Greek letters. "Lucifer's name in Heaven."

He continued walking me through the text. Excitement replaced the other emotions in his voice. "It mentions his companion, one named Amo, who fell with him to Earth. I've never heard of that, but much of this is new to me."

Amo. The name vaguely rang a bell. I'd met Lucifer and his witch back around Halloween. Her name was Amy.

Amy. Amo.

She wasn't just a witch.

She was Fallen.

I nearly smacked my head with my palm. I never expected this to be easy, but I sure as hell hadn't expected to need Lucifer's help to stop the Horsemen. "What else does it say?"

"*With flame and sword, Lucifer and Amo will lead an army*

against the bringers of Armageddon. The Beast will rise and the Whore of Babylon will strike it down, cutting off its head and smiting the evil within."

In the hallway, I heard the sound of footsteps. "Time to go," I told Sal.

"What about the other book?"

Shouts erupted and the footsteps started running. A check of their auras told me we were cooked. The trap had been sprung.

I shoved Sal toward the secret door at the back of the study. "This one tells us what we need. Get it out of here and back to Damon."

He ducked through the door, turned back when he realized I wasn't following. "Me? What about you?"

"There's no way we'll make it out if both of us go. I'll distract them so you can get out."

"Kali..."

No longer whispering, I flashed my demon eyes at him. "Go!"

He gave me his sad, weight-of-the-world look and pulled the door shut behind him.

Just as the secret door closed, the study door opened. I whirled around and found myself face-to-face with half a dozen Swiss Guard, several men in black and white attire and a female shifter I never expected to see again.

"You," I said.

Isi gave me her Disney princess wave, smiling, like usual. "Hi, Kali. Fancy meeting you here."

Behind her, the pope strolled in, sizing me up with wide eyes. He was short and plump, probably from too many cakes. "*This* is the one?"

"That's her," Isi sing-songed. "Isn't she amazing?"

The pope's wrinkled jaws and forehead grew deeper lines. His English was refined and lacked even a hint of Italian accent.

"Not much to look at, if you ask me."

Same to you, pops. The Swiss Guard trained their guns on me. Human weapons that could take a chunk out of my hide, but wouldn't kill me.

Mentally, I calculated how long it would take Sal to get downstairs and into the tunnels. How long it would take him to reach Cole and the Merc demon. I needed to kill time but killing the Guard, Isi and the pope would take three minutes, tops, and I'd end up with more humans on my tail.

Raising my hands, I tried to look scared and harmless. "I surrender," I said, lowering my eyes and bowing my head.

The rush of magic hit me right before Maria's scent did. "But of course you do, *mia bambina.*"

My head snapped up and my breath caught. "Maria?"

She was whole—no longer a ghost. The half-succubus ruler was back in flesh and blood and her aura screamed vengeance. "Welcome to my new court, Kalina. I'm sure you'll be right at home here."

29

Maria took me from my family in the late 1800s to be part of her supernatural court. I was nine years old.

My parents thought it would be a good thing, and in some ways it was. For them, at least. They were given titles and land in exchange for my servitude. Safety from The Church's persecution. They believed erroneously that Maria would provide me with a better education than they could and I would lack for nothing.

Between the ages of nine and seventeen, I saw my mother and father once, and by that time, Maria had brainwashed me into being her pet. A pet who tortured humans and other supernaturals for her pleasure. When I fell in love with a young Frenchman she coveted, my doom was sealed.

Rad and I fell in love and tried to hide it behind her back. Our attempts at subterfuge were pointless. Maria knew everything that happened in her court, and she didn't appreciate her pet stealing something she considered hers.

On the night Rad and I were to marry in secret, he never showed up. While I was looking for him, thinking he'd gotten cold feet, Noctifector assassins sent by Maria tortured and killed my family. Rad was gone and I returned home to find my life inextricably altered. My parents and little sister had been crucified, their bodies nailed to the floor, their demons exorcised, their heads removed.

Maria had trained me so well that I knew her every weakness. I channeled the suffocating grief into hate, and went after her with, shall we say, a vengeance. I tortured and killed her in the same manner as my parents, meting out justice for them and my sister.

Only Maria didn't stay dead. Her ghost had put in an appearance before Christmas, right before the other vitiums had showed up at my church. But I'd sent her ghost on its way too. Or so I'd thought.

Staring at my worst nightmare come to life, my instincts took precedence over my shock at seeing her in the flesh. My shields locked into place. Volante tightened on my arm, nearly cutting off my blood flow. "You're dead. I killed you. Twice, I believe."

Her smile was slow and deliberate. One of her fingernails —painted blood-red—pointed upward. "Friends in high places."

Heaven? "You don't have friends."

Her lip curled. "Neither do you. We're two of a kind, aren't we?"

Not even close. I had friends. Not many, but enough. Enough for me, anyway.

And I was going to get home to them. "Who raised you?"

Her red hair was beautifully coiffed, twisted up high on her head. The tall collar of her jacket, embroidered with scenes of a foxhunt, flared around her neck, emphasizing her porcelain skin. I honed in on the pulse beating at the base of her throat where a large garnet hung from a gold chain. She had a heartbeat and a pulse. Definitely alive.

"Your last attack sent me to Heaven, Kalina. The archangel Michael took a liking to me."

There were no curses in my extensive vocabulary to fit that statement. As if I hadn't had enough shocks in one day, my archenemy had returned, claiming an angel resurrected her.

With no warning, my demon growled low in my throat. "Looks like I have another entity to add to my vengeance hit list then."

"Come now, *bambina*, let's not fight. I have a special day planned for you downstairs in the torture chamber."

The pope cleared his throat, gave her a chiding look. She recanted. "The *interrogation* room is what I meant to say. All the supernaturals brought there have the most interesting time, I hear. But none have witnessed what I can do to them." The evil smile returned. "We're going to have so much fun, you and I."

Isi stepped forward. "What about Parker? She said to wait until she got here."

My gut sank even further. "Parker? As in Parker Burkett?" If there was anything that could distract me from the 'fun' Maria was promising, it was that particular Noctifector. "You know her?"

"She's my sister, silly. Well, step-sister, technically. Her dad, my mom." Isi shrugged. "You know how it goes."

No, I really didn't. "The sister you told me about is *Parker*?"

Isi bopped up and down on her toes, exuding pride. "She's a huge fan of yours."

Riiight. "Why is she coming here?"

"She and Maria have a deal to—how did you put it?" She looked at Maria. "*Sideline* Kali?"

Parker, you bitch. I was really going to wring her pretty little neck when I got hold of her. First Maria. Then Parker. I almost grinned at the potential ways I could make both of them miserable.

The pope cleared his throat once more. He wasn't used to

being ignored. "The Noctifectors believe it to be in our best interest to hold you for a period of time."

"For what?" I asked the old man. Might as well find out what they planned for me so I could derail it. "Why don't you just exorcise me and be done with it? That's what you're planning, isn't it?"

He strolled closer, and the Swiss Guard, already at full attention, grew even more threatening.

"Padre," Maria said with a nod of respect. "I would advise you to stay clear of her claws."

My *claws*? I mentally laughed. This scene was so ridiculous, it was surreal.

Volante gave my arm another squeeze, suggesting my 'claws' might not go for his throat, but she might.

He stayed out of reach, circling me with his long robe *shushing* against the marble floor. "I find it more than curious that you can stand in my presence, demon. Why is that?"

I wasn't in the mood to play twenty questions, but if my mental clock was right, Sal had to be out of the building and in the tunnels. A few more minutes couldn't hurt. "For the same reason Maria can."

One of his white eyebrows rose slightly. "She is blessed by the angels. You, I'm afraid, are not."

"Angels-schmangels. We're both original sins cast out of Mary Magdalene by Jesus. We are both virtue and vice. Hence, consecrated ground has no effect on us."

There was a lengthy silence, and then the pope burst out laughing. "You? A virtue?"

He nearly slapped his knee and hooted. Maybe my claws *were* going to find his throat.

While the priest laughed, I eyed Maria. Isi and the guards would be a snap to incapacitate—I didn't want to kill any of them, just get them out of my way. Maria, on the other hand, was the bad penny of the underworld. She kept turning up in one form or another. How many ways could I kill this bitch?

The Beast will rise and the Whore of Babylon will strike it down, cutting off its head and smiting the evil within.

My father's words—or perhaps I should think of them as my mother's—echoed in my ears. I could almost hear my father's voice saying them, sending me a message. A sudden thought bloomed. "You're the Whore of Babylon, aren't you?"

The pope blanched. Maria gave a slight tilt of her head, as if she were reevaluating her student. Her attention slid to the monsignor and they exchanged some kind of unspoken message. Then her gaze came back to me. "Sorry to disappoint you, but it's not *me* who is the Whore of Babylon..."

Always one for dramatics, she let the rest trail off, the inflection in her voice suggesting she expected her student to figure it out.

Games. Everyone wanted to play games with me. Challenge me. I was sick of it. "Just tell me, what is it you want me to know?"

A patient smile. Another glance at the priest. "*You* are the Whore of Babylon, Kalina, and—"

Before she could finish, Parker burst in, a handful of Noctifectors on her heels. "And we're going to make you pay dearly for all you've done."

One thing about Parker, she always brought out the tyrant in me. I let Volante's handle slide into my hand. "Well, then, let's get started."

30

I flicked the tip of my whip at her, let my demon shine through in my eyes. "Who's first?"

"Not so fast." Maria gave one of the guards a hand signal and he disappeared out the door only to return a moment later, prodding a bound and gagged Reese and Nicola in front of him.

Nicola's eyes were wild above her gag. Reese's were apologetic.

I lowered my whip hand. Hostages. That changed everything. "Let them go, and I'll come willingly to the interrogation room."

"You first," Parker said. "Once you're restrained downstairs, I'll personally escort these two out of Vatican City. You have my word."

"As if your word is worth anything."

That pissed her off. The pope stepped in before she could reply. "You have *my* word, as the highest authority in this land. We have no wish to hurt the father and his lover."

"The Church has done nothing but lie, steal, and persecute

my kind. Forgive me if I don't find your assurances any more comforting than Parker's bullshit ones."

His watery eyes sized me up. "Then we are at an impasse."

"Not an impasse," I said. "Reese and Nicola are innocent. They deserve your forgiveness."

Maria snorted. "You're one to counsel forgiveness."

I turned on her. "I will never forgive you or the Noctifectors for murdering my family and taking Rad away from me, and I will never forgive myself for the atrocities I committed under your rule. So here's the thing, I can never make up for the wrongs I committed against those humans, but I *will* defend and protect the humans I can now."

She rolled her eyes. This was getting us nowhere. Maybe a change of tactics.

"Where is your virtue, Maria?"

"My virtue?"

"All seven vices also possess virtue. I've never seen yours. Where is it?"

She reached out and grabbed Nicola by the hair, giving her a hard yank. The demon I knew existed inside her flashed across her face. "I don't have virtue, you pompous little demon. My job here on earth is to make everyone else's life miserable. And take my pleasure while I'm at it."

"Michael resurrected you so you could take back up where you left off?"

Releasing Nicola, she strode forward, putting her face in front of mine. Her dark energy swirled around me. "Why Michael resurrected me is none of your business, and if you don't walk your sweet demon ass downstairs to the interrogation room, I'll personally remove the hearts of these two traitors and eat them in front of you."

As she spoke, the pope, Isi, and most of the Swiss Guard backed up, putting space between us and them. Were they just now realizing what Maria truly was?

All the auras in the room overlapped, crashed, and mixed. The only one who didn't seem afraid was Parker. She eyed me with interest. "You don't want to see these poor innocent people die for your transgressions, do you, Kali?"

Backed in a corner was my least favorite place to be. I turned to the pope. "Jesus must be really proud of you."

He seemed unfazed. "He who lives in a glass house should not cast stones."

Oh, we were going all biblical now, huh? Okay, fine. "'*For nothing is secret, that shall not be made manifest; neither anything hid, that shall not be known and come to light.'*"

The pope's jaws dipped in contemplation. "I do not understand your reference."

Maria made a gesture and stepped back, shaking her head. We were keeping her from her fun.

"Luke 8:17." I waved a hand at the bookshelves. "You're keeping secrets. You and The Church have been hiding valuable information since you began. Controlling what humans think and the ways in which they're allowed to worship. You're in possession of my father's writings—writings that can secure the future of humankind—and yet you refuse to share them. You're the Beast mentioned in my father's writing. But your secrets are about to be exposed."

"Those writings were by a *demon*. The prophecies he wrote were given to him by a demon. There is no truth in them and your parents now burn in hell for their sins."

I swallowed the lump of fury in my throat. What was done was done. I couldn't save my parents. Even if I gave up and went on my own, I suspected Reese and Nicola were going to die, but the risk was worth it. I had to try and save them. "You and the Church have condemned innocents before and you're about to do it again, so let me be very clear, if Father Reese and Nicola aren't released unharmed, that along with Jesus, you'll answer to *me*."

If I couldn't appeal to the pope's or Maria's virtues, then I had to do what I did best...mess with their heads. "I've killed Maria twice before. I'll do it again. And when she's no longer protecting your papal ass, I'm coming after you."

He swallowed hard but didn't break eye contact. The man had a bit more steel than I expected. "As I previously stated, you have my word. I will swear it on a Bible if it reassures you."

That type of oath meant nothing to me, but it did to him. "Do it."

While one of the Nocts grabbed a Bible, I sent Reese a reassuring look. He seemed less than encouraged. The pope laid his hand on the book and recited his pledge that Father Reese and Nicola Giovanni would not be harmed if I went willingly to the interrogation room in the basement.

When he finished, I held out my wrists so the guards could handcuff me. Maria gave me a sly smile, knowing it was a futile gesture and I could easily break the bond, but she also knew I'd comply to save the humans.

Parker removed my cape of weapons, but Volante refused to leave my arm. "Command your whip to stand down," she said.

I did, and Volante reluctantly released me. Parker ran her hands over my body, finding the knives stashed in my boots, the thigh holster filled with holy water, and the gun and bullets Cole had strapped to the back of my shoulder blades. Standing there with nothing but my clothes, I felt naked.

Parker flashed one of her daggers at me. "Remember this? If you don't want another dose of it, keep your head down and your mouth shut until we reach the basement."

She put a black blindfold over my eyes, gave my wrists a tug to get me moving. I did as commanded, my demon laughing.

When we reached the basement, all bets were off.

31

Torture chamber was a more accurate term than interrogation room, although the papal version was high-tech and modern compared to the torture chambers I'd been in during my time on earth.

When Parker removed my blindfold, I'd had to blink several times against the bright lights. The spacious room was...clinical. Almost as white and sterile as the Bridge Institute's infirmary. The difference? This place had the usual assortment of torture equipment: whips, saws, weights, and knives.

A shiny electroshock device sat in one corner next to one of the numerous restraining beds. Pretty sure I didn't want to know what that was for.

"Feeling at home?" Maria swept by me, running her lacquered nails over the hardware. Probably picking out which instrument to use on me first.

"High-end, but lacks ambiance, don't you think?" I sniffed and my eyes watered at the strong smell of disinfectant. It only masked so much. I could still pick out dozens of different blood types that had been spilled here. All of them supernatural.

"Could use some chains in the walls, some skeletons on the floor, and a lot less fluorescent lighting."

She glided over to an electronic set of buttons on the wall and pushed one with her thumb. A wall moved, and a set of chains anchored to steel plates appeared. "Chain her," she said to two of Parker's Noct buddies who'd followed us down.

They seemed hesitant to get too close. One kicked me in the back of the knees. "Move!"

I went begrudgingly and held out my hands for him to unlock the silver cuffs. Burn marks ringed my wrists. The cuffs weren't just silver. They'd been dipped in holy water, and the welts on my wrists testified to the strength of it.

Willingly, I raised my wrists for him to chain me to the wall. "Where's the *strappado*? They didn't forget that, did they?"

The rope and pulley system dislocated the victim's shoulders and was a favorite of Maria's. She pushed a second button, and sure enough, another wall shifted to reveal the abhorrent torture device, complete with a heavy weight to attach to the victim's feet to increase the pain.

"By the way," Maria crooned. "Your friend Salmad, the mad monk, didn't make it far. He'll be joining us shortly."

My heart sank.

Maria caressed the *strappado's* ropes. "I'm reserving this for him. He'll never be able to cross himself again."

The Nocts chained my feet and added a leather belt around my waist that locked into the wall. Tight leather braces were placed over my hands so I couldn't touch my fingers together, keeping me from using my shields. Maria ambled over and struck my face with her hand—a warm-up of things to come.

She used her nails to tear through my clothes, exposing my flesh. Parker handed her a knife, and she cut the pants off my legs, drawing blood each time as she went past the material into my skin. The knife was pure silver, and its bite stung, creating small rivers of blood that trickled onto the floor.

I held my tongue, not wanting to give Maria any satisfaction. Things were going to get worse, much worse, and I had to reserve my energy until I had her where I wanted her.

My demon cried out for revenge. I clamped her down. *Not yet*, I told her. *Soon.*

For the next thirty minutes, I allowed Maria and Parker to take turns at me. Parker held off on using the angel fire blade. I wondered why, but trapped in a prison of pain and despairing over the fact they'd caught Salmad—and, in turn, my father's journal—I cared little about Parker's weapon of choice.

Contusions would heal. Cuts and wounds, too. When they started breaking bones, I couldn't help but resist. Those would heal as well—and yes, they hurt like a bitch—but I would need to be able to run once I turned the tables on my enemies.

Maria kept up a diatribe of insults and sexual innuendo throughout the process. As a succubus, she drew strength and pleasure from my pain. Sinking her succubus tentacles into me, she would spear a kidney or sever an artery and then kiss me passionately as I withered in agony.

The kiss, rather than the pain, made me wretch. Too bad she jetted out of the way before any vomit hit her.

When the guards brought in an unconscious Salmad, they had to drag him across the floor to the *strappado*. One of my eyes was swollen shut, and blood ran from a head wound into the other, so I had a hard time seeing him. Best I could, I inventoried his wounds and his aura. He'd suffered a blow to the head and had a broken wrist, but most of the damage was superficial.

Injuries aside, I hadn't expected him to be unconscious. That made escape more difficult since I was severely injured myself. My injuries healed at a rapid pace, but the number and extent of them kept me weak.

At least Sal was alive. You could grievously injure an original vice, bringing him or her to the brink of death, but as I'd learned recently, killing us was a whole other matter. Yes, I'd done it to Maria, but I'd only killed her earthly shell. She had come back as a ghost and infiltrated several human bodies and one supernatural—mine—before I sent her to the afterlife by sheer willpower and a whole lotta help from my friends. Now, she'd been raised by Michael. Hard to kill? Damn straight.

Maria became enamored with stringing Sal up on the *strappado*, leaving me with Parker. The Noctifector didn't have the experience Maria did, nor did she truly have the stomach for hardcore torture. Her aura had a decidedly queasy tinge to it.

Time to get inside Parker's head and turn the tables.

A large part of torture involves the mind. That's where fear and pain begin before the body's ever involved. The fear of torture is often a stronger emotion than physical sensations, which is why, in the past, I showed my victims the torture chamber and instruments I planned to use on them before I ever touched them.

But my head was as strong as my body. Took a lot to mess with it. And inflicting pain? Bring it on. Nothing my demon loved better. Right then, she was clawing at her prison to break free and clear the decks with Parker and Maria, but I wasn't ready to let her loose just yet.

"Why are you doing this?" I muttered to Parker as she used a scalpel to make an X over my heart.

She surveyed her handiwork and ran her fingers through the blood trickling down my breast. "You don't know?"

Smug. We'd see how long that lasted.

Maria had used Volante against me, wrapping the leather braid around my throat and choking me off and on in an auto-erotic fashion. Poor Volante had resisted, but Maria's magic was too strong to overcome. My throat was sore and speech difficult, but it was important that I confirm my suspicions about Parker's motivation. "Payback for me stealing your boyfriend?"

She laughed, a high, ringing sound that seemed too loud to

my ears. "Stealing my boyfriend? You think you took Radison from me?"

"He was never yours to begin with, so yes, I believe you're a scorned woman wanting revenge."

"Radison never left me or the Noctifectors. He's been playing you all along. His job was to infiltrate your little gang and bring you in."

Now who was playing mind games? "You live in a dream world, Parker."

"Do I?"

We stared at each other for a long moment, and realizing I didn't believe her, she sighed and jabbed me in the ribs with the scalpel. "That *was* his mission. He failed because you seduced him and played tricks with his mind, so I took over." Another jab. "Now I'm commissioned with bringing him in."

Searing misery in my lungs made it hard to breathe. "Which is why...you offered me...the deal."

"The deal you didn't take, but now you're here. Maria's going to help me trap Rad just like she trapped you." Another jab in a different rib. "Which works perfectly. Even as we speak, Rad's on his way to rescue you. Isn't that cute?"

Oh, no. No, no, no.

She licked blood from the tip of the scalpel. "And he's going to offer one hell of a trade."

My demon squealed from my sudden anxiety, and I had to close my one decent eye and take several deep breaths—which hurt like hell from Parker nicking my lungs—to keep the evil monster from blasting out of me.

Thank goodness my lungs were the easiest to heal, from the amount of blood pumping in that area. If Dru hadn't fed me directly from his vein right before I'd come here...

Focus.

"What kind of trade?" I wheezed.

Parker laid down the scalpel and rubbed her bloodied hands together in a mocking gesture. "He's bringing the pope all kinds of trade secrets and information on your precious Bridge Council. Damon, Kirill, Yasmin...we'll know everything about them. Their strengths, their weaknesses, all of it. And then?" She laughed softer this time. "Once Rad is here and has offered all of that in trade for you, we'll exorcise you, throw him in the prison next door, and I'll lead the Order in disposing of the Bridge Council."

"Rad wouldn't betray me."

She leaned forward and slammed her hands on either side of my face. "Yes, he would. I told you, he's the White Horseman. He's brainwashed millions of humans and suckered you into thinking he's a god."

I was naked and bleeding. Three of the fingers on my right hand were broken, my lungs punctured, my neck bruised. I'd suffered a slight concussion from Maria repeatedly banging my head against the wall. The artery in my left leg was shredded and my kneecaps were in pieces.

But never had I felt as wretched as I did at the thought that Rad would betray me once again. I had no doubt he *was* on his way if Parker had told him of my circumstances, but after all the crazy things she'd said in the past few days, I reached for denial and a belief that this was just another of her tricks. Rad had no love for Damon and the Council, but would he turn traitor?

No. I would have seen in it his aura if he were double-crossing me. Double-crossing the Bridge Council.

Would he betray them to rescue me?

Yes. *That* he would do.

My sole purpose in life was the Bridge Institute and what we did to protect and defend humans. Without that, what did I have?

Friends, I reminded myself. *You have friends and a new family. They need you, and they'll help you rebuild.*

I also had a whole new purpose in life...saving the world from the Horsemen.

"What do we have here?" Maria's voice interrupted my thoughts. She held up my father's codex so I could see it. "Stealing from the pope, Kalina?"

Parker left me, crossing the room to get a better look at it. I needed to stall to give my injuries time to heal. As long as neither of them was causing new damage, my body had a chance.

Keeping their focus on the book saved me and Sal from further harm. "That book belongs to me. It was written by my father."

"So I'm told." Maria handled the parchment with careless fingers. "What exactly does it say?"

"You can't read it?"

She didn't like my critical tone. Meeting my gaze, she shoved it at Parker. "Read it."

"I can't read Greek," Parker said. "If it was in Latin..."

"Sal reads Greek." I glanced at the priest, who hung limp and unconscious on the *strappado*. His aura showed signs of life, and he seemed to be coming around. "Splash a little water in his face. See if you can wake him up."

Maria narrowed her eyes at me. Suspicious. "Does this say something about me?"

"Ahh..." Best to play it cool. "Never mind. You don't want to know what it says."

That raised her curiosity even though her face said she still suspected a trick. "It reveals something about my destiny?"

That Maria cared about her destiny surprised me. It presented another tool for me to use against her. "Yours and mine."

She glanced at Sal, back to me. Calculating. Her aura suggested curiosity was getting the better of her. Logic—a foreign currency to her—suggested she had nothing to lose by using Sal to read the manuscript. The two combined convinced her.

"Wake the priest," she commanded.

Parker took out a bottle of holy water and splashed some in Sal's face.

Because of his vice, the holy water sizzled on his skin. He moaned and his eyes fluttered open. They were unfocused, and even though some of his wounds were spontaneously healing, he struggled to stay conscious.

A ruse or had his head suffered more damage than his aura suggested?

I hoped for the first, planned for the second. I'd give him another minute or so to gain strength.

My own was escalating by the second. While Maria and Parker focused on Sal, I flexed my broken fingers and found them partially healed. I drew in quiet, forceful breaths, compelling my heart to pump blood faster. The ribs on my left side repaired themselves in short order. My scalp stopped bleeding. Because of the restraints, I couldn't bend my knees, but the pain in my kneecaps eased.

Maria slapped Sal's face and pinched various places on his body looking for a response. He was fully awake now, but still disoriented. He struggled to push her away but dangling by his arms with a weight hanging between his legs, the insignificant amount of strength he had was quickly zapped.

"Read this text to me," she demanded.

Parker held up the book and Sal's face darkened with understanding. His eyes darted around the room, taking in the situation in a frenzied manner. His aura darkened to match his face.

As if I could read his mind, I saw the memories flashing in

front of his eyes. A different torture chamber in a different century. Maria and her pet inflicting pain and death on him.

His gaze returned to the here and now and landed on me.

He drew a deep breath, focused on my face, and relaxed.

Funny, that. I appeared to be in no condition to help him, but my mere presence ironed out the wrinkles in the corners of his eyes and shut down the fear rolling off of him. Even more ironic was that in his memories of a past torture session, *I* was Maria's pet.

Giving him a weak smile, I nodded at him to do Maria's bidding.

He understood and began reading from the text, halting and slow. That bought us time.

I soaked up the words as greedily as Maria did. The passages didn't always make sense to me. The images my mother saw must have been frightening and disjointed. In my father's hands, however, the odd descriptions and symbolism began to form a picture. A picture that told of hope as well as destruction.

Rather than the complete annihilation of the earth's populations, I saw a transformation. A new world order based on enlightenment. A real savior who would step forward and reunite heaven and hell...

But only if the Fallen won the coming battle.

After a few pages, Maria interrupted Sal and rounded on me. "You said this book revealed my destiny."

Her ingratiating tone made my skin crawl. She didn't see the big picture, only looking for her role in the future.

So be it. I poked my demon, priming her. "What I said was that it revealed *our* destinies. Haven't you been listening? If we don't stop the apocalypse, none of us—human or supernatural —will have a destiny worth living."

She crossed the floor and smacked me across the cheek.

"You demon bitch. I don't care about anyone else. Does it mention me specifically or not?"

"I don't know. I haven't read it."

"You lied?" Her indignation was palpable.

And humorous. "As you just pointed out, I'm a demon. A demon *bitch* to be precise. Of course I lied."

Another slap, her nails scoring my skin and drawing blood. My demon clawed at my chest, a bull waiting to charge the red cape.

Sal piped up. "This book and the Book of Revelation in the Bible mention you repeatedly, Maria."

Her head snapped right to look at him. "What do they say?"

Wanting to extend this conversation, I drew her attention back to me. "Why would God care about you over the rest of us?"

"Because in the end, I'll be the lone vice standing and I will devour any humans that survive."

Sal cleared his throat. "'*And when they shall have finished their testimony, the beast that ascendeth out of the bottomless pit shall make war against them, and shall overcome them, and kill them.*' Revelation 11:7. Many proponents of eschatology believe the Roman Catholic Church is the beast symbolized in the Revelation verses, but in reality..." He paused for dramatic effect. "It's Maria."

Maria seemed at a loss for words.

I wasn't. "And does either book suggest a way to kill her?"

"'*He that leadeth into captivity shall go into captivity: he that killeth with the sword must be killed with the sword.*'"

A sword? Damon's words echoed in my head. "Cut off the beast's head?"

"Yep." Unusual to hear Sal use such a common slang term. He'd been hanging around Maddy too long. "In your father's codex, it mentions the sword that will kill the beast is forged in angel fire. It belongs to Michael."

Wouldn't want it to be any old sword, would we? No, that would make it easy on the vengeance demon. I eyed Parker's dagger. She was staring at it as well. "Does it have to be Michael's sword?"

"Yes."

"Will that stop the apocalypse?"

"No," Sal sighed. But it would make me feel a hell of a lot better to see Maria die."

She hissed, wheeling around and raising her hand to strike him.

"Maria!" I yelled.

Her hand stopped in midair. Seething, she looked over her shoulder at me. "What?"

"Don't you want Sal to finish? Find out what your destiny is? Whether I'll succeed in cutting off your head?"

A humorous laugh parted her blood-red lips. "You know what I want, *bambina*?"

This ought to be good. "No idea."

"Parker?" She met the young woman's wide-eyed gaze. "Bring me a match."

Parker put the dagger away and hustled to do her bidding, giving me a questioning glance as she passed. From a cabinet, she withdrew a box of matches and handed them to Maria.

I didn't like where this was going. Neither did Sal. His focus went to the codex. "That book is holy. Destroying it will not stop providence or divine order."

"Well then." Maria lit a match, set the flame at the corner of the papyrus as she kept her steady, patronizing gaze on me. "It won't matter will it? The only ones who will know what this book says are in this room."

Meaning, Sal, me, Parker, and the silent Noctifectors waiting in the corners were going to die. Well, the humans would die. Sal and I would simply rot in the cold, clinical torture chamber, succumbing day after day to Maria's magic and torment.

Poor Parker had no idea what she'd signed on for, but she wasn't stupid. As Maria's words and their implication sank in, she began backing toward the door. Her Noct buddies registered her fear and looked around for their own way out.

The papyrus was so old and brittle, it caught fire instantly. My heart burned along with its pages. My father's writings. My mother's prophesies. At least I'd heard some of them. As smoke curled from the fiery remnants, Maria dropped the mess on the floor at my feet. "Your last link to your parents," she taunted. "Reduced to waste, just like they were."

Hate consumed me, and then nothing. My demon finally got her wish. Raising my gaze from the burning book, I met my enemy's eyes with cold detachment. "Pick a safe word, Maria."

Her lips curved in a grin. Parker stopped her surreptitious exit. "Safe word?" Her hand grazed the key lock, ready to punch in the code. "What's she talking about?"

Maria rolled her eyes. We were in a room pimped for sadism and masochism. Bondage and torture. Who wouldn't understand what *pick a safe word* meant? "Good help is so hard to find these days," she murmured.

My demon came roaring out, snapping the chains that held my wrists and ankles, and I stumbled, but my previously ruined knees held me up.

Taking a deep breath with healed lungs, I rolled my head around on my neck, loosening it up. As I did so, I stripped off the leather gloves and touched my fingers together, raising my magic. The cool, blue light engulfed me, and the cuffs on my wrists and ankles broke into pieces and fell to the ground.

I licked my lips, winking at Parker, my demon shining through.

She screamed and stumbled, her back hitting the door.

I cracked my neck again and shifted my gaze to the succubus in front of me, purposely stepping on the charred remains of the book at my feet. "It means, Parker, that I'm about to have some fun."

Maria parted her lips and smiled as if she'd been waiting for this all along. Maybe she had. "You can't kill me, *bambina*, but I'll enjoy the dance."

"According to my father and mother, I *can* kill you."

"Not if you don't have Michael's sword."

She had me there. Didn't mean I was backing down.

I stepped forward, my demon tired of the talk and ready for action. Gripping her around the neck, I leaned in and sniffed. The sharp tang of fear and anticipation seeped from her skin. She was scared of me, whether she wanted to admit it or not, but she didn't try to pull away or reach out to strike me. "One way or another, I'll get that sword. You can bet on it."

"The Whore of Babylon," she said in a mocking tone. "Always trading favors."

I struck then, raining down hell on Maria. Before she could react, I broke her neck and ripped her limbs, one by one, from their sockets, flinging them across the room. Blood spurted from the wounds. My demon let loose a howl that shook the foundation of the building.

Parker renewed her screaming and slapped at the keypad. My magic surged, shorting out the electricity and plunging us into darkness. A second later, my supernatural vision clicked in. Sal's aura was to my left. Parker to my right. The Noctifectors huddled in the corner.

Realizing she couldn't escape now that the electricity was out, Parker turned toward me, removing her sacred dagger from her waist and holding it out in front of her. The blade had a slight glow, but she didn't seem to see it. She acted blind.

The blade that had poisoned me. My demon snorted. Blade or no blade, this was child's play—killing a human who couldn't even see me coming. "Oh, *Parker...*" my demon chanted. "Come out, come out, wherever you are."

She whirled one way, then the other, no longer sure where I was. I made my way to Sal and released him from the *strappado*, catching him as he fell. The sound of the machine and chains releasing their weight echoed in the room as I lowered him to the floor.

Parker cocked her head, listening and feeling her way around the outside of the room toward a stainless steel tray that held a stun baton that could shoot two-thousand volts of silver-laced electricity into my skin. I knew because I had one back home.

Home. If my demon got out of here, she wasn't going home. She was going to annihilate the Noctifectors, the pope, and the entire population of Vatican City. Then she'd go to work on the rest of Rome.

At that moment, I didn't care. The past few days—hell, the past few months—had been nothing but one emergency after another. The stress, the confusion, the load to handle everything had built inside me like a pressure cooker. Seeing my mother's prophesies, so carefully written down by my father, being burned at Maria's hands finally blew the lid off it.

Leaving Sal on the floor, I stalked Parker inch by slow inch. She kept her dagger swinging from side to side, hoping to make contact. Her scent had deepened, the fear bringing out something dark and dangerous she probably didn't even know existed inside her—something inhuman.

That darkness sensed me as I neared, and the dagger pointed in my direction. It continued to glow. Angel glow. This was definitely the dagger forged in angel fire and mixed with the pope's blood.

The pope. Maria. Michael. A triangle of strange power I didn't yet understand. I tried to connect the dots but my demon was salivating. *No more waiting*, she entreated.

Vampire speed was impressive. Demon speed even more. Before Parker's heart finished a single beat, my demon reached out and snatched the dagger from her hand. The silver and holy water burned my skin, and my demon screamed, but in the next beat of Parker's heart, I flipped the blade around and sliced open her cheek.

No sense in rushing her torture.

She sucked air and stumbled, tripping over her robes. My demon launched itself at her, taking her down and beating her head and upper body. She had the presence of mind to flip the switch on the stun baton, but I batted it away.

My fingernails dug into her skin and tore chunks from her arms. She screamed. Sal yelled at me to stop. The other Noctifectors both passed out.

I was going to kill her, but I was going to make her suffer first. Not for me, but for Rad and all the other supernaturals she had tormented and killed.

Leave her be.

The words came out of nowhere and slammed into my frontal lobe. My demon shrieked in pain, and my back arched, hands going to my head as if they alone could block Damon's voice. At once, I was terrified and relieved.

Damon. I need you, the virtue in me yelled.

A spear of magic hurled at me. Damon's archdemon magic, bringing with it the smell of wood smoke and dominance. I tumbled off Parker, still gripping my head, and curled into a ball on the floor.

Contain your demon, Kali. Come to the square. We're waiting.

My body spasmed. My brain throbbed. Under my eyelids, all I saw were pulsing stars. I whimpered and rubbed my temples, anything to stop the pain.

Sal's hands gripped my shoulders. My demon cowered inside my chest once more. Damon had scared her once when she'd tackled the vamp Master, Toel Chase. He'd been forced to shut her down then, and no one, besides Lucifer, had ever scared her like that.

On the ground beside me, Parker cried softly. The virtue in me rose like floodwaters, chastising me for losing control with her, a human.

Vaffanculo, I told my virtue. Fuck off. Parker would have scars to last a lifetime, but I didn't feel guilty about it. In truth, I wished my demon had killed her.

Shaking inside and out, I shoved my demon back into her prison. Drew back the out-of-control magic and refocused on my mission.

The codex was lost. I was not.

Neither was Sal. I allowed him to help me up, steady me while I found my balance.

Once I was back in command, I stripped the passed-out Noctifectors, and threw their robes over our naked bodies. Then I went to the sink and splashed water on my face, cleaning it as best as I could from the blood. Sal did the same.

Volante lay on the floor, covered in my blood. I picked her up, stroked her handle. She responded by wrapping herself around my arm. Next, I took Parker's dagger and hid it in the pocket of the robe.

Damon's magic continued to come at me, but with less full-on assault. More soothing, cajoling. He was waiting for me in the square with someone else, and he was impatient. I had to get Sal out of there while the lights were out and Maria was dead. I hadn't cut off her head with Michael's sword, so no doubt, she'd be back one way or another and soon.

I touched the dagger in my pocket. Would it have the same effect?

No time to find out. I sent a mental message to my boss. *I'm on my way. Sal's with me.*

Hurry. Time is of the essence.

Kicking Parker for good measure, I stepped over her body and zapped the keypad with a dose of magic.

The torture chamber's door swung open. Sal and I hurried upstairs. We'd hit the first-floor landing when the lights came back on, and a high-pitched alarm sounded.

"Time to run," I said.

His face was healing from several bruises, but he still looked like hell. I must not have looked much better. "We should put our hoods up," he suggested.

Under cover of the material, we searched for an exit, watching priests, cardinals and staff sprint by us. None seemed concerned about the basement. Instead, they were all headed toward a veranda overlooking St. Peter's Square—the veranda next to the pope's private quarters.

Curiosity may have killed the cat and led to Maria's temporary demise, but I couldn't ignore it either. I stopped a man before he could pass. "What's going on?"

He shook his head, his eyes wide behind wire-framed glasses. "The end of days. Right here in Vatican City." Another shake of his head. "The dragon has arrived."

The dragon? Sal and I exchanged a look. This I had to see.

Our robes denoted us as Noctifectors, so we blended in with the other priests, and no one stopped us as we squeezed through the crowd and made it to the veranda. The crush of men on there was nothing compared to the humans in the courtyard. The sun was up but clouds darkened the sky, casting shadows inside the holy walls and blanketing hundreds of onlookers packed around the circle. I expected the clouds to burst any second and drown everyone.

The humans' attention was focused on the center of St. Peter's. Following their eyes, my gaze landed on a sight that made my breath freeze in my chest.

Sal, too, made a startled sound in his throat. "Who is *that*?"

In the courtyard stood six males, five of them denoting the

points of a pentagram. Magic zipped between them, lighting the ground underneath their feet and rising into the air. It called to my demon, demanding she bow and pay homage to the absolute mastery in front of her.

Legs going weak, I swallowed hard and grabbed onto the railing. Damon, Cole, Alexandru, Shayne, and Rad stood guard at each point around the central figure. A faint angelic glow floated around the center male...the kind I'd only seen once in three hundred years. Without looking at his face, I knew who had come for me.

Lucifer.

32

Sal, having never seen an angel, albeit a fallen one, promptly fainted.

Great. Very helpful.

You must come to us, Kali, Damon's voice instructed. *Quickly.*

I wasn't sure Damon and the others could see me, but the only way I could exit the papal apartments fast was to jump the railing and fall the twenty or so feet to the ground. The fall wouldn't hurt me, but I was damn strung out.

Plus, I couldn't leave Sal behind, and hauling a one-hundred-and-ninety-pound male over the railing with me was going to be interesting. Not because I couldn't lift him and toss him over. He was part demon, like me, and could survive that short of a fall. But he'd already had some pretty intense brain trauma. Could take days to recover instead of minutes or hours and I didn't want to make it worse. I needed him ready to help with the Red Horseman when we got back to Chicago.

If we got back.

The natives were growing restless. The humans watching didn't understand they were looking at Lucifer and five demons, but they knew something big was afoot. Magic is energy, and humans feel energy fields and react to them whether they understand what's causing them or not.

The holy men on the veranda suddenly parted, creating a path. The pope was coming.

I got it, Damon. Just let me take care of the priest lying at my feet.

There was no response, but his impatience drilled through the air like a shout. My demon cowered. I shook Sal's shoulders, slapped his face a couple of times. He remained a limp rag doll in my arms.

"You!" a voice behind me called out. I recognized it as the pope's. "How did you escape?"

"Escape?" The men around me murmured. "Who is that? What is she doing?"

They looked to their leader for answers. I looked at him for something else. Giving him a rude gesture, I hefted Sal over my shoulder in a fireman's hold, grabbed the railing, and rallied my strength.

Blood, magic, vice, and virtue all coiled inside me. Like on top of the Bean in Chicago, I sucked it all in, bracing. "Here we go, big boy."

I jumped.

We hit, and I directed us into a controlled roll. Sal banged his head on the ground, but there was nothing I could do to prevent it. From the balcony and from the human gawkers, a collective gasp cut through the cool morning air.

The first thing I felt was all that magic pouring off the males. Damon's archdemon magic, Rad's Chaos magic, Cole's War magic. Dru's vamp magic was different but just as strong, and Shayne's seemed to be the dullest. Probably because the other four males all wanted to run to me and help me out with an intensity that nearly lifted me from the ground by sheer willpower.

But Lucifer...oh, that magic felt completely different. As it had the first time I'd been in his presence, my brain screamed *danger*.

Danger or not, Lucifer was waiting for me. The others were waiting for me.

They'd come to help me.

I didn't need to read auras to know Lucifer's mood. He was pissed beyond reason.

Why? Why had he come? The only thing that made sense was that Damon had brought this to pass. How, I had no idea.

Lucifer was not a demon; he was a fallen angel. So, while Damon exuded authority, Lucifer exuded preeminence—superiority on a level that made my demon quake in fear.

Lucifer wasn't just king of the underworld. He was *god* of it.

The only way Damon or anyone else could enlist Lucifer's help was to cut a deal. Usually, that involved a soul. Damon was a demon—no soul to trade—so what had he done?

Getting to my feet, the agony I'd experienced during the Maria-Parker torture sandwich flared back to life. Most of my injuries were healed or healing, but I felt like a walking wound. In barely two days' time, I'd been beaten, infected with poison, strung up, and tortured. The night at the Bean, the night at Fierce Warrior Castle, and then a little sadism from Maria and Parker to boot. After the jump and subsequent roll on the ground trying to protect Sal, my body let me know it was damn tired of the rough treatment.

The other reason my body rebelled was due to the memory of what Lucifer had done to me the last time we'd met. As a young female in Maria's court, I'd undergone hideous torture sessions. Her teaching methods involved hands-on instruction that she then commanded me to use on other supernaturals who dared cross her and the humans who had the misfortune of catching her eye. The more pain she inflicted, the more intense the pleasure for her.

And because of her, I knew what deep physical and

emotional pain was, but nothing I'd ever experienced compared to Lucifer's swift and unmerciful punishment inside his girlfriend's ice cream shop a few months ago.

No wonder my brain warned me to run. Brain and body were in complete agreement. Lucifer may have come for me, but I refused to be on anyone else's torture menu today.

Hefting Sal into my arms, I started forward. Lucifer's energy superseded the others' but I could feel the tug of Rad's competing for my attention. Our eyes locked, and in his, I saw his desire, his anger, and an emotion I wasn't familiar with. He seemed ... disappointed.

I looked away. What had I done to disappoint him now?

Left him behind, stupido.

The palm-to-forehead moment passed as quickly as it came. He could be angry and disappointed all he wanted. This was my job, and while I didn't always like the conditions of my duties, I wasn't about to let down Damon, the Council, or the humans I protected because something annoyed me.

In the shadows, the humans surged, pushed back, raised their voices. Lucifer and the others were an unknown entity exuding weird energy, but a female jumping from the pope's balcony was sacrilege. Add to it the fact I had jumped with a robed man in my arms and then came to my feet seemingly unscathed created a sort of panic. They may not have seen the demon in my eyes, but they knew I was evil, regardless of the sacred robe I wore. As I carried Sal toward the pentagram, I heard shouts from the Swiss Guard. The sound of running feet followed. The air carried the smell of weapons and a fearful anticipation.

"Stop her!"

The voice was female, so not the pope. And it came from directly behind me, not from the balcony.

The voice of my nightmares.

Maria.

The damn bitch had revived.

Cole motioned at me to run. He and the others couldn't break formation or something bad would happen. I wasn't sure what, but I could tell from their tense auras and even tenser faces that they were under Lucifer's control. Even if they wanted nothing more than to rush forward and protect me, he held them bound.

How are we getting out of here? I asked Damon.

You'll see, was his only reply.

Fuck that. Maria wasn't going to let me simply mosey out of there like a tourist on holiday. A showdown with her in front of humans wasn't high on my list, but sometimes a vengeance demon had to do what a vengeance demon had to do.

I laid Sal down—he moaned softly, finally coming around —and turned to face my pursuer. Maria was leading the charge, with the guard following on her heels.

"I see you pulled yourself together," I called across the stone courtyard. "Literally."

Her hand shot out, fingers firing invisible but lethal magic at me. I touched my ring fingers to my thumbs and brought up my shields and magic in one swift movement.

"Vengeance is mine," I murmured, ready to deflect her magic and send some of my own her way.

"No," Lucifer said, suddenly beside me. "Vengeance is *mine.*"

With that, he flicked his hand at her. Angelic magic exploded in the courtyard, an intense white light engulfing us. I saw Maria lifted into the air and sent flying backward, knocking the Swiss Guards down like a bowling ball wiping out a dozen pins.

The white light blinded me, and I ducked for cover, throwing myself over Sal in a protective manner.

In the next second, we were both flying.

33

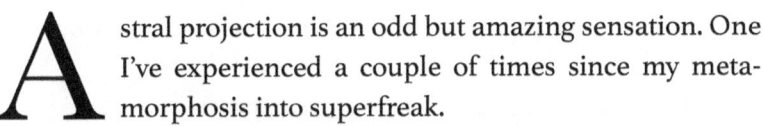stral projection is an odd but amazing sensation. One I've experienced a couple of times since my metamorphosis into superfreak.

What Lucifer did to us was more than simple projection. It wasn't only our astral bodies he projected into Father Reese's bookstore, it was our physical bodies as well.

It felt as though I were catapulted into the air and then sucked through a tiny sieve. Sharp pinpricks of pain ate at my skin. My internal organs turned inside out. My brain, already on overload, completely blanked out.

I landed with a crash in the bookstore, hands still clutching Sal's robe with him underneath me. Guess he took the brunt of the landing, but since he was unconscious, I doubted he would mind. I only hoped his head hadn't received another injury.

Rolling off of him and onto the floor, I groaned. Not because of the red-hot poker inside my body, but because the magic Lucifer had used to transport us through space made me want to throw up.

And since the devil himself was standing over me, having just saved my ass from another pounding by Maria and her minions, it seemed disrespectful to vomit on his expensive leather boots.

My moaning brought a host of attention from the others. Rad got to me first and helped me sit up. He seemed fine. Damon attended to Sal, a touch of his archdemon hand waking the priest from his fear-inspired fainting spell. Cole stood behind Lucifer, keeping an eye on him and me, and I noticed the War demon's hands were hidden. Surely he wasn't contemplating pulling a weapon on Lucifer?

I appreciated the thought. Cole would take on anything, even hell and damnation, to protect me. *Priceless.*

Dru and Shayne hung back in the shadows, both looking as green as I felt after our ride. To my surprise, Reese and Nicola appeared. Reese started to speak and Dru gave him a shake of his head, pointing at Lucifer and putting a finger to his lips.

Reese's eyes widened, but he obeyed, giving me a *glad to see you* nod.

I couldn't say the same. Before this was over, I was going to give him a piece of my mind.

Rad's hands distracted me, running over the few remaining cuts and bruises on my face and neck. "Maria did this?"

"Maria and Parker." Ignoring the look of shock on his face at Parker's name, I used him for leverage to stand, my guts still threatening a rebellion. Good thing I hadn't eaten in a while. "Maria's got some kind of agreement going with the pope. I don't know what it is, but they're on friendly terms. And she seems to be training Parker to take my place in her new court of torture."

Damon spoke to Lucifer. "How is it Maria walks the earth again?"

Sal realized Lucifer was with us and nearly keeled over a second time. Damon's hand on his shoulder kept him upright.

"Michael raised her from the dead," I told them. "She

claims that when I sent her to the afterlife, she went to heaven." I challenged Lucifer with a look. "How is that possible?"

He may have been the angel of darkness, but his aura was all light. He didn't move a muscle. Didn't appear to breathe. The magic oozing from his pores nearly made me high. "My brother, Michael?"

I nodded. Rad didn't like the way Lucifer's magic called to mine and he inched closer, placing a hand on my lower back. His ocean scent grew thick and salty in my nose. "Maria claims I'll need his sword to kill her," I said. "According to my father's book, I'll also need it to stop the Four Horsemen. How do I get it?"

Sal lowered his head. "My deepest regrets, Kali, for allowing myself to be captured and the codex to be burned."

Damon reared back. "The book was destroyed?"

My focus never left Lucifer. "I'll tell you about it later." My demon wanted to grovel at Lucifer's feet and, at the same time, throw herself into his arms. *Bad, bad demon.* "What about this sword?"

Lucifer's black eyes snapped with annoyance. At me or over Michael's actions? He shifted them to Damon. "My work here is done."

He stepped toward me, and I reflexively took a step back, running into Rad's solid support. His hand squeezed my arm, letting me know he wouldn't let Lucifer hurt me.

As if he could stop the god of hell.

"Be still, demon," Lucifer said, reaching out and touching my temple.

Merde. He'd touched my forehead at our previous meeting, using his magic to call up my memories. I knew what to expect from his touch, but it was still a jolt to feel him probe my mind.

My entire body went limp, but I didn't fall. His magic held me in place, turning my bones to air. The last of the aches and pains vanished and my vision went black.

In my mind, he rewound everything that had happened to me and Sal inside Vatican City. When he got to my encounter with Maria and her words about Michael, the mental video slowed. Rewound, played again. In thirty seconds, it was all over.

He broke the connection, and Rad caught me as my legs gave out. A frown pinched the corners of Lucifer's eyes. He gave me a curt nod. "We'll talk again. Soon."

With that he shimmered out of sight.

"Goddammit!" I shouted at thin air. "What about the sword? What about the apocalypse?"

A lot of good it did to yell at nothing. Anger flared low in my stomach and I made a gesture at the spot he'd been a second ago. "*Testa de cazzo.*"

"Kali," Damon reprimanded, but Cole laughed at me calling Lucifer a dickhead. "Testing Lucifer's patience is unwise."

Unwise? You bet it was. I was fed up with doing the wise thing. "What about my patience? I've been sent on a secret mission, beat up and tortured by my enemies and those who were supposed to be my allies, watched my father's work burn, been flung through space like a rag doll, and not *one* of my questions has been answered! I don't really give a demon's dark ass if Lucifer wants to reprimand me or not. I've had it. I'm done."

It wasn't a lie. I started to stomp away—who knows where I thought I was going—and a wave of lightheadedness washed over me. I made it past Dru when the floor tilted and I tumbled into a bookcase. My hands grabbed at the shelves, searching for purchase, and books went flying. I tripped over my feet, then over the fallen volumes on the floor.

Dru and Shayne grabbed my flailing arms and righted me, turning me around to face Damon.

"Are you done, now?" he asked, as though I were a two-year-old throwing a tantrum.

I hung my head. "I need to eat. Blood protein's low."

Dru jumped at the chance to help me out. "Where's your bedroom?" he asked Reese.

The priest lifted one brow and Rad all but knocked everyone aside to save me from the big, bad vampire. He grasped my arms and took me away from Dru and Shayne, then asked Reese, "The kitchen. Do you have any meat?"

Twenty minutes later, I feasted on a steak, pasta, and some delicious crusty Italian bread. Nicola made me a cup of espresso and served it with a slice of cake for dessert, keeping her distance, but watching me with observant eyes nonetheless. Before I'd eaten half the cake, I fell asleep at the table.

I woke sometime later, immediately tensing, ready for a fight, until I realized I was in a warm bed with Rad spooned around me. For a second I thought I was home at the church. That it had all been a bad dream.

It was so natural, so comfortable to be wrapped in his arms. To feel his hard, lean body next to mine. The past few days of hell came back in a rush. No dream, but they seemed like a distant memory.

I snuggled closer and felt his arm tighten around me. "You're safe," he whispered in my ear. "Go back to sleep."

Familiar, this. It had been nearly three hundred years since Rad had said the same thing to me while hiding our relationship from Maria until we could marry and escape Italy for France. A long, long time, but it still felt right.

Safe. How many times in my life had I ever felt safe?

The word echoed in my brain until I did, indeed, fall back to sleep.

34

Against my protests, we returned to Castle Fierce Warrior that night. Our plane was fueled and ready and Damon didn't bother going to the actual castle. That pleased me. I didn't know what had transpired between him and Valentina after I left, but I assumed he'd stayed away from her if he wasn't saying goodbye.

We boarded the plane and took off. As it taxied down the pot-holed runway, I glanced back at the castle. Valentina stood outside on the parapet, her long gown billowing out behind her as she watched us go.

We're not done, I thought at her even though I knew she couldn't hear me and Damon could. I was in a bitchy mood, even after eating and sleeping nonstop for twelve hours. It felt good to be pissy. I felt stronger being a bitch. *You come near me or mine again and I'll send you to hell.*

I expected a mental reprimand from Damon, but I didn't get it. In fact, he pretended he didn't hear my threat. He appeared distracted, and since we both had plenty to worry about, it came as no surprise he was ignoring me. I would have ignored me too.

Damon had his way of dealing with stress. I had mine. I needed to hit something. Hard. But I'd have to wait until we got back to the Institute. Cole had promised me a training session that would work out my anger and frustration.

Rad had promised a similar workout, although his would require me naked.

I wasn't sure which I was looking forward to more.

I slept again for a couple of hours. When I woke, the gang was all watching me. I checked the sides of my mouth for drool, ran a hand through my hair. "Was I snoring?"

"Nah," Dru informed me. Outside, the sky was bleak, and the Atlantic was dark and choppy. We're just waiting for you to finally tell us what happened."

I'd begged off giving them the full story, but Sal insisted I tell it since he'd missed crucial moments between Maria and me. Apparently, my grace period was over.

I gave all the details and answered questions. Many were answered with "I don't know." I told Damon that Reese had lied about the safe behind the painting and that we'd found the book in the pope's personal collection. Sal didn't argue about Reese lying.

I'd seen Damon give the man a hefty sum of folded bills before we left. Still feeling bitchy and self-righteous, I pinned Damon with a hard look. "That worthless SOB almost got us killed."

"Let's not sweat the small stuff," he replied.

Small stuff? Betraying Sal and me was small stuff? My mood didn't improve with that pronouncement.

After another half hour of bug-the-hell-out-of-Kali with questions, I reconsidered Lucifer's approach to mind reading. Sure was a lot more efficient.

In the end, I decided what they needed to know could be condensed into one sentence. "I need the sword, and we need the Fallen. Period."

Everyone got quiet after that. The rest of the trip, I looked out the window and speculated about Maria, Michael, Lucifer and whatever Damon had done to get the angel's help in rescuing me.

The temperature in Chicago was three degrees below zero when we landed. Quiet, cold, dark...the city welcomed me home and my surly mood lifted.

Detective Moreno was waiting for Damon. He pulled my boss aside, and they spoke in low voices. Dru kissed my cheek before climbing into his car and driving away. The rest headed for the Land Rovers in the parking lot, ready to head to the Institute.

I grabbed Rad's hand and waved at Damon. "We'll catch a cab and meet up with you later."

Under the weak lights in the parking lot, Damon's face looked unusually pale. His eyes went flat, hard. He said something to Moreno, who glanced my way and then walked away.

Damon paused, seemed to be thinking things over. "Be in my office by oh-three-hundred for a formal briefing on your next mission."

Even his voice sounded off. His aura pulsed with jealousy. Mr. Uptight was back with his military time and mission talk. Lovely.

I almost responded with a snarky comment, but I suddenly felt awkward—like a teenager caught making out in the back seat of a car. "Three a.m., I'll be there."

He left without sparing me another look.

My church home was deserted when we arrived. Here I thought we'd have to sneak upstairs and lock the door. "Where is everyone?"

Rad paid the driver and helped me out of the car. "The Institute. Kirill wanted them out in case he succeeds in luring the Red Horseman here."

"But we'll need all of them to fight him, especially since I don't have that damn archangel sword."

"Let's worry about that later."

He ran a hand under my hair and caressed my neck. A shiver ran down my spine. An empty house and Rad all to myself. I was suddenly feeling a lot better.

I laid my hand on the stone, felt nothing out of the ordinary coming from the house. Even with my demon metabolism and elevated body temperature, I was cold. I unlocked the door and ushered my boy-toy inside. "I want to forget about everything for a while."

He was already unbuttoning my coat. "Deal."

We made it to the living room, him steering me to an over-sized chair in front of the fireplace. While he removed my boots with slow, deliberate movements, skimming his hands over my thighs, calves, and ankles, I snapped my fingers, and a fire flared to life in the fireplace. The church was a castle made from stone. Chilly by nature, but that night, it was downright cold.

Knowing Rad, I'd be warm in no time.

I wanted to question him about Parker's charges. See how he reacted when I told him she claimed he was the White Horseman. Kneeling before me, he raised one of my feet and kissed my ankle, making all thoughts about Parker evaporate. "Promise me you'll never run away again without telling me where you're going and why."

"I didn't run away. I was ordered on a mission. I can't promise it won't happen again in the future. It's the nature of my job."

His lips worked their way up my shin. "I nearly went out of my head with worry."

This line of discussion made it hard for me to concentrate on the good stuff. "Did you win that award? The one you went to Hollywood for?"

"It's on the mantle."

Duh. I hadn't even noticed. "There are three of them."

"Favorite Song, Favorite Album, Favorite Band."

"Damn. That's good, right?" The odd little glass statues reflected the room's light, each one tapering to a point like the flame of a candle. "They're...cute."

"Cute? The Chaos Demons win three People's Choice Awards and you think they're cute?"

"Amazing, wonderful, fantastic. Just like you."

He gave me a rakish smile. "Stop changing the subject." Raising my leg higher, he used his tongue to lick the back of my knee. I nearly came right there. "Promise."

"Promise what?"

"No more sneaking off and putting yourself in danger."

"Top secret missions are extremely rare, but they do happen. I'm not going to make a promise I'll have to break."

"Rare." He lowered my leg and trailed his lips along the top of my thigh. *Devil take me.* "Good to know since I don't think I can handle your unexplained absence on a daily basis."

I sunk my fingers into his hair, jerking his head back so I could look him in the eye. "I'm sorry. I thought Damon gave you and Maddy some kind of explanation for my disappearance."

He arched a brow and shifted back. "Did you just apologize?"

Using my hold on his hair, I urged him forward and lowered his head again, encouraging him to resume his torturous seduction. "Yeah. So?"

He licked my skin, paused on his journey to the spot between my thighs. "This may be a first. Forgive me if I take a moment to enjoy it."

"*Non si preoccupi.* It won't happen again."

We both laughed.

"You did what you're trained to do, but this time was an exception. Damon's using you."

Mentioning Damon was a definite mood killer. "How so?"

"I think you know."

So done with this conversation. Leaning forward, I put my breasts in his face. "I thought you were going to make me forget the past few days. Not up to the challenge, Chaos demon?"

He cupped my breasts, gave the nipples a squeeze. A promise of things to come. "I lost you for two-hundred and eighty-three years. I won't lose you again. Damon can go to hell if he thinks he's going to come between us."

"Can we stop talking about him already?"

Why was talking about my boss bothering me so much? I wasn't sure, and I didn't want to think about it.

He searched my face. "We need a pact. I'll share the details of my work and you'll share the details of yours."

"You're not going to let this go, are you?"

He spread my legs and lowered his head, licking between my legs. I gasped and he lifted his head, a grin spreading those wicked lips of his. "This is the way it works. The only way it will work, if you don't want me to take out Damon. Agreed?"

I'd do or say almost anything to have his tongue back where it had been. "Whatever you say."

He sucked a nipple into his mouth, flicking his tongue back and forth over it. I moaned and he released it. "Say it, Kali. Say, 'I agree, Rad.'"

Damn. "I agree."

The grin returned. He dipped his head between my legs once more, and the contact of his hot tongue nearly brought me to the edge right there. Then *il pistolino* pulled up.

So close. "Don't stop," I begged. "Please."

Hands on my hips, he yanked me forward, forcing my knees farther apart. Anchoring his hands under my ass cheeks, he held his mouth just over my slick wetness. "Promise."

Gah. Growling in the back of my throat, I surged my hips. "You are so going to pay for this, Chaos demon."

His laugh was low and sexy. His tongue entered me with deliberate strokes, bringing me to the brink once more before he straightened and arched a brow.

Fine. I was too desperate to be held accountable for my actions at this point. "I promise. I promise. Now, get on with it already!"

Rad stood and undressed, leaving me in full lust mode, intensifying the ache between my legs. His gold eyes watched me watching him. First, the sweater came off, revealing hard abs and a thin trail of dark hair disappearing under his waistband. The boots and jeans went next, revealing his penchant for going commando.

When he was done, he lifted me from the chair and turned us around so he sat and I straddled him. I found his mouth, giving him a frantic kiss as I arranged my pelvis over his hard length. His hand stopped me, fingers slipping into my soft wetness. "I missed this."

"I was gone a whole twenty-four hours."

A finger slipped inside. "Too long."

Too long? I was about to explode and he was talking about too long? "I need you. Now."

"You were a very bad girl to leave me," he whispered against my skin, another finger slipping inside and finding the spot that throbbed for him. "You probably should be punished."

I moved against his fingers, building a rhythm. But the damn male grabbed me by the waist and held me still. A victim under his onslaught. "God, yes. Punish me. But do it quick, or I'm going to kill you."

He laughed and kissed me at the same time, removing his fingers and letting me come down hard and fast on his shaft. The impact made us both gasp.

I rode him hard and fast until the combination sent us into a mutual orgasm that literally shook the walls of the castle.

"Holy hell," he whispered, breathing as heavy as I was in the aftermath. "I keep thinking it can't get any better, and then you go and blow my mind all over again."

I blew *his* mind? I was lying on his chest, limbs weak as a newborn kitten's. Every cell in my body hummed with joy. I wasn't sure I could even form words but some popped out. "*Ti voglio bene.*"

He stiffened, and I thought *oh, shit. What did I just do?*

"Did I hear that right?"

In Italian, *I love you* sounded even more serious than in English.

Too late to take it back.

I didn't want to take it back. I didn't know how to respond, however, so I sat up and started to scoot off his lap, avoiding his eyes.

He stopped me. "First, you say you're sorry. Now you tell me you love me. This is quite a night."

The cockiness in his tone lifted my head. His aura was filled with passion, love, respect. He wasn't mocking me. He was truly amazed.

In that moment, I fell for him a little harder. I had to save the world, if only for the two of us. Selfish? You bet your damn ass. "For me ,too."

Kissing me tenderly, he ran his tongue around the inside of my lips and stroked my back with his hands. Coming up for air, he locked his gold eyes on mine. "I love you, Kali. I've always loved you."

For the first time in days, I felt happy. Hopeful. Whatever was coming, I was going to fight it tooth and nail. Rad didn't want to lose me again, and I sure as hell wasn't going to lose him.

35

A while later, Rad went to work in the kitchen, banging pots and pans and whistling as he cooked a meal. The homey scent of spaghetti sauce with basil and oregano filtered into the living room, where I slept on the couch, waking at the banging around. I was starving.

The castle's security alarm went off, but it was only Maddy and Arman. Wrapped in a blanket from the couch, I let them in. Maddy threw her arms around me, shrugged off her coat, and headed to the kitchen.

Arman gave me a nod, averted his eyes, and trailed after her.

I went upstairs to shower and dress, and when I returned, Di and Neve were setting the small table in my kitchen for a late-night dinner. We all hugged—initiated by me, in fact—and Di opened a bottle of wine. Neve had brought cookies and cannolis, and I snuck a cannoli while she slapped my hand away.

The spaghetti was simple but delicious. The best meal I'd had in forever.

"So what's the latest on Ranulf?" I asked Maddy and Arman. I wasn't ready to dive back into Armageddon talk.

"Nothing," Maddy answered around a mouthful of pasta. "You said to wait until you got back and we'd hunt him together."

"You actually listened for once?"

Arman snorted. "I wouldn't let her go after him."

I tipped my wine glass at him. "Good call. Whatever's up with the pack leader can't be good."

Neve asked a few questions about Ranulf, and I filled her in with what I knew, but that was small potatoes compared to what Arman knew. The kid may have been a cat shifter, but he idolized the alpha wolf. "There has to be something wrong with him. He would never throw away all the work he's done to socialize shifters into modern America. Never."

I wanted to agree, but his recent actions said otherwise. Actions always meant more to me than words.

Di swirled the wine in her glass. "Like what? What could be wrong with him?"

None of us had an answer. Rad pushed his plate back. "Possession?"

"Like as in demon?" I asked.

He shrugged. "Just a thought. Demons can possess shifters since shifters are human as well as supernatural."

I hadn't thought of that. Demons generally took the easy road. If they wanted to possess something, humans were the simplest vessel. A shifter's internal struggle with their supernatural side made them less appetizing. "For what reason?"

Another shrug. "To throw you off the track of the actual demon?"

Maria. Hmm. Not a bad theory. I'd never faced that scenario before but that didn't mean it couldn't happen. "But why? Ranulf's kill mimicked Lamir's. What kind of demon would mimic another demon and use a shifter to throw me off track?"

"Someone who doesn't want to get caught," Di said.

Maria, I thought again.

At least she was otherwise occupied at the moment.

My phone rang. Caller ID announced Dru. "Master Vamp, what can I do for you?"

Rad's eyes narrowed. Not a fan.

"I heard there's a party at your place. I'm hurt you didn't invite me."

Vampires and politics. I covered the phone and glared at Maddy. "Did you text Dru?" I whispered.

She gave an indignant scoff. "No."

How did he know we were all here then? Did he have someone watching my place? "Is Brianna outside?"

"I felt it important to guard my queen in light of recent events."

"Without my knowledge?"

"Stake me for being concerned about your wellbeing."

"Don't tempt me."

"Are you going to invite me over or what? Last supper and all that."

"What?"

He chuckled. "The Last Supper. As in Jesus and his apostles sharing a meal before the big crucifixion scene. Surely you're familiar with it?"

"Of course, I know that. What I don't understand is the context. What does that have to do with a spaghetti dinner at my place?"

A *tsking* sound came through the phone. "I thought perhaps you were gathering those closest to you for a final meal before taking on the Horsemen."

Ah. "It's just dinner, Dru. Would you like to come over?"

Rad came out of his chair, anger radiating off him in waves. I lifted a hand. *Down boy.*

With irritated reluctance and a tight jaw, he resumed his

seat. Dru's voice was chipper as he responded. "I would like that very much."

Poor vamp. For all his wild parties and political maneuvering so that every supe in Chicago owed him a favor, he was much like me. True friends were numbered on one hand.

We said our goodbyes and I faced the music...namely my insanely jealous boyfriend. "He's lonely," I told Rad. "And worried."

Rad shook his head, downed the last of his wine. "He wants to get laid."

That too. I looked at Maddy. "Is Cole still seeing Brianna?"

"Dude, he's totally in love with her."

Di winked at me. "Invite him over."

"I don't think that's a good idea," Maddy said. "The skank's not good enough for him."

Dru's last supper comments rang in my head. I texted Cole. What if this *was* the last time all of these people in my life were gathered in one spot? What if this was the last time we enjoyed ourselves?

"Cole's not particularly choosey," Rad added, refilling all of our glasses.

Maddy heaved a dramatic sigh. "You don't get it. Bri's in love with Dru. She's just toying with Cole."

Rad took his seat, eyed the dark liquid in his glass. "And who is Dru in love with?"

Everyone fell silent, gazes landing on me. Rad's gaze did as well. My cheeks heated.

Maddy sat back in her chair and rolled her eyes. "Oh, please. Dru's always been in love with himself."

Neve and Di chuckled nervously. I picked up my plate and took it to the sink. I didn't want to spoil the mood, but Rad had already done that for me. "Cole in love with a vampire. Wow. Hell froze over, and no one told me."

A few more chuckles. I switched the subject again, getting

really good at this skill. "Do you have any leads on where Ranulf might have gone, Arman?"

I had more on my mind than the local pack leader going psycho on us, but it was nice to think about something, well, *normal*, rather than the end of the world.

Arman transferred his weight to one side in order to dig a piece of paper from his jeans pocket. "Underground tunnels in uptown. A friend of mine says a new werewolf with powerful magic is running with the rogue shifters not far from here, but he stays under a bar called The Green Mill."

He handed me the paper with the Mill's address on it. The notorious Mill, once a Capone hangout, had tunnels under it leading to other buildings.

If I never went in an underground tunnel again, it would be too soon.

"Why is he running with rogue shifters on the South Side? Why didn't he leave town if he knew we were after him?"

No answers from my young companions. "That cop's been hanging around," Maddy announced.

"Moreno?"

She nodded. "Everywhere we go, he's there. He's stalking us or something."

Would it break privilege to tell them he worked for Damon? "Ignore him."

I turned the conversation back to Ranulf, and we discussed him until Dru arrived, bringing Brianna inside with him. Cole followed shortly after, but as I suspected, he grabbed a bottle of wine and some glasses and hustled Bri away from the crowd. Rad stuck close to me but was civil for a jealous Chaos demon. Hell truly had frozen over.

The other *vitiums* arrived. I once again had a packed house. As big as the church was, it felt small with all those bigger-than-life entities inside it.

Talk turned to the Horsemen and Armageddon. Once

again, I found myself explaining what had happened in Rome. Shocked stares from Neve and Di. Twenty questions from the others. Sal said little, his aura suggesting he still felt guilty for getting caught and allowing Maria to get her hands on my father's writings.

"Didn't you say there were *three* books? The one in the Bible, the one Maria burned, and another?" Maddy asked. "Why didn't you go back for the other one?"

"No chance. Once I broke Sal and I out of the torture room, we had to leave asap."

Seraphina sat on the breakfast bar, playing with one of her short, slender knives. "A shame, really. You were right there. You should have found a way to get back into the pope's quarters and retrieve it. We need that intel."

My hackles rose. Rad slipped his fingers under my hair and rubbed the back of my neck. I took a deep breath and calmed my stinging pride. "You don't understand, Sera. There was no way we could do that. Our rescue team was waiting."

Akimo turned to Shayne. "So that's where you went."

"And a bloody good time it was, mate." He leaned against the sink, grinning from ear to ear. "Lucifer is one badass motherfucker."

A chorus of voices rang out. Even Bronwen woke up from his usual stupor. "*Lucifer?*"

Suddenly wishing I had a trap door to escape through like Capone, I nodded at the dozen pairs of eyes on me. "Yes, Lucifer. He was...instrumental...in getting us out."

Alexandru sat opposite of me, his Master vamp energy calling to mine. "Like every other male that comes into contact with her, he seems quite taken with our vengeance demon."

Yeah, right. Lucifer had hated me since the day I walked into his girlfriend's ice cream shop.

Rad's hand tightened on the back of my neck. The glasses on the table wobbled on their bases. His voice was low and controlled. "He's a snake in the grass. I'm surprised Damon would call on him. Doing business with a snake will only bite us in the ass down the road."

I couldn't have agreed more, but I had the feeling Rad wasn't talking about Lucifer.

Dru gave him a challenging grin, understanding Rad's dig. "Snake or not, a deal with the devil is still a deal. Breaking it would be...futile and dangerous."

Okay. Time to wrap this up. "Dru, do you have any leads on Ranulf?"

"Why would I?"

"Because you know everything that happens in this city."

He took that as a compliment. "He's gone rogue, as I suggested to you the other day. Back to his beastly nature."

"Arman says he's staying in the tunnels under The Green Mill. Can you put some scouts out and confirm that?"

He gave me a graceful bow of his head. "Your wish, my queen, is my command."

Silverware clanged against the dirty plates. Rad's warm ocean scent went chilly. I rubbed his hand under the table, soothing. "Thank you."

"Forget Ranulf," Maddy said, picking up her knife and slashing at the air. "What do we do about the bitch that won't die?"

"Maria?" I sighed. What *was* I going to do about her? "There's nothing to be done except everyone watch their back-side. She may try to get to me through you guys again and I can't guard all of you."

"We'll be careful," Neve said, but the inflection in her voice told me she remembered all too well her last encounter with Maria.

Sal stared at the floor, pensive. I'd been meaning to ask him about Parker's dagger. "Hey, Sal? What you said about Michael's sword...will it kill Maria if he's the one who brought her back?"

He glanced up, looking nervous at being put on the spot. "About that. I sort of...lied."

"Lied about what exactly?"

"None of the biblical canon or your father's writings said anything about Michael's sword being the weapon that could kill the beast. I said that because I wanted to see Maria's face."

His eyes dropped to the floor again as if embarrassed.

"I like you more every day," I told the demon priest.

His gaze returned to mine, relief evident. "You're not mad?"

"That you lied? Hell, no. The look on her face was priceless. But now I'm wondering what else you lied about."

"Nothing." He shook his head. "I speak the truth to you. Always."

I believed him. He was one of the few who told me the truth, whether I wanted to hear it or not. "The sword is quite powerful, though, yes?"

"Yes, but..."

"Powerful enough to kill her?"

He thought for a moment. "Those who stand behind Michael receive his and the sword of heaven's protection. Those who get in his way are cut down by it."

"Why would he resurrect Maria?" Dru asked.

Why, indeed. "If he resurrected her, he has a plan," Sal said. "And the pope is in on it."

There was that triangle of power again. A triangle of heaven, hell, and humanity. "Michael raised her, and it must have to do with starting Armageddon."

The priest looked as troubled as I felt. "After the apocalypse, paradise will return to earth, according to the Bible."

Heaven on earth. "But what's in it for Michael? Surely he's already living the good life in heaven, isn't he? Why care about returning earth to paradise?"

Sal had a theory, but he held back and shrugged. "The angels, like God Himself, are a mystery."

Tell me about it.

"But this sword," Maddy said. "If it's forged in angel fire, won't it kill anything, human or supernatural, regardless of who's wielding it?"

Sal nodded.

She gave me a sly grin. "Where do we find that puppy?"

Good question. Outside of Lucifer, if there was any source that might know, it was in my office at Sweet Investigations. "Let's go see what Sophie can tell us."

36

Sophie was the best thing since God created mankind. Only JR had created Sophie.

The other *vitiums* had wanted to accompany me to Sweet Investigations, but I'd begged off, telling them this was simply a fishing expedition and my small office wouldn't hold all of us. That was sort of true. I wanted to ask my genius computer what she could find out about Michael and his sword.

That was Plan A. Failing that—which I assumed would happen because, let's face it, Michael wasn't just going to hand over his precious toy—Plan B would be to continue as planned. There had to be another way to kill the Horsemen and stop the apocalypse. My father had believed the Fallen could do it. All I had to do was figure out where to find the Fallen and how to get them to help us.

Piece of cake.

Maddy went to SI with me. Rad stayed behind, claiming he had an early morning meeting with a new producer anxious to sign the Chaos Demons to his label after their recent awards. Parker's father had been Rad's producer up until he'd broken their engagement and left the Nocts. Being a free agent with his band hadn't hurt Rad in the least. If anything, the breakup with Parker and dissolution of the band's contract with her father had only given them more exposure.

I thought about Parker's threats in the torture chamber as I drove. I hadn't mentioned them to anyone, and I was glad Rad hadn't thrown Damon and the Council under the bus to save me.

But I wondered if Damon had done something worse. I was going to find out at our upcoming meeting.

Maddy and I arrived at Sweet Investigations around two. Di came, as well, after dropping off Neve at her place. JR was inside doing geeky computer things. I preferred not to know what he did when I wasn't there, although the worst I'd ever caught him doing was playing some Star Wars role-playing game with a half-naked female on the screen as his side-kick.

I tossed my coat on the couch in my office and relaxed a notch as Sophie's cultured voice came from hidden speakers above my head. "Hello, Kali. What may I assist you with this morning?"

Sophie knew everything, from trivia about my beloved White Sox to world history starting with the beginning of time. I had a long list of questions for her. "What can you tell me about the archangel Michael?"

I should have set tighter parameters.

On the dozen or so screens on the walls of my office, pictures of the angel flashed on and off. Some were traditional paintings, some were modern-day renditions. Nearly all of them showed him with a sword in one hand and an angelic light around his head. Sophie gave me his history. "A high-ranking angel of the Lord who fought against Satan and his followers and defeated them in heaven. He is spoken of twice in the Old Testament and twice in the New."

Like Wikipedia on steroids, she went on for the next twenty

minutes serving up trivia about Michael. Maddy hung out for about five minutes before heading to the kitchen and coming back with microwave popcorn and a Coke.

"The name Michael means 'Who is like God'. The angels in heaven used Michael's name as a battle cry in the Great War of Heaven against Satan. Michael is the host of the angels and of humanity."

Sophie went on to give us information about Michael based on writings from the Christians, Jews, Catholics, Eastern Orthodox, Jehovah's Witnesses and others. She quoted scripture, listed the shrines dedicated to the angel and described massive art and literature tombs dedicated to him.

Michael, it seemed, was a god in his own right.

When she got to the Latter-Day Saints and their beliefs, I interrupted her. She'd given me all the human theories, but still hadn't answered one fundamental question. "Sophie, is the archangel Michael good or evil?"

For the first time since JR had installed her at Christmas, the computer didn't immediately answer. After a long pause, she said, "I'm sorry. I do not understand. Please rephrase the question."

I'd stumped Sophie. Maddy and I exchanged a look.

I rephrased. "If I encountered Michael, would he be friend or foe?"

Another pause. "Michael is a holy force against evil. You are a demon."

I was also a virtue. "So you're sure he's my foe, even though I was touched by Jesus."

"Michael carries the sword of truth and justice to protect humans and slay demons. He is the Chief of the Order of Virtues. You protect humans and carry out justice. You are a demon."

A one-word answer would have sufficed, and I still wasn't clear whether Michael would kill first and ask questions later or possibly be on my side. But Sophie's explanation got me thinking about the sigils in the catacombs. About the angel of vengeance. I'd have to ask her about that later. "This sword of Michael's. What can you tell me about it?"

The on-screen pictures changed to a variety of swords. Sophie continued her lecture. "Humans depict a flaming sword of power and strength cast in blue light. A two-edged sword, one side representing truth, the other side, justice. The blade, handle, and guard often show sigils and words of holy origin."

"Will the sword kill a Horseman?"

The screens went dark. "I'm sorry. No data exists for that question."

Story of my life. "Is there any way to kill a Horseman?"

The screens came back to life with depictions of the Fab Four. "The Four Horsemen of the Apocalypse will cleanse the world of sin. The dragon will be defeated by Michael and his army of angels, who will strike down Satan and remove demons from earth. No documentation found referencing *killing the Horsemen.*"

None needed. Sophie had just confirmed my suspicions.

Screw Michael's sword.

Lucifer and his army of Fallen were my only hope.

37

When I arrived for my meeting with Damon at the Institute, his office was once again empty.

I wasn't in the mood to chase him around the building so I texted Cole. *Is D with you?*

It took a minute for his response. *No.*

Curt. Hmm. He was still hanging out with Brianna. For some reason, that annoyed me. *Where are you?*

Busy.

An answer but not an answer. Definitely with the vamp chick. I wondered if I should tell him what Maddy had said about Bri being in love with Dru. My demon voted yes.

I decided against it.

It felt wrong not to tell him, but he was having such a good time with her, it felt wrong to lay the truth on him. I'd have to ask Di when I saw her. The goddess of love would know what to do.

If Cole wasn't there, Damon wouldn't be in the gym. Damon usually ate in his office and never went into the media center unless it was to do research.

Sitting at Damon's desk, I closed my eyes and concentrated

on him, opening up all my senses to see if I could detect his presence. I didn't want to call to him mentally in case he was indisposed, like taking a leak in the restroom down the hall. All I wanted to do was test my internal tracking system.

As I deepened my meditation, my astral self began pulling away. It tugged at my physical body, floating out from my center and making my fingers twitch. It felt good...like flying, except without the pain Lucifer's version caused.

Problem was, it felt too good. Astral projecting to Damon's location could be more embarrassing than talking to him while he was taking a leak. All I needed to do was pop in while he was showering or something. The image of him naked in the shower doing things to himself flooded my mind.

No! I was startled, and my astral self snapped back.

Sweat broke out around the collar of my shirt. I cleared my throat and blinked several times as if that would clear away the mental picture.

It didn't. I got up, paced the room, and fanned myself. What the hell was wrong with me?

If I was a shifter, I'd think I was in heat.

Forget tracking him with my senses. I left the room and headed to the media center.

Damon wasn't there and I was almost relieved. I needed to talk to him, but I also couldn't look him in the eye at the moment.

Deciding I could clear my head in my apartment, I took the elevator to the third floor. Just seeing Damon's closed bedroom door across the hall made my clothes feel too tight. I marched to my door and used magic to unlock it. The door behind me leading to Damon's room creaked open.

I didn't want to look, and I didn't have to. Instead of Damon's wood scent and impatient boss-man vibes, Kirill's aura hit me.

I turned, and he raised a finger to his fat lips as he quietly shut the door.

"What's wrong?" I whispered.

"He's sleeping."

Sleeping? Damon never slept. "Is he sick?"

Kirill's lips tightened and he motioned me to follow him away from Damon's door. When we were a sufficient distance down the hall, he shook his head. "I can't find anything wrong with him, but he's off his game. He hasn't been right since you two came back from Rome. What happened there?"

Valentina. I feigned ignorance. "I got beat up a couple of times and discovered Maria's back, but nothing out of the ordinary."

Kirill frowned, truly stumped. He didn't even seem surprised about Maria. Guess it was getting harder and harder to shock any of us. "Why didn't he tell Yasmin and me about your trip?"

"I wasn't aware he didn't tell you."

"He's acting strange."

Ya think? "There's a lot on his plate right now with the apocalypse and everything."

"Still..." He tapped his chin. "Something's amiss. His magic...it's different somehow. I can feel it."

Maybe it wasn't Valentina after all. "It doesn't feel different to me."

"You're not an archdemon."

"What? My deadly sin decoder ring doesn't let me into the clique?"

"Sorry, no." His tone turned superior. "Archdemon magic is distinctive. You can feel it, yes, but not the way *I* feel it because I'm also one."

I'd felt plenty of Damon's magic in my time. The latest bout at the castle had left a lasting impression. "Any luck with Pestilence?"

Kirill's face went from superior to annoyed. "He refuses to see or talk to me."

Damn. "Keep trying, okay?"

"You don't get it, do you?"

Of course not. I was just a simple ol' vengeance demon. "Kirill, you're an archdemon. Your magic is exceptional, isn't that what you just told me? Keep trying. Pest will come around to your incredible charms."

He was so easy. His face morphed yet again, this time to one of self-confidence. "I'll get back to you."

He left, and I padded quietly to my room. At the doorknob, I stopped. Damon would never blow off a meeting with me to sleep. Something *was* wrong, and I needed to find out what.

I knocked softly on his door, got no response. Laying my hand on the wood, I tuned out the endless questions circling my brain and the growing sense of unease in my chest. A wave of Damon's protection magic rose from the floor and mingled with mine, exploring, testing. Was I friend or foe?

The magic took its sweet time deciding. Impatient, I held still, allowing it to access whatever it wanted.

Demon, it whispered. Then...

Angel.

The word hit me like Lucifer's magic—hard, impenetrable. True.

Virtue and vice, the voice continued. *Holy evil.*

Holy evil was accurate. Holy hell on a stick was more like it. I jerked my hand back and frowned at the door. My vice was a demon, but my virtue was...

An *angel*?

My brain stumbled over the word. *No way.*

Reese's words now overrode Damon's protection magic. *Don't you see? You're part of the divine order.*

Heaven and hell. Good and evil. Angel and demon.

Damon's door opened. The archdemon blinked at me,

standing there in pajama bottoms and naked from the waist up. "Kali?"

"Hey." I stammered, shifting my weight and trying not to look at his well-muscled chest and its smattering of curly black hair. "We had a meeting. At three, remember? You weren't in your office, and Kirill said you were sick. If you want me to come back later..."

Stepping back, he motioned me into his apartment. I hesitated, remembering our last encounter alone in his private quarters. "Wouldn't you rather talk in your office?"

With a sudden move, he pulled me into the room. Shutting the door behind us, he gave me one of his intense gazes and backed me against the door. His magic and his aura surrounded me, heating my skin and making my stomach flutter.

He stared down at my lips. "I'm sorry, Kali."

The intensity of his eyes had nothing on the intensity of his magic. It circled me, taunted my own magic, running seductive fingers over the prison bars of my demon's cage. "For what?" I squeaked.

Then he did something I never expected.

He hugged me.

"I never should have let you enter Vatican City alone."

"I, ah, wasn't."

"Without me," he said the words against my temple. "I should have been there to protect you from Maria."

His arms were a vice around my chest. I patted his back a couple of times and tried to figure out how to extract myself. "You wouldn't have gotten any farther than Cole. I assume you were able to enter with Lucifer because he performed some kind of spell to protect you and the others."

Damon dropped his arms, stepped back, and looked at the floor. He shot a hand through his already mussed hair. "Lucifer..."

He retreated into his bedroom. I didn't need to be an archdemon to recognize he wasn't himself.

"Damon?" I followed behind him, disregarding the intimacy of the room. "What about Lucifer?"

"Nothing." He waved me off, standing in front of a window facing the lake.

"You called him, didn't you? Offered a trade so he'd help rescue me. Why? I would've gotten out on my own."

Silence.

"Come on, Damon, I deserve to know."

"Valentina betrayed me. Us. She figured out our visit wasn't just so I could show you off to the European branch. Although she wasn't sure what you were up to, she assumed correctly it involved breaching the Vatican."

"So it wasn't Reese who betrayed us, it was her."

A tight nod. "She sent Isi to notify the pope you were coming."

Bitch. I tried to lighten Damon's mood. "We nailed it, didn't we?"

He gave me a questioning look.

"Our little ruse. She bought it, and her ego demanded she get back at us."

"I fear she would have betrayed us anyway."

Of course, she would have. "Then I'm doubly glad we screwed with her mind."

A frail smile broke through. "When I found out you and the others were walking into a trap inside Vatican City, I couldn't sit by and do nothing."

"Cutting a deal with the devil was a little extreme."

He sighed, heavy and full of self-derision. "I should have put more faith in you."

Never thought I'd hear that. I searched for a proper response. "After my performance in the dome, I'm surprised you didn't."

"Me, too."

Again, I found myself at a loss for words. I needed to say something to release him from his guilt. "It was good you came for me. My demon was just getting started when you interrupted her."

He continued to stare out the window. "Do you know what I wanted to do the first time I saw you?"

A part of me didn't want to know the answer. He gave it to me anyway. "You were so damaged. Beyond anything I'd ever seen in a demon, and I've seen some severely damaged ones." He touched the window pane, his broad fingers creating steam against the cold glass. "I wanted to protect you. To repair the damage Maria had done. You were so fragile under that tough exterior. So...humanlike. I didn't understand it, but I wanted to mend what she'd broken inside you. What both she and Radison had broken."

The words were hard to listen to. The conviction in his voice was even harder. "It was never your job to fix me, Damon. Or to protect me."

He continued as if I hadn't spoken. "So I hired you to work for me. To become an enforcer where you must put yourself in danger every fucking day."

I wasn't sure I'd ever heard Damon swear. "It's what I do."

The hand on the window curled into a fist. "I throw you into the lion's den with every assignment." He faced me, agony distorting his features. "And then I pray to God you'll come back."

This was too much. Everything inside me wanted to run away. Wanted to erase the distress on his face. Times like this, I either throw punches or reach for my snark. "I always come back, don't I? You know me, I'm one stubborn-ass bitch."

One side of his mouth quirked and disappeared so fast I almost missed it. "The end is coming, Kali. Promise me something."

Promises, promises. Did every male in my life enjoy torturing me? "Anything for you, boss."

"I need to leave. Soon. While I'm away, I want you to be in charge."

I gulped. "In charge of what?"

He waved a hand. "The Institute. The Council."

A nervous laugh escaped and I applauded, then made like I was flicking sweat off my brow anyway. "Phew. Good one. You had me there for a moment."

Nothing in his expression changed. He wasn't joking.

"You can't be serious. Where are you going?"

"I'll talk to Kirill and Yasmin. They'll accept my decision."

The hell they would. "Where. Are. You. Going."

He faced the window again, his reflection distant and hazy. "While you're in charge, join forces with Alexandru. He knows what to do. Merge the Institute with the Vampire Nation and Lucifer's Fallen. But watch your back with Lucifer. Dru you can trust. Never trust the devil. If the Fallen fall again, you and Alexandru will be the only chance humanity stands against Michael and his army."

Now I knew Damon was smoking demon crack. "Damon, you're scaring me. What the hell is wrong with you?"

His eyes met mine in the window reflection. Sad. Doomed. "Lucifer will meet with us at sunrise to plan our defense. I'll call you when he arrives."

I was more confused now than I had been when I entered his room. I crossed the floor and laid a hand on his shoulder. Awkward, but necessary. "Damon, talk to me. Tell me what's going on with you and Lucifer. If you've made a suck-ass deal, I'll get you out of it. I know his girlfriend, remember? I have leverage. I can threaten her. I'll...I'll...find a way to sic Maria on her if Lucifer doesn't want to negotiate."

He stiffened under my hand. "You have no leverage with Satan. None of us do. A deal with him is ironclad."

"What deal? What did you promise him?"

Facing me once more, he touched my face, running a finger down my cheek. "The time has come for us to pick a side. Who will you fight for, Kali? The angels or the demons?"

"I fight for humans. So do you."

His hand dropped to his side. "Not anymore, I'm afraid."

"Damon." I took a step back, my voice low and concerned. "What have you done?"

He smiled a joyless smile. "Made a deal with the devil. A deal neither of us can break."

38

Shit rolls downhill. I seemed to be at the bottom.

Whatever Damon had promised Lucifer, it was my fault. He'd done it for me.

I drove through the streets of Chicago, my mind a salad spinner of ideas. Damon never showed emotion outside of annoyance and irritation. He *never* cursed. Aside from his deal with the devil, there was something else causing him to act so weird. A sure bet Valentina had her hand in it, whatever *it* was.

Therein lay the problem. I didn't know what had happened to Damon after I left Castle Fierce Warrior. I didn't know what deal he'd negotiated with Lucifer on my behalf. Without answers to those questions, I couldn't form a solid plan of attack against either.

The quiet time in the car calmed my nerves. It did little to calm my mind. I kept hearing Damon's protection spell whisper *angel* in my ear. I drove past Sweet Investigations and considered asking Sophie if it were true. Pointless, that. She'd already told me I was a demon.

When my mind started playing the same soundtrack for the

third time, I turned on the radio. Muse was singing about an uprising, and I sang along.

The music was interrupted by a news story. I wondered who else was listening at four thirty in the morning.

Officials report gangs on the South Side clashed around two this morning. Rioting broke out in South Deering and a group of Polish-Americans from Archer Heights descended on Morgan Park and set fire to cars, homes and the property of several Irish-Americans. Officers responding to the attacks and riots were driven back. SWAT Teams and the National Guard have been called in. Sixteen people are reported dead. Forty-nine injured. No arrests reported yet. Officials have no comment and eye-witness accounts give little insight into the motives behind these senseless attacks.

Lovely. Sounded like another Horseman had arrived.

War.

The South Side is a big place, and within its borders is a lot of ethnic and economic diversity. The cliques of different ethnic groups are no different here than any other big city. Conflict between groups is nothing unusual. During my drive, I hadn't seen the rioting because I'd headed north.

I needed to refocus on the Horsemen. Instead, I found myself wandering farther north. Toward the Master vamp's house.

Damon had said Lucifer would arrive at sunrise for our discussion. That gave me two hours. It was a long shot, but I had the inclination that Dru knew what had happened between Lucifer and Damon. Even if he didn't know the specifics, he might know enough to give me clout in that meeting. Better yet, he was an ally I could count on. Damon trusted Dru and so did I. He had his faults like the rest of us. He also would willingly throw his hat in the ring with me for no other reason than me asking him to.

I might not have leverage with Lucifer, but I did with Dru. He wanted something from me that no one else could give him...the ability to turn the Undead Nation into a preternatural superpower. How many times over the last few months had he insisted that together, we were unstoppable? He was right, and that's what scared me. I didn't want to be unstoppable.

And without Damon to rein in my demon on the off chance she got so high on Dru's plan she cut loose? Armageddon would be child's play.

My arrival at the House was unannounced, throwing the servants into a tizzy. A Queen garnered respect and there were protocols to follow even if the staff secretly hated me. They showed obsequiousness and proper reverence and I tried to do the same to them.

The minute I stepped through the entrance, the calm I'd found in the car evaporated. Vampire magic suffocated me and I was suddenly angry and upset all over again. Not at the vamps, just in general. The world was ending, humans were getting hurt and killed by the dozens, my boss was 'going away' and Lucifer was about to show up on my doorstep. He was apparently my only hope to fend off the Horsemen and Armageddon.

Throw in Maria's return and Parker's simple existence and I was a ball of fury.

I needed to hit something. Too bad I hadn't gone rounds with Cole earlier like I'd planned.

I was escorted to Dru's office, and my presence was announced. He rose from his desk and came forward to kiss my cheek. His normal lust magic sizzled over my skin. "You're upset. Trouble with the Chaos demon?"

He wished. "What do you know about Damon's deal with Lucifer?"

His aura went from lust to cautiousness. "Perhaps we should sit down. May I offer you a drink?"

I grabbed his wrist before he could walk away. "Tell me."

His gaze dropped to the hand restraining him. Breaking free

would have been easy, but he held still. "I know nothing that can help you dissolve their contract."

"But you know there *is* a contract between them."

He sighed. "There is."

I knew it. "What does the contract involve?"

"That I don't know."

"Damon thought I couldn't get out of Vatican City and none of you could offer assistance, so he called on Lucifer."

"I didn't realize Damon knew Lucifer until the deal was already done."

Neither did I. "I didn't need help, but he could have sent the other *vitiums* in to create a distraction or something. Why go to such an extreme?"

"You were in greater danger than you realized."

"How so?"

Finally, he broke away from my hold, running a hand through his hair and down the back of his neck. "I don't know the details. All I know is that Damon believed the European Bridge Council caught wind of what you were doing, and they were prepared to stop you if you made it out of Vatican City alive."

I paced over to the couch. "That bitch."

"Who?" Dru asked, coming up behind me.

"Valentina. She and Marco are not loyal to the Bridge cause. The opposite in fact. They're using the Bridge as a cover to train supernaturals and send them out to manipulate humans. I beat every one of their elite warriors to a pulp and I threatened her when I discovered she was messing with Damon's head. She had her hooks in him, if you can believe it."

"Love is a messy thing. It can turn even an archdemon into a ninny."

"Val was looking to take me out of the picture so she could have her way with him and bring him back into the demon fold. She warned the pope I was coming."

Dru went to his built-in liquor cabinet and poured us each a shot of bourbon. "The vampire you brought to his knees in the dome that night pledged his allegiance to our House several hours later."

I accepted the bourbon, downed it. "Smart male. But he's in Italy. He won't do us much good there."

"On the contrary." Dru edged closer, his eyes warm and comforting. "He's here at the House. For a certain exchange of information, I granted him sanctuary. I believe you'll find him a wealth of knowledge about Valentina and Marco's plans for European domination. He's waiting for you in the conference room."

The first bit of good news I'd had all day. Hell, all week.

The bourbon burned. The vamp blood in my veins burned as well. I was suddenly hot and Dru was entirely too close. "That won't help me with Damon's fucked-up contract with Lucifer."

He sipped his liquor, eyeing me over the rim of crystal glass. "Damon knew what he was doing. You do him a disservice by not honoring his choice."

Males and their honor. "I don't believe his choice was made willingly. He told me he's no longer on the side of humans. That's not Damon. He would never break his oath to the Bridge and humankind in order to save me."

I sounded like Arman defending Ranulf. The thought bothered me.

Dru brushed my hair from my shoulder and touched the faint silver scar on my neck left behind from his teeth. The blood under my skin rushed to the surface. "How do you know? Perhaps Damon was tired of fighting his baser nature. Perhaps he was ready to embrace being a demon again."

Dru was baiting me. "That was your theory about Ranulf, too."

He shrugged, his eyes dancing with mockery. "I'm a one-trick pony."

"No, you're not. You want an excuse to give in to your baser side, so that's what you see in others."

His thumb rubbed the pulse at the base of my throat. "And what do you want, Kali? The world is about to end, and here you are worrying about an archdemon who can't be saved. Isn't there anything else you'd rather do?"

His blood gave the siren call to mine. My body was already burning with need. The need to scream, to cry, to fight. Now it fought against his magic and his Master vamp entreaty. "Tell me what you know about the contract and I'll make it worth your while."

Shocked, he retreated ever so slightly. "You would sleep with me to save Damon?"

"Not sleep with you. I'll help you with your quest to exult the vampire nation over other supernaturals."

A second passed and then he chuckled. "If we survive Armageddon."

"We'll survive."

He studied me. "How can you be so sure?"

"You're going to help me manipulate Lucifer."

"Is that so?"

I was desperate. Time to go all in and appeal to Dru's baser nature. "The only way to predict the future is to hold the power to control it. You and I hold the power. We are, in fact, the two most powerful creatures on earth at this moment—outside of Lucifer and the Horsemen. But our capacity for absolute power lies in our solidarity. We work together and we might just be unstoppable."

Ever the politician, he couldn't resist the sound of that. Exactly what I was counting on. "Power corrupts. Isn't that what you're always preaching?"

"Power corrupts, evil corrupts. What do you care? It's the

end of the world, Dru, and you're looking for a reason to let the monster inside come out to play." I stepped closer, flashing my demon at him. All war is based on deception. "Be evil, Master vampire. With me."

My challenge sent his magic on a rampage. He dropped his glass, letting it shatter on the floor as he grabbed me and pulled me to him. The move crushed my breasts against his chest; our hips ground together.

He lowered his lips mere centimeters from mine. "Don't offer what you're unwilling to go through with, my queen."

"Oh, I'm willing, Master." Bluffing was a forte of mine. "Damon is leaving the Bridge Council and has elected me to take his place."

Letting that bit of news sink in, I dropped my glass to join Dru's on the floor and raised my wrist to his lips. "I offer my demon blood to make you stronger, faster, better, and I swear to you and the Undead Nation on that same blood that I will elevate vampires to a status becoming their magic when I take over the North American Bridge Council. You and I will be partners, Dru, and we will run the Council and the Undead Nation our way."

His eyes snapped with the conquest. "If, and only if, I tell you what I know about the contract between Lucifer and Damon."

"You already told me what you know. This deal hinges on you agreeing to help me get Damon out of the contract."

I waited for his answer, his aura flooding me with lust and desire. His magic as well. If I got out of there in one piece, it would be no small miracle.

But I could, and would, handle him. It wasn't my finest hour, lying to him, but I'd do whatever it took to save Damon. I owed my boss that much.

Act first, apologize later. I'd keep my word as best I could with Dru, but I'd never be able to give him everything he wanted.

His desire overcame his misgivings about sincerity. He kissed me, long and deep, sealing our deal.

I held still and waited for it to end, and yet, somewhere along the line, something snapped inside me.

His tongue teased mine into playing. He drew back and plunged again. My legs went weak, my arms went around his neck. He cupped my ass cheeks and lifted, encouraging my legs to go around his hips.

My demon laughed. I ran my hands over his shoulders, ringed his neck so I could feel the solid thickness there. The lack of a pulse.

I tightened my hold. Or rather, my demon did.

Tightened it, in fact, until I was choking him.

He broke my grip, a new surge of power emanating from him. "Like it rough, do you?"

I didn't like it at all. But my demon did. She jumped him, taking him down with a howl. He fought her, but she was strong. Flashes of Parker cowering under me filled my mind and made my demon grow wilder.

The fight I'd been itching for happened. I beat on Dru. He beat back.

Mostly, I suspected, in an effort to keep me from killing him.

I fought my inner demon as well. It did no good.

"Vampire," Dru finally yelled at me as I circled him with a piece of glass from his now broken coffee table. "I command you as your Master to stop."

My body arched and froze. The vamp blood inside me sat up, clicked its shoes, and saluted.

That's what brought me back to reality. Combined with the virtue wrestling inside me with my demon, the two managed to throw her back into her prison cell.

Dru saw me change. He took a few cautious steps forward and gingerly took the glass shard from my hand. We were both bleeding, and the smell of his blood was like the finest wine calling to me. I licked my lips as my legs folded under me, and I sat down heavily on the glass-strewn floor.

"I'm so sorry," I whispered.

He sat next to me, put an arm around me. "No apologies. That's the best row I've had in ages."

His touch sent a wave of lust crashing over me, and I jerked away, horrified at how close I'd come to losing control. I might have killed him.

Hell, I'd tried to kill him.

Needing some space, I splayed my hands on his chest and tried to shove him back a couple of feet. I hit an unyielding mass—he stayed put, and angry, I shoved again, harder.

I went flying. I slid through the blood and glass, my back smacking hard against the far wall when I finally came to a stop.

Vampire strength or demon?

Did it matter anymore?

"Kali." He rose and came toward me, one hand extended. He was breathing hard, and so was I. "I'm the one who should be sorry."

He'd crossed the line. The line he'd wanted to cross all along. But now, he knew what could happen if I crossed that line as well. My monster was nothing to fuck with.

Ignoring his bleeding hand, I scrambled to my feet. "I have to go."

I flew out the door of his office, his entreaties to stop falling on deaf ears.

What is wrong with me?

I was a demon, goddammit. I didn't get caught up in emotions. Didn't let others get to me. Not their feelings or their magic. I had to get myself under control.

I'd just hit the front steps of the house when my phone buzzed.

With shaking hands, I answered. "Damon?"

"Lucifer is here." His voice was flat and unemotional. Almost normal.

I knew it was a sham. "I'm on my way. Don't say anything until I get there."

I jumped in my car, revved the motor. Wiped my bloodied hands on some napkins in the glove compartment. As I started to pull away, the passenger door opened and Dru hopped in. "You're not leaving without me, are you, partner?"

Giving him a dirty look, I pointed a finger at the door handle. "Get out. I'm on my way to a meeting with Lucifer. You're not invited."

"Tough." He smiled. "I'm going anyway."

I could see from the set of his jaw and the determination in his eyes, arguing was futile. I was in a hurry and didn't care. "Fine. Put on your seatbelt."

He did as told. I flipped on the radio and cranked up Iron Maiden.

We're off to see the devil, my mind sang. *The wonderful god of hell.*

All I needed were my magical red shoes.

39

Lucifer was magnificent.

No matter how angry I was at him, no matter how much I feared for Damon's life, there was no ignoring the fact Lucifer was like nothing I'd ever seen.

The fallen angel stood at the window of Damon's office, arms crossed over his chest as he stared out at the lake. In my mind's eye, I glimpsed his hidden wings spreading around us.

His eyes saw something beyond the gray waters and cloudy sky over Lake Michigan. That stare was unfathomable and I suspected I didn't want to know what he was thinking. "Michael has begun the countdown to Armageddon."

Like that was news?

Damon sat at his desk, normal as could be. He toyed with a pen, his face a mask of concern. Nothing in his aura suggested that his concern was for himself or for me. He was one hundred percent focused on the current situation and how the Bridge would protect humanity.

Interesting, since he'd informed me he was no longer on the side of humans.

Kirill and Yasmin were absent. Dru and I were silent. I

needed to ask questions, to work out a strategy. Each time I opened my mouth to say something, my voice refused to work. The fallen angel mesmerized me.

He mesmerized my demon as well. She alternated between hiding and throwing herself at the prison bars wanting to bow at his feet. Seduce him even.

Can you imagine? Me and Lucifer?

I almost snorted.

When the two of us first entered, the devil demanded Dru leave. "The Child of the Night is not welcome," he'd said.

I'd seen Damon's relief at Dru's presence, and combined with a sudden surge of anger at Lucifer, I'd countered his demand. "Alexandru and the Vampire Nation will be important when this goes down. He stands with me."

Damon flinched and flicked a damning look across the desk at me. Lucifer didn't like being challenged. From the scowl on his face, I expected to take a trip across the room and have a repeat performance of what had happened in Amy's ice cream shop a few months ago. I braced, prepared for the worst, and Dru slipped a hand into mine.

Solidarity in the face of the enemy. How sweet.

And probably suicidal.

Dru's magic zipped up my arm, heading for my heart. I wanted to jerk my hand away but held still, slapping his magic with my own to halt its progress.

Lucifer saw our hands and sized up what it meant. Finally, he'd recanted, allowing Dru to stay. It had less to do with our show of solidarity and more to do with acknowledging the commitment between us.

Lucifer recognized that a deal had been struck between me and the Master vamp. I saw it register in his eyes. He thought we were lovers. He thought of Amy.

The thought of her softened him.

Amazing.

Dru and I now sat on Damon's black leather couch. I forced my attention away from Lucifer at the window and stared at my boss. My heart pinched thinking about him and his earlier confession. Seeing him back to normal gave me hope. It also helped me collect my thoughts. "Isn't that God's job? Kicking off Armageddon?"

"Michael does our Father's bidding. He's broken the necessary seals to begin the countdown."

"I don't get why angels care what happens on earth."

Lucifer was so still, I wasn't sure he was breathing. Did he need to breathe? "We recently had an encounter...he tried to defeat me and send me back to the pit, but he failed." Again, his aura projected thoughts of Amy. Had she been instrumental in defeating Michael? It seemed so. "He's bringing the battle here this time in another attempt to separate me from...earth." He meant Amy, but whatever. "And this time, he's bringing the entire army of heaven with him."

Good times. *Not.*

Dru piped up. "All of this end-of-the-world stuff is over you?"

Lucifer gave him a condescending glare. "The war between heaven and hell has *always* been about me."

There you have it. I kept my attention focused on Damon so I could think straight. Every so often, I sent him a mental message. *Could he be any more full of himself?*

No response.

Alrighty then. I wanted my questions answered. "Why did Michael raise Maria from the dead? Was it to open a seal?"

"Employing the presence of the seven deadly sins on earth at the same time is not a seal. You're an excuse."

Well, weren't we less than important? Funny, I didn't see it that way, but I played along. "An excuse for what?"

"For him to get his way. If all seven of you walk the earth at the same time, he has another reason to come after me. Heaven and hell believe I put all of you here."

"A setup," Dru said, chuckling. "Clever guy, this archangel."

"He's blamed me for many things since our first fight."

Heaven wasn't immune to sibling rivalry. Big deal. I had no love of angels, fallen or not. "Can you get his sword?"

Lucifer faced me and spoke with a tone suggesting I was an ignorant child. "Neither you nor I can separate Michael from his sword. It is his and his alone."

"What if we kill him?"

Lucifer arched a brow, very Damon-like. "Kill an angel?" He glanced at my boss as if it were his fault I was so stupid.

I thought of Cole's bottom line when facing a deadly opponent. "Does Michael bleed?"

"You cannot kill him. He's immortal, and you are nothing more than an ant under his foot."

If I was an ant, I was a fire ant. "You forget, I'm virtue and vice. A hybrid, you called it. Michael may see me as inconsequential, but that's to your advantage."

Damon and Lucifer both perked up.

Damon stopped toying with the pen. "What are you suggesting, Kali?"

I wasn't suggesting anything. Not yet. I wanted to know about Lucifer's Fallen. "If we can't stop Michael before he brings Armageddon, the key to winning against him and his army is the Fallen."

Lucifer tensed. "What do you know of the Fallen?"

"If you hadn't bugged out of Rome like your pants were on fire, you'd have heard me tell Damon about my father's codex. He wrote the Book of Revelation and two other texts based on my mother's..."

"I know about John and his prophetess," the devil interrupted. "What did she see about the Fallen?"

His stare was so intense my skin heated. "The Fallen can defeat heaven's army."

He shook his head. "The prophesy states God and his army will defeat me and the humans I command, ridding the earth of sin and restoring paradise."

Dru sat forward. "That's one possible outcome Kali's mother saw. There were others. One of them states that Fallen will defeat Michael. The Church hid those texts. They didn't want God-fearing humans to think you stood a chance in hell —pardon the pun—against God."

Gears turned in Damon's head. He looked at Lucifer. "Can you raise the Fallen?"

Lucifer's attention went back to the window. "The Fallen are scattered across the earth, reincarnated as humans. Others are imprisoned in the City of Lost Angels on another plane."

Humans and a mysterious city. Not much to work with. Better than nothing. "The reincarnated angels...do they have powers?"

He seemed to sigh although nothing about him moved. "There are those who have suppressed magical abilities. A rare few who know what they are and how to use their full arsenal of angelic power."

"Can we find the others and break them out?" Dru asked. "The ones in the city?"

His jaw tightened, relaxed. "We are working on that."

"We?" My father's words surfaced—the ones Sal had read to me inside the pope's chambers. "You and Amy? She's Fallen, isn't she? She's one of the reincarnated angels."

He shot me a look that blistered my skin. "If you breathe a word of this to anyone outside this room, I will chain you in the pit for eternity."

Nice.

Threatening me was never a good idea. Damon and Dru went on alert. My jaw tightened. My demon took offense.

I mentally commanded them all to stand down. "How many Fallen walk the earth?"

The heat on my skin lessened. "A few thousand."

"A few thousand humans who don't know they're angels are our only hope in fighting the wrath of heaven? Great. I love impossible odds."

He took the bait. Lucifer's angelic aura turned defensive. "A dozen angels with only a speck of their original heavenly power could scrub this planet clean."

Our odds were looking better. "Then round them up. Dru and I will recruit the supernatural population—every demon, vampire, shifter, and deadly sin we can get. You also have Gabriel, right? He's hanging out at Amy's shop. All combined, our forces will bring Michael to heel. We'll clip his wings and send him back to heaven where the dog belongs."

A spark of hope flashed in Lucifer's dark eyes. "You enjoy suicide missions."

Enjoy them? Hell, no. Cole and I had a motto that seemed to fit the situation. "Only pussies run from trouble."

Damon blanched at my base language and direct challenge to the god of hell: If he ran, he was weak.

Dru tried to hide a smirk. Lucifer walked over, grabbed me by the front of my shirt, and lifted me from the couch. My feet dangled in the air as my nose touched his. Inside, my demon groveled. "For an ant, you're a pain in the ass."

Protective magic poured off Damon and Dru. I laughed. "Ants can lift twenty times their body weight, form highly structured and organized colonies, and are one of the few insects to infiltrate every continent on the globe except Antarctica. Soldier ants defend their leader, forage for food, protect the colony, and fight to the death. They've even survived a previous apocalypse...the mass extinction event that killed dinosaurs. I'd say ants are underrated, wouldn't you?"

Lucky me, hiding my snark inside a science lesson seemed

to intrigue Lucifer rather than piss him off. "I'll enjoy sending you behind enemy lines to see what you can do."

He dropped me back onto the couch and turned to Damon. "We'll talk soon."

A simple statement loaded with hidden meaning.

I started to stop Lucifer—he wasn't leaving without me discussing the terms of his and Damon's agreement—but my phone rang, and the readout said Kirill.

Damn. There was only one reason he'd be calling me.

I hated to stand him up, but my first concern was stopping Lucifer from shimmering out of sight. "Wait," I said. "I need to talk to you. Privately."

Lucifer's eyes locked on mine. Something passed between us...did he read my mind?

He grabbed me by the shirt once more, and a second later, we were alone on the roof of the Institute, me and my demon groveling in our proper place at his feet.

40

The sun peeked over the horizon, a weak glow behind the clouds. Snow covered the trees, ground, and cars in the lot. To the west, smoke from the riots rose in dark plumes. Wind whipped hair in my face and stung my ears.

Lucifer's blue-black hair stayed perfectly coiffed. "Your desperation is unbecoming for a demon of your rank."

Struggling up from the ground, I tried to calm the nerves jumping around in my stomach. "True, but you've made me *very* desperate."

"How so?"

Fear. Worship. A two-headed dragon. I was torn between the extreme emotions and it irritated me. Lucifer irritated me. He was too damn everything. Sexy, conceited, proud. Intoxicating.

Focus, Kali. Don't get emotional. "What did Damon offer you in exchange for my rescue?"

He smiled into the wind. His teeth were bright enough to make the sun pale in comparison. "He said you'd try to bargain."

Did he, now? "No bargains." Blackmail wasn't out of the question, though. "What did he agree to do for you?"

"The deal is done. You can't change it."

"I know that, but I also can't let you take him."

That tweaked his curiosity. "Again, you can't change that."

We'll see about that. "I'm asking you nicely to let him out of his deal."

Lucifer wasn't one to play games. He knew I was up to something. Would he bite? "Be careful, demon. Threats will not be tolerated."

"Not threats. A promise. Free Damon from the deal he made on my behalf and I'll protect Amy when Michael comes."

His full attention rained down on me. I forced myself not to squirm, not to look away. "You alone cannot protect her."

"Damon will help. Between the two of us, we'll keep her safe. If that's what you want. She's Fallen, remember. She should fight beside you."

A muscle jumped in his jaw. He seemed to wrestle with himself over his next words. "She's with child. My child."

I sucked in a cold breath. *Game changer.* Scrambling to find a new argument, I stayed with the logical one. "Even more reason to put the best of the best on the job."

He fell silent, brooding. Even his brooding was beautiful. "You are not a bodyguard."

"I'm an ant in your metaphor, and as I mentioned earlier, ants protect their leader to the death."

More brooding. My phone buzzed again. Kirill was getting panicky. I hit the ignore button. "What do you need Damon for?"

"None of your concern. The deal is done. He has twenty-four hours to wrap up what he needs to here. Then he's mine."

Stubborn SOB. "Take me instead."

He cut his eyes to me. "I thought you weren't going to bargain."

"What can Damon do for you that I can't?"

It was a fair question. "Damon is an archdemon."

That said it all, didn't it? "I'm part angel."

He turned to face me full-on, slight amusement on his face. "Who told you that?"

"Damon." Well, Damon's magic had told me. Close enough.

The amusement faded. His eyes narrowed. "How would he know your origins?"

I shrugged as if it were obvious. "Archdemon, remember?"

He shook his head and returned to gazing at the lake. "If it were true, I would know you for an angel."

"You said I was a hybrid of good and evil. What's the opposite of demon?"

"Jesus cast you out. You're touched by Him, I'll grant you, but you're no angel."

Truer words had never been spoken. My bluff wasn't working. I almost threw out the fact I glowed when I climaxed, but that seemed like TMI between me and Satan. "If you don't cancel the deal with Damon, you'll force me to do something unpleasant. Like I said, I'm very desperate."

He wasn't exactly shaking in his thirty-thousand dollar designer boots. He changed the subject as if my threat meant nothing. "Even for a demon of your beauty and grace, you have an excess of lovers. Why does Damon tolerate the others?"

Beauty? Grace? What?

The devil thought *I* was beautiful.

I nearly swooned and fell off the roof. "I have one lover. Damon is not in that category."

"The vampire?"

"Only a close friend."

"There is more than friendship between you."

Not going there. "I only love one male."

"Ah, yes, the Chaos demon."

"My Achilles' heel. He's my Amy."

Amy. Her name always hit a nerve. "I'll protect her from Michael."

"While you're fighting him? How does that work exactly?"

Silence. A muscle in his jaw danced. "You are a pessimist, aren't you?"

"'Pessimist: One who, when he has the choice of two evils, chooses both.' Oscar Wilde said that. Fits me perfectly."

He nearly rolled his eyes. "I have made arrangements for Amy's safety. She will be in capable hands."

The way he said *capable hands* made a warning bell go off in my head. It was the same tone he'd used when he'd said, *Damon is an archdemon.* "Wait. Damon is going to guard Amy? *That's* the deal?"

Disgusted, he nearly flattened me with a look. "You thought I would cast him into the pit?"

Well, *yeah.* "He's no more a bodyguard than I am."

"I assure you, she's safer with him than you."

"Why is that?"

"Maria ring any bells?"

He had me there. "We're facing the end of the world and she's still after me."

"Like a hellhound on a sinner's bones."

"Amy could end up collateral damage."

"Amy and the baby. I could strike Maria dead, but Michael would only raise her again."

"Two of a kind, aren't they?"

We stood for a moment, lost in our respective thoughts.

"After this is over and Amy is safe, you'll free Damon from his contract?"

He shook his head. "He's bound to me, no matter the outcome."

"So you *are* going to throw him in the pit."

"My prerogative. But no, I have other plans for him."

Plans he wasn't going to share. My ire rose. My original idea surfaced once more. An idea that would make him take me seriously.

Unfortunately, threatening Amy held no appeal. I liked her and couldn't stomach hurting her, whether she was a human witch or a reincarnated fallen angel. On top of that, she was pregnant.

A pang of jealousy hit. A strange sensation that made me shift from foot to foot.

Me, jealous of a pregnant female? Laughable. I had no desire to have a child. I'd be a horrible mother. The child would constantly be in danger. Another Achilles heel making me reckless.

But the idea was so normal, so *human*, I was jealous anyway. The devil and his witch were in love and expecting a child. The stuff of fairy tales and romance novels. Why couldn't I have that?

Did Rad want children? I didn't even know.

Facing Armageddon, the thought smacked me in the face. Whether he did or not, it was no longer a viable option unless I fought Michael and won.

Sometimes you have to overthrow heaven. Michael and his army were waiting for me and Lucifer. I needed to make sure Amy's baby had a chance. That Rad's did. "Earlier you said something about sending me behind enemy lines." I rubbed Volante's handle. "As a sleeper agent or a guerrilla soldier?"

A sleeper agent would have to buddy up to Michael somehow and double-cross him.

Not likely.

A guerrilla soldier would have to sneak into the enemy's camp and bring back intel that would help our side overthrow the bastard.

Sneaking into heaven seemed even more unlikely.

The devil looked up at the sky. His body grew hard as steel, and his nearly invisible black wings fluttered open.

I followed his gaze and saw nothing. What I felt, though, was a different story. An oppressive weight smothered my skin and made me lightheaded. Someone on high was watching us, eavesdropping on our conversation.

Big brother perhaps?

Lucifer lowered his voice. "We'll speak again soon, demon."

Bam. He struck me down with a look, totally without warning, and I hit the ground hard. I sputtered; he shimmered out of sight.

"Nice talking to you, too." I lay on my back on the rooftop, stunned and confused. The blow had been hard enough to topple me, but not as hard as Lucifer was capable of doling out.

Wiping blood from my lip, I gazed up at the boiling clouds overhead. Whoever was watching us had seen the show.

And that's what it was. A show.

I did my part by cursing Lucifer in Italian, English, and the bit of French I'd learned from Rad. The oppressive feeling disappeared, leaving a sticky, oily sensation on my skin. A sensation even lye soap wouldn't dissolve.

My phone buzzed. *Gah*, Kirill. "Sorry, Kirill. I've been tied up with Lucifer."

No answer. Nothing but air. I pressed the phone closer to my ear, leaving the windswept roof to go back inside.

In the quiet interior of the building, no sound came from the other end of our connection, not even someone breathing. But the line was open, I was sure of that.

Not good. Whatever Kirill was into, he couldn't talk, and he needed help.

I spoke just above a whisper. "I'm on my way home, Kirill. Press one for yes, that's where you are, or two for no, I shouldn't go there."

A second passed. Sweat broke out along my hairline. *Come on, come on. Give me some kind of clue.*

I was about to issue a different verbal command when I heard the slightest noise. Kirill shifting ever so slightly.

Beep.

One. I waited.

Only one.

"Okay. Hang on. I'm coming."

I ran all out, down the stairs, through the hallways, nearly knocking Lainie over in my haste. "Sorry!" I called as I blew past her.

Dru was in Damon's office with Cole. Damon was MIA.

"He said he had something to do," Dru said when I asked where Damon was. "Said he wouldn't be back for a while."

Damn. Nothing I could do about it now. Cole nodded at the phone in my hand. "What is it?"

Taking a deep breath, I tried to calm my racing heart. Parker's dagger grew heavy inside my cape pocket.

"Show time," I said. "Pestilence is waiting."

41

S trategy is seeing the end goal, the finish line, and working backward.

Preparation is key. Know your enemy, know yourself. Damon had taught me well.

I'd had little time to prep for my meeting with the Red Horseman, but I'd had three hundred years of experience fighting supernaturals.

I'd also had a boatload of Damon's teachings jammed into my head, and Cole's fighting techniques beat into my muscles.

Initially, my goal was to destroy Pestilence. After much deliberation on the way over, I'd changed the end goal to capturing him. If I could take him alive, he might pony up valuable information. He might be a commodity to trade for.

Either way, heaven would take notice.

I planned to capture him on my own, no backup necessary. Plans go astray in battle, so on my orders, Cole and Dru sent out the word to the vampire troops, the *vitiums*, and the Institute's soldiers. All hands on deck. It annoyed me to admit I might need their help, but this was the first step in our war against heaven. I wouldn't risk losing this one to satisfy my prideful ego.

It began to sleet before we reached my place. Cole stopped the car two blocks away for recon. He, Dru, and I circled the church and took up positions on the north, south, and west sides. I itched to run in and attack Pest to save Kirill. Instead, I watched silently from my hidden spot in the cemetery while sleet caught in my hair, melted, and ran down the back of my neck. Within a minute, I was soaked to the bone.

The church sat desolate and seemingly empty. No movement past the windows. No sounds or smells coming from the interior. I lowered my shields and opened my senses wide.

As a precaution, I had multiple layers of magical security as well as a high-tech human security system. It took me time to weed my way through the magical layers, lowering the house's defenses without setting off any alarms.

Hang in there, Kirill. Busting in with guns blazing might put him in more danger than he already was. It certainly would put me in danger. I worried little about what was waiting for me, but I wouldn't risk Kirill's life on top of it.

After ten minutes of watching and waiting, I was running out of patience. The ghosts in the cemetery clung to me, their evil energy pressing on me and making me irritable. They messed with magic, calling it out to play. Keeping my focus on the church, I sensed a supernatural presence inside...

Only one and very, very weak.

Kirill.

My stomach churned. What the hell had happened?

I used the comm link in my ear to connect with Cole and Dru. "I'm going in."

Cole's voice argued. "Backup's not here yet. Hold your position."

Damon would have agreed. I mulled the advice over, found

I couldn't sit still any longer. "Target is not inside. I repeat, Pestilence is *not* inside. Injured party is. I'm going in."

"I'll accompany you," Dru said, his voice calm and reassuring in my ear. My blood did a happy dance. "I'll approach from the south."

"Wait 'til I've breached the entrance in case it's booby-trapped."

"Copy that." He paused. "Be careful."

Cole huffed. "Could be a trap. I'll cover the outside."

Smart demon. I should have considered that. I sighed, realizing I had much to learn about being in charge. "Copy that. And thank you."

Leaving my position, I made my way slowly out of the cemetery, skirting the edges of the iron fence and staying as hidden as possible behind the gnarled trees and ancient grave markers. The gate squeaked as I opened it, sticking in the snow. A touch of my fingers silenced the rusted iron, and I pushed through, heading for the back of the church.

With the security systems diffused, the only sound was my boots on the snow-packed ground. I stood outside the kitchen door and laid a hand on the stone wall. The residual energies of my friends assaulted me. The tormented energy of a demon in pain stung my palm.

Had Kirill made it here on his own in such pain? Managed to get through my various security systems without setting them off?

I dug deeper, trying to find a second energy that was recent and being suppressed by Kirill's pain. Deeper...deeper...

A thorn of white-hot electricity shocked my hand. I jumped back and rubbed at my injured palm. Kirill had been brought here by a preternatural creature, that much was true. The magic wasn't dark, nor was it light. It was simply...powerful.

"What is it?" a hushed voice came from behind me. A wave

of Dru's protective magic wrapped itself around my arms, my hips.

I glanced over my shoulder, and my blood skipped another skip. His hair was wet, and his bangs were hanging low over his eyes.

Why did he have to be so sexy? "Pestilence was here, but he's gone now. We need to help Kirill."

He nodded, the action an urge for me to lead the way.

Kirill was lying on my kitchen floor in a puddle of green pus, blood, and other body fluids I didn't want to examine. Blood ran from his eyes, his nose, his ears. It seeped from under his fingernails. His chest moved in slow, jerky motions, a wheezing sound issuing from his lips.

His eyes were open, but he appeared to be blind, his head tilting toward the sound of Dru's boots scuffing against the tiles.

The archdemon's voice was barely more than a whisper. "Kali?"

I was frozen. "What happened to you?"

It seemed to take all of his energy to answer. "Pest... happened."

In my ear, Cole barked at me. "Report in. Status?"

Dru crouched next to Kirill, looked up at me. "We should get him back to the Institute."

I hit the ear comm. "Bring the car around. Transport needed to Institute."

Dru, who was always so meticulous and fussy about his clothes and appearance, picked up Kirill like he was a child and carried him toward the front door.

"Hurry," I added to Cole. "We don't have much time."

42

This is my fault.

I stewed as Cole drove us back to the Institute. Kirill had told me my plan to draw out the Red Horseman wouldn't work. I should have listened.

And now the Institute's resident doctor was dying. Who would take care of him?

Kirill lay across the backseat of the Land Rover, losing consciousness, then regaining it, crying out in terrible pain.

Bits and pieces of what had happened came out when he was awake, but he was less than lucid even when his eyes opened and his lips moved. He'd manipulated Pest into taking him back as a soldier of disease, told him I was gunning for him, and Pest needed to dispose of me. Hence leading him to my place.

Kirill was convinced Pest believed him...right up until Pest hit his disease specialist with a dose of his own medicine. Or in this case, a dose of the bubonic plague.

Dru notified our backup army to convene at the Institute. My hands shook as I stared at my phone trying to figure out what to do. Damon was gone; Yasmin would be of little help. Who should I call?

The letters skipped under my fingers as I texted Rad and told him what had happened. I had to keep deleting and retyping, my fingers shook so hard. Finally I hit send.

A minute later, he texted back that he was out of his meeting and would join us at the Institute. He knew nothing about diseases, nor did he seem overly concerned about the approaching apocalypse. He'd probably do nothing but distract me from my duties. Yet, he was the only one I wanted to see.

The route to the Institute was a circuitous one. Rioting had broken out in various neighborhoods. Houses and cars burned, dark smoke hovered in the air all over the South Side. Mobs of ordinary people roamed the streets, mixing and clashing with legitimate gangs. Supernaturals combed the back yards, alleys and empty lots, looking for human snacks.

A part of me wanted to jump out and confront the supernaturals preying on the innocent, but I ignored it. Instead, I laid a layer of protective magic over the Land Rover so we cold muscle our way through the worst. Here and there, we caught the eyes of various miscreants, but all let us pass without confrontation.

Twenty minutes later, Dru and I hoisted Kirill into a bed in the infirmary. He'd had two seizures in the car, his lymph nodes were swelled up, and he was vomiting blood. Lainie put a hand over her mouth when she saw the archdemon, but offered to clean him up while I looked for supplies to treat him.

In the lab, I grabbed streptomycin, doxycycline, and ciprofloxacin—medications I'd read about when I Googled bubonic plague. Would they work on a demon? There had to be some reason Kirill kept them around.

I'd had many IVs over the years and quite a few shots. With my current overactive immune system, I hadn't needed anything but the yellow goo lately. I found a stash of bottles with green liquid in them in one of the refrigerators in the lab. If the variety of antibiotics I'd scored didn't work, the yellow goo was next.

Seraphina entered the lab without a word and gathered the components to set up an IV. Together, we descended on Kirill like a couple of EMTs, and soon had the IV pumping drugs and fluids into his system, an oxygen mask helping him breathe, and Sera drew several syringes full of blood to test. We'd both infused our magics into everything entering and covering his body.

"Can you save him?" I asked her, not questioning her medical expertise, only his condition. "It's bubonic plague."

She scanned him with her soulful, turquoise eyes. "I've never seen a demon infected with plague. Human diseases don't affect us."

"Lucifer gave it to me a few months ago. Then he took it away a few minutes later. I can truthfully say, during the minute or two I was ill, I wanted to die."

"Lucifer is all-powerful." Her lips thinned in concentration. "Without that type of intervention, there's no way of saying whether he will live or die."

Kirill stopped vomiting and slept. Fitfully, but at least he seemed to be in less pain. While Seraphina went to work looking at slides of his blood under a microscope, I headed for Damon's office.

On the way, I passed the conference room. Lots of voices rising and falling. The troops were restless, on edge. I'd address them soon. First I needed a minute to myself. A minute to form a new plan and come up with a motivational speech.

Yeah, right. My plans had worked so well up to this point. My motivational speeches were nothing but garbage.

The door to the office was locked. Not magically, just a simple mechanical lock that flipped open at my touch. Inside, the lights were off, dust motes floating in the weak light by the window. Damon's wood smoke smell was faint but I breathed it in, expanding my lungs as far as they would go to hang onto it. Exhausted, I dropped into his leather chair and closed my eyes.

I had failed. Everything. Everyone.

Kirill. Damon. Dru. The other *vitiums*. Even Ranulf.

I'd failed my father, my mother.

Myself.

For several minutes, I sat like that. Beating myself up and enjoying a good pity party.

But pity parties aren't my style. I scrubbed my eyes with the back of my hands, flipped on the lights, and scanned the rows of books on Damon's shelves. I pulled out three, sat down, and started reading. First up, the Bible.

Book of Revelation.

The text was confusing and soon I was thinking about my parents more than the words on the page. I left the Bible and opened a file cabinet where Damon kept personnel files.

Dulce, Kalina, wasn't a hard one to find. It was right on top.

I'd sneaked a peek at the file before. Knew there was information about my parents and how they'd died. My tired eyes went over page after page of my assignments, my background, the past. There was nothing new, but I felt a fresh connection to my family.

I started to close the file when a line of handwriting on the inside flap caught my attention. *Do what you are.*

Damon's handwriting. I sniffed the ink. Fresh.

Do what you are.

A message?

If so, I didn't understand. *Do what you're good at. Do what comes natural.* Those things I understood. But *do what you are?*

I sat back and forced myself to think like Damon. I was a vengeance demon, the Institute's enforcer, a deadly sin and righteous virtue. I was the earthly daughter of a prophetess and a scholar who'd authored several biblical books.

I was also the Queen of the Central United States Undead Nation. A friend, a lover, a soldier. The monster Damon had made me.

Do what you are.

My thoughts were interrupted by Yasmin when she stormed into the office and grew angrier when she saw me sitting in Damon's chair. A deadly finger pointed at my face. "Who the hell do you think you are?"

After ten minutes of considering exactly that question, I answered truthfully. "Your new boss. What's the problem?"

Flabbergasted, she sputtered and huffed. "What's the problem? *You're* the fucking problem." She stabbed the top of the desk with her fingernail. "Whatever you did to make him leave, undo it. Bring him back. Fix this disaster right now. Kirill and I will not stand for you kicking Damon out and inserting yourself in his place."

"Unfortunately, Kirill is unable to state his preference at the moment, and I don't know where Damon is. If I did, I'd beg him to come back. For the time being, I'm in charge. You're free to leave and face the outside world on your own, but I hope you'll stay and help us fight the Horsemen and the Archangel Michael."

"What's wrong with Kirill? What did you do to him?"

Where the hell had she been? "He and the Red Horseman, Pestilence, had a run-in. Kirill's in serious condition."

A second passed. Her face reddened. "You bitch. You planned this all along, didn't you?"

Being accused of purposely setting up Kirill pissed me off enough to bring my demon to the surface. I contained her, but she must have flashed in my eyes because Yasmin caught her breath and removed her finger.

I leaned forward. "I would never hurt Kirill. Or Damon for that matter. I made a poor judgment call with Kirill, but he's an archdemon like you. I never dreamed he could be poisoned by a human disease."

"I suppose you also want me to believe that you had nothing to do with Damon leaving his position on the Council?"

Yasmin might have been a Council member, but Damon had kept her in the dark even more than me. I understood her anger. "He made a deal with Lucifer. A deal I knew nothing about until it was over."

She leaned across the desk to put her face in front of mine. "You've been planning to take over the Institute since Damon brought you to work here."

That got a laugh out of me. Outside of Sweet Investigations, I had no desire to be in charge of anything. I hated being vamp queen. Hated that the *vitiums* looked to me as their leader. Taking over the Institute would be a nightmare for me, not a career goal.

But Damon was counting on me. Whether he was there or not, I was going to do the job he'd given me.

I sat farther forward so our faces were even closer. "I don't want to be in charge, Yasmin, but I am, so deal. Like I said before, you're free to leave if you're hostile to the change of leadership."

I even sounded like Damon. She straightened, screwed up her mouth as if she were going to argue, and then stomped out of the office.

"That went well," I said to myself. "Really, really well."

Rad appeared in the open doorway. "What crawled up her ass?"

My insides did a flip to see him. So familiar, he was. So perfect in the midst of everything else.

"Me." I scrubbed my eyes again. They felt swollen. My stomach growled. When was the last time I'd eaten? "And unfortunately, I'll have to do it again if she continues to threaten me."

"She threatened you?"

"Not in so many words. Her aura, though, was a shining beacon of I'm-gunning-for-you."

He flopped into the chair opposite the desk and drew it closer. He looked good. Tight jeans, a wooly fisherman's sweater, a full night of sleep. "Better watch your back. She's evil enough to come after you."

His presence calmed me. "Yeah, well, she'll have to get in line. At last count, Maria, Parker, Valentina, Pestilence, Michael, and a few others were ahead of her."

I brought him up to date on everything from my discussion with Lucifer to Kirill's physical state. He shook his head. "The drama never ends, does it?"

Drama? "I'm dealing with real life here, Rad, not a glorified reality TV show."

He slouched in the chair, fiddled with a string on his sweater. "My meeting went well, thanks for asking."

He was having business meetings like everything was normal. "Sorry. I'm a little preoccupied with the world ending."

He had the nerve to roll his eyes. "You said it yourself, Kali. This is a pissing match between Michael and Lucifer. It has little to nothing to do with wiping sin from the world and restoring Eden. Our best bet is to lay low, let them kill each other—or whatever angels do to each other—and survive the fallout. Things will settle down and life will go back to normal."

I stared at him. "Are you on drugs?"

"I haven't even had a hit of your blood today." He waggled his eyebrows. "We should fix that."

"I can't decide if you're really that selfish or if you're trying to take my mind off things."

His eyes flashed with irritation. "*I'm* selfish? All I hear is Damon this, Dru that, Lucifer yada, yada, yada. I'm telling you, they've sucked you into this game and you're the one that's going to end up screwed when all's said and done."

"What about the innocent humans that have died in the past forty-eight hours? The ones who've been injured or are lying in a hospital bed with an incurable disease? Tell me again, who's getting screwed in this scenario?"

He tipped his head back and stared at a spot above my head, then sat forward, elbows on the chair's arms. "Look, I know you're dedicated to saving humans. I support that. But you can't save them all, especially when the forces that be are working against you. Your mother prophesied this would happen. Your father wrote it down. Cultures across the globe, since the beginning of time, have predicted the end of the world. It's going to happen. You can't stop Armageddon, Kali, even if you kill the Horsemen and fight side-by-side with Lucifer. You know that, right?"

The hunger pains turned to nausea.

"It's a noble cause, but this battle isn't yours." The sincerity in his eyes was real. The intensity in his aura even more so. He was scared for me. Scared I was either going to end up Lucifer's bitch or Michael's. "Don't let them use you as a pawn in their fight. Once the dust clears, the world will return to normal. It may be a new normal, but even if Michael defeats Lucifer and sends him back to the pit, sin will still exist. *Demons* will still exist. You and I will be here to help the humans who survive, and we'll go back to protecting them."

Was I a pawn? Would the earth and heaven and hell simply start up where they'd left off once this was over?

He gave me a look that reminded me of Damon's stern *you should listen to me* expression. "We can't do that if we don't survive. You've got three strongholds—the Institute, your castle, and Nudra's house in Oak Park. Personally, I vote for Oak Park. It's far enough away from the South Side rioting and full of weapons."

Nudra, the vamp who'd made me his blood slave, had an arsenal in his house. A house that passed on to me when I killed the bastard. Rad wanted to hang out there because it was well-fortified and filled with luxurious amenities. I had the feeling the arsenal of weapons was of secondary importance to him.

Oak Park was no safer than where I sat, and the big heaven-hell picture was impossible to see. I doubted even Damon could see it.

Do what you are.

All I could do was fight the fight handed to me. I was sorry Rad wouldn't be fighting the same fight by my side. "I'm not a pawn, and I'm not hiding out while heaven and hell duke it out in my town."

He let out a disgusted sigh, sat back again and tapped a thumb on his thigh. "Parker's back in Chicago."

The sudden change in topic confused me. Or maybe I was too tired to care. "So?"

"She's coming for you and only you. Orders from the pope."

I shrugged. "I have bigger problems than Parker Burkett."

"See, that's just it. Parker's an assassin and her mission is to kill you before sunset tonight."

"The pope's pissed I trashed his place and showed him up, huh?"

"You're not *a* pawn in the game, Kali. You're *the* pawn. Heaven wants you destroyed before Michael even mounts his horse. Parker's been tasked to do the job, but the pope's not taking chances. He's sent Maria as insurance."

Rad's go-to-ground philosophy suddenly made sense. "How do you know the pope's plan?"

He cleared his throat, played with the string again. "Parker told me."

I needed a second to wrap my head around that. "You've spoken to Parker? Recently?"

"She's still trying to convince me to return to the Nocts."

Of course she was. *Should have killed her when I had the chance.* "She wants you back, period. Nocts or no Nocts."

He made whatever gesture. "I need to get you to a safe place. Here, the castle, Nudra's compound, wherever you feel safe. But I will not stand by while Parker or Maria or anyone else tries to harm you."

Talk about noble. My heart pinched, torn between wanting to give in to him—wanting someone to take care of *me* for once —and knowing I could never leave the people and supernaturals who were counting on me in order to save my own skin.

Damn Chaos demon. I had a job to do and he was making me doubt myself. "I can't, Rad. I can't abandon this cause."

"Please, Kali. Do this for me."

"I want to—I do—but you know I can't. It would be wrong."

Anger flared. "It's okay to think about yourself for once. To put yourself and your well-being ahead of others."

No, it wasn't. I looked into his pleading golden eyes and it tore the heart right out of me to disappoint him. "Not gonna happen."

He set his elbows on his knees and hung his head. "She's pulling out all the stops. Everyone you care about is in danger. And she won't quit until your head is on a stake in Vatican City."

"Let her try." The best defense was a good offense. "The only one losing her head by sundown tonight will be Parker. You can bet on it."

"You really plan to kill her? A human?"

She'd given up her human card a long time ago. "I'm going to relish every minute of it."

He sat there looking at me like I'd morphed into someone else.

Maybe I had. My demon hadn't even peeked out.

"What?" I challenged. "A minute ago you wanted me to sit

back and let thousands, if not millions, of innocent humans suffer and die because Michael's got a bug up his ass, and now you're disappointed I'd kill Parker who's done nothing but threaten and torture me?"

I didn't let him respond. "Not only me, Rad. She's tortured hundreds of supernaturals in the basement of the pope's apartments. I felt their residual energy, their pain and suffering. She and her Noct buddies have killed thousands more. She threatened to harm you right to my face and now she's gunning for me again. Human or not, why would I cut her one ounce of slack?"

"I'm not asking you to. But you said it yourself. Her track record is impeccable. Whether you want to admit it or not, your life is in danger. Be smart and stop getting distracted by the Armageddon mess or you won't be around to fight it."

I didn't want to argue anymore. Rad was not only my lover and blood slave, he was also a good resource. I needed him—not the angry him, the smart him. The one who could help me defeat Parker because he knew her weaknesses.

I shifted in the chair, fidgeting with the uncomfortable feeling lodged in my chest. "All right. Your concern and credible information are duly noted. Outside of hiding from her, what do you suggest?"

"Use me as bait."

I barked a laugh. "You can't be serious."

He met my gaze with his, cool and steady.

Okay, serious it was. In the silence, I considered the idea like an objective commander would do. Parker wanted my head on a stake and Rad back in her bed. Which one did she want more?

Duh.

Sun Tzu advised to 'hold out baits to entice the enemy'. Who was I to argue with the master? "I'm listening."

Rad's mouth quirked to one side. "Meet me at your place in

an hour and you'll see." He stood, leaned across the desk, and planted a toe-curling kiss on me before strolling to the door and looking back. "And wear something sexy. Like that thing with all the ties."

"The leather bustier? What does that have to do with killing Parker?"

"Nothing, but when your boobs are pushed up like that, I'll fight twice as hard to save you."

Asshole.

He left me with my mouth open, his footsteps echoing in the hallway. As he left, I heard him whistling the notes of the latest song he was working on.

I laid my head down on Damon's desk and groaned.

"What's cookin', home fry?" Maddy bounced into the office, took one look at me and closed the door behind her. "Whoa, girl. You look like the Jersey Shore after Hurricane Sandy. What's up?"

"Besides the end of the world?"

"The look on your face isn't apocalyptic." She skirted the edge of the desk, held my face between her palms, and studied it. "Nope. This here is your man-trouble face. Which one is it? Rad? Dru? Damon?"

She winked at me, popping her gum. "It's Dru, isn't it?"

"Him and every other male in the place," I said, putting my head back down. The desk was cool against my skin. "I hate them all."

"There, there." She hopped up on the desk and patted my shoulder. "Maddy's got just the thing to cure that problem."

I looked up. "A mani-pedi at that vampire salon you love isn't going to cure jackshit."

She made a frowny face. "Testy much, my dear vengeance demon?"

"Hell, yes. Rough doesn't begin to cover my day."

She smiled again and snapped her fingers over her head in

a gesture that was pure Italian. "Arman! Chop, chop. My queen needs nourishment."

The shifter appeared, white bags of takeout with my favorite restaurant's logo on the side in his hands. "We come bearing food, oh queen of the Undead."

The smell of grease and seared steak hit my nose. My stomach rumbled. I might have drooled.

With one sweep of my arm, I cleared the desktop of papers. A very un-Damon-like thing to do. Then I wiggled my fingers at Arman. "Come to momma, werecat."

43

After I had consumed the last piece of steak and French fry, I thanked my young friends and went to see my lieutenants. That's how I was thinking of Dru and the others now—lieutenants in my hodgepodge supernatural army.

The emotions and magics inside the conference room were still running high. Dissension was rampant. Troops fall apart when their leader is absent.

Maddy and Arman followed me and stood amongst the others. Yasmin was noticeably absent. Juliana Ballou Jackson, the Creole vamp queen of the Southern Region, and her cohort, Rafael DeMarco, the Godfather vamp king of the East, had joined us. They looked as happy to be there as everyone else. Both regaled me with questions, so I took a minute to bring them up to speed.

Once everyone had the lowdown on what had happened so far and what *might* happen in the next twenty-four hours, I divided our army into five units, assigned each a lieutenant from those gathered, and then divvied up Chicago's South Side into four quadrants.

"Dru and Brianna" —I pointed to a map on the wall outlining the various quads— "you and your vampire teams will police the east from Bridgeport to South Shore. Shayne, your team of Institute soldiers and shifters will take the green areas from South Chicago to Hegewisch. Akimo, your team gets the orange sections encompassing McKinley Park to West Lawn. Seraphina and Sal will stay here and handle communication, injuries, and weapon detail. Cole, you're with me."

"And what exactly are we doing?" Brianna asked. She had *haughty vampire* down to an art. "Controlling the human population or fighting the Horsemen?"

"Both."

Her red glossed lips puckered in distaste. "I thought *you* were going to handle the Horsemen."

Behind me, Cole stiffened.

"Brianna," Dru admonished.

Damon's written words rang in my head. *Do what you are.*

I was Brianna's queen. Being defensive wasn't the answer, but her attitude was unacceptable. Especially in front of the other regional managers. "Cole, show Brianna the front door since she's unhappy with my leadership."

Cole sucked up whatever angst it caused him and marched toward the vamp. She was unhappy alright but had no intention of living as an outcast whether she had hours or centuries left of her Undead life. It was too cushy, and she deemed herself above most of her fellow vampires. Being exiled meant no more Dru, no more Cole.

She stopped Cole with an upraised hand and tipped her head in a show of subservience to me. "My deepest apologies, queen. Current circumstances weigh heavy on my mind. My tongue gets away from me."

"Watch yourself, vampire, or your tongue will be removed."

The silence in the room was deafening.

Point made.

"Yes, my queen," Brianna said, her hate simmering under her submission. "I am at your service."

"Moving on." I motioned Cole to return to his spot near me. "You may encounter one of the Horsemen before I do. In that case, don't engage them. Get in touch with me and we'll work out a plan based on the circumstances. In order to do their jobs, the Horsemen have to stick out their necks. I'm working a plan to attack them when they're most vulnerable."

Brianna wasn't pacified, but many of the others were. They believed in me. She set her lips into a grim line and offered no further argument.

"Look," I said to all of them. "My first skirmish didn't go as planned, but I'm better prepared now. The Horsemen are virtually unstoppable and behind them is an army of angels led by Michael. But on that front, we have an ally. A powerful one. When the time comes, we stand with him."

Feet shuffled. Voices murmured. Some of them knew I was talking about Lucifer. Others guessed. I waited for discussion and dissent from the vamp regional managers. None came.

What alternative did they have? I hoped they were sticking with me because they believed my plan would work, but supernaturals weren't welcomed by heaven and its emissaries. Earth was their only home unless they wanted an extended vacation in hell.

The door opened and Kirill appeared, white hospital gown tied awkwardly around his middle and his IV pole in tow. "Did I miss anything?"

He looked too pale and unsteady on his feet, but by hell and damnation, he was up and walking. I nearly jumped over Sal to get to him. "Kirill. Are you sure you should be up so soon?"

Seraphina moved from behind Shayne. "Feeling better, love?"

"You." Kirill pointed a finger at her, his gown falling open in the back. "What did you do to me?"

I grabbed the gown and tried to fix it. "She saved your life."

"Miss Do-gooder. Couldn't resist, could you, Nightingale?"

The archdemon was delusional. "That's Seraphina, Kirill. The *vitium*. Not Florence Nightingale."

"She may have changed her skin color, but I'd know the magic in those hands anywhere."

I looked at the female, as did everyone else in the room. She hid a sly smile. "One of my gifts is shifting appearances. Kirill has known me as Florence Nightingale."

Maddy clapped in glee. "You're a Metamorph? How frickin' cool is that? I didn't think you guys existed anymore."

A Metamorph was a shifter, only one that shifted her human looks to appear as whoever she wanted. There was no animal in her.

Sera nodded, glanced at Kirill. "We have a history together. I thought it best to adopt a new appearance before coming here."

Kirill started forward. I grabbed his arm and held him back. His chubby cheeks shook with anger but under that, his aura shook with unrequited love. "You tricked me."

Oh, jeez. Sexual chemistry burned bright between them. "Relax, Kirill. Trickery aside, she saved your life, and we don't have time to fight amongst ourselves."

"He's in no condition to fight," Seraphina advised.

Kirill stiffened and made a noise in the back of his throat, but she was right. I could tell it was adrenaline and anger keeping him upright. "Back to bed, archdemon. We need to talk."

I dismissed the rest of the group. Seraphina led the way to the infirmary; Cole and I guided Kirill back to his bed. I asked Cole and Sera to leave us alone for a few minutes.

A pale Kirill closed his eyes once they were out of the room. "So you've taken over."

"If you want the job, it's all yours."

"Where's Yasmin?"

"No clue. She left after she found out Damon had handed me his position."

"Damon's lap dog." He sighed, opened his eyes. "You're better off without her. She'd only try to sabotage you. She's in love with him, you know."

"And he's in love with Valentina. Do you know her?"

Kirill waved a weak hand. "He was never in love with her. She was nothing but a distraction. A substitution for a female he wanted and couldn't have. But he got caught up in Val's dream weaving shit and he couldn't remove the barb she left in him."

"I noticed."

The IV continued its drip. "Where did he go?"

"He's slumming with Lucifer. Best guess? He's in a small river town west of here. Lucifer's got him guarding Amy Atwood."

Kirill *tsked*. "A deal with the devil. Should've known. For what, though?" He eyed me suspiciously. "What would make him give up being head of the Bridge Council to go to work for Lucifer?"

His tone suggested he knew what. I looked away. "I didn't ask him to make that deal. He did it without my knowledge or consent."

"Because he knew you wouldn't go along with it?"

"I was out of commission when the deal went down. He didn't have a chance to ask."

Kirill thought for a minute. "You believe he did it to save you."

I glanced at him. "You don't?"

"Damon doesn't put anything ahead of his commitment to the Bridge Council. Not even you."

Memories of the past and my dealings with Damon

surfaced. Kirill was right. "You think he cut a deal for my safety with Lucifer because it benefited the Bridge? How so?"

"He needed you alive and in fighting condition for this war."

"I'm just a soldier, Kirill. Damon was our commander-in-chief. He's worth more than a dozen of me in any battle."

"He must not have seen it that way."

I chuckled under my breath, as confused as ever. "I've never understood the way he thinks."

Adjusting his blanket, Kirill snorted. "Makes two of us."

Back to business. "We struck out with Pestilence. Any other ideas?"

His cheeks rose in a smile. "*Au contraire*, enforcer. We didn't strike out."

The gleam in his tired eyes sparked hope in me. "What did you do?"

"My blood. Have you drawn any?"

"Seraphina took a couple of tubes."

"His calling card is in my blood. When he infected me, he left a breadcrumb."

I wasn't following. "A breadcrumb?"

"Every disease has a calling card. An originating source. We can track his calling card. Like GPS."

Satan be praised. "I can find him by using the breadcrumb he left in your blood."

He nodded, pleased with himself. "Actually, I'm the one who can track him since it's my blood."

"How soon can you be up and ready to travel?"

"Give me a few hours of sleep. I'll be good as new."

Sleep. Sounded good. "You got it. I have one issue to resolve at sunset and then I'll be back for you."

"You still have to figure out how to kill him once you find him."

Some of the air left my balloon. "I have the dagger that

poisoned me. The one forged in angel fire. Will that do the trick?"

"Let me see it."

It was strapped in my boot. I removed it and handed it to him.

The blade flashed under the fluorescent lights as Kirill turned it over and over. He sniffed the blade, closed his eyes, and channeled magic at it. When he opened his eyes, I saw the archdemon behind his human façade. "Where did you get this?"

"Parker. It's the blade she used on me in the park."

"Hmm." He tasted it, running his tongue along the flat side of the blade. "Interesting."

"What?"

"It's indeed forged with angel fire, but there's another component I don't recognize in the makeup of the silver."

"Angel or demon?"

"Maybe both."

Both? "Is that good or bad? Can I kill Pestilence with it?"

He sighed, handed it back to me. "I doubt it. The energy is..."

"Is what?"

"Off."

This was getting me nowhere. "Can you be more specific?"

"If I didn't know better, I'd think it was forged by Death himself."

"Death, as in the last Horseman?"

He nodded.

Great. How did Parker get a weapon forged by Death? "And if the weapon is forged by a Horseman..."

"It won't kill a fellow Horseman."

Exhaustion weighed heavy on me. Or maybe I'd lost the earlier spark of hope. "Any other brilliant ideas?"

He yawned, eyes at half-mast. "Let me think about it."

He was asleep before I walked out the infirmary's door.

44

Sleep. The mere idea made me stumble as I trudged to the third floor. I eyed Damon's apartment door, where his magic still stood guard. The room beckoned me to slip through the security and come in. That type of thing—breaking into a guarded place and snooping around—didn't usually bother me. I was a demon, after all. But my stomach was comfortably full, Kirill was going to survive, and my brain was mush. Entering Damon's room seemed like a violation. A sacrilege.

My apartment was too quiet. Too still. Perfect for a few hours of shut-eye if I could turn off the voice in my head.

I undressed, put on my favorite Hello Kitty flannel pjs and crawled under the covers. I'd just settled in when a soft knock on the door got me back up.

Di was on the other side. "Sorry. Were you sleeping?"

Seeing her standing there in all her goddess beauty, I nearly wept. Since I'm not a crier, I threw my arms around her and hugged her tight.

I'm not a hugger, as evidenced by her grabbing my arms

and setting me back so she could look me over after she returned my hug. "Are you all right?"

"Not in the least."

"Saving the world is a thankless job, isn't it?"

I motioned her into the room. We sat together on the luxurious white settee Dru had given me. I'd brought it to the apartment to escape Rad's wrath.

Di fixed the pillows around us and opened up a soft chenille throw to drape over our laps. We propped our feet on the coffee table and Di scanned my face. "Talk to me."

"I need Michael's sword to stop the Horsemen, and even if I succeed in beheading each of them, Michael himself is coming to wage war against Lucifer. Damon cut a deal with Lucifer to guard his witch in return for Lucifer rescuing me from Vatican City. In order for Damon to fulfill his side of things..."

Di stopped me. "Forget about all of that. Let's talk about what's really bothering you."

I'd never had a friend like Aphrodite. She saw through my outer layers and into my heart. "What's really bothering me? Di, I'm trying to..."

She interrupted me again. "Is it Rad? Did he do something to bring up the past?"

Rad *was* my past. He was also my present. "He's imposing restrictions on me and our relationship."

"You feel fenced in."

"Not fenced in so much as..." I hesitated, searching for the right term. "I can't live up to his expectations. I know I'm going to fail and fail big."

"The same issue you've experienced with Damon on multiple occasions."

She knew me so well. "On some levels."

"You believe you've let Damon down many times, but he's entrusted the care and keeping of the Bridge Council and this

Institute to you. Doesn't sound like failure to me. Does it to you?"

Not when she put it that way, but Di always saw the glass more than half full. "I'm in love with Rad."

She followed the conversation's right turn seamlessly. "That scares you."

"What scares me is letting him down. I've never put anyone above my work, and today, when he asked me to hide instead of fight, I wanted to. For him, not me."

"But knowing you, you told him to fuck off."

"Not in those exact words." We shared a small laugh. "He knows my job means everything to me. I can't stick my head in the sand because I'm in danger."

"I think he understands that. He'd do anything for you, Kali. Protecting the woman he adores is part of his genetic male makeup. The human side and the demon side."

Tipping my head back, I closed my eyes. "I should be protecting him. I'm stronger, faster, and more...well...everything, thanks to *my* genetic makeup and the recent boost from Dru's blood."

"Logically, he knows that. Emotionally, he hates it."

"Then we're going to keep having problems."

She was silent, the heavy air of love-goddess analysis descending on me. I cracked open one eye. "What?"

"In work, you enjoy problems. They energize you. In relationships, you fear them."

"And by the look on your face, that's wrong. Right?"

"Actually, it's completely normal. You're secure in your job. You've made a name for yourself, built a reputation. Supernaturals respect you for who you are and what you do. Your relationships—with potential mates and with friends—aren't as cut and dried. They're messy and unpredictable and they tend to confuse you because you don't rely on emotions when making decisions. In your case, your love for Rad screws with your female mojo. It keeps you off balance."

Boy, did it. "Sometimes in a good way. The problem is when it interferes with my job. How do I avoid that?"

"You can't. None of us can avoid conflict between our jobs and our loved ones. If you give everything to one, the other suffers. It's called devotion."

I wiggled my feet under the blanket. The truth was hard to hear even if I already knew it. Coming from the goddess of love, it held more weight.

"The good thing," she continued, "is that women have been making it work for millions of years."

"I'm not an ordinary woman."

"Neither am I."

"No offense, but you suck at long-term relationships."

"Maybe I don't want a long-term relationship."

"You believe in soul mates. How can you not want a long-term relationship with yours?"

Now it was her turn to look away. "I haven't found him yet."

Sadness and guilt flooded me. The goddess of love had never found the very thing she symbolized, while I, a demon of vengeance, had never loved anyone but Rad. In turn, he loved me back.

I thought of Lucifer and Amy. Obviously a love story that had survived everything heaven could throw at it.

Heaven, hell, earth. They all came together somehow and shifted inside me. Perspective was a wonderful thing. "I'm sorry for being so selfish, Di."

She chuckled and patted my hand. "It's your nature to be selfish. Never apologize for being true to yourself. Besides, you're my best friend. I'm here for you, no matter what."

Loyal, selfless, and full of heart. My friends were pretty amazing, especially this one.

Thinking about my nature reminded me of my last intimate

run-in with Dru. He hadn't acted any different since our kiss and subsequent fight, but the memory stayed just under my skin...dynamite ready to explode. "I kissed Dru."

The surprise on her face was comical. "Why, you little minx."

Yasmin's label burned in my ears. "Slut is more like it."

Di waggled her eyebrows. "Was it good?"

"Aphrodite!"

"What? Did you have sex, *too*?"

I covered my eyes with my hands and groaned. "Thank Satan, no, but bottom line, what's the difference? I cheated on Rad."

"It was just a kiss, Kali." She forced my hands away from my face. "Right?"

"My demon made an appearance."

"Damn." Her face said it all. "Must have been some kiss."

"His blood...his magic...I don't know what it was. All I know is that it can never happen again."

"You sure about that?"

For the first time that day, I was sure about something. "Dru and I share this weird bond, but I don't love him. Not like I love Rad."

"Love and sex aren't the same thing. You can desire someone you don't love."

"I don't want to desire him. He's a freakin' vampire!"

"A sexy Master vampire who has deep feelings for you and wants to please you. Why wouldn't you be attracted to him?"

Suddenly too hot, I sat up and tossed the blanket off my legs. "You're not helping."

While I picked at my nails, she sat forward so we were shoulder to shoulder. "If Rad finds out, he'll be extremely disappointed. That's what scares you more than admitting you want to jump Dru's bones and scratch that itch."

"Disappointed? Try devastated. And he'll try to kill Dru, which will end up with one or both of them getting hurt."

"Dru can take care of himself."

"I don't want them fighting over me."

She wrapped an arm around my shoulder. "That's what males do. It's supposed to make you feel desired."

"It makes me feel nauseated."

She squeezed. "Oh, Kali. You are truly one of a kind."

"Why do relationships have to be so hard?"

"They're hard for all of us, but I'm proud of you. You're not a one-man island anymore. You're spreading your wings and letting all of us who care about you in."

"Being an island was a hell of a lot easier."

Her infectious laughter got to me and I smiled. In Maria's court, I'd never had a friend. No one to talk to about Rad or my love life. No one in three hundred years to tell me these complicated, human-like feelings were perfectly normal. "Does this qualify as a heart-to-heart about boys?"

"You bet it does. Now," she rose from the settee and pulled me up with her. "Time for you to get your beauty sleep, defender of the world. We'll talk more later."

We meandered into the bedroom and she watched as I climbed under the covers. Our conversation hadn't actually resolved my issues with Rad or Dru, but I felt better anyway. "Thanks, Di."

"I keep telling you, that's what friends are for."

"If I don't save the world, will we still be friends?"

Her forehead pinched. "Of course, silly. We'll go down in flames together. Thelma and Louise style."

After she left, I lay there looking at the ceiling and feeling odd. "What just happened?" I said out loud.

The walls and furniture had no answer, but my demon did.

Kali Sweet, vengeance demon, has gone soft.

45

A buzzing in my blood woke me a few hours later. The room was cast in shadows and I sat up like I'd been shocked, eyeing the corners of the suite for intruders. I smelled blood. Felt it in my bones. Blood my body craved.

Dru.

I scanned the shadows again but he wasn't hiding in them. Throwing back the covers, I followed the scent of his blood until I reached the apartment's door.

Through the heavy wood, Dru's voice spoke. He knew I was on the other side, sniffing him out. "Kali, I thought you should have a pint of my blood before you do battle tonight."

Satan be damned. He wanted me to drink from him.

My body shuddered. I licked my lips.

Laying my forehead on the door, I squeezed my eyes shut and tried to calm my racing heart. "I don't think that's a good idea."

Damn. My voice betrayed me, coming out low and breathy.

There was a strained pause. "I know you find drinking directly from my vein unappetizing, so I've prepared a glass of blood for you. I'll set it down out here and you can drink it if and when you're ready."

I heard a tray settle on the carpeting. Heard heavy footsteps walking away.

I flung open the door, and sure enough, there was a crystal glass of warm blood at my feet. Dru's back retreated down the hallway.

My throat was tight. I managed to speak through it. "Thank you."

It was barely a squeak, but he heard it. Without looking at me, he stopped, nodded. When he started to walk away, I called out his name. "Dru?"

His body was so tense, I could have bounced my wooden stakes off it.

"Be careful out there."

Again, nothing but a nod with his back still facing me. "You, too, queen. Remember our deal."

Watching him walk away, I raised the glass to my lips with a shaking hand. The blood was thick and tart, puckering my lips, but I downed it.

The velvety liquid slid across my tongue and down my throat, and even though it was still warm, none of the heady feelings I'd experienced feeding at Dru's wrist came with it.

Disappointing. That was a high I'd never be able to duplicate otherwise. There would be no more feeding directly from him.

After forcing the rest down, I went back inside the apartment. I felt revived and confident, ready to fight Parker, Maria, and anyone else who got in my way.

I showered, did my hair, and took stock of my weapons.

Then I dressed, making sure to wear the leather bustier... and a whole lot of sharp weapons.

46

Kirill was still sleeping and I left him alone, figuring our quest for Pestilence could wait until after I'd dealt with Parker.

Cole was in the training center. Damon would have insisted he stay there, getting the teams ready for their scouting missions. Doing things Damon's way no longer appealed to me. It was time I embraced my own way of handling things.

"I'm heading to my place," I told Cole once I pulled him away from a group of soldiers. "I need backup."

His brown eyes sized me up, lingering on my décolleté neckline. My request for help wasn't that unusual and yet he seemed a little surprised. "I'll get my stuff."

We met up again in the parking lot. "What gives?" he asked.

"My place. Parker. Possibly Maria. Rad is baiting them."

The control freak War demon insisted on driving. We were out the gate before he commented. "I know you don't want to hear this, but it could be a trap."

"You think everything's a trap, but this time, you're right. It is a trap for Parker. I have to deal with her before I go after the Horsemen."

He kept his eyes on the road, avoiding the clogged streets and roaming marauders as best he could. His right hand was tight on the wheel. His left hand held a loaded gun on his lap. One finger lightly caressed the trigger as if itching to pull it. "Something you should know about Guitar Boy."

Now what?

"Little bird told me he's been meeting with Parker in secret."

"He told me. She wants him back. Beyond that, he has this plan to draw her out so I can kill her."

Cole shot me a look of jaded disbelief. How could I be so naïve? "You can't trust him, Kali."

"But you trust your source?"

"She's credible."

She. Hmm. "This little bird wouldn't happen to be Brianna, would it?"

His eyes stayed pinned on the road. The hand on the wheel tightened. All the answer I needed. "Dru doesn't trust Rad, and had her follow him."

If that was true, Alexandru and I were going to have a discussion. One that involved me shoving a stake up his ass. "Did Dru tell you that or did Bri? Have you considered she's lying and using you to get to me?"

An incredulous snort. "How exactly would *that* work?"

"It's no secret Brianna doesn't like me. It's also no secret that she's deeply connected to her Master. A Master vampire who wants *me*."

The finger caressing the gun trigger stopped. "Before Damon left, he told me to cover your ass at all costs. I'll shoot first and ask questions later, whether it's Guitar Boy or someone else. Got it?"

Oh, I got it. "I don't want to do this now, but you haven't left me much choice. Brianna's in love with Dru."

"I know."

Wait. "You *know*? Then why are you hooking up with her?"

Belligerent. "Why is that your fucking business?"

"Because you care about her, and I care about you. I won't stand for her using you."

He turned right, accelerated around a car lying on its side. Gave me a quick, assessing glance and a renegade grin that said he knew jealousy when he heard it. "Maybe I want to be used, ever think of that?"

To my astonishment, I realized I was enjoying our argument. It was like old times. Good times. "You're right. It's none of my business, but I know vampires like Brianna. She'll turn on you in a heartbeat. I don't want to see you get hurt."

He exchanged his hands on the wheel, used his right one to make a fist, and punched me in the arm. "Stop it."

"Ow." I rubbed the spot. "What the hell?"

"You're getting mushy."

He was right. But it felt okay to get a bit mushy. "Me? Nah. I'm a hardass vengeance demon. Not a mushy bone in my body."

"Good, 'cuz you need to face facts. Guitar Boy isn't telling you everything."

Paranoia is so ingrained in my system that I spent half a second on Cole's suspicions before shaking them off. One thing about Cole, he called it like he saw it, and I knew he was worried and trying to look out for me. I appreciated that. No way I believed Rad was screwing me over, but to make Cole feel better, I nodded my head. "Just don't shoot his male parts. If he's double-crossing me with Parker, those parts belong to me."

"Good." Cole accelerated onto the interstate. "That's more like it. I knew you were wearing that distracting shirt for a reason."

Besides entertaining Rad? "Something like that."

He glanced at my chest out of the corner of his eye. "No

male in his right mind wouldn't be mesmerized by those babies. If it *is* a trap, he's going down."

I chuckled under my breath. "Did Damon say anything else before he left?"

"Just to look out for you, and, you know, be there for you when the shit hit the fan."

"No words of wisdom? No secret messages?"

"Nope, sorry."

Ten minutes later, he took the turnoff to my place and then passed my block and parked in the shadows of a vacant lot. Cole's idea was to come at the church from the backside like we'd done before when we found Kirill on my kitchen floor.

"I hate that damn cemetery," he said, "but so does every other supernatural creature. It's our best cover while we stake out the place and make sure Parker and Maria aren't lying in wait for you."

Someone *was* waiting for me. Lights blazed in all the downstairs windows. Music blared through the walls. The curtains and blinds were drawn, but shadows moved here and there behind them.

"I count at least three," Cole murmured as we took cover behind a mausoleum on the east side.

I checked my phone. Rad hadn't responded to my earlier text, and nothing was showing up in missed messages or calls. Was he already in Maria's and Parker's hands?

Anger gelled inside me. I opened my senses, going through the same routine I'd used before to locate entities inside my house. What I picked up was a mixed bag. Whiffs of Maria, Parker, and Rad, but suppressed. Vague impressions of other creatures. A shifter, maybe, and someone else.

I strained harder, sending out a light dose of magic along with my five senses. Slowly, it bled through my security system and into the church. I closed my eyes and let my inner eye travel with the stream of energy, picking up impressions as I went.

A weight pressed in on my chest, making it hard to breathe. Astral projection caused that sensation. Trying not to fight it, I imagined my bones were light as a feather, the way Lucifer had made them feel. As my astral being passed through the stone wall and into the kitchen, I was enveloped by a mystical fog. It swirled around me, cutting off my sight and dulling the voices I heard coming from the living room.

Rather than fighting the fog that dulled my senses, I stood still. No point in giving away my tactical advantage, and although I wanted to rush in and attack, I wasn't sure what I was facing. Better to remain immobile and see if I could feel Parker's and Maria's auras.

The loud music dulled even as my nose went to work. Blood. Sweat. Overripe fruit. The scent of decay, rotting flesh, beeswax candles. Damp, ocean air.

Someone was in the throes of sex. I could smell the tang of desire, hear the moans. I felt the moment of release, a tiny death. My heart skipped uncomfortably. Parker and Rad?

Don't go there.

I forced myself to move on.

Someone was eating. Gorging themselves. But the more they ate, the hungrier they became.

Maria?

None of it fit. Everything I came in contact with was off.

Next, I detected the split personality of a shifter. No wait. Two shifters. One canine, the other feline. Their animalistic selves were fighting, snapping and hissing at each other.

The air around me changed suddenly, raising goose bumps up and down my arms. A different kind of magic struck me hard, and a figurehead of a bearded man appeared in front of my astral self. The scent of dead and decaying flesh stole into my throat, choking me. "Join us, will you not, Ms. Sweet?"

Jerking out of the projection, I flew backward through the kitchen, stone wall and yard, tumbling to the ground at Cole's feet when my astral body snapped back into my physical one.

Snow puffed around me as my ass hit the ground, and I sat there, stunned. "Holy shit," I whispered to no one in particular.

The cemetery's ghosts huddled around me, stroking my back, massaging my magic. Still crouching behind the marble façade, Cole offered a hand. "What happened?"

On my feet again, I brushed snow off my backside, not bothering to hide anymore. With a flick of my hand, I sent the ghosts and their black magic back to their corners. "We're made."

"Maria?"

"She's in there. So are Parker and Rad. But there's something else in there. Something I don't understand."

Cole double-checked the gun's clip, a nervous habit he'd already completed at least three times. "Evil?"

"Oh, yeah, but not in the normal sense of the word. Necessary evil is more like it."

His forehead creased. "What are you talking about? What did you see?"

"Death." I removed Parker's dagger from my cape pocket and gave it a couple of turns in my hand. "And he's waiting for me."

47

I was right on all counts.

Death, Pestilence, and War waited for me inside.

A quick inventory of the room showed Parker writhing naked on top of Rad in front of the fireplace, their eyes unfocused and glassy. Maria kneeled between Death's legs, servicing him, her head bobbing hard and fast as he urged her on with one beefy hand buried in her hair.

At a large wooden table someone had dragged into the room, Pestilence was being fed by Arman. At least I assumed it was Pestilence. He didn't shift into a rat or flea, but he was shifting. He and Arman both kept switching between human and animal forms so fast, they were a blur. Pest would shift to a wolf, reach out and bite Arman's neck. Arman would shift to werecat and scratch him, making him laugh. Like Parker, Arman's eyes were glassy.

The wolf seemed vaguely familiar in human form.

Ranulf?

No way. Now I was really pissed I hadn't busted his ass sooner.

I almost missed War standing in a shadowed corner by my

office door. The seven-foot giant was sharpening a wicked-looking knife as long as my arm. The blade sang under his ministrations. When our eyes met, he grinned, displaying a wide gap in his front teeth. Over the thumping music—the Chaos Demons, no less, he asked, "Where be your friend, the War demon?"

He knew Cole was there. Not good. It shouldn't have surprised me. He could probably sense Cole's blood like Pest could sense Kirill's.

"Which one?" I asked with a touch of flippancy. I shut off the music with a snap of my fingers. My communication link was open, so I knew Cole heard his question. "I have so many."

He pointed the end of the knife at me. "I shall enjoy drinking his blood before the sun rises."

Cocky. Perfect. Under my cape, I rubbed the dagger's handle. Nothing better than taking down a Goliath who believed he was invincible.

Cole, on his end, said nothing. He was there, though. I could feel him. Planning. Strategizing.

I couldn't see Maria's eyes as I crossed the room to face the bearded form of Death. He seemed to be the leader, watching me with an evil smile as I drew closer, and climaxing when his gaze landed on my double D's in all their glorious height.

Since I'd been spotted by him in astral form, there'd been no point in hiding. Believing the Horsemen didn't know Cole was there, I'd left him to send out a call to the troops and sneak in after I had the Horsemen's attention.

Attention captured.

Death needed no time to recover from his climax. Still eyeing my breasts, he used Maria's hair to lift her off, twisting her around so she faced me on her knees. "The *vitium* graces us with her presence. Gaze on her beauty. Fairer than you, she is."

The Horsemen's accents were hard to place. Maria's glassy-eyed stare connected with my boots first, then traveled slowly up my legs, over my stomach, never pausing before it reached my face. Her head tilted as if curious, but not an ounce of recognition showed in her face. Her succubus magic was muted, lifeless.

Ignoring Parker pounding away on top of Rad, I met Death's forceful leer. My plan was to keep them distracted until reinforcements arrived. Then we'd divide and conquer. "Have to say, I like Maria better this way. What's your secret?"

Death shoved her off and sat back, spreading his knees wide. "Come sit on my lap, demon."

I sensed Cole's distress on the open comm even though he was silent. My code word was 'mouse', and Cole knew I wouldn't use it to bring him in until I had to.

Death's pants were unzipped and he was ready to go again, standing at full attention. The sight revolted me; the idea of getting anywhere near him was instantly rejected. Sensing my hesitation, he slammed me with a wave of his foggy magic. Hot, clammy, disgusting against my skin. My blood warmed, my limbs tingled.

Was his magic supposed to mesmerize me like it had the others? Seemed to be his plan. It had worked on Maria after all. Parker, Rad, Arman...why not me?

My demon shivered and my vampire blood went on the attack. On its own, it might not have repelled his magic, but combined with my demon blood, it absorbed the energy he sent out and dissolved it without any trouble.

Death cocked his head, sent another wave of magic crashing over me.

Sucking up the *ew* factor, I decided it was best to play along. Nothing like getting up close and personal when taking down an enemy. Not my favorite way to fight, but still effective.

Swaying on my feet, I let my eyes go dull and flat, pretending to be under Death's spell. Then I walked past Parker

*—the bitch—*who couldn't seem to finish the job with Rad and crawled onto the couch.

I didn't just sit on Death's lap like an errant schoolgirl. I straddled him so my breasts were in his face and my legs went on either side of his. He was big. Not as tall as War, but wide and thick-muscled. His stiff member poked my butt and I shifted to press it down and away from me, trying not to gag.

Death pawed me and I went to my happy place. *Happy place* for me translated to the moment when I yanked Parker off Rad and used her as a shield when I went vengeance demon on a couple of Horsemen's asses.

"Where is the other one?" I asked Death as he sucked at the soft mound of my left breast. "I thought there were four of you."

War was watching us, so I made sure to keep the flat affect in place as I ground my hips into Death's lap. His hands went up under my cape and I held my breath, praying he wouldn't find the weapons stashed there. He didn't notice, his hands busy gripping my hips and groping my ass cheeks as he tried to position me where he wanted me.

Good luck with that, buddy boy.

"All four are here," he muttered against my neck. The scar on my neck from Dru burned when Death's tongue trailed over the silvery outline. "You'll get your chance with each of us, that is a promise. But then you've already experienced a thorough fucking from the Prophet, now, haven't you?"

Dread slammed into me. "What?"

Death drew back, frowned. Females under his spell weren't supposed to ask questions. I stared at a mirror on the far wall, keeping my face impassive. In the mirror, Rad's three awards gleamed like glass soldiers on the mantle.

Seemingly satisfied that I was still fog-happy, he pinched my nipples through the leather bustier and bit the sensitive skin over my clavicle, drawing blood. "Radison Beaumont. The White Horseman."

My blood froze on the spot. It couldn't be true.

Emotions were for the weak. Logic, a welcome friend, came to my rescue.

If Rad's a Horseman, why is he under Death's spell?

Was he? I resisted the urge to look at him.

Death grabbed my panties and ripped them in half. The demon in me hissed.

"Unfortunate that he be half human." Death grabbed Mr. Winky and rubbed him against me. "Humans be weak. Not of use to us."

I threw up a little in my mouth at the feel of his hot skin against mine. I calculated my next move as he continued, licking his lips as he spoke. "Leading the masses be a worthless skill, unlike infecting lowly humans with plague. We watch them die slow, tortured deaths."

That does it.

Logic didn't have time to talk me out of my next move. Parker's dagger was in my hand before Death nipped the top of my breast again.

I slammed it home, going up under his ribs and driving it into his heart.

48

Fighting three of the four Horsemen on my own was akin to juggling chainsaws.

A dagger to the heart wouldn't kill Death. Cutting off his head with it would take too long. Time was the one thing I didn't have.

Okay, I didn't have my army either, but they'd be here soon.

I hope.

War was watching from his corner when I drove the dagger into Death's heart. The back of the couch hid us from War's direct view, so I kept the trance-like look on my face, grabbed Death by the back of his neck with my left hand, and tightened my legs around his lower body. Shifting my weight backward, I toppled us off of the couch, making it look like Death was throwing me to the floor and driving Mr. Winky home.

The bearded Horseman was a limp noodle by the time we landed. His body on top of mine jerked a couple of times and then went still. I rolled him to the left where Maria still lay in a fog. How long did I have before he came to? Minutes? Seconds?

Having never fought a Horseman before, I went with the worst-case scenario: *Thirty seconds, Kali. Make it work.*

Out of War's sight behind the couch, I came up on hands and knees. I was only a few feet from Rad and Parker, who were still going at it like rabbits in a daze. There was no kissing or fondling. Just a lot of endless, meaningless humping. The fact Rad was, indeed, the White Horseman gave me pause. Had he been lying to me all along about his False Prophet status?

My gut told me no. He'd been used unwittingly. Why, I wasn't sure, but there's no way he could have kept that kind of secret from me all these months. I would have picked it up in his aura if nothing else.

Of course, I hadn't realized he was meeting Parker on the side until he confessed.

The *ziiing* of War sharpening his knife snapped me back to the present. *Deal with War and Pest. Then figure out what to do with Rad.*

War's knife was nearly sword-length. Sharp enough from his meticulous whetting to cut through bone, I'd bet. If I could get it away from him, it might do the trick to cut off the Horsemen's heads. But would they stay dead?

Kirill claimed a weapon forged by a Horseman wouldn't kill one. Guess it was time to find out if that was true.

To my left, Death came back online, moving a bit and moaning. It was a moan of pain, but I hoped War would think it was a satisfied sex moan.

I would only have one chance to surprise War and Pest. Pestilence was still entertaining himself with Arman, and my protective instincts wanted to take him on first and save my blood slave.

But Arman would have to wait. War was my next target. I needed that knife.

Parker sat on top of Rad. She didn't take notice as I crawled the couple of feet to her side. I held her dagger in one hand, Death's cold blackish blood covering my skin and making my grip slippery. Volante curled around my waist, trembling and wanting in on the action.

Soon, my pet.

I toyed with the dagger, turning its handle around and around in my palm. The demon in me wanted to drive the dagger into the base of Parker's spine and use it to shred her intestines. Instead, I switched the dagger to my free hand, took a centering breath, and grabbed Parker by the back of the hair.

In one swift motion, I rose to my feet, hauling Parker with me.

I intended to use her as a shield in case War threw his knife at me, which was what I hoped he'd do: throw the knife, hit Parker, and allow me to remove it from her body. At that point, I'd use it on Death first, then War and Pestilence.

But when I came up with Parker in front of me, War didn't seem all that surprised. Like a Greek god of old, he simply looked annoyed, rising to his full height and giving me an *I'm going to enjoy hurting you* look.

We'll see about that.

Parker's haze broke enough for her to realize she was no longer on top of Rad. She stumbled in front of me, my hand still holding onto her hair like the reins on a horse. "Put down the knife and let's talk," I said to War, even though I knew he had no intention of letting go of his toy.

That made us even. I had no intention of talking.

He chuckled, and the low, gravelly sound made the hair on the back of my neck stand up. Raising the knife and pointing it at me, he said something that sounded like Latin but with his odd accent I couldn't be sure. "*Hasta la victoria siempre.*"

Until the eternal victory.

Huh. War was quoting the Marxist revolutionary Che Guevara. Never imagined heaven's soldiers being Communist. Maybe War gave Che his start?

War circled me, that wicked knife doing an elegant dance in

the air as he drew closer. Death groaned again, but he'd lost a lot of blood...blood that pooled around him and Maria. Pestilence finally realized all was not right in his animal world and morphed into his human form as Ranulf and stayed there. Arman collapsed at his feet, and Rad lay motionless in front of the fireplace.

I backed toward Rad, keeping Parker in front of me. "Yeah, well, better dead than Red."

It was the only solid anti-Communist comeback I could think of.

"Cole?" I said into my comm. "Could use some help in here."

"Already inside," he said, emerging from the shadows of the kitchen.

War and Pest did a double take. I just chuckled. "Damn, you're good."

"I keep sayin'."

Bri, Dru and a dozen or so Chicago vampires stood behind him. How had they arrived so fast? No time to speculate. "War, here, is pushing Communist propaganda. What do you say we show him how Capitalists fight?"

War looked confused. Pest backed up, so he stood behind the table.

Then War gave another deep chuckle. "Shut up and fight, demon."

Dividing his attention between me and Cole's small army, the Horseman brandished his knife and snarled. Definitely had to get that blade away from him. It might not be Michael's sword or even forged in angel fire, but from the way he was doting on it, it packed some righteous power. Power, I bet, that could kill him and his buddies, no matter what Kirill believed.

"Hey, War."

He looked at me. I waved Parker's dagger. The second his gaze focused on the blade, I tossed it in the air. His attention followed and that was all the distraction I needed. I picked up Parker and threw her.

Though not big in her own right, she was a large projectile. War ducked and Bri took a running slide, hitting the floor and knocking her booted feet into his ankles. Parker, screaming all the way, would have missed him if she hadn't flailed her arms and managed to grab his hair.

War's legs went out from under him from Bri's kamikaze move. At the same time, his head snapped back as Parker grabbed hold. The three of them landed in a messy pile, but War didn't lose his knife.

"Kali?" Rad's voice came from the fireplace, sounding baffled. "What's going on?"

I hauled him to his feet. "We're fighting for our lives. Now man up and ...oh, my god."

Speaking of manning up—my gaze fell on his very large, very engorged manhood. Heat flushed my body. My demon licked her lips. Could I pick a worse time to be in heat?

Shaking it off, I forced my attention back to his face and cleared my throat. "Get ready to fight, Beaumont, or I'll kill you myself here and now."

"Kali!" He lifted a hand like he was going to grab me. "You need to—"

"Not fucking now!"

"Behind you," Cole bellowed, and I realized a second too late that Rad was trying to warn me.

Death grabbed me by the neck with both hands. His fingers encircled my throat, crushing my windpipe. He lifted me from the floor and kept me at arm's length, shaking me in front of the others. "Put down your weapons or she dies."

I couldn't breathe.

"You can't kill her," Dru volunteered. "She's one of the original sins."

War tossed Parker off and jumped up, stomping on Brianna

as he did so. She was a tough bitch and sprang up just as fast, going for the knife in his hand.

Dark spots danced in front of my eyes. I wanted to tell Dru to shut up...challenging Death to see if he could, in fact, kill me was a bit too brazen for my liking. Since I couldn't form words, I did the next best thing.

Maria had risen to her knees, propping her upper body on the couch cushion. Using her to gain my footing, I ran up her back, kicked off from her shoulders, and flipped my feet ass-over-tea kettle, using Death's strong-arm stance as a lever.

My neck didn't fare well, but the heels on my boots scored as they came over my head. I twisted out of his grasp. One spike landed in Death's eye, the other in his cheek. He howled and jerked back, releasing me.

I dropped like a rock, my boot heels making a satisfying suction sound as they popped out of Death's cranium. Flipping the rest of the way over, I somersaulted and landed on my feet like an Olympic pro.

War, enraged, charged me with his knife. I fumbled for the dagger lying on the floor as I ducked behind the couch. Strong legs appeared in my peripheral vision and I looked up to see Rad hurl the pointed end of one of his People's Choice Awards at War's chest.

Pestilence jumped into the foray, and the vampires descended on him, taking him to the floor. Blood and hair flew in all directions as he tried shifting back to wolf. War staggered when the glass point embedded itself in his heart, and Cole jumped on his back, taking him down as well. Death—recovered but with one eye damaged and bleeding profusely—let out a war cry and attacked me once more. As his compact body took me down, Rad raised another award over his head and brought the pointed end down on Death's back, driving it through to his heart.

The next few minutes were a confusing, blood-thirsty battle

between good and evil. Maria, Parker and Arman woke up fully from Death's magic fog. Maria and Parker attacked me while Death nearly bled out again. He didn't die, however, and kept rising to come after me.

Rad—who'd found his pants and put them on—fought by my side, shirtless with his bare feet poking out from under his frayed jeans, sliding through the blood and debris. He fended off Maria and Parker as best as he could while I worked on Death.

The vampires and Pestilence continued their fight. Arman went down early. Dead or just hurt, I couldn't tell.

Cole, Brianna, and Dru advanced on War, retreated when he overcame them and advanced again. War would hurt Brianna, Dru would jump in with his sword and try to disarm him, and Cole would manage to get in a punch or two. Then War would injure Cole, and Brianna would jump in.

Back and forth our dances went. No one winning, no one losing.

In the bowels of the house, I heard the security alarm go off. A little late for that, but I hoped it signaled the arrival of more troops.

I wanted to unleash my demon, but Damon's voice was as clear in my head as if he were standing beside me. *Evil may win battles, but it cannot win this war. Good before evil, Kali. Save the world. Save yourself.*

It scared me, that voice. *Save the world.* No pressure there, right?

Worse...*save yourself.*

The past days and months went by in a flash. All the failures. I was no leader, too reckless and selfish to make the decisions that had to be made.

Di was wrong—I *was* still an island—and an island was a poor friend, selfish lover, and disastrous leader. I hadn't even been aware Rad was a freakin' Horseman, for Satan's sake.

What if I don't want to save myself? I argued with Damon's imaginary voice. *Not sure I'm worth saving.*

A loud explosion rocked the church. Debris fell from the ceilings, beams crashed around us, and we paused in our various fights to take cover as the front of the church exploded, leaving a gaping hole.

I blinked in surprise at the woman standing there. My voice croaked since part of my windpipe was still injured. "Amy?"

Lucifer's witch led dozens of men and women into the disaster area I'd once called a living room. Maddy followed on her heels, a wide grin on her face until she saw the shambles of the place.

"What are you doing here?" I searched the crowd for Lucifer. I saw Father Reese, Nicola and...wait. Was that Detective Moreno? Even Reese's Merc demon was present. No devil, though. He would never let the witch out of his sight. "Where's Lucifer?"

She smiled and waved as if she'd crashed a tea party instead of a fight. "He'll be here soon." From under a blazing red trench coat, she pulled a sword that sang brightly when released from its scabbard. It also glowed. "Meanwhile, thought you might need this."

She threw it. The sword sailed through the air, the handle, decorated with a pair of elegant, swirling gold wings, arched perfectly toward me. I reached out and it landed in my hand, the second my skin touched the hilt, a charge of electricity shocked me from head to foot.

My skin burned. The sensation reminded me of being tased. I cried out, my body vibrating with the intensity of the charge, but I clenched my teeth and tightened my grip.

Turning, I swung the blade at Death's neck.

49

War moved at the same time, throwing his knife.

The two blades connected, a golden light bursting forth from the sword. The impact was so intense, the reverberation stung my palm and sent me sideways, making me stagger and nearly fall.

In the next second, I registered two things: Rad's hands steadying me, and a sharp, deep pain in the side of my neck. War's knife had bounced off the sword and embedded itself a few centimeters from the base of my throat.

There was a bunch of screaming, yelling, and commotion, but everything sounded distant and muffled in my ears as I slumped into Rad's arms. All I heard distinctly was the beat of my heart and the sound of Damon's voice. *If you won't fight for yourself, fight for me.*

Dots swam in my vision and my knees turned to water. Rad dragged me toward the couch, and Death laughed, the sound echoing off what was left of the high rafters of my living room.

Fight for me.

The scent of wood smoke filled my nose. My eyes fluttered closed even though I tried to keep them open. *Damon?*

"Kali."

His voice seemed so real. Not in my head. I forced my eyelids open.

My vision was blurry, but I saw his face in front of me. *Am I hallucinating?*

Hot blood poured down my neck. All around me, supernaturals and humans shouted my name like a battle cry. The clashing of metal resumed.

All I heard was Damon's voice saying, "I'm here."

It took me a moment to realize he really *was* there, not just a figment of my imagination. My heart did a hop and a skip and I reached out to touch him.

You're back. I couldn't speak, except mentally. I couldn't even sigh. But my fingers trailed over his aristocratic jaw and high cheekbones. I felt lightheaded. *I can't do this, Damon. I can't be you.*

Of course you can't. Be what you are, Kali. A vengeance demon.

What about the other things?

Those...components...of your being don't matter at the moment.

Components. Even in the middle of a fight, Damon couldn't bring himself to use a common word like *things*. I would have laughed if I'd had the strength.

I wasn't even sure what the *other* things were anymore. Everything was fuzzy. Rad had removed the knife and was pressing a cloth against my throat. Fighting continued around us, the clash of magics and weapons pounding against my senses. Amy's crew seemed to be holding their own against the Horsemen, but the sword was still in my hand.

Rad was talking to me. Maddy was talking to me. I couldn't focus on anything but Damon.

I stared into his eyes—so dark, so unfathomable. His magic reached for mine, soothing me and encouraging my neck to heal. Damon's magic, Rad's hands, Dru's blood...everything inside me suddenly flooded with heat. A rush of adrenaline.

My neck stopped bleeding. My vision cleared.

Even better than Rad's healing rune.

Sword in hand, I sat up. A new rush of warmth suffused my head. Not Damon's voice, but my own. *You didn't come to help me. You came because of Amy.*

He spoke out loud. "I came because of *you*."

I didn't believe him and was about to tell him so when without warning, Death appeared and grabbed him from behind. He flew across the room, taking Damon with him.

I shot off the couch, following them, sword raised. Death had wrapped a meaty arm around Damon's neck and continued hauling him backward, using him as a shield.

Copycat.

The soldiers with Amy parted. The fighting around us stopped. An eerie silence descended as Death glared at me from the corner of the room. "Try it, demon. Take your best shot."

From the side, Pestilence, in Ranulf's wolf form, launched himself at me. I reacted on instinct, my reflexes working as one with the sword as I turned my body to face him and sliced the glowing blade through the air.

It cleaved him in half at the breastbone. The sword made another swift cut and the Horseman's head hit the floor at the same time the rest of his body did.

He might not stay dead, but by golly, he was in pieces for now.

War came next with a war cry. Without any command, the sword lifted, and no thanks to me, buried itself in his stomach. There was a popping sound and the sword released a small burst of light.

War dropped to his knees. I withdrew the sword and beheaded him where he knelt at my feet.

I faced Death, a strange ringing in my ears. He still clutched Damon in front of him, but now he also jammed Parker's dagger at Damon's neck. Damon didn't struggle, only fixed on my gaze with his sure, unwavering dark eyes. *Cut off his head.*

I shook my head. *I'll cut off yours as well.*

All eyes were on me. Death snickered, seeing my hesitation.

Be what you are, Kali. I promise, all will be well.

The demon inside me smiled. *Vengeance is mine.* The sword warmed in my hand.

No. I'd just gotten Damon back. *I will not sacrifice you.*

The sword vibrated. Around my waist, Volante did too. If I could use her to injure Death without injuring Damon...

"Cut off his head!" Damon demanded of me. His magic crackled in the air. "Now!"

Against my will, my hand rose with the sword. *I will not*, I mentally yelled. At Damon or the sword, I wasn't sure.

Seeing the sword, Death reared back, digging the dagger deeper into the skin under Damon's chin. Blood poured from the wound. "Swing that sword and your lover dies."

At the word *lover*, all eyes turned to me.

Including Rad's.

A biting wind swept through the open front of the building, whipping past me and the others and throwing snow and ice into our eyes. The flaps of my cape lifted and debris from overhead rained down. The fire in the fireplace roared to three times its original size, flames licking up the sides and catching the furniture on fire. Every light fixture, glass window, and mirror in the place exploded.

Rad lunged. The sword flew from my hand. The two connected in the air, and with a graceful spin and arch of his back, my real lover brought the blade down and across.

Damon's and Death's heads rolled.

50

I'm not a screamer.

Seeing Damon's dismembered body, however, turned me into one.

My screams shook what was left of the walls. I rushed Rad, grabbed him, and threw him across the room. He hit the kitchen wall so hard, he went through it.

Dru was by my side in an instant but I shoved him away as well. Not as hard, but hard enough to get my point across. He slammed into the stairs.

I fell on my knees beside Damon's headless body and wept.

Minutes went by. Hours. Around me, bodies moved, voices spoke in low tones, a collective relief fell. The Horsemen did not rise again.

Those who had known Damon gathered around. Salmad cradled his head and brought it back to his body. After Cole and Dru dragged me away, the body was then covered.

Cole and Dru sat me on what was left of the couch, blabbering nonsense at me while Maddy tried to get me to drink some tea. I stared into the now-dead fireplace and focused on breathing slowly and evenly. My demon paced just under my skin, furious at Rad, mad at the whole fucking world, and ready to take it out on everyone.

Amy came over and shooed Dru out of the way so she could sit next to me. Her sister and her best friend, Keisha, the voodoo priestess who worked at Amy's shop and slept with Gabriel, crowded around. They kept one eye on Amy and another on the dead Horsemen.

Amy was once again in possession of the sword and she laid the scabbard across both our laps. The blade had been wiped clean before reinserted but I could smell the faint scent of Damon's skin. My eyes burned with more tears.

The humans who'd fought with us were all dead. Father Reese, Detective Moreno, Nicola. Their bodies were carried out. Reese's Merc demon gave me a stiff nod and took his leave.

Maria and Parker were subdued. They disappeared under guard by a battalion of vampire soldiers and Shayne.

Amy put an arm around me as if we were friends. I stiffened at the contact. "I'm so sorry. I know the two of you were close."

Close? *Close?*

Tears streamed down my cheeks. I concentrated on breathing in through my nose and out through my mouth. Using one hand, I dashed at the waterworks. I looked up at Dru. "Where is he?"

They all knew who I was talking about. Dru played dumb anyway. "Arman? Maddy's tending to his wounds. He'll be fine in a day or two."

Traitor. I turned to Cole. "Where is *il pistolino*?"

What I really wanted to ask was, *how could he do this to me?*

A deafening explosion hit the church, worse than the previous one. Everyone dove for cover.

Everyone but me.

I faced the front opening, feeling angelic magic flooding my house with a fiery concentration of power and strength.

But the angel didn't come through the front door. He ripped off the roof.

Michael, on a mission to regain his beloved sword, descended from heaven on a horse, breathing fire and brimstone. Revenge was in his eyes.

51

Would the sword work against its master?

I didn't know, nor did I care. I raised it, mimicked War's battle cry and launched myself into the air.

We met in what was previously my second-story bedroom. All that remained was a hole in the center and the walls around the outside edge.

I swung the sword blindly, not sure how I was managing to fly. My feet peddled air—a Wile E. Coyote imitation—and yet I continued to rise instead of fall.

My demon burst forth in a show of black lightning bolts, reflecting the flames shooting from Michael's steed. Both the angel and his horse were ginormous. I must have truly looked like an ant attacking a giant.

I didn't care. I cursed Michael, calling him every name in my wide lexicon of swear words. Shaking the sword at him, I blasted him with evil energy. "This is my home, my town. These are my friends. You're not welcome here on Earth."

My tantrum was short-lived. He took one look at me and

sneered. White light exploded from his eyes, twin laser beams of death and destruction. They hit me in unison, ripping through me and catapulting my body end over end until I lost momentum and fell toward the ground.

I was out over the cemetery, the marble grave markers and snow-covered ground speeding toward me much too fast. Welcoming it, I let the sword fall from my hand as I prepared myself to die.

The beat of giant wings filled my ears. A powerful rush of angelic mojo caught me, and suddenly, the sword was back in my possession.

"Your raw gutsiness is admirable," Lucifer said in my ear as he wrapped those beautiful wings around me. "But your life is not forfeit today."

He swooped through the air, avoiding a blast of fire from Michael's horse, then landed with me in the cemetery. A protective bubble of magic formed over us.

My demon bowed her head, disappointed she didn't get to take a swing at Michael, but relieved too. The rest of me was simply raw, miffed I'd been cheated out of death. "Damon's dead."

Lucifer scanned the sky and brought his attention back to me. "He never should have let Amy come here on her own. He was tasked with keeping her safe."

"You can't control her either, can you?"

He sighed and I knew I was right.

"She brought me the sword," I said, wanting him to forgive her. "Without it, I couldn't have killed the Horsemen. You have to give her credit for doing the right thing."

The archangel galloped overhead, searching for us. Lucifer ignored him. "You didn't kill all of them."

"Why didn't you tell me Rad was the White Horseman?"

"Would you have believed me?"

No. "I would have been better prepared."

He chuckled. "Even your lover didn't know. How could you prepare for that?"

How indeed. "Will I have to kill him?"

"He's no threat to you or the humans without the other three. Leave him be."

Thank Satan. Literally. "Where's Michael's army?"

"He cannot lead it without his sword."

"So it's just you and him, *mano-a-mano*?"

"Appears as such. Without the sword and the Horsemen, he can't start Armageddon. This fight is between the two of us. There's not much he won't do to get that damn sword back."

I handed it to him. "Kick his ass. He deserves it."

Lucifer didn't take it. "I'm surprised you care."

"I don't. I just like a good fight."

His cocky smirk told me he didn't believe me.

Stupid fallen angel. "Bring Damon back. I know you have the power."

The smirk faded. "I cannot undo what Michael's sword has done."

"Bullshit."

He shook his head, sadness clouding his black eyes. "Damon trained you to be strong. To take his place. It's time for you to live up to that."

Spreading his wings, he rose into the air, the bubble of protection evaporating with his absence. For a moment, I watched the two angels fight...fire, wings, and magics clashing in a chaotic frenzy.

Those inside the church poured out to watch as well. Behind them, fires burned in the skeletal remains of my house.

In the crowd, I saw Maddy, Cole, and Dru looking for me. Absent was Rad.

Good thing too. The numbness inside me hadn't spread far enough to stop me from killing him.

I turned my back on all of it—the fight, my friends, and

Damon's death—and started walking, dropping the sword on the ground.

52

Four hours later, I sat in Damon's dark office, rocking in his leather chair.

The Institute was deathly quiet even though the majority of residents and visitors had all returned. Eavesdropping on their whispered conversations, I confirmed Lucifer had repelled Michael. An outcome I'd watched in the distance from a bench in Millennium Park.

The humans in the surrounding areas thought it was a fireworks display, a meteor breaking apart in the atmosphere and raining down fiery bits and pieces, a freak aurora borealis no one could explain, or an alien landing...

While walking through Chicago that night, I heard dozens of excuses for the fire and brimstone display—every possible reason under the sun except the real one.

Whatever reason they picked to believe, the humans stopped fighting and rioting. That was a good thing. By the time I arrived back at the Institute, reports were being received all over the Chicagoland area that the epidemics had peaked and were subsiding. The red water in Lake Michigan had returned to its normal, wintery gray.

Two days later, the first person to break my silence was Amy. She burst into the office, where I'd camped out, flipped on the lights, and smiled at me. "I want to make a deal."

I wasn't up for talking. My throat was healed, but it still felt tight and unwilling to make sounds and converse, especially with a perky witch who wanted to make demands on me.

But she was Lucifer's mistress. His *pregnant* mistress.

And she'd saved my ass.

I motioned her toward a chair. "How did you get Michael's sword?"

She made herself comfortable, the golden wings of the blade in its scabbard peeking out from under her coat. "Ever heard of the angel Raguel?"

I sat back, the memory of the catacombs surfacing. "The angel of vengeance."

She glanced at Damon's library of antique books. "He appeared to me in my shop. He gave me the sword and told me to get it to you, regardless of what Lucifer wanted."

"Why did he go through you? Why didn't he give it to me himself?"

"Right? I asked the same thing." She acted frustrated. "He said it was better if the two of you didn't meet. That if you did, you'd set off some kind of a weird karmaclysmic explosion."

"Karma?" I couldn't keep the irritation out of my voice.

She made air quotes. "'Divine unbalancing' is what he called it."

Huh. Sounded like he was chickenshit to face me. Like someone else I knew. "So what is this deal you want to negotiate?"

"I need a place for a couple hundred of the Fallen to stay and train. To recoup from being held prisoner for so long."

I gave her my blank face. She couldn't seriously be suggesting...

"You have room here at the Institute," she continued.

"Lucifer said there's an entire wing that's empty and you have one of the best training programs around."

Swallowing my disbelief, I saw an opportunity. "I want Damon back."

She screwed up her lips. "I can't offer that."

When she saw me set my jaw, she put up a hand. "I already tried to get Luc to release him from his contract. He said he can't. For now, Damon's in the pit...the sword sent him there. While there may be ways around Damon spending eternity in hell, the means are few and...well...you should leave that kind of magic alone or risk your own well-being."

I rocked the chair, thinking. "Your vodun priestess. She ever raise anyone from hell?"

Amy blanched and I knew I'd hit gold.

"Who was it?"

"Me. Sort of. She didn't do it alone, though, and I wasn't really dead."

Interesting. "She ever raise a demon?"

"Don't know. Don't *want* to know." Removing the sword, she laid it on the desk. An offering. "This in exchange for housing the Fallen and training them to be the warriors they were born to be."

"How did you manage to keep it from Michael?"

"Luc's creative when he wants to be. You should hide it. Michael will be back for it."

"Not interested."

She slowly let the air out of her lungs, reaching for something, anything that would make me bite. "I'll talk to Keisha. See what she says about raising a demon. Between she and I— you know I'm a Fallen, right?"

I nodded and she continued. "Between the two of us, we can probably figure out a way to get Damon topside again. But Luc won't let him out of his contract."

"Does Lucifer know you're here? That you want me to hide Michael's sword?"

"He sent me. You know, a woman-to-woman thing. Thought I might have better luck getting you to agree. He says you're a malapert." She made air quotes around the Damon-like term. "I don't even know what that means, but he says you don't see things his way and piss him off. A good trait, if you ask me."

She winked, but I kept my face stone.

The forced brevity left her aura. "Luc wants you to know that he appreciates your sacrifice for our child. So do I."

I'd frozen my heart into a solid lump of granite. Nothing could penetrate it. Not pats on the back, not bribes, not thank yous.

But, dammit, something about this fallen-angel-turned-human-witch got under my skin. Satan take me, I liked her. "My sacrifice?"

"You took on the Horsemen to save the human race from the apocalypse, and lost not one, but two men you loved. You gave us and our child a chance. Prophecy says this child is destined to reunite heaven and earth one day. All the Fallen can go home."

Yeah, good luck with that. "Why would Lucifer ever want to return to heaven?"

She looked sad for me. "I used to think that way, too, but I've changed my mind about it. It's not all bad."

I almost asked her how she knew. Tried to harden my heart again. "I wish you well with your baby."

"Do you have children?"

"No." And I never would.

"Can I tell you something I haven't told anyone else?"

Oh, jeez. "Sure."

"I'm scared shitless. I don't know anything about being a mom."

I thought of my own mother. My little sister. Maddy. "Have patience with him and with yourself."

"Him? It's a girl."

Nope. I had the distinct impression it was a boy. His aura pushed through hers, reaching for me. "How far along are you?"

"Only a few weeks, but I know it's a girl. I have, um, insider knowledge."

She jumped a little, like something had pinched her, and her eyes widened. "Oh, God. I think she just kicked me." Her hand rubbed her abdomen. "That's not possible, is it? I'm not far enough along to feel the baby move."

Hell, if I knew. What I *did* know was that the child was not female. "Amy, I don't want to burst your bubble, but the baby is a boy. I can read his aura. One-hundred-percent male testosterone. Angelic male testosterone like his father."

"What?" She sat back down. "That makes no sense. The baby's supposed to be a girl."

Kirill was no baby doctor, but I wondered if he could confirm my belief. "Would you like to see our resident doctor?"

The air in the room heated and shimmered. Lucifer appeared, moving toward Amy before he was fully solid. "What is it? I felt your distress."

Amy looked into his face and her expression softened. "It's nothing. Stop freaking out over every little thing."

I really liked this female.

Lucifer's jaw tightened. He took her hand and kneeled beside the chair. At the same time, he shot a damning look my way. "What did you do to her?"

I locked in my shields, repelling the heat rolling off of him. "Told her the truth about the baby. It's a boy."

Nothing could prepare me for the way the devil's face morphed into surprised joy. "We're having a boy?"

Amy glanced at me, back to him. "I...I don't know. I was sure it was a girl."

And then, I felt it. A small, shy trickle of magic, hiding behind the forceful male energy. I couldn't help but smile. "*Mamma mia*. I don't believe it."

They both looked at me and, in unison, said, "What?"

I rose from the desk and waved at them to follow me. "Let's go see Kirill."

53

Kirill, healed and back to his old ways, confirmed it around a mouthful of chocolate fudge cake. "Twins. A boy and a girl."

"*What?*" Lucifer and Amy said again in unison.

"That's not possible," Amy mumbled.

I gave her a *you've got to be kidding* look. "You're a fallen angel. Lucifer loves you. You just faced down the Horsemen of the apocalypse and won. How is having twins an impossibility in your book?"

She gave a sheepish grin. "It's just I ... I don't know how to handle one baby, much less two."

Lucifer kissed her forehead. "This will be a piece of cake compared to what we've already been through."

"Speaking of cake." She eyed Kirill's quickly-disappearing slice. "Is there more of that somewhere?"

I led them downstairs to the cafeteria, made sure they had all the cake they wanted and accepted Lucifer's strained thanks.

Before I could escape, he drew me aside. "The Chaos demon is in great pain."

Good.

Every time the memory of him and Parker fucking in front of my fireplace flashed through my mind, *I* was in pain. Every time I remembered how he'd fooled me and met with her behind my back, the pain turned into anger.

And when I remembered how he'd grabbed the sword from my hand and killed Damon in front of my eyes, the anger morphed into revenge.

I'd stayed away from thoughts of Rad since then, but Lucifer's comment snuck up on me.

Steeling my emotions, I trained my eyes on the ugly linoleum at my feet and made a note to myself as the Institute's new director: *update the cafeteria's flooring. Check.* "I hope he's agonizingly miserable."

"He did what you wouldn't do. He deserves your thanks, not your hate."

"Seriously? You, defending a lowly half-human, half-demon?" I met his hard gaze. "He cut off Damon's head. That's unforgivable."

"He followed Damon's orders to save you from having to do it because he knew you'd never forgive yourself."

My breath stuck in my throat.

I hadn't considered that. Still... "He should have left the job to me. I had a solution to work around Damon and still behead Death."

Lucifer didn't believe me. "You've lived a long time, vengeance demon. Your heart is stone."

"Keeps those ugly emotions at bay."

"Does it? You find righteousness in being alone and miserable."

Damn right. "Not all of us have lived a charmed life like you."

My malapert insolence irritated him. "Forgive the Chaos demon. He did the right thing."

"Have you found a way to release Damon from the pit yet?"

"Yes, but he still must complete his end of our bargain."

Hope unfroze part of my heart. "Is he okay?"

"He lives."

As if that were enough. Maybe it was. "He's not guarding Amy."

"Michael has returned to heaven. You possess the sword. When my brother returns, and he will, he'll come after you. I have other uses for Damon's skills at this time."

So much for appreciating my sacrifice. The devil wanted his archenemy hunting me and not him and Amy when he came back. "Damon belongs here."

"Damon is serving a greater purpose."

I almost laughed at the ridiculousness. Lucifer was being purposefully ambiguous and enjoying my frustration. "When will you cut him loose?"

"When the time is right."

"Can he earn leave? Just for an hour or two? I need to talk to him."

He sneered and my skin burned, his magic shredding my shields like they were paper.

I pleaded. "Please. I need to see him and know he's okay."

The sneer faded. "I'll see what I can do."

I left the cafeteria, my pride and righteousness stretched to the limit, but with hope making my heart softer than it had been in days.

54

I lived on that hope for the next week. Meanwhile, I threw myself into Damon's job, resumed my duties as vamp queen, and let Maddy completely redo Yasmin's empty room into a bedroom for her. Think Goth princess meets Aeropostale. Arman, healed and back to normal, spent a lot of time in there with her.

Seraphina and Kirill shacked up in his apartment and set up a proper lab to care for all the new and incoming guests we had. Damon's room sat exactly the way he'd left it. I never attempted to cross the magical barrier again.

I reorganized the Institute's soldiers into squads, set up a training schedule for the Fallen, and hired more help. An assistant for me, six housekeepers for Lainie, and two dozen cooks for the kitchen. Within days, we had nearly two hundred supernaturals living, eating, and working on the Institute's grounds.

Cole brought in Brianna to help train our new soldiers and he took a couple of his best students and promoted them so we had enough lieutenants to handle the squads. When they weren't training, the squads went into the surrounding neighborhoods and helped South Siders rebuild their houses and their futures.

Maddy wanted to be my assistant, but she was the least organized female I knew, so I hired my friend Neve instead. She ran a tight ship and never hesitated to call me on the carpet for screwing up. Her electric wheelchair buzzed in the hallways at all times of the day and night and everyone loved her motherly hen-pecking even though they groaned good-naturedly when they heard her coming.

Di held down the fort at Sweet Investigations, and I trained Arman to take over some of my cases there with JR's help. Maddy pitched in when needed, and I spotted her and Arman holding hands outside near the back dock.

Cole kept a close eye on our prisoners.

I missed Damon and my hope that he would show up dwindled. One day, I went to see the women in the prison below my feet.

I felt nothing when I looked in on Parker. She lay cold and naked in her cell and immediately began begging for her life. I spit on her and went to examine Maria.

Strung up by her favorite instrument of torture, I'd also placed various wards and spells, thanks to Amy's friend Keisha, on the cell to keep her contained. Every few hours, one of the *vitiums* would behead her to keep her from gaining enough strength to break through our security measures.

Assured Maria was harmless and in great pain, I opened the door to Victoria's cell and asked her a question. "What does it take to raise a demon from hell?"

She raised a hand to shield her eyes as the light from the hallway hit her face. Her red hair looked like she'd been electrocuted. Deep lines had formed around her mouth during her stay in solitary confinement. She hadn't spoken in weeks and her voice came out a croak. "Fuck off."

"If I offered you your freedom, could you do it?"

That got her attention. "What demon?"

"An archdemon."

Her eyes narrowed. "Archdemon? Why would you want to raise such a thing? Don't you have enough of them here already?"

"Can you do it?"

"Not for you."

"Not even for your freedom?"

"You'll kill me either way."

True. "I haven't killed you yet."

She considered this. "Give me my freedom first. Then I'll raise your demon."

Like I was stupid. "I'll think about it."

And I did.

Amy dropped in every day at four o'clock. The sword sat on the desk where she'd placed it. I hated the blade but the gold wings had turned black after Lucifer's success against Michael. That pleased me.

"Don't you think you should hide that?" Amy said as she shimmered in unexpectedly early that afternoon.

I jumped and nearly fell out of my chair. I'd been Googling Rad.

Lucifer had convinced me that he'd done the deed of killing Death and Damon to save me grief, but grief ate at me night and day. Everything was upside down. Trust was dangling by a thread. I needed to talk to him, but for an innocent male, he wasn't trying to exonerate himself.

Why didn't he show up and see how I was doing?

I kept my grief locked up. Grief was an emotion I couldn't afford. I had to be a strong powerhouse of leadership now, not some wimpy love-sick, grief-stricken female. I let work consume me and made sure I never had time or energy enough to go looking for the Chaos demon.

Maddy had mentioned that morning that he was totally off

the grid, so I'd Googled him to see where and when his latest appearance had been. His name alone generated millions of links to blogs, forums, photos and more, but his last appearance had been at the People's Choice Awards. The forums ran amok with speculation about why he'd disappeared.

Speculation, I was embarrassed to be caught reading.

I quickly clicked off the internet and sneered at Amy. The sneering I'd picked up from Lucifer. "Don't you ever knock?"

She set down her latest ice cream concoction in front of me. "Sorry. This shimmering from place to place is all new to me, but I love doing it. And look." She pointed at the ice cream. "I brought you a treat. You said you like cherries, so I want you to try this new blend of cherry chip with white and dark chocolate and tell me what you think."

Every day she brought ice cream. My initial resistance to being her taste tester wore off after the first day. Yeah, yeah, shoot me for being weak in the face of ice cream. Sweets were a definite chink in my armor, and so was this witch.

I took a bite. Then another. Gave her a thumbs-up so I wouldn't have to stop eating long enough to talk.

She settled into her favorite chair across from mine. "Doesn't it make you nervous having the sword?"

She knew Lucifer had given it to me for her safety, not because of my grand gesture. Guilt oozed from her aura even though she kept up the pretense that it was a gift for my sacrifice.

I spoke around a mouthful of heavenliness. "I like having it within reach."

Her eyes turned solemn. Rare for her. "You like to fight, don't you?"

"Byproduct of being a vengeance demon."

"What if Michael returns?"

I shrugged. Why did she insist on talking? "I'll handle him like I've handled Lilith and the Horsemen."

A knock on the door interrupted us. Lainie stuck her head in. "I brought you breakfast."

Since I worked at night and slept most of the day, my breakfast was at dinner time. Lainie didn't care. She carried in a tray loaded with an omelet, toast, hash browns, and steaming coffee. Her attention landed on the empty ice cream bowl in front of me. "Did you already eat?"

"I'm still hungry." I took a sip of coffee and grabbed the tray. If not for her and Amy, I would be starving. I hadn't had much appetite anyway, and I rarely left the office. "Thank you."

"What can I get for you, Ms. Atwood?"

Amy lifted a triangle of toast off my plate. "I'm good, thanks."

I tasted the coffee again. "Is this a different brand? It's much better than the stuff you brought me yesterday."

"Your friend dropped it off. Said it was your favorite blend."

The cup suddenly felt too heavy in my hand. "My *friend*?"

Lainie blushed. "He made me promise not to tell you he was here, but I don't keep secrets from my employer."

I swallowed hard. "I appreciate that. If he comes here again, let me know, will you?"

She nodded and left. Amy kicked back. "How long do you plan to make him pay?"

I didn't want to discuss it. "He hasn't even texted me."

"Have you reached out to him in any way?"

So not her business. "*I'm* supposed to call *him*? Text *him*? He's the one who screwed up. And I mean that literally. Screwed his ex right in front of me!" I didn't add that he was under Death's magic spell. I needed my anger. "No. He needs to reach out to *me* and say he's sorry."

"I get it. You miss him, you love him, and you're hurt, but you're being an ass."

Yes, I was. "And a bitchy one at that."

"He brought you your favorite coffee."

"You brought me ice cream. Doesn't mean I forgive you either."

"Me? What did I do?"

"You made me like you."

She screwed up her face. "What's wrong with that?"

"I don't have friends. Too stressful."

At that she laughed, a nice sound in the big office. "You're blessed with friends, Kali. Oodles of them. Now get over yourself and go makeup with that hot rock star."

She shimmered out and I pushed back the plate, no longer hungry.

A minute later, unable to concentrate on the files in front of me, I grabbed the cup of coffee and drank it. All of it.

And then I stood up and went to find the hot rock star and kick his ass.

55

I opened the back door of the Institute, heading for my car, and came to an abrupt stop.

There, on the other side, was a sight for this demon's sore eyes.

"Damon!" I threw my arms around his neck and stood on tiptoe to hug him. He hugged me back and my magic did a happy dance inside my chest.

After a thorough bear hug, I stepped back and looked him over. He looked good. Really good. His hair was a little longer, the corners of his eyes held a few more wrinkles. But he was dressed in Italian silk and smelled like good old wood smoke.

Hot damn.

"You're back." Relief laced my voice, and lightened the heaviness in my chest. "Come in, come in."

He smiled and stepped over the threshold. Behind him came two females. Magic—weak but angelic—drifted from them.

Fallen. I'd been around enough of Amy's group to recognize it.

Damon stared at me like I was one of Amy's ice cream concoctions. Good enough to eat. "It's good to see you, Kali."

To my embarrassment, I giggled. Hugged him again. Ran my hands and eyes over his frame to make sure he wasn't a figment of my imagination and that he wasn't hiding any injuries from his trip to the pit.

He stopped my roaming hands. "I've brought you guests."

I'd already forgotten them. The females' auras were battered and suppressed. In their eyes, mistrust and disheartenment were evident. Long ago, I'd seen the same look in the humans I tortured.

I nodded at each of the females. "You're welcome here. No harm will come to you."

A flicker of hope flared in one of them. She bowed her head slightly, not daring to believe me, but not willing to disbelieve either.

So broken.

"I hear you're doing well as director."

Like I wanted to discuss that. "I thought I'd lost you forever."

"You can never lose what is truly yours."

The air seemed charged between us. A spell over us. Was Damon causing it or was I?

Damon pulled me aside, his hand firm as always on my elbow. "I can't stay, but I need to tell you something."

I grabbed hold of his sleeve. "You can't leave. You just got here."

"Eden and Malo are from the City of Lost Angels. It's a type of purgatory and they've endured more than you and I put together. They'll need special care."

"Damon..."

He shushed me. "I'm proud of you, Kali."

I didn't know what to say. "I'm only filling in until you get back. And I'm making a mess of everything, so you better come back soon."

"My new job requires a great deal of time and energy."

His seriousness was welcome for once, and yet, I couldn't help lightening the tension. "Look at you, an archdemon rescuing angels."

"There are more Fallen to rescue. It will be a while before I can return."

"How long?"

His forehead creased and he held my hand. *Bad news coming.* "It could be months. Maybe years."

Damn. A small thread of panic, hot and mean, spread in my veins. "I'll give you until the end of this year. Work fast."

He gave me a patient smile. Squeezed my hand. "Yes, boss."

Hearing the expression I'd used on him many times made me laugh. The sound was tense and rang oddly in my ears. I felt vulnerable.

Clearing my throat, I tried to return his smile. Miss Emotionless Powerhouse melted. "I miss you."

Another squeeze. "I miss you every day. We're both doing important work, but I wish we were together."

My throat closed up. *No tears*, I warned myself. *You will not cry, dammit.*

I stood there, saying nothing for a few seconds, so just damn glad he was all right. Damon stayed quiet too. It was a comfortable quiet and I relaxed for the first time in days. Damon was all right. *I* was all right. He believed in me and I wasn't going to let him down.

He leaned down, locked eyes with me. "Radison did the right thing. Stop torturing yourself and him. I should never have asked you to swing that sword. My bad, as Maddy would say."

No tears. "I know. It's okay. You can make it up to me when you get back."

This time, he hugged me. "Watch your back for Valentina and Marco. They'll be coming for you."

Let them get in line. "I know. We'll be ready when they come."

We broke apart and I wiped moisture from the corner of my eyes. Damon pretended not to see, reassuring Eden and Malo that I would take good care of them.

With one last glance over his shoulder, he walked out the door.

I gave him a wave and my most confident smile.

The minute the door closed, I let out a huge sigh and hung my head.

"Are you okay?" Eden asked.

Pulling myself out of my pity party, I smiled at the fallen angels. "Of course. Let's get you two upstairs."

I took the two of them to Seraphina and Akimo, who would act as mentors for now. Together, we made sure they each had a meal, a hot shower, and a bed.

Two hours later, I texted Rad.

Where r u?

His reply was slow in coming and by the time it reached me, I was tapping a foot.

Got my coffee, huh? There's more if you want it.

Not exactly remorseful, was he? *Don't make me hunt you down.*

That's exactly what I'm counting on.

Ugh. I nearly threw the phone across the room.

Fine, he wanted to play games?

Game on.

56

I n the car, I commanded my phone to dial Maddy's number. "Where is he?" I asked when she answered.

"At the church. Where else?"

My home was a burned-out shell of a castle. "What's he doing there?"

"Guess you'll have to drop by and find out."

Vampires. "I'm going to stake you one of these days."

"You can try."

I made the turn to take me west to my place. "Win-win for me. You won't be around to steal my stuff or piss me off."

"Nice. You're such a good friend. Feeling better, I take it?"

"Damon came to see me."

"Ahh. He's okay, then."

Sort of. "I don't want his job, but it looks like I'm stuck with it for a while."

She smacked her gum in my ear. "Wah, wah. You're damn good at it. You'll do fine."

"Maddy?"

"What?"

"Thanks. For being there for me."

There was a long pause. The smacking stopped. "Are you feeling all right?"

Not really. "Do you want to catch a movie in the media center tonight?"

"Be there with bells on, sweet thang. Let's plan on two. I'll invite Arman. If that's okay with you."

I said it was and we disconnected. My heart felt lighter.

My place came into view. The tall column on the front was gone. The stained glass windows, blown out. The stone walls had huge chunks missing, the roof had collapsed over the nave. One whole wing was nothing but ash.

The sun was setting behind the church, the cemetery more visible now. As I drew closer, I noticed lights inside. Shadows moving. The smell of cut wood, tools and male sweat drifted on the air. The sound of power tools did as well.

The west side had been rebuilt with beautiful stones. Even from a distance, I could smell the mortar was fresh.

I picked my way across the debris in the yard, stepped through a new, temporary doorway, and found myself staring gaped-mouth at the inside.

The living room's beams were back in place—not the old ones that had splintered and burned during the fight, but new ones. The beams also held up a nice, new ceiling. The wall between the living room and kitchen had been rebuilt, with fresh drywall mud still visible.

The furniture had been removed, the floors sanded and stained. The worst of the interior walls had been patched, and plastic hung here and there. Under the scents of new construction drifted the smell of a calm ocean.

I followed a trail of tools and the sound of two male voices talking and laughing in my kitchen. Rad sat on the kitchen counter, shirt unbuttoned, a beer in hand. Dru sat at the kitchen table, eating half of a chocolate cream pie and drinking wine. They startled when I entered.

Rad jumped down from the counter. Dru stood up so fast that his chair tipped backward.

Guilty, much?

"Kali," the Master vamp wiped his mouth with the back of his hand. "I didn't feel you come in."

I hadn't felt him in my blood either. Another benefit of my self-imposed emotional lockdown? My demon had been quiet, my magic unused for the past week. I hadn't had a drop of Dru's blood. Didn't feel like I needed it. "You two are working together?"

Rad's eyes drank me in. "Common purpose."

"And what is that exactly?"

Dru waved a hand around. He was dressed in ripped jeans and a flannel shirt. I'd never seen him so casual. Sawdust dotted his hair. "Restoring your grand abode...and hopefully, your outlook on life."

My outlook was just fine. Mostly. "Did you kill the lumberjack you stole that shirt from?"

The vampire flinched, brushed at his slumming clothes. "Maddy said it was awful."

"She's right." I glared at Rad. "Since when are you a carpenter?"

He shrugged and tapped the beer bottle against his leg. He also wore ripped jeans and a cotton button-down, but on him, it looked perfectly natural. Probably because it was unbuttoned, showing off his luscious chest and abs. "I've picked up a few skills in three hundred years."

"Like being the False Prophet? A.k.a the Antichrist? The White Horseman?" He flinched, and I snapped my fingers as an idea came to me. "You and Jesus, both carpenters. You two have more in common than I thought."

Dru skirted the table, then me. "I just remembered I have business at the House to take care of." He pecked me on the cheek. "I'll see you tomorrow?"

Twice a week, I did my queen duties there. "Bet on it. We have a lot to discuss."

A tight sigh escaped his lips, and he nodded a solemn goodbye.

Rad and I circled each other for a minute. "Want a beer?" he asked.

"How about an explanation."

"I needed a project. I couldn't work on you, so I worked on your house instead."

I sat at the table, sipped Dru's wine. Stuck my finger in the pie and ate a chunk off the end. Rad's gaze zeroed in on my lips. "I needed time to think things through. To grieve. At first I didn't realize why you did what you did. You and Damon weren't exactly buds."

His eyes came up to meet mine, saw the hidden meaning there, and he plunked down the beer bottle on the table. "You thought I killed him on purpose?"

"I did."

Shaking his head and snorting, he paced back and forth a couple of times before grabbing a chair, flipping it around and straddling it. The room was lit with a single bulb hanging from the ceiling and it swayed with the intensity of his emotions. "Wow."

His disappointment was palpable. He wouldn't look me in the eye.

"I know better now, and...I'm sorry I thought that to begin with. It was...wrong."

He hooked the bottle with a finger and took a drink. Several heartbeats of silence passed. "Okay."

I wasn't all that familiar with the whole apology process, but *okay* seemed a little anticlimactic. "That's it? *Okay?*"

He eyed me across the table and his magic came to attention. "You want me to hold out? Make it harder on you than it already is?"

"Hell, no. I just didn't think you'd let me off the hook that easily."

"Oh, you're not off the hook. I'm going to keep you dangling there a long, long time."

Something kicked hot and needy in my stomach. I arched a brow, practicing my Damon aloofness. "Funny, because you aren't off the hook, either, Guitar Boy. I haven't heard an apology yet."

"I'm holding out, hoping you'll make me pay for my insolence."

He was going to pay all right. But not tonight. "Rad, this is not a game. Damon's death..."

He rose and came to me, pulled me out of the chair, and kissed me. Soft, uncomplicated, sweet. Our magics mixed and swirled.

When our lips broke apart, he rubbed my back. "A thousand apologies wouldn't be enough for that. But it had to be done and I did it. For you and for Damon. He never should have put that responsibility on your shoulders."

"That's what he said."

"He's back?"

"Not per se, but he will be one of these days. Right now, he's still working for Lucifer."

"Are you okay with that?"

"Do I have a choice?"

The back rub continued. "Damon may be gone, but the rest of us are still here."

That rock-solid emotionless powerhouse inside me shook. My magic stirred deeper, my demon softening under the feel of Rad's hand on my back. "I'm so tired."

"Stay here tonight. Rest."

My eyes dropped to the open shirt and his naked chest underneath. Spending the night with Rad would *not* be restful.

He saw the thought flash across my mind. He pointed three fingers in the air. "Scout's honor. I won't touch you."

I was physically tired, but not *that* tired. I wanted him to touch. Wanted his arms around me, his fingers trailing melodies over my skin, and his comforting voice whispering in my ear.

Facing the truth about what I really meant by *tired* made me uncomfortable but I thought he might understand. The next words were hard to say. "I'm tired of saving humans. And supernaturals. Everyone needs me. *Save the world, Kali.*" I rubbed my head, guilt hitting me square in the face. "I want to save them, but I'm fucking exhausted."

He brushed hair from the side of my face and chuckled. "Even Wonder Woman needs a day off now and then."

"Ah, but there's the difference. Wonder Woman is a goddess-slash-superhero. I'm a demon-slash-superfreak."

"You both have lassos."

Volante, curled around my arm, flicked her tail, offended.

I laughed. "For the record, I have a whip, not a lasso."

"You and the WW both have sexy legs, big boobs, and kickass attitudes."

True. "Don't forget the boots. It's really all about the costume."

He untied my cape, removed it from my shoulders. "Less costume is better."

"What happened to *I won't touch you*?"

"Just helping you get comfortable."

He did too. He poured me a shot of Frangelico and brought me a clean fork for the pie.

I preferred using my finger and did so. He sat again, watching it dip into the cream, rise to my lips, and be sucked off. "We need to talk about Parker."

"Parker who?"

Funny. "I didn't kill her. Yet."

"Why not?"

I stopped feeding myself. "She has information I may need down the road about the Noctifectors and the pope. I'm keeping her, Maria, and Victoria in the isolation chambers at the Institute. For now."

He looked at me. "And?"

"When the time comes, I may have to torture her to get the information I'm looking for."

His brows dipped. "Are you asking for my permission?"

"Just reminding you that she's a prisoner of war, and I will use her for my purposes the way she tried to use you."

"I understand. And I owe you an apology for that."

"For seeing Parker behind my back or for fucking her in front of me?"

"I don't even remember that. The fucking part."

"I know." I blew out a sigh. "You were under Death's spell."

"So you are—or aren't—mad at me over that?"

Another fingertip of cream went into my mouth. "Haven't decided."

He blew out a disgruntled breath. "I only saw her once behind your back, and that was to fool her into thinking I was double-crossing you. It was the only way to control how and when she and Maria showed up here. I never dreamed they were bringing friends."

I sipped the Frangelico and kicked off my boots. "Anything else you want to admit to?"

"Keep torturing me with that pie and I'll confess all my secrets."

Now we were getting somewhere. "Why haven't you been making public appearances?"

He stilled. His magic stilled. "I've been busy here. And I'm looking for a new job."

My finger froze half-way to my mouth with a fresh dab of cream. "You're giving up being a rock star?"

"Not completely. Just thinking about a new option."

"Why? You love your music, fame, and fortune."

The chaos in him could not rest for long. He fiddled with the beer bottle, picked at the label. "I do. I'm not walking away from that, but I have skills well suited to the cause."

"What cause? *Oprah for president*?"

"Don't underestimate my powers. I helped Obama get all the way to the White House."

Huh. I saluted him with my glass. "Nice job."

"Thanks." He stood and placed his empty bottle in the sink. Set a hip against the counter and crossed his arms over his chest. I nearly drooled. "I want to work for the Institute."

The glass bobbled and I nearly choked. "Come again?"

"You're busy doing Damon's job. You need a new enforcer."

I laughed loud and hard. "You? A Bridge enforcer?"

His eyes snapped. His chest expanded. "I was a Noctifector for two hundred years. I think I can handle it."

I forget sometimes that he's more than a pretty-faced rock god. More than a gorgeous Chaos demon. "Not the same."

The tension in his body increased. "*Exactly* the same. I know everything there is to know about supernaturals and the ways in which they think and act. I know what they crave, what actions they take against humans, and I know how to stop them."

He had a point. One I didn't particularly like. "It's dangerous work."

"That you've been doing for several hundred years."

"But you're half human."

"I can't believe you just went there." He made a disgusted noise in the back of his throat. "Yes, I have human genes and human weaknesses, but I survived all the torture and brainwashing the Nocts did to me. I survived all the encounters I had with supernaturals once I was in the field. You can't use that against me."

I'd never seen his humanity as a weakness. I went to him, unfolded his arms and slipped up on my toes to kiss his lips. They were stiff, unyielding.

My fingers brushed his waist, lightly made their way up his back. I admitted the truth against his firm lips. "I can't stand the thought of losing you."

"You won't," he murmured back, catching my lower lip between his teeth.

The bite was gentle, provocative. I yearned for more. "If I take my clothes off, will you forget this crazy idea?"

His hands went under my shirt and found their favorite targets. He cupped my breasts and massaged them, making me weak in the knees. "Only for as long as you keep them off."

While Dru and some of the males—and a few of the females—at the Institute might not mind that, it was generally hard to take your director seriously if she was naked. "Deal."

He carried me to the table, sat me on the edge, and undressed me. His pants hit the floor along with my clothes, and we feasted on each other's bodies.

Literally. He laid me back, spread my legs, and placed dollops of chocolate cream pie in strategic places before licking it off. Our lovemaking was soft and slow. Languorous, as if we had all night.

We didn't. My cell phone rang, bringing me back to reality. "Could be the Institute," I said, shoving him aside and fumbling for my cape.

Rad grabbed my wrists, brought me to heel, and refused to let me answer. He kept me restrained as he bent me over the table and entered me from behind.

I quickly forgot the phone.

It rang on and off the rest of the night. Continuing to ignore it, I took what was left of the pie and made my own special treat out of his body, licking, sucking, and restraining him my way.

He came in a rush of magic, my evil powers giving no quarter to his breathless begging for me to stop.

When he recovered, he blindfolded me. "Trust me."

Naked and at his mercy, I did.

"Show me what you want me to do to you," he murmured against my neck at the exact spot my vampire scar rested. I shivered under his lips. "For the next hour, it's all about you and only you."

Be what you are.

Something inside me broke loose. Something dark and dangerous. Being the selfish demon I was, I showed him exactly what I wanted him to do to me and reveled for the rest of the night in my debauchery.

Funny thing was, it wasn't about the sex.

Sunlight woke us, bright and blinding on the snow outside the kitchen windows. We squared off across the table again, this time with coffee and donuts.

"I won't hire you unless you completely give up being a rock star."

He bit into a glazed pastry, licked his lips, and said, "Okay."

Wait. He was supposed to balk at giving up his career. Music meant everything to him.

This brilliant idea had hit me as I lay half-dozing in his arms. I'd thought it was the perfect way to foil his plan to replace me as enforcer.

"I mean it. Everything. No concerts, no albums, no benefits. You can't work for the Bridge and be in the public eye the way you are now."

"I know. I was thinking about it last night. The band will have to find a new frontman."

Merde. "Your fans will never buy it. The Chaos Demons will fail without you. You know that. You don't want to disappoint the guys or your fans, do you?"

"I've always said I wanted to go out on a high note." He finished off the donut. "Now's the perfect time."

So much for reverse psychology.

I leaped up, downed my coffee, and grabbed my cape, still lying on the floor and stained here and there with chocolate. "I have to go. I have, uh, Bridge things to do."

He rose too. "You'll think about it? Hiring me?"

Avoiding his puppy-dog eyes, I adjusted my cape and wrapped Volante around my arm. "Bring me your resume. I'll have to take it to Kirill and get his approval. Hiring decisions are a joint process."

Two hours later, I was back to business. Despite having had little sleep, I had too much restless energy to go to bed. I checked on the new Fallen guests—they were adjusting nicely —spent an hour on the phone with Di discussing the latest SI cases, and ate a hearty breakfast with Cole. He laughed at my predicament with Rad.

"What's so funny?" I asked.

He laughed again around a mouthful of bacon. "I'm thinking of all the ways I can make Guitar Boy's life miserable when he's here every day."

"I'm not hiring him."

"The hell you aren't. He's right. He's perfect for the job."

Why was Rad always right? I slammed down my napkin and left Cole smiling into his orange juice.

Rad showed up, resume in hand, at noon. He brought Kirill with him.

Busted.

I hadn't spoken to Kirill yet to recruit him to my side.

The archdemon was munching on an apple. Seraphina had put him on a diet. From his sour mood, it wasn't appreciated.

He slammed the apple on my desk. "I vote yes. Give the boy your job."

Rad grinned. I scoffed. I had one last card to play. "No sleeping with the boss."

The grin fell off his face.

Kirill frowned. "There's no rule against that."

There wasn't?

Time to make one up. "Bridge Mandate, Code Six A, Section Eleven. Look it up."

Kirill shook his head, making his jowls bob. "Liar."

Rad crossed his arms. "I'm announcing my retirement tonight on the Late Show. I already talked to the guys, and they're cool with it. They've reached out to a couple of other frontmen and will continue the band. Meantime, I'll lay low, make myself over so fans don't recognize me when I'm out."

The Kali approach wasn't working. I sat back in the chair, reached for a pencil, and started turning it end over end, drilling the point into my blotter. Channeling Damon, I called up an impassive face. "Why are you doing this, Radison?"

The two males looked at each other. "Scary," Kirill said.

"You sound just like Damon," Rad added.

Good. "Answer the question."

He squared his body and looked me in the eye. "I want to be an enforcer so I can help humans."

Now who was lying? "That the only reason?"

"I want to be with you and my current lifestyle makes that difficult."

Finally, we were getting somewhere. "Why be an enforcer? Why not, say, a carpenter?"

A glint of challenge registered on his face. "I want to help you save the world. Take some of the strain off your shoulders."

I believed him, but I still tried to come up with an argument.

He pulled out all the stops. "Give me a chance. Just one chance. Trust me, Kali. Let me do this for you."

Don't get emotional. Don't take it personally. My mottos coming to my rescue.

How have those worked out so far, there, Kali girl?

After three hundred years of battles, scrimmages, and all-out wars, I was just learning that emotions served a purpose and that I needed to take things *more* personally.

"All's fair in love and war," I said to no one in particular.

Rad and Kirill exchanged another look. Rad shifted forward. "Does that mean I have the job?"

I tapped the pencil against my cheek. "After a thirty-day trial period, I'll review your performance and make my final decision."

"Yes." He did a fist pump and he and Kirill high-fived each other. "You won't be sorry."

"No, but you might."

He grinned. "Challenging me already, boss?"

I returned his smile with an evil one of my own. "I'm going to put you through hell, Chaos demon."

He planted his hands on the desk and got in my face. "Bring it on. You don't scare me."

I grabbed him and kissed him.

A second later, I heard the door close—Kirill leaving us to seal the deal.

We did, right there on the desk, the future shining as bright and dangerous as Michael's golden sword.

GLOSSARY OF TERMS

biblical pseudepigrapha—refers to books of the New Testament canon whose authorship is misrepresented

castello: castle; from Latin root castellum

guerriero feroce—fierce warrior

Hasta la Victoria Siempre: Until the Eternal Victory—Marxist revolutionary Che Guevara's famous slogan

il pistolino—dick, prick

merde—shit

Noctifector—demon slayer belonging to the Roman Catholic Church's secret organization; slang terms Slayer, Noct

porca miseria—miserable pig

mio fratello—my brother

mon petit chaton— my little kitten

non si preoccupi—don't worry formal, singular

rifugio—refuge, sanctuary

semper paratus—always ready; motto of the U.S. Coast Guard

soldato della notte—soldier of the night

ti voglio bene—I love you

verba volant, scripta manent: words fly away, writings remain

VISIT MY STORE

Did you know you can buy directly from me? When you do, the retailer doesn't take a cut and I can pass on the savings to YOU!
https://mistyevansbooks.com/shop

Benefits:
You can find ALL my books in one place
SAVE money
EARLY access to new releases
Special Collections, Boxed Sets, and Limited Editions
Support a small business (and support a dream!)

Why Buy Direct?
When you purchase a book by your favorite author, electronic or print, on retailer platforms, the company keeps 30-70% of the sale, leaving the author with little to no profit (after the company deducts delivery fees, taxes, and other fees).

Buying directly from the author means that more goes to them so they can keep turning out stories for you. Every published story, every book, requires cover art, editing, and hours and hours of the author's time simply to create it. Not to mention overhead costs, such as websites, newsletters, writing software, graphics programs, advertising, taxes, etc.

In addition, one of the big-name retailers requires exclusivity, and all of them have terms of service and rules and regulations that make it challenging and time-consuming for an indie author to navigate the publishing world.

Most of us would MUCH rather spend our time creating more stories for YOU, rather than trying to jump through the hoops at the retailers. Buying direct from your favorite authors (where available) helps ensure that an author you love is not subject to unexplained account closures, withholding of royalties, censorship, and other issues that can affect their livelihood.

I've experienced ALL of these. By buying direct, you help put control of my work back in my hands—and I can continue to write more.

Either way, thank you for supporting me! I understand buying direct doesn't work for everyone and even if you use the retailers to buy my books, I appreciate you!

Happy reading,

Misty

https://mistyevansbooks.com/shop

YOU'RE INVITED!

Do you have a passion for my stories?

Want more from my characters?

How about early access to ALL my new releases?

My reader community is for YOU!

Try my **VIP reader community** for a month! It's ONLY $5—you're buying me a coffee—and in return, you get all these perks:

 Writing Updates so you know what's in the works and how soon you can get it

 Special Charmed Content, including episodes in my GrimVerse and Kali Sweet worlds, character interviews, alternate endings/deleted scenes, future story plot ideas, and cover reveals

 Early Access to new stories—I always have multiple books in the works and I release a chapter(s) early before the stories are on retailers

 Charmed Coupons for discounts to <u>my online store</u>

 Pics of my pets (all are rescues and they "help" me write and edit)!

You're invited! What are you waiting for?

I'm in! Give me more stories!

PNR & UF BY MISTY EVANS AND NYX HALLIWELL

Paranormal Urban Fantasy:

The Accidental Reaper Paranormal Urban Fantasy Series Special Collection

Killin' It (short story for newsletter & Ream Stories subscribers only)

The Vampire's Kiss (an exclusive short story available in Misty's Store. *Intended for mature audiences 17+*)

Grave Girl

Grave Magic

Kali Sweet Urban Fantasy Series Books 1-3

Sweet Curse, Kali Sweet Urban Fantasy Series, Book 4

Paranormal Contemporary Romance:

Witches Anonymous Step 1

Jingle Hells, WA Step 2

Wicked Souls, WA Step 3

Dark Moon Lilith, Witches Anonymous Step 4

Dancing With the Devil, Witches Anonymous Step 5

Devil's Due, Witches Anonymous Step 6

Dirty Deeds, Witches Anonymous Step 7

Wicked Wedding, Witches Anonymous Step 8

Paranormal Romantic Suspense:

Soul Survivor, Moon Water Series, Book 1

Soul Protector, Moon Water Series, Book 2

Cozy Mysteries (writing as Nyx Halliwell):

Sister Witches Of Raven Falls Mystery Series

Sister Witches of Raven Falls Special Collection

Of Potions and Portents

Of Curses and Charms

Of Stars and Spells

Of Spirits and Superstition

Confessions of a Closet Medium Cozy Mystery Series

Confessions of a Closet Medium Special Collection

Pumpkins & Poltergeists

Magic & Mistletoe

Hearts & Haunts

Vows & Vengeance

Cupcakes & Corpses

Tea Leaves & Troubled Spirits

Sister Witches of Story Cove (Formerly Once Upon a Witch) Cozy Mystery Series

Cinder

Belle

Snow

Ruby

Zelle

THRILLING ROMANTIC SUSPENSE & MYSTERY

SEALs of Shadow Force Romantic Suspense Series Box Set, Books 1-7

SEALS of Shadow Force Series: Spy Division

Man Hunt

Man Killer

Man Down

Covert Affairs

Covert Tactics

Covert Obsession (2024)

SCVC Taskforce Set Books 1-10

SCVC Taskforce Romantic Suspense Series Books 11-13

Super Agent Romantic Suspense Series Books 1-7

The Justice Team Series (with Adrienne Giordano)

Stealing Justice

Cheating Justice

Holiday Justice

Exposing Justice

Undercover Justice

Protecting Justice

Missing Justice

Defending Justice

SCHOCK SISTERS MYSTERY SERIES w/Adrienne Giordano

1st Shock

2nd Strike

3rd Tango

The Secret Ingredient Culinary Mystery Series

The Secret Ingredient, A Culinary Romantic Mystery with Bonus Recipes

The Secret Life of Cranberry Sauce, A Secret Ingredient Holiday Novella

MEET MISTY

USA TODAY Bestselling Author Misty Evans has published over ninety fiction novels, as well as nonfiction inspirational journals. She loves writing urban fantasy, paranormal romance, and mystery/suspense. Under her pen name, Nyx Halliwell, she also writes supernatural cozy mysteries.

When not reading or writing, she enjoys music, movies, and hanging out with her husband, twin sons, and three spoiled rescue dogs. She's a crafter at heart and has far too many projects to finish.

Don't want to miss a single adventure? Visit www.mistye vansbooks.com to become a VIP and find out ALL the news!

LETTER FROM MISTY

Hello Beautiful Reader!

Thank you for reading this story! It is an honor and a privilege to write books for you. I'm an indie author and every fan is important to me. I pour my heart into each story and do my best to bring you an escape from the real world.

I hope you enjoyed this one, and if so, would you mind leaving a review at your favorite retailer? Or share your enjoyment of it with a friend or family member? I'd really appreciate it, and reviews help other readers find books they will love, too.

Readers are the key to my success—not a traditional publishing deal (had four), an agent (had two), or a publicity team (yep, you guessed it, had several of those as well.)

Those of you who read my books and love my characters and worlds, and who then tell others are the best of friends. I adore you and will keep writing if you keep reading!

If you'd like to learn about my other books, sales, and

special promotions, please sign up for my newsletter at **www. mistyevansbooks.com.**

Support me directly (no retailer taking their cut), grab special edition box sets, and get new releases before they are out at retailers by visiting my store **https://mistyevansbooks. com/shop** or **joining me on Ream Stories.**

Last but not least, if you enjoy clean, cozy mysteries, visit my pen name **www.nyxhalliwell.com** to see those books.

Thank you and happy reading!

Misty